IN THE GRIP

IN THE GRIP
a novel

Myer Kutz

Thanks to my wife Arlene, daughter Merrilyn, and son-in-law Bill for their work on the book and their encouragement. My sincere thanks to Theron and Joan Raines for their insightful editing and to Joe and Eileen Schuyler for their work on the cover photo.

Library of Congress Cataloging-in-Publication Data

Kutz, Myer
In the Grip/Myer Kutz
ISBN: 978-1478389699

For Arlene and Merrilyn

PROLOGUE

"**I** love to watch a woman get up from a chair," Sanford said. "When she's sitting down, she can let you look down at her cleavage or show you her legs, but when she stands up, it's then that she reveals all of what she really looks like. All you have to do is undress her with your eyes. Just take a look at the woman who just stood up - back there, a few tables behind you. Lovely. Go ahead, Mordecai, turn around and take a look. Don't make a big deal of it, just sneak a look. It'll do you good."

Sanford smiled at me. It was a tender smile, I had to admit. Around his eyes there was a hint of playfulness. I knew that he thought he had to be careful with me. But he was determined, in his own way, to help me move on from my troubles. Nevertheless, a game was a game. There were rules (Sanford made them up, always), there was a winner (Sanford, always), and there were losers (everyone else, at one time or another). And it was one game after another, it seemed.

I didn't move a muscle. I kept my eyes on Sanford's.

He looked across the room again. I had no idea where in the restaurant the woman in Sanford's crosshairs was. She could have been at the table right behind me, for all I knew. Sanford, of course, wasn't finished with her.

"Dark," he continued, "sturdy, built for a long afternoon of pleasure in more positions than are known to be available for such activities in what was once called polite society. Then a well-earned rest as the light dies behind filmy curtains. Now she's putting on her raincoat, to keep the elements off that lovely body. Ah, the mere thought of the delights it could offer makes the heart in this ancient breast flutter. Mordecai, indulge. Please."

I remained eyes front.

Sanford and I were sitting with two other people at our table, kept available for us every lunch time, in an alcove in the back of the restaurant that extended deep into the ground floor of the building where we had our offices. The place seemed to be in perpetual twilight, with just enough light for you to see what you were eating. But Sanford Glickauer affected to be able to pick out details in far reaches of the room, even without the spectacles that he would slowly place on his nose and then around his ears, but only when he was in the mood to do so, as he would put it.

He was seventy-three. With the skin still taut on his face and a leonine mane of grey hair that came down to the base of his neck, he didn't look it. He spoke *sotto voce*, not because he didn't want the woman in his sights to notice his attentions – I didn't think he cared much about whether a woman realized he was talking about her. No, he wanted the three us – I had become the third of his habitual lunch companions whenever he wanted to pop in down here – to have to lean across the table to catch his every word, just as everyone had to lean forward to hear him clearly when he was taking a deposition. That was one of his tricks: speak clearly, but softly, until the moment he deemed right to suddenly raise his voice with a question intended to elicit information damaging to the other party in a divorce proceeding.

Sitting next to me, Maggie Hartnett, the number three lawyer in Glickauer's firm, laughed, as Sanford himself leaned back in chair and erupted. I'd fallen for it the first time Sanford had done this shtick, but not since.

"It's a game," Maggie had said. "He gets you to turn around, he wins."

"What's the prize?" I'd asked.

"There is no prize," she'd said. "He just wants to make you do what you really don't want to do, that's all."

Bill Kramer took his turn: "And this delightful fantasy would come to pass, Sanford, because? Delightful for you, that is. For the other party, not so much, I'd guess." Bill had been Sanford's second banana, as he called himself, for fifteen years. He was of medium height, pudgy, and without a hair on his head, the physical antithesis of the ascetically lean and tall Sanford, but only on the surface. Beneath Bill's flabby exterior lurked an accomplished athlete. Intellectually, however, Bill complemented Sanford seamlessly, which was why they were still together after fifteen years. Maggie had been part of the firm for half that time.

It was Bill who'd first invited me to join the three of them for lunch. I'd met him on the golf course a few years ago, and we'd become friends. For the last few months, whenever Sanford was in the mood to take the elevator downstairs for "a bite and some babble," as he put it, Bill would pop down the hall from their suite to my cubbyhole and ask me to join them. We made up a foursome a couple of times a week.

Sanford looked up at the restaurant's ceiling, then back at Maggie and me. He had an answer for Bill. "Because I deserve anything any lovely woman will do for, or to, me. Look at all I accomplish in pursuit of justice and mercy for women who find themselves in tragic circumstances," he said. "Indeed, I deserve whatever might come my way to satisfy my voluminous appetites."

We all groaned, as he knew we would. We were his Greek chorus, after all. Then his eyes drifted over to the woman, and followed her as she walked past our table on her way out of the restaurant's back door, which led to the building's lower lobby. Up one flight was an exit to the street that saved going around the building in the rain. I kept my eyes on Sanford's, a thin smile on my lips. Best not to look triumphant, I knew, lest Sanford up the stakes in another game of his choosing.

Maggie murmured something that sounded like "Not that Gwennie gives a flying fuck," but I wasn't sure that I'd heard her correctly. Sanford and Bill seemed oblivious to the murmuring. Then Maggie raised her voice and said, "And justice and mercy is precisely what you wouldn't get from Gwennie, not if she caught you *in flagrante delicto*, not on your life," Gwennie had been married to Sanford for forty years, but with an interruption of five years after the first twenty. "She'd pluck all the hair off you, and then put you on a slowly revolving spit above a roaring fire. Not that any of this has the slightest chance of coming to pass. Maybe it would have when you were younger, but not now."

"Not worth two minutes of glorious friction, eh Maggie?" Sanford threw his head back and laughed. Maggie snorted. She brought her hands together around the glass of ice water in front of her, as if to cool fingers lit on fire by her bright red nails. She tapped her engagement and wedding rings against the glass. The Hartnett Maggie was married to was a hunky police detective named Tim. He'd been a football star, from Pop Warner through high school and college. He'd run out of the backfield, often putting his head down when he tried to run through a bigger defensive player he couldn't get around.

I turned to look at her. A satisfied smile played on her full red lips. She was a beautiful woman in her mid-thirties, tallish, slim, her lacquered blonde hair parted on the side – a larger version of Veronica Lake. She favored light colored suits, with short jackets and pencil skirts, plus patent leather high heels that showed off toned legs. Her jewelry was expensive, but understated. The finishing touch was the glasses she always wore, with their sparkling large lenses. "Blind as a bat," she'd told me, when I admired her glasses, "and I prefer them to contacts." She had numerous pairs, and wore different ones with different outfits.

"Not worth even a proper twenty minutes," she said to Sanford. I was just a spectator now, as was Bill. Sanford laughed again, heartily, in obvious appreciation. One tour of his large suite of offices, and it was evident that he liked to have attractive women around him.

"And he adores them when they give him shit," Maggie told me, "which I'm very good at, because I know all about him."

CHAPTER ONE

Thirty years earlier - it was spring, 1980, the year Ronald Reagan convinced enough voters to take a chance on him – I watched a very pretty woman, in her mid-twenties, I'd guessed, get up – unwind, really - from a chair.

"Where will it ever end?" she murmured, as she straightened up. Her eyes rose to nearly the level of mine. She caught me looking down at the backs of her long, narrow feet. "Flats," she said, "I'm six and a quarter." She seemed to be telling me that she was a bit over six feet tall, without actually telling me. "Would you care to dance?" I'd asked. "I'm good at the slow ones."

Her simple beige dress flowed nicely over her slim body. I liked the width of her shoulders. Her shoulder length blonde hair was combed in thick bangs over her forehead. I looked into her large gray eyes. They were set wide apart in a pale face with clear skin. It was a strong, alert face.

It was her face that had drawn me across the room to her. Now, the fact that she was tall drew me closer. "I like tall women," I said. "I have this idea that when they're confident about themselves, they don't have a need to be bossy. Sorry," I stumbled on, "I guess that was kind of a dumb thing to say." Ever the philosopher. I seemed to have misplaced the smooth approach I usually employed in this place. The young woman looked at me speculatively.

It was a Saturday night. We were in the lounge of the big hotel just off the highway, out near the airport. It was a place I liked to go to on Saturday nights. There were always plenty of single women there, most in their twenties to early thirties, some older. My hairline was beginning to recede, I had a goatee, and I wore a sport jacket and tie, so I could pass for older than the twenty-three that I was, at least in the lounge's dim light.

A couple of women who'd taken me home for the evening did act curious about my age, but I put them off with an "Oh, old enough" and a laugh. They didn't seem to care. Nothing was going to come of those one-night stands, and those nights seemed risk-free. Not that one-night stands were necessarily what I was looking for. But they were what seemed to me to be available at this hotel on Saturday nights. Or maybe that was what I really was looking for, but I wouldn't admit it to myself.

In any case, I kept going back there on Saturday nights, by myself, perhaps because I wanted to keep this part of my life hidden from everyone I knew. Not every week, but often enough so that the bartender had a scotch and water ready for me as I approached the bar. It was a harmless habit, I supposed, one that I could break at any time. I don't have to go there - I'm not looking for a serious relationship at this stage of my life, I told myself.

The music worked for me. There were enough slow numbers so I could get out on the dance floor without making a fool of myself - big guy, nearly two hundred pounds on a six-foot-one-inch frame, flailing around haplessly to a mindless, pounding beat. And the slow ones let you talk.

There was a bar on one side of the room, with stools and several tables and chairs. A dance floor, ringed by large upholstered chairs arranged in pairs, took up the rest of the space. The music was supplied by a trio, set up at one edge of the dance floor, with a woman on guitar and men on bass and drums. The guitarist and the drummer were doing a duet on "Polka Dots and Moonbeams" as I ushered the tall blonde onto the floor. It was filled with couples in their forties and fifties, but there was room to maneuver. The band played two more slow numbers, "Darn that Dream" and "I had the Craziest Dream Last Night," which the girl singer introduced with the line, "there's a theme here somewhere."

I held her close, but not tight. I'd learned that you'd get further here if you eased into things. Her head was next to mine, and we could hear each other talking softly. Her name was Patricia Murphy, and she was working on a PhD in art economics at the local branch of the state university.

She was the first grad student I'd ever met here, but I didn't tell her that. She was in her third year of grad school, which meant that she might be a couple of years older than I was. I was finishing my first year in a master's degree program at the Institute, up on the hill, north of here. I didn't tell her that, either. And I didn't tell her my real name, Mordecai Bornstein. Instead, I was Mike Born, as I was whenever I was here, and I said I'd gone back to school after working a few years, which wasn't true, either. But I'd had a lot of practice with a story that supposedly covered the past several years, and I felt at ease telling it. I left no clues that I might be fibbing.

Instead, I kept it simple. "You like this kind of music?"

"Not when they make it syrupy," she said. "I like it when the jazz singers – you know, Ella Fitzgerald, Sarah Vaughan, Billie Holiday – sing these slow songs. They bring out the best in the music."

"And not just the big three, as I heard a guy with a jazz radio show call the ones you just mentioned. He wouldn't play records by any other female singers."

"Not even Carmen McCrae?"

"Not even Dinah Washington."

"Chris Connor?"

"Not even Teddi King."

"Bessie Smith?"

"He might have bent his rules for her. Ma Rainey, I don't know." I could feel Patricia's warm breath on the nape of my neck. "You seem to know something about female jazz singers," I said.

"I knew someone once who had a fantastic LP collection. She used to play vocals whenever I came over, and she had me read the notes on the jackets. I could give you a long list of female jazz singers, and I could tell you a lot about each one."

"So let's start with your top ten. Then I'll give you mine. I think I know a lot about jazz, including the vocalists. I'm what they used to call a 'jazz fiend'." As we discussed our top ten lists for the next several minutes, I felt alone with Patricia in the midst of a crowd of people on the dance floor. I left the identity of the person with the LP collection to another time.

I wouldn't be leaving with Patricia, it turned out, though I wanted to, if only to keep on talking with her. We'd been talking non-stop since I'd first asked her to dance. She sat on a barstool and I stood next to her. She leaned against me. I wanted very badly to kiss her. "I came with two friends, and it's my mother's car," she said. "I can see they're going to need a ride home with me." She nodded toward two brunettes, who were sitting at a table by themselves, nursing glasses of white wine.

"Next Saturday night there's a big band at the Inn on the Lake," I said. "They play for dancing."

"Oh, I like that place," Patricia said.

Half an hour later, address and phone number in hand, I walked Patricia and her two friends out to her car.

She'd asked me to pick her up at home after dinner. She lived in a suburb of mainly single-family homes. Some dated as far back as the 1920s, but most were of more recent vintage, I guessed. I got there by driving out one of the city's older streets, lined with wooden two- and three-deckers. About a mile after I passed a movie theater, I went over a bridge. A large wooden sign indicated I was now in Patricia's town.

I had to keep stopping to check the directions I'd written out. The streets were winding, and one looked pretty much like another to me. I had to back up to read a street sign before I realized that I'd arrived on her street.

She was waiting for me on the front step of a small colonial. It was a warm spring night, and she was wearing a white blouse and a straight black skirt that came down to the tops of her knees. Her legs looked very slim. I could see by the way the beam from a low light in front of the step reflected off her legs that she was wearing pantyhose. I noticed she was wearing heels.

"Come in, Mike, my mother wants to meet you before we go out." We walked into the living room, which ran from front to back of the house, and walked over to the fireplace. Next to me, Patricia stood straight, an inch or so taller. I was glad she wasn't slouching, and I decided there was no point in sucking in my stomach and stretching up to try to match her height. I relaxed. I felt comfortable next to her. To my surprise, her mother seemed rather small, with a pretty round face, glasses, and permed blonde hair. She remained seated in a rocker, a pile of yarn and the beginnings of a garment in her lap.

"This is Mike Born," Patricia said. I made no move to enlighten mother and daughter about my real name.

Mrs. Murphy offered a cool dry hand, which I shook gently. "Please don't keep her out all night, young man," she said . "We have a date for mass tomorrow morning - remember, you promised," she said to Patricia with a smile. I silently complimented myself on my alias strategy.

On the way out to the car, I said to Patricia, "your mother's a small woman."

"I suppose you're wondering where I get my height from," Patricia said.

"The thought did occur." I wanted to sound casual about her height, but the truth was, I loved it.

"From my father, of course. He was six-four. When I asked one time if I could buy him a Brooks Brothers shirt, he told me he had a thirty-eight-inch sleeve."

"Impressive." I took Patricia's hand in mine. She locked our fingers together.

"When he told me that, he said, 'I suppose you're going to tell me you believe in evolution now.'"

It sounded like something I would have said. Patricia and I laughed together.

"I would have liked to have met him tonight."

"That's not possible, I'm afraid. He died fighting a fire when I was nineteen. It's been just my mother and me since then."

"I'm sorry."

We'd reached the car. I opened the door and Patricia lowered herself onto the seat. She looked up at me.

"Thank you, Mike," she said. "I'm sure he would have liked meeting you." Then she swiveled around on the seat and slowly drew her long legs into the car. I shut the door quietly but firmly.

The band at the Inn on the Lake was a classic sixteen-piece ensemble that played for dancing, except for ten minutes during each long set when they blasted a couple of hard driving flag waivers from the Woody Herman book. Only two or three expert couples took to the floor then. Patricia and I stood holding hands. Her head bobbed in time to the music. She turned to me and whispered into my ear. "They're pretty good, aren't they?" I tightened my arm around her waist in response.

We had a chance to step out on a couple of Basie numbers, "Corner Pocket" and "Shiny Stockings." On the slow tunes, I held Patricia very close to me, my eye socket pressed against her high cheek bone. She leaned back and directed my attention to a woman dancing a few yards away from us.

"I should get a pair of shoes like those," Patricia said. I saw that the woman was wearing kitten heels.

"You don't have to get them," I said. "I like us the way we are. Are you OK with it?"

"I wanted to wear heels, Mike," she said softly. "But I was worried you might not like my being taller."

Then Patricia melded into me, her cheek bone fitting into my eye socket again. She felt very warm, slender and tall, in my arms. With her long legs and the high heels, her waist was at the middle of my chest. I wondered how much maneuvering it would take to have sex with her standing up.

"We fit together perfectly," I said, very softly. When her arm tightened around my shoulders and she squeezed my hand, I knew she'd heard me. At intermission, we got ourselves something to drink. The bartender rooted around the fridge and found the cranberry juice that Patricia had asked for. He found a Molson's Ale for me without any trouble. We drifted out to the porch that wrapped around the front and sides of the inn. We stood near a pillar, sipped our drinks, and talked about visits we'd made recently to the Museum of Modern Art. We both liked the Kandinsky's and disagreed about the Picasso's.

"Just plain ugly," I said.

Patricia smiled. "I'll teach you how to appreciate them."

"Murphy," a woman standing next to me said. I turned to a pretty redhead in a waitress uniform. She was holding a tray of soiled glasses. She looked up at me quizzically.

"Oh, hi Mary," Patricia said. "Mary, this is Mike Born."

"Hi," I said.

"Hi," Mary said, and then turned to Patricia. "Have a good time, Murphy. I'm sure you will." She took another appraising look at me, and then sauntered away.

I felt as if I'd been ticketed for an offense. "Who was that?"

"She's someone I know from high school."

"A friend?"

"A classmate."

We stayed until eleven-thirty. It was a half-hour drive back to Patricia's mother's house. We got in my car and headed out of the Inn's parking lot. "Want to stop somewhere for a nightcap? I don't have to get you back until whenever." With a slight detour, we could stop for a while at my ratty apartment near the Institute, but I didn't expect Patricia to suggest that we do so. Nevertheless, I paused in hopeful anticipation. When her answer came, I didn't know quite what to make of it.

"Why don't we pull over somewhere dark and quiet," she said, "where no one will intrude on us." I thought of red-haired Mary, and wondered what the relationship between her and Patricia really was. Then the signals became mixed. "We can relax and talk," Patricia said. "I love talking to you, Mike." I reached over and brushed the back of my hand lightly against Patricia's cheek. As I drew it away, she caught it and squeezed it. Then she let it go. I put it back on the steering wheel. I was confused, but I was starting to get an erection.

I pulled into a driveway I knew that led to a strip mall with a secluded parking lot. There were a couple of cars there, and lights still on in the diner in the center of the row of storefronts. I'd eaten there; it was cheap and surprisingly good. The family who ran the place must be cleaning up after a busy Saturday night, I thought.

I coasted to a stop at the far end of the lot and tucked the car in against the trees. I killed the engine and lights. It was dark. I figured that with the diner cleanup the cops would ignore my car, at least for the hour or so that we had. And if the other cars in the lot drove straight out the way I'd come in, their headlights wouldn't rake over us.

"I thought the band . . . ." Patricia put a finger on my lips, and I stopped talking. She looked at me, and I slid out from the steering wheel to the middle of the front seat. My car was a late model Buick, with bench seats front and back. I always drove with the front seat as far back as it would go, so there was plenty of room for Patricia's long legs.

She reached down and pulled her shoes off, then snuggled against me. I put an arm around her and rested a hand on her thigh. I pulled her skirt up over her knees as I twisted in front of her and kissed her. I pulled back to look at her. The large gray eyes were looking into mine. She put her hand behind my head. I kissed her again, harder this time. But when I tried to push my tongue between her lips, she didn't open her mouth. I slid a hand under her skirt and slowly up her thigh. I'd thought she was wearing pantyhose, but when I encountered cool, bare flesh, I felt for, and found, a garter. "Well, well," I said.

"Shoo," Patricia said. Just that: "Shoo." And she kept repeating it as I stroked her legs. She was calm when my hand brushed over her slim knees and traveled down her nylons, but when my hand went back up to her bare flesh, she tensed, I could tell, and firmly pushed my hand back toward her knees. "Shoo," she kept repeating. She continued to kiss me, but chastely.

I gave no thought to unbuttoning her blouse. After many more closed-lip kisses and strokes of nylon-clad legs, punctuated with the obligatory exclamations of "shoo," Patricia pulled back. She held my face in her hand. "Mike, I think we should go," she said quietly. "You heard my mother." She smiled at me.

I slid back behind the steering wheel, surprised that I was still erect. If I wanted to talk about what had just happened, or not happened, I wasn't about to get any satisfaction there either, for Patricia immediately launched into a diatribe about Reagan and what would happen if he managed to get elected. She seemed content with what had just transpired in the front seat of my car, as if some mild petting defined passionate activity for her. The word flabbergasted crossed my mind. I groaned.

"That's the way I think about politics nowadays, too," Patricia said. So we talked politics the rest of the way to her house.

She put her hand in mine and leaned her head against the side of my face as we walked to the front step. I could smell the clean scent of her hair. She turned to face me. We kissed, lightly. "I'd like to take you out to dinner next Saturday night," I blurted out. My mind seemed empty, even of confusion.

"I'd like that," she said.

"I'll pick you up at six. We'll go someplace nice. I'll call you to let you know where."

She kissed me lightly again, then turned and went up the step. I looked at her legs, then up at her face as she turned and smiled. I waited until she had closed the door behind her, and then stumbled back to my car.

I went for a long run on Sunday morning, and spent the rest of the day finishing a paper that was due in a couple of days. I tried not to think about Patricia, because, I told myself, I hadn't a clue about her. Was she just a sheltered Irish Catholic girl, even into her mid-twenties? I didn't believe such girls existed anymore. Was she waiting for some sign from me that I was serious about her before she let me get further with her? Or was it that the front seat of a parked car wasn't the right place for sex as far as she was concerned? Would she have preferred the back seat? I had reached the point where I was telling myself dumb jokes.

Monday was very warm, with a cloudy sky, but little threat of rain, according to the weather map and forecast in the *Times*. I walked down the hill to the heart of the old city. As usual, there were cars parked at every meter, but hardly any foot traffic. There were few stores still operating downtown, and few restaurants still in business. I ate at the Chinese place in the ground floor of the old hotel, which had been converted to offices some years ago. I had the newspaper for company, which was fine with me. I drank tea for a while, and then began the walk back up the hill.

It's a steep climb, but I was keeping a steady pace, despite the warm, humid, still air. The exercise was doing me good, I figured. Halfway up, I noticed a woman coming down toward me. From my vantage point below her, I saw white high heels first, then shapely legs, a pleated white skirt, a wide black belt, a black tee shirt, and, finally, a cute face framed by short dark hair. We paused as we drew abreast. She was compact, but well built. She looked up at me.

"Aren't you going to ask me out for coffee?" Her voice was lower than I'd expected, and her tone was playful. I guessed she was pushing thirty, but not too hard.

I laughed. "You always ask strange men to take you out for coffee?"

"Only if they've been giving the once-over without leering and they have nice faces. Besides, you don't look strange at all."

So coffee it was, and a lot more for three weeks. I barely had time to finish the term paper and get some daily exercise, or so it seemed. Nights and weekends I was at Tina's apartment, in bed, the shower, or the bath, and never in any of these places without her. She lived in a garden apartment in a complex a few miles north of town. It seemed to be an anonymous place. No one said hello, or seemed to being paying attention to the comings and goings of someone new to Tina's place. Every meal I had there was breakfast: fried eggs, bacon, toast. I drank a lot of coffee and beer. Tina did, too. She liked Miller Lite – said it went great with cigarettes. She chewed mints after she smoked. We lay in bed all day Sunday, fucked, slept, and watched television. The Sunday *Times* went unread.

Tina kept her place neat and clean. On her way out the door in the morning, she never failed to remind me to make the bed. She had just the one bedroom and bath that we shared. The furniture in the living room and dining area didn't look expensive, but she fussed over it as if it were. The dishes and silverware looked new. The glasses sparkled.

She worked as a bookkeeper in an engineering company at the foot of the big hill downtown. She was returning from delivering blueprints to a professor up at the Institute when we met. She left the apartment each morning dressed perfectly, not a hair out of place. Evenings she spent in her panties, or wearing only a bra. Wearing both at once was against her religion, she told me. She was very cute, a little on the small side, except in certain places. I couldn't keep my hands, or my mouth, off her. She wouldn't leave me alone, either.

After the first couple of days, I began to feel guilty about Patricia. The way things were going, I knew I wouldn't be able to keep our dinner date on Saturday night. On my way to Tina's late on Thursday afternoon, I stopped at a drugstore which I knew had an old-fashioned phone booth, where I could talk privately.

Patricia answered on the second ring. I took a deep breath and spoke quickly. "It's Mike Born. I'm sorry I haven't called you like I said I would, but I haven't had a minute to myself since Monday." Which was true, but I couldn't say why, of course.

"Oh, I've been busy, too."

"That's good. Busy is good." I felt stupid. I didn't say anything more, and the phone line was silent for several seconds.

"Have you picked a restaurant?" I pictured her sitting with the phone, bending over, her hair falling forward, her long legs crossed. I felt sorry for her. She seemed so innocent. Suddenly, I felt sorry for myself, as well. I couldn't escape this thing with Tina just now, even though I knew it would run its course fairly quickly.

I felt awful. "The thing is, I can't make it this Saturday. There are too many projects I have to get done and too little time." I felt the beginning of a headache. If she asked me what things I had to get done, I wouldn't know how to answer her. There was another pause. "I'm sorry," I said into the silence.

I heard Patricia take a deep breath. "Call me when you have time. 'Bye, Mike." The line went dead. I pushed the folding door open and staggered out of the telephone booth. Then I went to Tina's.

The Tina idyll, as I called it, lasted less than three weeks. Two weeks to the day after my sad little phone call to Patricia, Tina came into the bedroom dressed for work. It was 7:30 in the morning. She sat on the bed next to me. I opened one eye. She tousled my short hair. I felt myself getting hard. "You need to go home now," Tina said. "My boyfriend's coming in tonight."

"I didn't know you had a boyfriend." I felt stupid that I'd gotten hard.

"You never asked. We were too busy, I guess. Anyway, he's a captain in the army, and he'll be here for a week."

"So you want me out, like you said." I wasn't hard any longer.

"I'll be coming home early this afternoon to get the place ready. Then I have to go food shopping." Apparently the captain ate better than I did. "It's been great, Mike. Have a wonderful life. I know you will make some lucky girl very happy. Believe me." Tina laughed, then leaned over and kissed my cheek. She bounced up off the bed and headed out of the bedroom. "Don't worry about the sheets or anything. I'm very speedy with housework. Just lock the door and push the key under it." It was very quiet in the apartment after the door closed behind her. I felt relieved.

When something like the Lisa idyll happens when you're twenty-three, it's great, I suppose, but I was glad it was over. Now it felt like three weeks of one-night stands. And for the first time in three weeks, I had time to think.

I'd left the scrap of paper with Patricia's address and phone number on my desk. I studied it. I really like the way she looks, I thought. We talked to each other so easily. Hadn't we hit it off? Why was I so focused on what had happened when I'd parked the car? What did I have the right to expect? What on earth had Patricia done wrong? I decided I needed to call her, but it was several days before I worked up enough courage.

My heart pounded with nervousness as I dialed the number in her mother's house. I wasn't sure why. A voice that sounded like Patricia's mother's answered the phone with a tentative hello. "It's Mike Born," I said. "Is Patricia there?" I heard her name called, and then the phone was put down. After a few seconds I heard Patricia say, "Mike?"

"I'm sorry about our dinner date," I said, speaking quickly but softly. "Can I see you again? Oh, sorry, how have you been?"

She didn't answer my last question. Instead, she said, "I can meet you for a drink on Sunday night. Unless you get super busy between now and then." Her tone was dull, and not very encouraging. I wondered whether I had made a mistake in calling her.

"That sounds good," I said, without thinking any further. She named a street corner in her suburban town. She would be waiting outside a friend's house, so there wouldn't be a risk of her being hassled.

"I'll meet you there at eight, Mike," Patricia said. You needn't call again before then." There wasn't much enthusiasm in her voice.

I parked my car on the quiet suburban street a couple of minutes before eight on Sunday night. As I walked up the street in the dimming twilight, I saw a tall blonde standing at the end of the corner house front walkway. She was wearing a dark dress that came to mid-thigh. Her long legs still looked quite slim, but stronger now that I could see more of them. The effect was accentuated by the very high heels she had on. My breath caught in my throat. I stopped in front of her. She was several inches taller than I was. My eyes seemed to be level with her mouth.

Patricia's large gray eyes widened as she looked down into mine. "It's just down the block," she said. I assumed she meant a bar. I kept looking up at her as she covered the ground with long strides. She seemed to manage the shoes expertly. I wondered if she had practiced with them. She looked straight ahead as we walked. She stopped abruptly in front of a store window.

I drew up beside her. We were reflected in a mirrored wall in the empty space behind the dark window, she taller and slender, me a bit shorter, but much broader. I thought that if she were to stand behind me, she would be nearly hidden, with only the very top of her blonde head visible. I smiled. She, however, had a different idea of how we looked together.

"We look ridiculous," she snorted.

"You're being awfully conventional," I said. "I certainly look like I can protect you," I continued, but she had already turned and headed down the street. I followed her into the bar a few doors down from where we'd been standing.

Heads turned as we made our way to a table in the back. I heard a murmur of laughter and a muffled "Wow!" as I pulled out a chair for Patricia. The heads turned away as she folded herself down into the chair. I went to the bar and got a couple of beers – I hoped she didn't catch my involuntary wince when she asked for a Miller Lite – and sat down catty-corner from her.

To my surprise, when I looked up at the clock over the bar for the first time, we'd been talking non-stop for nearly two hours. We'd barely touched the beer. We'd given each other our full attention. Her hands were folded on her lap, mine were on the table. We avoided contact. Once, her knees fell against mine, and she quickly straightened up. She sat erect; I slouched. I had to look up to her as we talked. "I think you like it that I'm taller than you," she said.

"Only in heels," I said.

"Well, I guess that's right." Patricia sounded disappointed. "That's why you asked me to dance that first time, isn't it," she said. "You wouldn't have if I wasn't tall." She made it sound as if she were looking for a way out of something.

"OK," I said, "I admit it. Look, I'm comfortable with you. Barefoot, heels, it doesn't matter to me. I liked walking in here tonight with you wearing those very high heels, taller than me. I liked seeing all those heads turn. I guess it's because I'm a fairly big guy that people notice the two of us more than they would if we were half a foot shorter."

The bar was nearly empty now, and there was no one sitting near us. The television set in the corner droned on steadily with a ball game. It felt as if we were sitting in a room sealed off from everyone else. "But I can't be the only guy who likes tall women."

"Where were you in middle school when I needed you?" Patricia looked into my eyes. "Boys can be so cruel at that age. They called me "stilts" and "Olive Oyl." You know, that skinny, ugly character in the Popeye comic strip. The girls could be especially cruel, though now a lot of them probably envy my legs."

Without thinking about it, I brushed her bangs away from her forehead. "Were you as pretty back in middle school as you are now?" She took hold of my wrist and brought my hand away. I dropped it back on the table. "Sorry," I said. You'd look better with your hair combed off your forehead, I thought. "Wasn't there even one boy who fawned over you?" I asked.

"There was one in eighth grade. I was five-eleven by then, I had only an inch to go, but my parents didn't know that and they were getting worried. Anyway, there was this one boy," Patricia smiled at the memory, "who was about six inches shorter and really skinny. He always wanted to walk me home from school. I tried to be nice to him, so I let him do it a few times. The other boys in the class would follow us and yell at us, roll around on the grass laughing, so I begged this boy to stop asking me."

"A case of unrequited love. Poor fellow."

"The funny thing is," Patricia went on, "he had a sudden, tremendous growth spurt in the tenth grade. They even thought there might be something wrong with his pituitary gland. He topped out at six-nine eventually."

"Now you could walk down the street with him without anyone laughing," I said.

"Except that once he got to be so tall, he wasn't interested in me anymore. He liked girls who came up to his elbows. He liked to drape his long arms over their shoulders."

Patricia dug her thumbnail under the label on her beer bottle. I took a sip of warm beer. We were quiet for a long moment.

"But being tall wasn't even my main problem. And, no, it wasn't that I was so skinny, either." She didn't wait for me to ask what the main problem might have been. She shifted in her seat and crossed her legs, jarring the table slightly. The top of her knee must have hit the underside. The beer bottles rocked slightly on the table's surface. "The real problem, I think, is that I was smarter than everyone else in high school, or, at least, everyone was led to believe that I was."

"How could anyone know who was smarter than whom?" I leaned forward and spoke softly, trying to keep any skepticism out of my voice.

"Well, there was this teacher, a woman." Patricia was speaking softly, as well. "She taught art in the high school. I guess I should tell you what she looked like before I say any more about her. She was tall, almost my height. She wasn't built like me; she had a big bosom and big hips. To make the most – or the least - of her figure, she wore pants suits and heels. She was always stylishly dressed. She wore makeup. Dark red lipstick. She had dark straight hair, which she wore short, with thick bangs in front." Patricia had started to scrape the label away from her beer bottle again. She turned and looked at me. "You're staring at me, Mike," she said. "OK, yes, I started wearing bangs when I became friendly with this teacher."

I couldn't help it. I reached over and brushed Patricia's bangs off her forehead again. "You look so much better with your hair this way," I said.

She pushed my wrist away again. "Please," she said. "I wear my hair the way I like it."

"Sorry," I said. "Go on. I'll be good."

"I don't know why I'm telling you this," Patricia said.

"Maybe it's because I'm a good listener."

"Maybe it's that," Patricia said slowly.

"Anyway, I can picture this teacher. What else was there about her? Was she married? Single?"

"She was married, all right. Her husband was a great big guy, with a bushy beard and a huge belly. He was a physicist, and he made beer at home, in the basement. They didn't have any kids." Patricia paused, then continued. "I guess you would say she was a feminist, if being a feminist means you think women are always superior to men, and you think high school girls are superior to the boys, or at least the girls are smarter and will achieve more than the boys if only society would let them. I know that sounds simplistic, but it's one of the things I remember she was adamant about when we used to talk, although I don't think she spread her views around to anyone else.

"When it came to me personally, she knew that I did really well in both the verbal and mathematical subjects. She couldn't get over how unusual she thought that was, especially for a female. She told some of the other teachers what she thought, and that's how the idea that she was convinced that I was smarter than everyone else got around."

"Were you class valedictorian? That would have settled any questions about how smart you were."

"Yes, Mike, I was. But in my junior year, it wasn't guaranteed. There were other smart kids, some of them smarter than me, I was convinced. But this teacher - I might as well tell you that her name was Joanna Stanton – had decided to sing my praises to anyone who would listen to her."

"It sounds a bit strange. Did it cause any trouble for you?"

"Well, of course, some of the other kids talked about me and wouldn't have anything to do with me. But I had some good friends. And Joanna went out of her way to compliment and comfort me."

"You must have spent a lot of time with her."

"I did in my junior year. She told my mother she was preparing me to make sure I could get into a top women's college, which I did, as it turned out."

"Smith," I said.

"Right, you remember."

"So it sounds like she was a terrific mentor."

"I guess you could say so." Patricia fell silent.

"What's wrong?"

She held my gaze for several seconds. "I don't know why I'm telling you about this, Mike, you of all people. I know you hardly at all, and I wasn't happy to be going out with you tonight, not after you stood me up. Oh, don't deny it." I made a show of opening and closing my mouth without a word. "Or, at least, I wasn't happy to be here with you," Patricia went on quickly, "but now you've had me talking to you for two hours non-stop, and that's never happened with anyone before, not even at a prom or some other big occasion. And I'm almost twenty-five, for heaven's sake. Plus I'm basically a shy person, so I should find it hard to tell anyone anything about myself, let alone this."

"Why me?"

"I don't know, I really don't. Just let me finish."

"OK, I won't interrupt."

"Things seemed to going along just fine. We spent most of the time on art history, in a way that made the subject come alive for me. One night, in April, I think it was, Joanna asked me to sit down next to her on her couch. She said she wanted to show me the pictures in an art book she'd just purchased. The first few were awfully crude. They were paintings of nude women in positions so you could see everything. Some of the women weren't very attractive, it seemed to me.

"I told Joanna I didn't want to look at the book. She closed it and rested her hand on my thigh. 'I'm sorry,' she said, 'I don't mean any harm. They're the kinds of pictures you might encounter when you immerse yourself in studying the artistic impulse,' she said. I remember that 'artistic impulse' phrase. 'They're only pictures of women's bodies,' she went on, 'and you'll find as you get older that all women's bodies are beautiful.'

"I tried to get up off the couch, but she pressed her hand down against my thigh. Then she turned my face to hers and kissed me. I remember that it was a gentle kiss, but it frightened me, of course. I told Joanna I wanted to leave. She let me, without another word."

"Jesus," I said. "Did you tell anyone?"

"No, not my mother certainly. It would have killed her. And not my father, either. He would have killed Joanna first, then her husband. I didn't go to confession to tell some priest, who wouldn't have understood anyway. There weren't any teachers I wanted to run to. I didn't tell any of my friends. They might not have believed me. As for Joanna, I didn't blame her for what had happened. She couldn't help herself, I told myself. Besides, she'd been wonderful to me. She'd taught me so much, and she'd set the direction for my academic and professional life. That was the phrase she'd used: the direction for my academic and professional life. It meant something to me, and it was real. I wasn't harmed. It was over and done with. Why punish her?"

I sat in silence. I thought back to one of my mother's friends, who lived with another woman. Growing up, I'd thought the two women did that to share expenses. A friend, no doubt more worldly than I was, took it upon himself to explain to me why these two particular women lived together. He used a word I'd never heard - "lezzies." What had happened to Patricia was different, of course. Did it explain anything about her? I had no idea. "I'm sorry that happened to you," I said. I didn't know what else to say. "I'm sorry about a lot of things."

Patricia looked up at the clock over the bar. "It's way after ten," she said. "I'd better be going." She stood up and started walking quickly out of the bar. A couple of heads turned to follow her progress.

Outside, she covered the ground back to her friend's house with smooth, long strides. I caught up to her just before she reached the walkway leading up to the house. I reached for her hand, but it darted away. She stopped at the end of the walkway and turned toward me.

"I'm going out to California to take a job in a museum," she said. "I'm leaving on Thursday. I'll finish my dissertation out there." I stood there silently. She stretched up to her full height, put her hands on my shoulders, bent from the waste, twisted her head, and planted a kiss on my lips. I watched this operation in awe. Her lips felt dry. They didn't linger on mine.

"Goodbye, Mike," Patricia said. She turned, walked up the path and the steps, opened the door, and was gone. I hadn't said a word in response to her sudden announcement. I had a feeling I hadn't been expected to.

CHAPTER TWO

The program I was enrolled in at the Institute in 1980 was a new one. It was funded by Fred Baxter, a 1950s graduate.

Fred had made his fortune by using some of his father's large pot of money to buy petrochemical companies cheap, combine several of them into a single massive organization, restructure every internal unit, and sell the resulting, smoothly running behemoth whole or in pieces at a colossal premium. Improved profitability was by no means achieved entirely through worker layoffs, although there were always plenty of them. They were, according to company annual reports, a natural result of combining organizations with similar back-office and other departments with multiple people doing the same job.

Fred had a genius for finding efficiencies not only throughout his companies' structures, but also through their technical and business operations, as well as for redirecting his companies' strategies to maximize profits. So great were his energies and his intellect, that he could summon the wherewithal to devote his time to other pursuits.

He purchased a prominent newspaper. With the Baxter name, as chairman, on the masthead, the paper's editorial stance shifted to a point commonly thought to be on the far right of the political spectrum. The paper did stand for low taxes and a strong defense, and it spoke out against any environmental regulations it deemed harmful to business, especially the petrochemical industry. At the same time, some readers were surprised and others annoyed whenever they noticed the paper take a centrist position on some social issues and promote the welfare of the arts.

When his pile of money had outgrown his father's, Fred started to give a lot of it away. It was the typical American robber-baron story: A tycoon is reviled for the ruthless way he amasses his fortune, and then celebrated for his generosity. So there were plenty of eager and grateful recipients of his largesse. There was no more than a muted objection when the Baxter name went up on theaters in two major cities. Fred was welcomed onto the boards of a museum and an opera company.

Yet, when it came to Fred's funding the new Institute program, he did put a foot wrong. His people let it be known that the money would be coming with some restrictions attached. Fred's people would want the final say on faculty appointments and curriculum development. They issued a white paper that was, for Fred and his people, uncharacteristically heavy-handed.

The new program was to focus on scientific and technical communications. It was to be rigorous in its training methods. Anyone completing the program would know how to construct and complete a report for an organization or a magazine article for the general public.

The program was to be designed so that recent graduates from engineering programs who enrolled in the program would learn skills beyond those they'd been taught as undergraduates. They might have learned how to report experimental results or describe how they'd designed a component or an assembly or a system. In this new program, they would learn how to sell an idea, and the white paper wasn't shy about what the selling job would be intended to accomplish: to cast a commercial organization in a positive light, or to sell the idea that commercial organizations could do great things in the public interest. Government regulations, especially environmental regulations, which interfered with business prerogatives, were to be subjected to the strictest scrutiny in any reports and articles. Regulations were never to be accepted at face value.

Only faculty sympathetic to these notions would be suitable. Socialists and left-wing environmentalists – people with unhelpful views of how the real world could work in the public interest – need not apply.

Press accounts of the affair stated that the Institute's provost, who was at pains to describe himself as a political moderate, would have none of the white paper. He recommended that the Institute reject Fred Baxter's gift out of hand. He was straightforward in his communication to Baxter's people. He told them in a one-page letter that the terms under which the gift would be given were unacceptable.

All of this - Fred's white paper and the Institute rejection - was public. There was, of course, no account of Fred's response when he heard of the rejection. But a few days later, an Institute press release announced the establishment of the Fred Baxter Program in Communications. The Institute, the press release noted, would have sole control over faculty appointments and the curriculum.

Evidently, Fred knew when to cut his losses, I thought, when I read about the affair. And his word could be taken as good. There was never any talk of interference on his part, or on the part of his people, during my first year in the program.

In fact, I'd entered the program as an engineer with a keen appreciation of the need to regulate industry to prevent it from polluting the environment, and I intended to leave it as a writer better equipped to explain that need, as well as how technical personnel went about designing pollution controls and putting them in place. I wasn't an ideologue - far from it. If there was a story to tell about how government and business had worked together to minimize, or even eliminate, pollution, I was as ready to tell it as I was to point to any industry transgressions. I wanted to see things clearly, without preconceived notions, and write accurately and without prejudice. I wasn't at all sure that I could make a living if I was so open-minded, but I didn't know any other way to go about my chosen professional activities.

My theories were tested while I was still at the Institute. I'd arrived fresh out of one of the strong chemical engineering programs at a Big Ten school. I'd done reasonably well there, finishing in the top third of my class's engineering graduates. I'd found a good summer job at a small engineering firm near Dublin, my hometown, a suburb of Columbus, Ohio, so I had a reputation as a kid who might know at least a little something about the subjects I'd studied for the better part of four years.

I might have been a bit suspect for not having gone on to get advanced degrees in chemical engineering, but the fact of the matter was, my ambitions were pushing me in another direction. Besides, I didn't relish the long slog toward a doctorate, even though I might have propelled myself into an academic career with all the trimmings, which didn't look like a bad life at all. But I didn't have a burning desire to investigate some esoteric engineering problem – the tip of a leaf on the end of a twig on a branch high up on the trunk of the tree, as it were - which was what it would take to produce a respectable dissertation, and no dissertation, no doctorate, of course.

Nor did I harbor a desire to start my own company eventually. The guys who ran the small engineering company where I worked summers seemed caught in a web of bowing and scraping as they chased an elusive big payday, probably by selling what they would be able to build up to a larger organization and becoming wealthy working stiffs, albeit at a supposedly exalted level. So when I made my own calculations about how I might find a satisfying level of success, I decided I could make a greater impact on my own future, and possibly on the world around me, as a writer rather than as an engineer.

At the end of my first year, a few days after Patricia Murphy had said goodbye to me, I was asked by the program director to see a professor in the environmental engineering department, who needed help with a project he was working on. His name was Rodney Barrett.

"That's Barrett with two tees," he said, when I shook his hand, "but just call me Ron." The office was in one of the newer buildings that overlooked the football field in the center of campus. Everything was in disarray. Not a single book seemed to be standing straight up in any of the bookshelves. I spotted a typewriter, but there was a pile of typing paper on top of it. There were piles of papers, journals, and more books on the window ledge and on nearly every surface of the standard issue gray metal furniture, even on the chairs. I looked around for a place to sit. Barrett read my mind.

"Don't bother trying to find a place to sit," he laughed, "let's go to the faculty club for lunch and I'll tell you what I have in mind."

I'd recognized Rod Barrett's name. It was on the cover of the environmental engineering textbook assigned for a senior course I'd taken. "It outsells all the competitors combined," he said over our turkey clubs and iced teas. A piece of bacon hung from a corner of his mouth. He stuffed it back in with the sandwich wedge he held in both hands. "The publisher's very happy with it. But it's been out awhile now, and the used book market is starting to cut into sales."

"Can't you do something about that?" I asked.

"You can't sue the college bookstores, who put used books on the shelf next to new ones, and there's no way you can force students to buy new books. Not when they're so expensive, and are a significant addition to the money kids and their parents are spending on tuition, room and board. Even giving away study guides with purchases of new books doesn't help, nor does bribing professors with free ancillary materials like teaching guides and tests. The free stuff helps convince a professor to adopt your book in the first place, but it doesn't help with used books replacing new books."

"Do you and the publisher get any money from used book sales?"

"Don't we wish. Not a penny. The bookstores, or the kids who sell them after the course is over, pocket all the dough."

"So what's the answer?" I asked. The turkey club was great. I'd ordered it on whole wheat toast, which had been browned just enough.

They'd used real turkey, not some deli stuff loaded with salt. Even the potato chips on my plate were fresh and crispy. Maybe there was something to being a professor, after all. I smiled at the thought.

"I bet you did it, too." Rod said. He looked directly at me. "I bet you bought *my* book for a course and sold it when the course was over."

"Actually, I didn't," I said. "I think I'm going to need it when I need to write in technical terms about environmental issues."

"Good, good. Anyway, the best way to combat used books is to put out new editions with enough changes and new material that the previous edition becomes obsolete. That buys author and publisher a few years, until they have to get on the treadmill again."

"So that's what you're doing?"

"Right."

"And it's going well?"

"Yes."

"So why'd you want to see me?"

"Well, I have a problem." Rod leaned back in his chair and looked up, as if what he was about to recount was written on a wall behind me. "Before I got started on the textbook revision, I'd agreed to put together an edited reference book on environmental engineering issues, specifically on how engineers have dealt with problems and mitigated the harm that polluting industries have created. I'm the editor, responsible for coming up with a list of articles, or chapters, finding people to contribute them, and seeing to it that they deliver."

Rod looked directly at me now. "Unfortunately, I haven't gotten very far with this project. I've done a table of contents, but that's it. I haven't contacted any potential contributors. I can't abandon the project. I'm working with the firm that publishes my textbook, but with a different editor. Still, I don't want to disappoint them."

"So where do I come in?" I asked, although I was beginning to catch on to the purpose of the nice lunch.

"I asked the director of that communications program you're in if he knew anyone who could help me – you know that his field is environmental engineering, too – and he recommended that I talk with you, Mordecai. I'll come to the point. I want you to go down to New York and talk with my acquisitions editor for this book I've been dawdling on. That's what they call the guy who sits behind the desk and gets company approval for book projects.

"He and I have discussed your taking over the business of finding contributors – I'll be available for a little help now and then – and getting the chapters in. He's receptive to the idea. It will take up your summer, but they'll pay you quite well, more I'd guess than you'd earn elsewhere. If you're amenable to this idea, I'll buy your train ticket down to New York. A meeting's been set up for a week from now, on a Tuesday afternoon."

Rod Barrett's editor was a man named Jim Upton. He worked for a publisher with offices in Midtown, and I'd anticipated a nice walk through the canyons from Penn Station. It was a warm, sunny day in early June, and I put my folded blazer over my arm and loosened my tie, but after only a couple of blocks at a brisk pace, my shirt was sticking to my back.

I'd left myself enough time for a short detour to Grand Central, so I could have lunch at the Oyster Bar, on the lower level. I stood still once I was inside the cool, cavernous restaurant and let the air conditioning work on me. After a minute or so, I found a seat at one of the long counters and ordered a bowl of Manhattan clam chowder and a seafood salad from a pleasant waitress who had an Irish accent. I was feeling optimistic about what the meeting might hold in store, and under the circumstances a nice lunch seemed a proper treat.

I loved the city. It was full of attractive women and great restaurants. There wasn't anywhere near the number of jazz clubs as there'd been in the Forties, of course, but where else could you find so many still going strong? I liked the noise and the bustle.

The publisher's address was a large, architecturally undistinguished glass and steel building. The reception area was paneled in dark wood and lined with bookshelves. Quiet reigned. I felt privileged. Wouldn't it be something to have my name on the cover of one of the books!

My reverie was interrupted by the arrival of a middle-aged, motherly woman, who was dressed in a blouse, a long flowing skirt, and low-heeled sandals. She looked ready for a brisk walk in the afternoon heat.

"Hi, I'm Estelle," she said, and shook my hand. She led me through a door into a hallway with fluorescent lighting and white walls. It was lined with filing cabinets, with books and thick reports piled on top. The hallway ended in an open area that ran the length of the building. Desks were positioned in front of offices that lined an outer wall of the building. We went through a door into one of the offices and stood in front of a large, gray, metal desk. A chair was tilted against the back of the desk. I couldn't see the occupant of the chair.

"Your guest is here," Estelle said in a loud voice. "I'll leave you two now," she said to me, her voice lowered.

The occupant of the chair must have pushed off from the window ledge because the chair swiveled quickly around until he was facing me. A lock of black hair had fallen across his forehead. His tie was loosened, and his shirt looked as if it had put in more than one day's duty. He looked at me with bleary eyes.

It was coming up on three in the afternoon. Jimmy Carter might have abolished the three martini lunch everywhere else in America, I thought, but not here. I had to assume I was looking at Jim Upton, Rod Barrett's editor, because the man didn't introduce himself. I looked at the open door to see if a nameplate might be on it, but a suit jacket was hanging where the nameplate might be. The man behind the desk motioned me to a seat.

"What makes you think you can pull this off, kid?" he asked.

Rod Barrett and I had met on the previous Friday afternoon. He'd gone over his plan for the book in detail, and provided me with a preliminary list of chapter titles. He'd given me a short written description of the book and its intended audience. He'd also given me a list of potential chapter contributors, with their phone numbers. I was to call them, one by one, and ask each one if he or she was interested in contributing a particular chapter. If yes, I would convey the information to Jim Upton, who would arrange for a contract to be issued. If not, I would ask about leads to other potential contributors. The net would get wider and wider, until I'd filled out the roster of contributors.

Throughout this recounting, the man I assumed was Jim Upton sat slumped in his large chair, his eyes half open, focused on the surface of his desk, not on me. His chin rested on his chest. He waved a cupped hand at me occasionally, as if to urge me to hurry through my story.

When I'd finished, there was silence in the office. I looked out the window, at office and apartment buildings and the blue sky. Then the man I assumed was Jim Upton leaned forward in his chair. His arms rested on his desk. He looked directly at me with red eyes. He began to speak in a loud voice. I wondered if he could hear himself.

"Rod Barrett's a valuable property. We trust him to deliver good work that we can sell. I'll take his word that you can pull this off. You look older, but I think you're just a kid. I'll give you five grand to get you started, another five grand when you give me a TOC – that's the table of contents - complete with names of contributors, and five grand more when you deliver a completed manuscript. Get the TOC to me by the end of the summer and the book nine to eleven months after that, but I'll give you some leeway if you need it. No royalties, but I'll pay your phone bills, postage, and any other itemized expenses you send me. Just don't take any of these people out to lunch and send me the bill. That work for you?"

I sat there stunned, but I must have nodded.

"Good," the man I assumed was Jim Upton said. "Leave your address and phone number with Estelle. Legal will draw up a contract and send it to you in a few days. I'll push them to get a move on. Oh, and by the way, you do a good job on this project, and I'll have more for you. Now say thank you and get out of here."

I said "thank you" and turned to leave.

"Don't fuck it up," the man I assumed was Jim Upton barked at me. "Estelle, get me an Alka Seltzer and a glass of water," he bellowed.

"You'll like working with Jim," Estelle said, as she ushered me out to the elevators. "Under that gruff exterior, he's really very nice." As I entered the elevator, reasonably sure now that the man I'd assumed was Jim Upton was indeed Jim Upton, Estelle patted my arm.

Six months later, on a cold December morning, Estelle called me. "Jim's pleased with what you've done on the Barrett book," she said, "and he's got another project for you. He's free on Thursday morning to go over it with you. Can you be here at ten? I think you'll find it's a good time to meet with him."

And so it was. Upton seemed much livelier than he'd been at that first memorable meeting. We talked for two hours. This project was further along than Rod Barrett's had been when I'd taken it over, and we could discuss the new project without the professor who'd originated it having to be there with us. We seemed to have exhausted all necessary topics by a couple of minutes before twelve. Upton offered me the same contract terms as he had for Rod Barrett's book.

As I was thanking him, he said, "Sorry to push you out, kid, but I've got a heavy lunch date." On my way out I noticed a buxom redhead in a black power suit and high heels waiting by Estelle's empty desk.

Another six months went by before I had another invitation to meet with Upton to discuss a third project. I'd turned in the manuscript for the first book, and a full roster of contributors was working away on chapters for the second one. Upton would call me once a month to discuss the progress reports I regularly submitted. As time went on, he'd ask me more and more questions about how I was doing personally, not just with the book projects. He seemed satisfied with the little I revealed, and he told me a few things about life in Connecticut with his homemaker wife and the three kids. We seemed to be getting along rather well, I thought.

I was feeling good about how I'd managed my relationship with him when Estelle called to tell me to meet Upton and a professor from the Civil and Environmental Engineering Department at Brigham Young University for lunch the next day at an Italian restaurant in the East Forties.

Before we got down to business, Upton ordered a vodka martini and urged me to join him. I wasn't shy about drinking, but I hadn't had much experience with alcohol at lunch. I figured a bloody Mary was my safest bet and ordered one. The professor, a tall thin man with a tan that set off his carefully combed thin white hair, said he'd stick with water. He stuck with his glass of water when Upton ordered a bottle of Barolo and two glasses.

The waiter poured the wine into a decanter and swirled it around. The glasses he poured it into were the largest I'd ever drunk from. The wine was utterly delicious, and I said so, and admitted that I didn't know an awful lot about wine. "Well, if it tastes good, it is good!" Jim Upton exclaimed. The professor, whose name was Don Burdette, looked pained.

We all had a salad, and I had half the bread in the basket. I held a slice of bread in my left hand while I took down what Don Burdette was saying with my right. Halfway through my veal Marsala, fried potatoes and string beans, which Upton had recommended and ordered himself, the waiter replaced the wine glasses with fresh ones and filled them with an inch and a half of wine from a decanted second bottle.

I pushed my papers to the empty place at our table and put my pen on top of them. "I think I've got enough," I said to Don Burdette. He looked at me and folded his hands in front of his plate. He'd eaten half of his steak, one or two bites of potato, and all of his spinach. "I'm sure you have," he said.

Upton remained silent for the rest of the lunch. He'd eaten little of his meal, apart from the salad. I'd finished everything, including the entire basket of crusty bread. After the plates had been cleared, Upton ordered a cognac. "The usual?" the waiter asked. Upton nodded. When the waited turned to me, I said I'd stick with the wine. I had some in my glass; the decanter was empty. At that point, Don Burdette got to his feet and announced that he'd better get a taxi to the airport. We shook hands, and he left without another word.

Upton and I walked down to his office building in silence. He veered off to the revolving doors. Over his shoulder, he said, "Estelle will be in touch, kid."

I continued south to my new apartment. I walked up the three flights, opened the door, and, without closing it, staggered into the bedroom and fell face down on my narrow bed. I was still woozy when I woke up in the dark, five hours later. The apartment door was still open, my keys still in the lock. I had no memory of the walk home. I fumbled in the inside pocket of my jacket for my notes. They weren't there.

My apartment was on the top floor of a tenement in the East Twenties, between Third and Second Avenues. I'd moved down from upstate right after I'd completed the third, and final, semester of the communications program. The first payment for my second project with Jim Upton was in the bank, and I had plenty of money for the escrow on a cheap apartment. It was a small place, just a living room, two pocket-sized bedrooms, a small kitchen that could accommodate a tiny table and two chairs, and a bathroom that might have been original to the building's construction a hundred or so years earlier.

There were a couple of gallons of white paint, a roller and paint tray, and two brushes, one wide, one narrow, on the living room floor, when I went up to the apartment on the morning I signed the lease and paid the escrow plus a month's rent. It took me two days to paint the place. I scraped paint off the windows and cleaned them inside and out, leaning out over the sills as much as I dared.

For the first week, I slept in a sleeping bag I bought in an Army and Navy store. A very large black man carried an enormous floor sander up the three flights of stairs and polished the floors. I went to a thrift shop in a church nearby and found a usable couch, an armchair, a dresser, and a small kitchen table with two chairs. The couch was Victorian, the armchair was Sixties vintage, I guessed, and the wood furniture was from several eras in between. I paid a young guy who worked in the thrift shop to help me carry my new furniture through the streets and up the three flights to my new apartment. I gave him a few dollars more to hold any bookcases that came into the thrift shop for a day or two for me.

I kept checking in, and a week later I was the owner of two tall pine bookcases, stained dark mahogany. They took up most of one of the living room walls. I found some working lamps, pots and pans, a toaster, a coffee maker, dishes, and flatware at flea markets over a weekend. I rented a small van and moved my clothes, books, records, high fidelity equipment, and a black and white television with rabbit ears down to New York. Macy's delivered sheets and towels and the narrowest mattress and box spring I could find there.

I paid more than I should have for two double-drawer filing cabinets and a rolling desk chair in an office supply store. I was careful about the chair. I knew I'd be sitting in it a lot, and I didn't want to scrimp on it. Finally, I carried an unpainted door home from a lumber yard. I put the door on top of the filing cabinets, put a lamp and my portable typewriter on top of the door, sat in the chair and rolled it into position.. The phone guy had installed a jack so I could put the phone on the desk. I was in business.

My office was in the narrow little bedroom adjacent to the living room. The two rooms were in front of the building and had Northern exposure. But because the buildings across the street and for several streets beyond were no taller than mine, I could see the hypodermic-needle top of the Empire State Building, and the two front rooms were bright a good part of the day. I used the other bedroom, which looked out on an airshaft and was dark all the time, for sleeping on the mattress and box spring, which stood on the floor.

I kept the small refrigerator full. I bought a fresh baguette every other day and a case of inexpensive Cote-de-Rhone every three weeks or so. I liked to eat lunch out, and breakfast and dinner at home.

I went to an animal shelter and adopted a gray cat who howled more than any of the others there. I figured he needed a new home more than the rest of the cats in the cages. When we got home, I showed him his litter box and fed him. He curled up on the Victorian couch and fell asleep. The attendants at the shelter had told me the cat was a male. I named him Balzac.

Estelle called a day after the lunch with Upton and Don Burdette. "Jim has your notes," she said. "He picked them up at the restaurant at lunch today." I sensed she'd put her hand over the phone's mouthpiece. "Wait," she said, "he wants to talk to you."

It was three-thirty. I figured I was going to get the bad Jim, not the good Jim, and I was right. Unfortunately. "Burdette says he wants to put the project on hold indefinitely," he said, the words slurred. "'Nuts to the contract,' he told me on the phone late this morning. His exact words. 'Nuts to the contract.'" Upton paused. "I blame you," he said, after what seemed like an hour. Then he hung up.

I sat without moving while the light died in the room. I'd spent the day moping listlessly around the apartment. I'd tried listening to Errol Garner, figuring that his bouncy, joyous piano playing would get me going, but that didn't work. I'd had toast, a soft boiled egg, and hot tea, and had asked myself why the delicious food and wine I'd eaten at the disastrous lunch had made me feel so bad, even though I knew the answer to the question. Now I had to face the possibility that the exciting career I'd fallen into was in grave jeopardy.

I was under no illusions. I'd always told myself I needed to live a life without illusions. I knew I'd been lucky. Starting with the Rod Barrett book, I'd fallen into the beginnings of a career. The Upton projects were a good base. When I told several of the contributors, who weren't academics, but worked at engineering companies, about the Institute's communications program, I found myself with writing assignments, even before I'd finished the program. I began writing reports and promotional materials for new products and services.

On a tip from a professor, I went over to the Engineering Societies Building, on the East Side, near the United Nations, worked my way into the offices of directors of publications for several of the societies, showed them samples of my work, and came away with a couple of assignments for stories in the societies' monthly magazines. I had loads of energy, and I was too young to realize how utterly brazen I was. One assignment seemed to follow another seamlessly. Everything I turned my hand to paid handsomely, as far as I was concerned. I had no idea where this odd little career of mine was leading. I'd decided to enjoy the ride for the time being.

And now this.

The morning after Jim Upton had lashed out at me, I put in a call to Estelle. "Do you think Jim would mind if I called Don Burdette and tried to put things right?"

"You really don't have to worry," Estelle said.

"But yesterday afternoon Jim sounded like the project was dead, and it was me who killed it."

"Mordecai, it'll all blow over. Trust me, it's happened before."

"With Don Burdette?"

"With Don Burdette, and with several others." Estelle's voice was a motherly purr.

"I'd still like to call. I need to explain myself." How I would do that, I had no idea.

Estelle's motherly purr put an end to the conversation. "Go ahead, Mordecai. I think it'll do you good."

Don Burdette was affable over the phone. "Not your worry, Mordecai," he said. "I could see that you weren't a veteran of Jim's lunchtime shenanigans. Besides, you're a nice Jewish boy. Your people aren't drunkards. A small glass of Manischewitz on Passover, that's the sum total of a Jew's involvement with the grape."

I flinched, wondering what was coming next. Would I be told that Jesus would save me if let myself be embraced by him? Was that what a Mormon would say?

"I should know better than to go to lunch with Jim, no matter what he tells me beforehand about his being on the wagon. Then it's same old, same old, I get annoyed, and I try to throw a scare into him. The project's still a go." Don Burdette laughed. "You have your notes, don't you?"

I hoped the bad Jim hadn't discarded them. "Of course," I lied.

"Great!" Don Burdette shouted. "Call me if you need more help."

After I hung up, I put on a Thelonious Monk record, with Charlie Rouse on tenor, and danced in a small circle, like that gifted, damaged man did when he couldn't contain his joy. I was full of relief, more so than joy, but it didn't matter. Then I went out for a run. I needed to sweat properly – and for a good reason.

To put the matter succinctly, during my first two years in New York, my love life, or sex life, to be blunt about it, didn't keep pace with my editing and writing life. Oh, Balzac had the opportunity every now and then to wind his way around and between a pair of ankles that didn't belong to me, but only every now and then. He liked to sleep next to the top of my head when I slept alone in my narrow bed, which was the case most of the time, but he didn't change his mind about the attractiveness of his accustomed place even when there was another person in that bed with me. Three was company, not a crowd, as far as Balzac was concerned. Besides, the other person was usually much smaller than I was and, though still on the mattress, was pushed against the bedroom wall, so Balzac had the same amount of space to curl up in as he did when I was alone.

For those first two years, no woman spent more than one night in my apartment, but not for lack of trying on the part of some of them. A PhD candidate, who looked surprisingly lumpy and out of shape when she took her clothes off – the nice legs had totally fooled me – left a pair of earrings behind, which, as even I knew, was one of the oldest tricks in the I-want-you-to-call-me book. I got her address from the couple who had fixed us up – I didn't tell them why I needed it – and put the earrings in the mail.

Another young woman, a bookkeeper I'd met on a hot day at the Twenty-third Street stop on the Lexington Avenue line, borrowed a cotton turtleneck from me on the morning after. She was a big girl. When I'd tried out a line about how hot it was on the platform, she'd said, "I'm taller than you are." I'd pointed out that she needed her stilettos to pass me by half an inch or so. In any case, the turtleneck fit her long torso pretty well.

Instead of putting her in a taxi, I let her take the train back to the Bronx, where'd I'd picked her up at her friend's place the previous afternoon. She was sitting at the kitchen table when I arrived, watching with great interest her friends fussing over several babies. Her skirt had ridden up so that her dimpled knees were exposed, and her legs, which she complained were too heavy, looked great in high heels. She talked a lot about her friends' babies at dinner, before we went to my apartment.

A week later I picked her up at her yoga class. I had to guess which pair in the sea of shoes near the door was hers. They were the wide high heels. We had a pleasant dinner, I liked her, she was tall, but there was no spark. I saw her in front of Grand Central a couple of months later. I was walking with a guy from one of the engineering societies who I sometimes ate lunch with. She came over to me and said, "Call me." I didn't, so I didn't ask for the turtleneck back, either.

New York was filled with great-looking women, but when I went to bars to find one, they were filled mainly with other men on the same mission I was on. Some were interesting – guys I could pass the time with – but others, like the guy who spent all evening staring at the mirror behind the bar and rearranging his hair - seemed weird. Perhaps the weird guys kept the girls away. I couldn't find any place like the hotel upstate that I used to frequent on Saturday nights.

When I told an older friend, who was married to a younger woman he'd met on a business trip, about my dilemma, he cautioned me against going to bars. "You'll meet someone at your publisher's," he said, "or on the tennis court, or at the beach." One afternoon, I went through all four floors at the publishing company, but didn't see anyone I wanted to chat up, except for the buxom redhead I'd seen outside Jim Upton's office. She was off limits, of course. The women at the engineering societies looked up from their work and their eyes met mine when I walked past their desks. Evidently, they were on a mission of finding love, or sex, as well. But they all looked too old for me and too wise in the ways of the big city. On the tennis court, I played tennis. I didn't care for the beach.

So I was surprised when I met Marci Treadwell in a bar on Third Avenue, late one afternoon. I'd checked to see whether Jim Upton was still in the office, and when Estelle told me that he'd gone for the day, I dropped off a manuscript with her. I thought I deserved a celebratory glass of single malt whiskey, something I didn't keep at home, so I stopped in at the bar a few blocks south of the publisher's offices.

As I ordered, my eyes locked onto the eyes of a very pretty, dark-haired woman, whose face was reflected in the mirror behind the bar. When I turned to seek her out in the crowd, the same pair of eyes locked onto mine, but this time directly. The very pretty, dark-haired woman got up from her barstool and began walking toward me. She was dressed in a dark power suit and high heels, the uniform of choice for New York businesswomen. She had a large chest and was slim below the waist. She was tall. On her high heels, she was just a couple of inches shorter than my six-one. I could tell that she was young – in her early twenties, I guessed. She was smiling at me. "Where have you been?" she asked. Her voice had a slight trace of the Midwest.

"Looking for you," I said. I kept it short. I didn't want her to know how hard I was trying.

"Well, you found me," she said. "Marci Treadwell," she went on, holding out her hand. She had a delicious smile on her lips. I wanted very badly to taste it.

"Mordecai Bornstein," I said, taking her cool hand in mine. I'd said goodbye to Mike Born in another life. I decided to take the plunge. "Would you like to have dinner with me?"

"Just let me say goodbye to the girls," Marci Treadwell said. "Then I'm yours."

On an autumn evening three years later, I sat at my desk in my small walk-up apartment. It was the same desk I'd always had in that apartment. I liked the large surface, which I'd covered with glass. I'd had the glass delivered; the thought of carrying a piece of glass that big through the streets and up three flights of stairs, even in bubble wrap, had terrified me.

I'd upgraded the living room furniture, except for the bookcases, which were still in great shape. There was a Persian rug on the floor, which still had a high gloss.

I was running, playing tennis a couple of times a week, having lunch with people in publishing, going to hear jazz in the clubs. I'd added contemporary classical music to the jazz I listened to at home.

My career was going gangbusters. I still had the gig with Jim Upton. He'd cut me in on royalties, so the projects were increasingly lucrative. I still did the occasional writing extolling industrial products, as long as they were environmentally friendly, and my relationship with the engineering societies continued, as well. I'd begun writing for general interest magazines on a variety of topics, not limited to environmental issues. I had an article on the rebirth of the Hamilton Watch Company as a maker of digital watches coming out in an airline magazine in December. I'd been talking to a major magazine about becoming a contributing editor and to a trade publisher about a book.

Balzac was still with me. Marci wasn't.

We were an ideal couple, Marci and me. Everyone said so. "Beauty and the beast," I said, more than once. "You're a beautiful man, Mordecai," Marci always said in response. I had no doubt that she meant it.

We had all the trappings of an ideal couple. We looked great together, we talked easily with each other, and we liked being together. I had my career, and Marci had a good one, too. She was a publicist for a publisher very much like the one I was involved with. We went on great vacations – the first year to London and the Lake District in April, the second year to Italy in March. We discovered cute little restaurants with sassy food and clever wine lists, and people who knew us followed in our footsteps. They heeded our movie recommendations and paid attention when we talked about what we'd seen on and off Broadway. We ran, and we kept fit. Marci swam while I played tennis. We had our own small apartments, and we were saving up to buy a single, bigger place together. After sex, Marci clung to me and whispered "I love you" in my ear. I thought she would love me forever.

She was barely twenty-two when we got together. I was five years older. She seemed to want me to be the dominant partner in our relationship. "As soon as I looked into your eyes," she told me more than once, "I knew I'd found a real man." The rest of the men she'd met in New York were all boys in her eyes, she told me, no matter how old they were. In bed, the littlest thing I did sent her into spasms of ecstasy. She asked me what I wanted her to wear, or asked if I approved of what she had already put on, no matter what the occasion was. Stepping out of the shower on a Sunday morning, when we were going out for breakfast, I'd find her in a tiny pair of shorts and red high heels, waiting for me to flash a smile of appreciation for the way she'd made herself look.

In front of me, at my desk that autumn evening, was a black and white photograph. It showed a woman in her full bloom of youth, with wide-set eyes looking directly into the camera. She has an expression on her face that says to the viewer, "Get real." She isn't smiling; her lips look lightly pressed together. It's as if she's confirming what ought to be blindingly obvious. The woman's shoulders are bare, except for two broad straps holding up a dark blouse that flows over her breasts. I knew those breasts, of course. The woman in the photograph was Marci.

After I'd taken it, Marci asked me to sit down, and I lowered myself into one of the Morris chairs in my living room. Marci sat on the couch opposite me. She leaned forward, her forearms on her thighs, her hands cupped together.

"I've been seeing a man whose name is Harold," she said, looking into my eyes. "I leave work early, spend a few hours with him, and then I come here."

My mind emptied out. I had no idea what to say. I'd had no clue. I sat quietly, and then I burst into tears. I screamed, my jaw twisted in rage. My throat felt raw instantly. Then the crying stopped, as abruptly as it had begun.

"Why tell me his name?" I asked.

"So you'll realize it's serious, and the relationship has a future."

"No, you're just being cruel. I don't understand any of this, what it means." I swallowed hard. "Why should I believe any of this shit?" I spat out the words. "I never smell him on you."

"We cook his dinner together. Then he does things for me and to me that you don't. Then we take a bath together. "

"What the fuck are you talking about?" I screamed. I was on my feet now, looming over Marci. She shrank back, as if I might strike her. Instead, I crumpled to the floor at her feet, put my arms around her long, slim legs, rested my cheek on her knees, and closed my eyes.

We said nothing more for several minutes. Then, without moving, I asked her in a calm, quiet voice what she intended to do She sat still and said nothing. Finally, she put a hand on the top of my head. We stayed where we were for a very long time, until Marci said, "he's older than you, and a lot more experienced. He knows less about technology and writing than you do, but he knows a lot more about people."

"I'm just a nice Jewish boy from Columbus, not much in the way of competition," I said miserably. I could feel no rage against Marci, not even against this Harold person. I felt very sorry for myself and ashamed of it.

Marci took a leave of absence from her job and went out to the West Coast with Harold for several months. Before they left, she told me that Harold needed to visit antique stores in California and Oregon. He supplied them with old furniture that he found in homes in Vermont and New Hampshire, and he needed to discuss what was selling and what the store owners wanted him to look out for.

On the day they returned, Marci let herself into my apartment with her key and set about preparing dinner. I made no move to stop her. I didn't ask about her trip, and she volunteered nothing. Her relationship with me simply resumed, although it wasn't exactly the same as it had been in the pre-Harold days.

Yes, we made no effort to avoid each other and went back to doing the same things we always did together. But there was something different in our relationship now: a lower level of emotional intensity. We never spoke of Harold, and never fought over him. He seemed to have faded physically away from Marci's life. I never asked why.

I never noticed a faraway look in her eye that might have indicated a longing for her former lover. But his ghost seemed to invade our space, or at least my space. I sensed his presence when Marci and I were having sex. Her movements, her urgings, her desires, everything she did when we were making love seemed directed toward channeling me into providing the streams of pleasure that Harold had helped Marci enjoy when she'd been with him on those furtive afternoons.   Or so I imagined.   I'd thought I'd provided her with pleasure during the first two years we'd been together – she'd told me so – but what had once seemed to satisfy her was no longer enough.

As the months slid by, Marci continued to eagerly help me provide her with more and more pleasure. I had no illusion that she was training me so that our relationship would evolve into one that would fulfill us as a couple committed to each other forever.   Instead, I realized that the relationship would end when Marci decided that she had gotten the most out of me, when she understood that she could get no more, and when she felt confident enough to set out on her own.   It did end, in the fall of 1985.

CHAPTER THREE

On a late fall afternoon, five years after I'd settled in New York, and after Marci was finally out of my life, I picked up a girl in front of the Public Library on Fifth Avenue and Forty-Second Street by telling her that we could walk up to Fifty-First Street almost entirely indoors by going through passages running the length of buildings in the middle of the blocks from Fifth to Sixth Avenues and then through the Rockefeller Center underground.

You could enter a lobby on one side street, walk through a connecting passageway, then exit another lobby on the other side of the building onto the next side street. It was just starting to rain, and she'd told me she wanted to get up to Fifty-First without getting drenched, so she was game.

I bought an umbrella at a newsstand in the first passage we went through, so we stayed dry while we dodged the traffic on the cross streets between buildings. I kept up a steady barrage of patter about my maneuvering skills that even I found pretentious. Still, she laughed all the way, hugged me at the end, and was willing to have a hamburger and a beer with me. Her errand was forgotten.

She was cute, but she wasn't very interesting, unfortunately. I persevered nevertheless, and she was more than happy to get in a cab with me to go pick up my car in the garage where I kept it, and then let me drive her home to someplace in Jamaica, Queens. After some awkward fumbling, she got out of the car. I didn't ask for her number. Then I had a god-awful time getting back to Manhattan, rueful that this dumb little girl had gotten dinner and a ride home, and I'd had a wasted evening.

This misadventure, typical of those first New York years, came to mind when I reached Karen Kolter's building on Broadway on the Upper West Side at around nine o'clock in the evening on December thirty-first. Her invitation had promised "a New Year's Eve party that would live in memory forever." Well, I needed something in my life that would fulfill such a promise, I thought, as I entered Karen's building and remembered that you could walk through it from Ninety-seventh to Ninety-eighth Streets. I had hoped the memory of that fall afternoon walk through midtown office buildings would soon fade away, but it was back.

The party was very loud and in full swing when I walked through the front door of Karen's apartment. It wasn't very cold that night, at least I didn't think so, and I'd made do with an open-collar oxford cloth dress shirt and a heavy tweed jacket. There were people dancing and standing talking in the large square foyer, the living room straight ahead, and the dining room to the left.

I decided to look around before I got a drink, so I made my way through the crowd into the living room. The windows at the far end of the room were wide open, but it was still warm. The crowd looked fairly young, and there were some attractive women. Whether any were unattached was anyone's guess. Either I'll get lucky, or it's going to be a long evening, I thought. Well, maybe the drinks and the food will be good. An energetic, husky couple bounced against me. To get clear of them, I backed into a hallway that led away from the living room.

"Mike?"

Karen, our hostess, swept past. I'd met her when she'd been the production editor on one of my books. Her invitation had come out of the blue. "Mi – i – ike?" she mimicked, and laughed.

I turned and looked up into large gray eyes.

"Isn't your name Mike?"

"Only when I ask Irish girls out on dates," I said.

"You remember me, then," Patricia Murphy said. She smiled at me.

I looked down at her feet. "I remember you, and I remember those shoes." The shoes that you said made us look ridiculous together, I thought, but didn't say.

"Oh, those. Karen told me to wear them. There's supposed to be some seven-foot guy here, Mark something or other, and I'm supposed to be the catnip." She smiled again. "So, Mike, what should I call you when I use your real name?"

"Mordecai Bornstein," I said. "Now you understand the strategy."

"Don't think I didn't have an inkling. But I respect the strategy, even though it wasn't necessary for me, then, or now."

"Would my having such a Jewish name have mattered to your mother? As I recall from that night I took you out dancing, she wanted you home early enough so that you wouldn't sleep through mass the next morning."

Patricia laughed. "Back then, I'm not sure, but not anymore – definitely," she said, a smile still on her face. "My mother's accepted the fact that I'm a lapsed Catholic. We stopped arguing about my not attending mass some time ago. So what do your friends call you?"

"Mordecai, just Mordecai."

"Wait a minute! Didn't I see your name on an article in an airline magazine? Let's see, wasn't it on the Hamilton Watch Company and digital watches? I thought that article was great!" She flashed a dazzling smile. It was blinding. "You know, when I saw that name, Mordecai Bornstein, I said to myself, "Hmm, self, could that be Mike Born?""

"Smart girl," I said. She flashed another smile. I felt untethered from where I was. "So what do you think of this nice Jewish name?" I asked.

"I really like it," Patricia said. "I really do." She looked away, then into my eyes, her gaze steady. "I thought of you now and then during these past, what has it been, five years? Six? Sometimes I was angry with you, for standing me up on that dinner date. There were days when I couldn't get that out of my head, which seemed like a complete overreaction, I know. I mean, we hardly knew one another. And I thought I might even try to look you up when I go upstate in the spring to defend my dissertation."

"I'm sorry about standing you up." I didn't know what else to say.

"Then I remembered the way we talked that last night I saw you, only the third time I was with you, I know, but you had this amazing effect on me, I realized later, because I talked to you so openly about myself. It was a total departure for me, because I was always so guarded."

"I've remembered those two hours," I said. "One time, a couple of years ago, I thought I saw you at a counter on the first floor of Saks. From the back, but I thought the tall blonde was you. So I rushed over, but it was girl who couldn't have been more than fifteen. I backed away as quickly as I could, while a heavier version of the girl, it must have been her mother, looked at me strangely. I thought she might call the store detective over, if there is a store detective."

Patricia laughed. "Nice Jewish boy arrested for child molestation."

"I didn't know where in California to find you exactly. Besides, I thought you were angry with me."

"Are you Pat Murphy?" said a voice from above and behind me. "Karen told me you'd be here. Hi, I'm Mark." He moved past me and stood next to Patricia. He had to be nearly a foot taller than me, although his legs didn't seem to be any longer than mine. His height seemed due to an elongated torso. The top of Patricia's blonde head was even with his jaw. Me, I thought, six-one and I feel like I'm standing in a hole.

"How about dancing?" Mark said. "Then we can get to know one another."

Patricia looked up at him, and I looked her over as quickly as I could. My time was undoubtedly limited. She had changed in the five years since I'd last seen her. Whether the change was due to her not being so shy any more, I had no idea. She still dressed simply, tonight in a gray belted wool dress, with a crew-neck collar and long sleeves. It fell loosely to the tops of her knees. Her jewelry was simple, too. Just a watch on her left wrist and a gold chain around her neck. No rings on her fingers.

The bangs of five years ago were gone; her hair was brushed back from her face and gathered in an arrangement at the back of her head. There used to be no makeup, I remembered, but now there was a little, just light eye shadow and pale pink lipstick. She looked gorgeous – to everyone, I was sure, and particularly to me. And to giant Mark, of course; he breathed eagerness from every oversized pore.

"Not just now," she said to him. "Mordecai and I have some catching up to do, and it's going to take a while. It always does." She turned to me. My heart banged against the wall of my surprised chest cavity.

"Which means never," Mark snarled. As he stomped out of the hallway, he banged the long neck of the beer bottle in his hand against the wall. It broke off and clattered to the floor. I reached for it.

"I don't want you stepping on broken glass," I said. Ever so gallant, ever so stupid. I picked up the glass and felt a sting of pain in my thumb. Bright red blood bubbled up. I sucked on the wound.

"We'd better take care of that," Patricia said. She took my free hand and with those long strides I suddenly remembered, led me down the hallway to an open bathroom door at the end. "Put it under the cold tap," she said. She locked the door behind us. While I held my thumb under cold water, she looked through the contents of a tall glass cabinet between the toilet and the sink.

"This should do it," she said, as she shook a brown bottle. "Hydrogen peroxide. It'll help cleanse the wound."

"How do you know about this stuff? OK, stupid question."

"Not at all. A man I knew in L.A. had young grandchildren, who were prone to cuts and scrapes."

"I'm not sure if I should ask who this man was."

"You can, but later. You can ask whatever you want."

"And you can ask whatever you want." I was suddenly insanely happy.

Patricia put my thumb over the open end of the peroxide bottle, then turned my hand and inverted the bottle. She held it there for a few seconds.

"Here, hold this while I open a bandage." She leaned forward, intent on wrapping the bandage around my thumb. When she'd finished, she turned her head toward me. Our lips touched, and then pressed against one another. I pushed my tongue out, her lips parted, and my tongue went into her mouth. Her hands flew up to the sides of my face. I pushed her against the glass door of the cabinet, but carefully, so as not to break it. I buried my face in her neck, as she stretched to her full height, so tall before me, her hands on the back of my head.

"Now you're standing me up properly," she said. She hiked up her dress. She still favored stockings and a garter belt, I noticed. She lifted her right leg and planted a high heel on top of the toilet lid. Her legs were apart, and my hand went to a place in Patricia it had never been. She unzipped my trousers.

"Hurry, just this once we have to hurry," she said. "Someone might want to use the bathroom." We laughed a lot about that line later that night.

"Mark tells me you two know each other," Karen Kolter said. Patricia and I were back in the hallway, out of the crowd, leaning against each other, our backs against a wall. Karen was holding two plates filled with stuffed grape leaves, a rice salad, hummus, feta cheese, tomatoes, and cucumber slices. "I call it Mount Olympus," she said. She was famous for her party food, I'd been told. "There's garlic in the hummus, but if you both eat it, everything will be all right." She fixed us with a meaningful stare as she handed us the plates, which weren't too heavy to hold with one hand, and put forks and napkins in our free hands. "Enjoy," she said.

We took the plates into what looked like the largest bedroom in the apartment. I cleared a pile of winter coats off a loveseat. "Tell me about California," I said.

"Everything?" Patricia asked. We sat close together on the low loveseat, our shoulders touching. I could feel her hip pressed against mine. Her legs were crossed, her knees at the level of our chests. I put my plate on the floor, leaned over, and kissed her exposed thigh, where her dress had slid down over her stocking. "That's very persuasive," she said when I'd straightened up.

"The job I went out to California for was at the museum in L.A. that I told you about in the hall just before Karen handed us the salads. I worked in the publications department. There were three of us at the top level - the department head, a marketing person, and me. I was responsible for the editorial side, sort of like what you do yourself for the publisher where that Jim Upton you told me about works."

After we'd straightened our clothes and left the bathroom, I'd told her what I'd been doing professionally during the past five years, including my catalogue of Jim Upton stories. Patricia took a bite of her salad.

"We published books connected with the exhibitions we mounted ourselves," she went on, "plus other titles having to do with the collections. In addition, people approached us with ideas for art monographs, and we commissioned even a few more titles in the five years I was there. The program was a pretty heavy one for a three-person department. The most time-consuming part for me was shepherding manuscripts with tons of illustrations through to production. I did have a small team – a copyeditor and an assistant to chase after illustrations and copyright permissions."

"You told me earlier that you're defending your dissertation in a couple of months. So you must have had work up to here." I brought my hand up to my throat.

"I'm a smart girl, Mordecai. Remember?" I nodded. "There was more than enough time for everything," Patricia said. I saw that we'd emptied our plates. I took Patricia's plate from her and reached down to put it on top of mine on the floor beside the loveseat. When I straightened back up, she cupped her hand under my chin and turned my face toward hers. She planted a quick kiss on my lips. I remembered the kiss she'd given me at the end of the evening five years ago. This one felt very different. "Let's go home," Patricia said. I knew where she meant.

On our way out, I saw Mark dancing with a dark, sexy girl whose breasts came up to his crotch. Her back was to him, as they wriggled in time to the pounding music. Mark opened his eyes and spotted me. He happily flashed me a peace sign. I grinned and threw a two-fingered V back at him.

Patricia had changed to low-heeled black leather boots. Her high heels were in her shoulder bag. She took my arm when we hit the street.

"Let's walk for awhile," she said, "and I'll tell you how I came to bandage kids out in California."

We headed south down Broadway, on the wide sidewalk jammed with people an hour and a half before the beginning of the New Year. Our long strides matched. The story Patricia told me now had overtones of the story she'd told me five years earlier about the high school teacher who'd initiated her into the world of art – and had tried to initiate her into something else entirely. The mentor this time was male. He was a major collector of pre-Colombian art, and he was sponsoring publication of a lavish book celebrating his collection.

His name was William Gaines, he was in his mid-sixties, and the kids Patricia had bandaged now and then were his grandchildren. He was a large, handsome man, and a widower with four grown daughters, all of them older than Patricia.

"He insisted on being intimately involved with every detail," she said. "He spent a lot of time with me." Her face was close to mine as we walked, our pace a little slower now. "It was a very intense relationship, Mordecai." She paused as we crossed Seventy-Ninth Street, south of Zabar's, which was still crowded. "We tried to keep part of it secret, but that was ridiculous," she went on, when we reached the sidewalk. "Everyone in William's family must have known what was going on between us. No one spoke to me about it, but every so often I'd catch one of his daughters giving me a knowing look."

I didn't interrupt Patricia to ask her to spell things out for me. I didn't need to. And it was equally obvious that she was very different from the woman I'd surmised her to be five years ago. Besides, what good would it do me to have details of her relationship with an older, more powerful man? I felt my heart coming up through my throat. We'd stopped walking and stood close together, facing each other. The stream of people moving along the sidewalk had to flow around us. She took me by the hand and led me over to a darkened storefront. She looked at me with concern. "Talk to me, Mordecai," she said.

I took a breath, looked down, and then back into her questioning eyes. Then I rolled the dice. "Were you in love with him?" I asked.

"I was falling in love with him. I can't deny that." Patricia looked as scared as I was. I thought she had to be wondering whether she'd made the right choice in bringing everything about California into the open so early.

"And?" I felt my question hanging in the small space between us.

"And we finished the project. The day the book went off to the printer, William announced that he and I shouldn't see each other anymore. It would be the best thing for me, he said."

"And you agreed, just like that?"

"William can be extremely persuasive. That's how he's gotten where he is. He made me see his point. The age difference was too great, I needed to have control over my own life, not be dominated by him. I pleaded with him, but only once. He convinced me that I'd known all along that the relationship had no long-term future. In the end, my heart agreed with what my head was telling me."

"So that's why you left California?"

"No, silly. As I told you, I was recruited for a bigger and better job here. I'll be the department head."

"Will you see him again?" Even as I asked the question, I felt like an idiot, a weakling.

"He comes to New York, but infrequently. If he asks to have lunch with me, I won't refuse him. Look, Mordecai, I'll be working in a museum with beautiful books. My department isn't the biggest one in the museum by far, but board members will take an interest. I may be interacting with other powerful men. It's inevitable.

"But if you, Mordecai, and I are together, the thing that happened with William won't happen again. I can promise you that." Patricia took one of my jacket lapels in her hand. Her face moved closer to mine. I could feel her warm breath on my chin. "I'm a grown-up and I want to be with someone who's a grownup, too," she said, her eyes beseeching me. "Can you be that person, Mordecai? Can you handle the kind of job I'll have, with the kinds of interactions I'll have to deal with? I need to know. Oh, darling, I desperately hope your answer is 'yes.'"

"Of course it's 'yes,'" I said. "It has to be, or I'll go mad." I kissed her, hard, and we held the kiss for a long time. Then I began to tell her about Marci.

We crossed over to the East Side at Fifty-Ninth Street. When we reached Lexington, Patricia pointed her chin uptown, in the direction of the Barbizon, where she was staying. "I don't need anything there tonight," she said. We kept walking east and turned south on Third Avenue.

"I can see how what I've told you about my relationship with William would be upsetting to you," Patricia said, when I'd finished the Marci story. We'd just crossed Forty-Second Street. "But you have to understand one important thing: I'm not Marci, and I'll never do what she did to you."

I had my arm around Patricia's waist. I drew her closer to me, as we made our way to my apartment. What she'd told me tonight about her relationship with William would have to do, I told myself. I also told myself that if my relationship with Patricia had any chance of success, I would have to believe that there would never be a need to ask her any more about her time with William.

Balzac fell in love with Patricia immediately. As soon as she sat down and took her boots off, he began to rub against her stockings. She stood up, and he looked up at her and howled. When she picked him up and cradled him in her arms, he purred louder than I'd thought he was capable of.

Patricia had stopped me when we were halfway up the outside steps of my building. She'd turned toward me and said, "When I saw you tonight, for the first time in five years, I knew that I wanted you." There was urgency in her voice. "I wanted you forever, Mordecai, not just for tonight, or for a week, or a month, or a year. Forever."

I held her close and looked into her large gray eyes, at the intelligence I saw there. I didn't speak. I waited for Patricia to continue with what she had to tell me.

"I needed to tell you about William tonight, before we'd started on our relationship. I wanted the painful memory, and the need to tell you, out of the way, so nothing would interfere with us." She smiled and tossed her head. "Oh, Mordecai," she said, her mouth close to my ear now, "I know I'm being too presumptuous. But I also know, even before we walk up the stairs, that once I'm in your apartment, with you, my darling, I'll be home."

I found her lips and kissed her lightly. "I'm so glad you're here, Patricia," I said. "I'm beyond glad. I've been waiting my whole life for this moment."

Upstairs, we stood facing each other and undressed each other slowly, uncovering our bodies carefully. When we'd finished, our clothes pooled around our feet, I picked Patricia up and carried her into the bedroom. I lay her gently down on the narrow bed. She stretched her limbs, and I crawled up her long body, exploring every inch of her, outside and inside, with my mouth and my hands. We made love hungrily, greedily even, until we fell asleep in each other's arms midway through the night.

I woke at six and turned toward her. Her eyes were open, and she was smiling at me.

"I can't believe we'll ever get much rest in this tiny bed," she said, "although it's actually long enough for the two of us."

"Hard to believe," I said.

"Hard, indeed," Patricia said, a laugh in her voice. She patted my erection. "Like I said earlier tonight, hurry, Mordecai, before somebody needs to use the bathroom." Then we made love again.

We acted like we were making up for the five years we'd been apart. We went to the Barbizon to collect Patricia's things that afternoon. Somehow, we made room for her clothes, in addition to mine. We cooked a simple spaghetti dinner together and ate it at the kitchen table with a bottle of the Cote du Rhone. We talked while we finished the wine, and then we washed the dishes and put them in the dish rack. We dried each one carefully, as if teasing ourselves with anticipation.

We took the clothes off each other in the kitchen. It didn't take long. I was wearing only a tee shirt and a pair of running pants. Patricia was wearing only one of my shirts and underpants. And high heels, which she'd slipped on after dinner.

"As a treat for you," she'd said to me. We made love slowly, then urgently. Balzac slept on a pillow Patricia had placed on the floor in a corner of the bedroom.

Patricia's job started at the beginning of the second week in January. For the next several months, we fell into a comfortable existence, laced with bursts of excitement and ecstasy. We felt as if we were introducing each other to a rebirth of our sweet new life together every day. We acted like a newly married couple.

On weekday mornings, we rose very early, well before six, and went for a run together. I made breakfast, while Patricia got herself ready for her day. She left for the museum a little after eight. By nine, I was at my desk, immersed in my projects. After dinner most evenings, we worked together on finishing her dissertation for a couple of hours.

"You supply the brain power," I said, "and I'll do the typing," which got a laugh and a roll of those large gray eyes.

Her dissertation had to do with museum economics. Patricia was interested in how certain things affected rich people's bequests of works of art they owned – tax and other government policies, market prices for the art, and such psychological factors as altruism and familial demands. In the end, I did function as more than a typist. We had several no-holds-barred debates about analytical techniques and how the wealthy thought about themselves. We weren't above calling each other a fool and an idiot, and then having furious sex an hour later.

That was the fun stuff, of course. The other stuff was just hard. There were equations, charts, and tables – a boatload of complex typing chores. This was a doctoral dissertation, after all. But I'd done such typing on my own projects, so I helped Patricia produce the finished project in a very short time.

Late one afternoon in early May, we took the train upstate. Patricia was scheduled to defend her dissertation on the following day. Her mother, Mary, picked us up at the train station across the river. She hugged us both in the waiting room. I knew that Patricia hadn't kept the fact of our living together a secret from her mass-attending Catholic mother. I wasn't sure what to expect. But when Mary hugged me, she looked up at me with approval on her scrubbed face. Then her look changed to one of appraisal – the same look I'd seen on her daughter's face. Mary leaned back a bit, still holding me.

"I know you'll take good care of my daughter," she said, "and I know she can trust you."

"Mother!" Patricia snapped.

Later, alone in Patricia's old bedroom, where we were sleeping – "on a decent-sized bed, for a change," Patricia had said – I asked, "What was that all about back at the train station?"

Patricia sat down on the bed. I sat down next to her. She took my hands in hers and turned towards me. For the first time in four months, I thought, she isn't smiling.

"I wasn't entirely honest back on New Year's Eve, when I told you how the affair with William ended," she said.

"Does the ending matter? It's over and done with."

"Yes, it does matter." She looked down, and then back into my eyes. Her eyes glistened.

"Then how did it end?" I asked. I didn't want to know, but I had to.

"I discovered that William was cheating on me." There was a catch in Patricia's throat. "With my boss, no less," she said quietly.

"So he hurt you, the son of a bitch." My voice had risen, and Patricia put her finger on my lips. "And you still loved him." It wasn't a question.

"No, no, Mordecai. I didn't. I couldn't. Please believe me."

"I believe you," I said. Then I kissed her. I didn't see any point to more questions. I would have to trust her.

We got ready for bed and slipped between the crisp sheets. We lay silently, holding each other, our skin melting together. I slid down and kissed her nipples, then slid down further. We made love quietly, so as not to disturb Mary. Afterwards, we lay side by side. "All that matters, Patricia," I whispered, "is that we're together."

She turned her head and put her mouth next to my ear. Her warm breath made me shiver a little. "I love you, Mordecai Bornstein," she whispered.

"I love you, too," I whispered back, "More than you could ever imagine. Now get some sleep. You've got a big day tomorrow. No more hanky-panky." I heard a giggle, then a sigh, and then, after a short while, I knew she was asleep. I fell asleep, too, hoping that the past was spinning further and further away from us.

The next morning, I drove Patricia to her dissertation defense. She was dressed in a lightweight, conservative gray wool suit, the hem of her narrow skirt at mid knee. The jacket was short and open at her throat. She wore a string of pearls that I'd bought for her in an antique store on a Sunday out of the city. She wore low-heeled shoes.

"I don't want to scare my department chairman," she'd said. No one but me knew that she wasn't wearing pantyhose; instead, she'd put a garter belt on, with light, sheer nylons. I put my hand on her knee as I drove Mary's car.

She'd asked, but her advisor wouldn't let me attend the defense. So I watched her from the car, as she strode toward her meeting, a tall, slim, blonde figure in gray, clutching her shoulder bag containing the slides she needed for her presentation. She turned and waved to me, just before she opened the door and entered the brick building.

I parked the car on the street and went for a long walk. By the time I reached the edge of downtown, I took off my tweed jacket and folded it over my arm. The plan was to meet in the school cafeteria at around eleven-thirty.

"I'll spend the time there checking out the local talent," I'd said. Patricia had hit me in the chest, hard, and I'd grabbed her fist and kissed it.

She was there on time, a big grin on her beautiful face. I stood up when she reached the table where I'd been reading the *Times*.

"Can I call you Doctor Murphy now?" I asked. Then I bent over and twisted my head to look up at her. "You know how I love looking up to you," I said. She cupped her hand under my chin, and I straightened up and kissed her.

"I prefer Doctor Bornstein," she said. The grin was back in place.

"Wait a minute! Are you proposing to me?"

"You catch on fast, kemo sabe."

"Oh, yeah? I'm way ahead of you. Just watch this." I knelt on one knee, and took a small, pale blue box out of my jacket pocket. I noticed that the crowded room had become silent. I sensed that all eyes seemed to be on us.

"Patricia, Will you marry me?" I opened the box and took out the ring. I'd bought it at Tiffany's with a huge portion of a royalty check. I'd had it sized with a ring of Patricia's that I'd taken out of her drawer. She held out her left hand, and I slid the ring over her knuckle. It fit snugly. "I hope you like it," I said. The stone was sapphire. I'd had the band made wider than usual to accommodate Patricia's long fingers. "We can always get a diamond, if you don't." How I would manage that, I hadn't a clue.

"Not on your life," she said. "Now get up, please. Everyone's staring at us. Oh, and yes, I'll marry you. Wait a minute, I think I already said that, sort of." I got up, and Patricia threw her arms around me. Then the cafeteria burst into applause.

When we went outside, Patricia asked me if I'd planned that movie scene we'd just performed in.

"No, Doctor," I said, "you forced my hand." She giggled.

She went off to call her mother with the good news about her dissertation defense, and then to lunch with the committee. I drove to a Chinese restaurant I knew. The food wasn't on a par with what you could find in Manhattan, but it was good enough. We met outside the library at three, as planned, and walked to the car. "I'll drive," Patricia said.

"Jesus, we've been engaged less than four hours and already you're wearing the pants."

"Get used to it, buddy," she said, and pecked my cheek.

She drove into the country and pulled off the two-lane road onto a small parking area. She led me down a short lane to a low, flat rock that served as a bench of sorts. Thirty yards from us was a fenced-in meadow, where several horses galloped back and forth, then stopped by the fence to drink. A couple of them nuzzled. A breeze came up, and I put my arm around Patricia's shoulders. She leaned against me.

There was an Italian restaurant she knew, about fifteen minutes away. We ordered a glass of champagne. The wine list had a Barolo on it.

"Promise you won't look at the bill," I said.

"I promise," she said.

We finished the champagne and all of the wine. Patricia got back behind the wheel. I slumped down in the seat and closed my eyes. I opened them when the car bounced into the parking lot where we'd gone after dancing at the Inn on the Lake five years earlier. Patricia steered the car over to the dark spot at the edge of the lot and killed the lights and the engine.

"Let's get in back," she said. We settled ourselves on the back seat. Patricia slipped her shoes off and pressed her lips against mine. Her tongue entered my mouth. I put my hand under her skirt.

"What happened to your panties?"

"I took them off in the ladies room back in the restaurant. It helps with the driving." She laughed. So did I. "But I did wear them the rest of the day. I wouldn't have wanted to have crossed my legs and scandalized the committee."

My hand caressed her between her thighs. She didn't push it away.

"This is very different than the last time we were here," I said.

"Wait a minute, Mordecai!" Patricia sat up straight. She let my hand stay where it was. "Don't you remember the cranberry juice?"

"I guess so." I wasn't exactly sure what she was talking about.

"You drink cranberry juice when you have a bladder infection, which I had that first night we went dancing. That's why I couldn't let you touch me down there. I didn't want to have to explain about it. So I pushed you away. I couldn't get started with you. Somehow, I thought you'd understand. But what were you really thinking five years ago? That I was a Catholic school virgin who wouldn't put out for you?"

"I didn't know what to think." I said, miserably.

"So you dumped me. No sex, no Patricia. Then you made up some cockamamie excuse about why you broke our dinner date and didn't call me for three weeks." Patricia looked at me fiercely. At the same time, she squeezed my hand between her thighs. "Well, who was she, and how much bigger were her tits than mine?"

"I told you that I'd gotten very busy and had to drop everything but my work," I said.

"Mordecai, I want you to promise me something. Promise me you won't ever lie to me."

"I can't promise you that," I said. "I'll promise that I'll never hurt you. And I want you to promise me the same thing."

"First tell me about *her*," Patricia said.

"Her name was Lisa. A couple of days after the night I took you dancing at the Inn on the Lake, she came on to me when I was walking up the hill to the Institute after lunch. I was minding my own business, believe me."

"I'll bet."

"No, really." Patricia was glaring at me. "Lisa stopped me and asked me if I wanted to have a cup of coffee. That's how it started. And she did have big tits, but they weren't as nice as yours are now and they won't be as nice as yours will be fifty years from now. Look, she knew how to handle me. She was twenty-nine, six years older than I was, and I was relieved when it was over. A few days later, I finally worked up the courage to call you, and, if I remember correctly, we had a great time, talking for hours, and then *you* dumped *me* and took off for California."

"Wait, she was twenty-nine, six years older. So you were twenty-*three* five years ago. And I was twenty-*four*. I'm a cradle robber!"

"Come on, Patricia, the age difference is only thirteen months. I checked your license, while you were in the shower." As soon as the words were out of my mouth, I knew I'd made a mistake.

"I wondered why I had the privilege of taking a shower without you for once. Well, now I know. And you knew that my birthday is in the summer, a month before yours. You just didn't know which birthday was coming up. So you had to snoop on me, you little shit!" She was still glaring at me. If she'd blinked in the agonizing seconds since my blunder, it hadn't registered with me.

"You had a high forehead back when I first met you, and you have the same high forehead now," Patricia snapped. "You've always looked thirty-five. And you'll still look thirty-five twenty years from now, when I'll be fat and pushing fifty and look every bit of it."

When a beautiful woman you outweigh by more than sixty pounds calls you a little shit, you know you're in a lot of trouble. Worse yet, I realized, I'd never heard the word shit, or words like it, pass Patricia's lips. She seemed too refined for crude language. And another thing: unlike me, she didn't make stupid mistakes. I tried to find a way out, no matter how lame. "I seriously doubt that you'll ever get fat. Your mother's as skinny as a rail."

"I'm beginning to wonder about us, Mordecai."

I felt sick. How could such a terrific day be turning out so badly? Had I thrown Patricia away *again*?

"Do you want to give the ring back?" My hand remained trapped between her long thighs, which felt more powerful than they had at any time during our months of making love. I had the good sense not to try to yank it out.

Her eyes grew larger. The satisfied expression on her face seemed to say, "I've got you where I want you." I wasn't about to disagree with that assessment. Despite the situation – or more accurately, because of it – I was getting an erection.

"Are you kidding?" Patricia said in response to my question. "I fully intend to marry you and make you miserable for the rest of your life."

She looked at me in triumph. It didn't seem possible, but her thighs squeezed my hand even harder. "By making you my sex slave. Of course, that won't make you miserable, just extremely lucky. And very tired."

She laughed, and then there was a serious look on her lovely face. "Please don't ever do anything to hurt me, Mordecai," she said quietly. In the dim light, I could see that an emotion somehow including both yearning and fear had suddenly taken over her large gray questioning eyes. "I love you so much," she whispered.

"I love you, too, with all my heart."

"Don't ever leave me. If you did, I couldn't go on with my life. I'd rather die." Then she kissed me hard on my mouth. Our tongues collided. It took some gymnastics for twelve feet of human beings, one of them with very long legs, and the other big and broad, to have sex in the back of that small car, but we managed it, with satisfying results. Not having to deal with Patricia's panties made things ever so much easier, we agreed. Afterwards, I drove us back to Mary's house, while Patricia slept quietly, her head resting against my shoulder. Her big day had finally caught up with her.

CHAPTER FOUR

Patricia and I were married in her mother's back garden. My parents flew in from Columbus. Patricia's museum colleagues and publishing people I knew drove up from New York. A judge officiated, a compromise which pleased no one and pacified everyone.

My parents were enchanted with Patricia. My dad couldn't take enough pictures with his new daughter-in-law, who towered over his stocky five-eight. My sensible mother, a tiny woman – I got my size from some ancestor, I was always told - made sure to be sitting down when she and Patricia talked.

"She's so smart and gorgeous," my mother whispered to me. "I'm so proud of you."

"I thought you were going to ask me how I managed to snag such a prize," I said, with a smile. "I owe it all to mom and dad, I would have told you."

She leaned back and studied me. "Don't be silly, you deserve her." I didn't believe it entirely, I told myself, but I swallowed any doubt.

Two days later, Patricia and I flew to Paris. We were in coach, which was full. In our cramped seats, we couldn't stretch out, so we hardly slept. We spent most of the time reading. We held hands while we leafed through the two guidebooks that we'd brought with us. I'd been to Europe twice with Marci, so I considered myself a seasoned European traveler. Patricia had never been across the Atlantic.

We were on our way to the Frankfurt Book Fair. Our overnight flight landed at Charles de Gaulle in mid-morning. We picked up our luggage and put it in the trunk of a rental car. I had to get one of the clerks to show me how to put the manual transmission into reverse. Once I'd straightened that out, we were on our way. I got onto the N4 eventually, and we headed east, across France. After a couple of hours, Patricia asked me, "Aren't you tired?"

"I feel fine," I said.

"You're not human," she said.

I pulled off the road and went into a gas station's convenience store. I came out with a package of cookies with a dark chocolate coating on one side. Patricia opened the package and bit into a cookie. "I've never tasted such delicious chocolate!" she exclaimed.

"Welcome to France," I said.

We spent our first night at a chateau that had been converted into an elegant hotel. They served a whole chicken in two courses, first boiled, then braised. We ate the chicken, and a cheese plate afterwards, with a bottle of moderately priced red wine. I watched two middle-aged French couples order for their cheese course two bottles of Burgundy, each costing six times what I'd paid for the wine that Patricia and I had enjoyed. I told her that I felt outclassed. She told me she had to go upstairs for another one of the cookies I'd bought for her.

"Maybe I have simple tastes," she said.

When she plugged in her hair dryer that night, to see if it worked, all the lights in our room went out. I stepped into a darkened corridor. Apparently, the outage was widespread. I crept down the stairs and found myself outside the kitchen. A large platter of cheese sat on a serving stand. The platter was covered with flies. Then the lights come back on, and I went back upstairs to bed. Patricia was already dead to the world when I got back to our room.

She was still asleep when I woke in the early morning. Outside, a very large dog attached himself to me and led me on a long walk past fields and into some woods. When I returned, Patricia was tucked into a sumptuous breakfast of croissants, brioche, bread, cheese, and coffee. I joined her. The cheese was particularly good. I hoped that it hadn't been recycled from the previous night. I didn't have the heart to tell Patricia about the flies.

It took me the better part of a day to drive us to Frankfurt. At one o'clock, I spotted a restaurant just off the road. "There's a lamp in the window," I said. "The food's bound to be good." Patricia looked at me.

"You can tell from *that*?"

"Trust me," I said.

There was a buffet inside. We filled our plates. Patricia dumped a pile of sliced carrots on hers. She put a piece of carrot in her mouth. "I've never really tasted a carrot before this!" she exclaimed.

"That's what they really taste like," I said. "Not like from the supermarket back home."

"I'm not sure I can go back home, not after these carrots."

We stayed in a suburban town, Bad Homburg, which is on a rail line to the main Frankfurt train station. We'd picked a large, commercial hotel, the Steigenberger. It had a lot of shiny wood paneling. The room was large. I made the mistake of requesting a wake-up call. The ring was incredibly loud.

We joined a stream of people walking from the station to the fairgrounds. It was a crisp autumn morning, but with gray skies. The book fair was spread across multiple buildings. After checking in, Patricia headed to the building where art book publishers had set up their stands. She was at the fair to scout titles she could buy the American rights to. She wanted to add to the books she published herself at the museum. I headed toward the scientific and technical publishers' stands, to see for myself what the action was in the environmental engineering and science fields.

We made a plan to meet up on the art books floor at one – or at thirteen hundred hours, as we were getting used to saying.

"I'll find you," I said. "There can't be that many tall blondes here, even though it's Germany." She looked stunning in her black wool turtleneck and slacks. She'd left her raincoat at a coat check. She gave me a quick kiss and headed off.

I hadn't counted on the size of the floors. They were enormous, packed with publishers' stands, and crowded with people from all parts of the globe, walking, talking, eating, and drinking. I recognized many of the publishers' names, but not all of them. It took me a couple of hours to make my way through the stands lining four long aisles. I found a few people to talk with, and I took some notes.

I cut my tour short and went to look for Patricia a half hour before we were scheduled to meet. I was worried that it might take me the entire afternoon to find her. But I saw her almost immediately. She was walking through a large German publisher's stand with a tall, gray-haired man in a blue blazer. They went through a door in the back of the stand. I walked briskly toward the door. A large young man stepped in front of me.

"I'm just trying to catch up with Patricia Bornstein," I said.

He held up his hand like a traffic cop. "She's in with Doctor Grosz," he said. "Why don't you wait over by reception? I'll tell her when she comes out that you're waiting for her. And you are?" He spoke English with a British accent.

I busied myself with a pair of gorgeous books that dealt with German painting in the early Twentieth Century, before the Nazis took over. The text was in three languages – English, French, and German. The illustrations were superb. I became engrossed with the books. When I looked up, Patricia was walking toward me. She was holding the arm of the tall, gray haired man in the blue blazer. She looked very happy. Her face was flushed. A wisp of damp blonde hair lay across her forehead.

"Werner," she said, "this is my husband, Mordecai Bornstein. Mordecai, Doctor Werner Grosz." She pronounced the W as a V. He and I shook hands. He was in his sixties, I guessed, and looked as if he belonged in the diplomatic corps. He gave me a quick glance, and then turned to Patricia.

"Why don't you and your husband join my staff and me for dinner tonight, Patricia?" It was a question, but it didn't sound like one. "We will go to Charlot. It's just across from the Opera. You can't miss it." He checked his watch. It looked like it cost more than a small Mercedes. "At nineteen hundred hours, good?" He checked out my tweed jacket and gray slacks with another quick glance. "You both look elegant. You won't need to change. If you want, you can stop by my hotel – the Frankfurter Hof - and freshen up."

He rubbed his chin. "On second thought," he went on, "you might find the Frankfurter Hof a bit crowded. The lobby is filled with young women on expense accounts, having tea and cake they wouldn't even consider ordering if they had to spend their own meager funds for such overpriced snacks." He laughed lightly, patted Patricia's hand, and then turned on his heel to greet another woman. I felt dismissed.

"Did he show you his etchings?" I asked Patricia. We were outside, sitting at a long picnic table. I bit into a delicious bratwurst.

"Werner can be very sweet, underneath that Prussian exterior," Patricia said. She smiled at me. "It was so hot in that little room. I felt flushed when I came out. Did I look it?" I let her question hang in the air.

"Did you do any business with him?" I asked.

"It was very worthwhile. But I have more publishers to see." Patricia took a bite of her bratwurst. She licked a dab of mustard off her upper lip. "Good god, isn't there anything in Europe I don't want to eat by the barrel full? I'm going to gain twenty pounds on this trip."

We rendezvoused at seventeen hundred hours at the picnic table where we'd had lunch. We had two hours to kill before dinner – not enough time to go back to Bad Homburg. We found a hotel, the

Hessischer Hof, not far from the fairgrounds. We collapsed on a sofa in the lobby, read the Herald Tribune, and talked about the day. We'd been on our feet for over eight hours, but we told each other we felt energized.

Patricia stood next to me at the entrance to the restaurant. In her kitten heels, she was almost my height. A dark-haired girl in high heels in front of us stood a couple of inches taller than me. Patricia looked at the top of the girl's head. "I should have worn my heels," she said into my ear.

"Don't tell me you're competitive about height," I said.

"Of course." She raised up on her toes. "See? I'm taller than you are. But I still love you, little man." She laughed and blew into my ear.

"Beats being called a little shit," I said softly. I found to my dismay that I was still smarting from her characterization of me on the night months ago in the parking lot. What the hell was wrong with me?

"Take it easy, babe" she said. She pressed the length of her arm against the length of mine. "I really do love you. I always will."

Then, like I always did when I was standing next to Patricia, I relaxed. "I really love you, too, big girl," I said. My voice was still soft, but husky now. She put my hand on her ass and made sure it stayed there as we sauntered across the restaurant. It wasn't the sort of thing Patricia normally did. I had no doubt that this expression of possessiveness was for the blue-blazered smoothie's benefit. I started to get an erection and worried about how I might conceal it.

We ate dinner with Werner and five of his staff at a large table. He put Patricia next to himself, with me at the far end. I talked about movies and New York with the young women on either side of me. Whenever I looked over at Patricia, she was laughing. Werner had pushed his chair back from the table, and Patricia was turned halfway around in hers. I noticed that she hadn't eaten much, even though the food was terrific.

After dinner, we took taxis to a small dark club where everyone smoked and the disco music pounded. Everyone danced energetically. One of the women I'd talked to at dinner pulled me out on the dance floor and stomped and shook herself to the beat in front of me. I looked over her head at Patricia, who was dancing with Werner. I knew that the flush on her face was back.

Shortly after midnight, Werner led Patricia and me outside and put us in a taxi. He handed the driver several large bills and told him the name of our hotel. We dozed off on the trip to Bad Homberg. As soon as we were in our room, Patricia stripped off our clothes, pushed me down on the bed, and crawled on top of me. She put my already erect penis in her mouth, then straddled me and fucked me in a frenzy, her eyes screwed shut, her hair tossing wildly.

Frankfurt completed the transformation of our still-young relationship. For the five days we were there, Patricia was the dominant partner. She was catered to by the European publishers, always seated next to the head honchos at dinners. Several times a day, after I'd arrived on the art book floor from my rounds at the sci-tech stands, she would disappear with yet another of these smooth European gentlemen, always in yet another blue blazer, behind yet another closed door, while I amused myself with yet another excessive, lavishly illustrated art book. Or so it seemed.

She brought a pair of stilettos with her to the fair and checked them with her raincoat. She put the shoes on in the evening, when we were wined and dined.

"They complete the look," she said, unnecessarily. It was a look that took my breath away. I told her so, of course. I also told her that I didn't mind being the candy on her arm. Just watching her being the center of attention made me crazy with sexual anticipation.

The feeling ebbed away as we drove west, past the broad fields of France shimmering in the golden afternoon light. Halfway to Paris, Patricia ate her first *frisee* salad with *lardons*, and polished off half a baguette with it. She'd shown me, by holding the waistband of her slacks out from her stomach, that she'd lost weight in Frankfurt. "They're falling off me," she'd said.

"*Ess, mein kind*," I said, in my best imitation of my grandmother. "Tell me," I asked later, "did you lose the weight because of the *tete-a-tetes* with the blue-blazered smoothies, or because of the sweaty sex with me?"

"Both," she answered. "Obviously."

There was more sweaty sex in Paris, but it didn't prevent Patricia from getting back to her normal weight, despite the miles we ran and walked each day. It was the irresistible food that did it, of course. We stayed in the Seventh, near Rue Cler, the shopping street, where we found a café that served baguettes sliced longitudinally and slathered with butter, together with steaming cups of café au lait.

We ate our breakfast at tables outside, in the midst of mothers with toddlers, every kid dressed to the nines, it seemed. We ate three-course meals at brasseries and bistros twice a day. Among our favorites were Allard, where we had boeuf aux carrots, a dish of remarkable sweetness – those carrots again - Chez Rene, Boeuf sur le Toit, and Brasserie Flo, where Patricia let the waiter empty the entire silver pitcher of hot chocolate sauce over her profiteroles and proceeded to get some of the sauce on her white blouse as she devoured her dessert.

We splurged on a Sunday tasting-menu lunch at the Jules Verne restaurant high up in the Eiffel Tower, where an attendant checked us in at the entrance to the elevator at ground level, but only after we'd run an appalling gauntlet of what appeared to be Gypsy children begging for money. Afterwards, we walked back to the hotel, changed into more comfortable clothes, and walked in the gathering darkness across a bridge to the Right Bank.

Midway through the week, we had an afternoon of business appointments. Patricia went off to have lunch and a meeting with another of the blue-blazered smoothies at his offices. I met with the head of a successful environmental engineering consulting firm in his offices on the Left Bank. He had invited me to lunch, and I looked forward to a meal at some fantastic, high-end place that even Parisians could only dream about.

When I arrived, however, I was ushered into a private dining room, where we were joined by the firm's general manager. A middle-aged woman in a black waitress uniform with a white apron served us a clear soup, smoked salmon on dark bread, some unspectacular Camembert, and, for dessert, a respectable, but hardly fabulous flan. We drank a chilled Rosé with the meal. I tried not to sulk, and I hoped the two Frenchmen didn't notice any rude, childish behavior. Fortunately, the discussion more than made up for the disappointing meal.

Naturally, Patricia arrived back at the hotel with a tale of lunch at Brasserie Balthazar near the Sorbonne. I put my hands around her lovely throat and pretended to strangle her while she shrieked with laughter at my embellished account of the lunch in the private dining room.

There'd been an hour before we were due to meet at our hotel room, and I'd found a bench along the river. In my notebook, I'd quickly written a poem about the evening walk after our lunch at the Jules Verne. I read the poem, called *Locked in Memory*, to Patricia at the hotel:

We leave the hotel in the late afternoon and walk to the bridge
Halfway across, we stop, alone
Everywhere we look it is dusky blue-gray
Buildings, the river, the sky
In the last few minutes, lights have come on
Traffic seems to move without a sound
"It's so beautiful," you smile
"I wonder why it's just the two of us"
"At this moment we're the only people in the world"

On the far side of the river
We find a bench facing giant black horses
Rearing up, their nostrils flaring
Guarding the door to a museum
We do what lovers in this city always do
On benches in the gathering dark

Later, we pass a small restaurant
Warmly lit, paintings on the walls
"Not after that lunch we had today," you laugh
We remember how jealous that woman looked
When the waiter in the tower restaurant led you past her
You so tall in your red suit, everyone attending
To the corner table by the floor to ceiling windows
The orange roofs of the city
Spread out below in the sunlight
The pale stone of the cathedral
Glowing on the distant hill

We sit with drinks in a brasserie
Across the street, in a second floor apartment
Behind filmy curtains, figures move
We are connected to them
And still alone together
You put your hand in mine
It has always been there
It will be there forever
As on this Paris evening,
Now, forever, locked in memory

The Frankfurt trip became an annual event. I began to write books for general audiences, and I tried to convince myself that it would be a great idea for me to add the big trade book publishers' stands to my book fair itinerary. But truth be told, there really wasn't much reason for me to be at Frankfurt, except to support Patricia, which I was more than happy to do. I understood the importance of staying out of the way of everyone in the art book world, and I managed to do so well at it that even the blue-blazered smoothies didn't seem to voice any displeasure to Patricia about my shadowy presence.

"After all, they can always take you behind closed doors," I joked to her.

With each passing year, Patricia and I extended the post-Frankfurt part of our annual European trips a little further. It might have made sense for me to fly to Frankfurt at the end of her work time there, but before I decided to put this plan into effect, I discovered there were people for me to visit at German education and research centers. So we were both usefully engaged during our days in Germany, and outside of our nights in the same bed, we didn't spend much time together for four or five days. I figured that one or two of the blue-blazered smoothies must have been pleased.

In addition to Paris, which we returned to often, we spent time in Provence, London, and the Cotswolds. One year, we did Scandinavia. One weekday evening, in a fine, and nearly empty, Copenhagen fish restaurant, we were sitting side by side on a banquette. I recognized a famous orchestra conductor and his beautiful, soloist wife as soon as they entered. They were seated, also side by side, at a banquette on the opposite wall. I whispered their names to Patricia, who whispered "I know" into my ear. The conductor eyed my spectacular wife. I eyed his spectacular wife. After a couple of minutes of this, he summoned the waiter, who returned with a sheaf of paper. The conductor began to attack the paper with a pen.

"Probably penning a sonata for his lady love," I whispered into Patricia's ear. "I've been one-upped." She held her laughter until we were outside.

Ireland and Italy were on our travel wish list. I told Patricia I wanted to walk Scotland's moors and to visit the Isle of Jura, where George Orwell, one of my heroes, had lived near the end of his short life. But Paris kept drawing us back.

Soon after our first European trip, Patricia and I moved into a two-bedroom apartment on the Upper West Side. A few years later, we determined that we were doing well enough to buy a three-bedroom co-op, and we managed to find one in our price range – the third bedroom was tiny - with a river view when the leaves were off the trees, on a lower floor in a large older building on Riverside Drive. We were up near Columbia, and a short walk to the cross town bus that took Patricia to the museum.

I used one of the larger bedrooms as an office. It was big enough for an Eames chair, in addition to a desk, padded leather desk chair, files, and bookcases, and we put the TV in there. The living room was for reading, listening to music, and entertaining. We loaded the built-in bookcases with art books and music.

When it came to the art on the walls, we favored the Twentieth Century. Both of us. Patricia told people that she had the taste of a guy with good taste. We put up paintings, drawings and photographs, mainly of industrial and built-up America. From the beginning, we bought originals when we could afford them and whatever limited-edition prints our decorating budget would allow. We didn't stint on frames.

A lot of our art was black-and-white. We did splurge on a Louis Lozowick limited-edition print – made by his wife, actually – showing a high-steel worker on a skyscraper girder, with a cityscape in the background and an elevated train running underneath him. During a casual pass through an antique shop while we were on a Cape Cod vacation, we found a charcoal of four men in a law library by Courtney Allen, an illustrator active in the 1920s through the 1940s.

When we felt we were doing better financially, we looked for more color in the art we bought and began to frequent a shop, located in a Manhattan antique market, run by a dealer in the kinds of art works we liked. On weekend trips upstate, we found an artist who did night paintings of buildings, and we became minor patrons of his.

The apartment had an eat-in kitchen, and a large dining room, where we installed more bookcases and a cherry dining set with straight lines. While I made solid, unspectacular breakfasts and occasional dinners of broiled salmon or chicken with baked potatoes and steamed veggies, Patricia somehow found time to become a competent chef with a decent repertoire.

I wasn't surprised when the couple we'd invited to our first dinner party in our new apartment gave the chef a round of applause.

"The veal stew was delicious," Rita Cassidy said. We'd been friends of the Cassidys for the past several years, and we were all comfortable together. "Where did you get the recipe, if I may ask? Or did you dream it up on your own?"

"Oh, no," Patricia said. She was beaming. "I couldn't make up something that wonderful. I used a recipe that was created at Monet's home in Giverney."

"You art babes," Brian Cassidy cracked, a big grin on his round, smooth face. He was a large man, taller and heavier than I was. My tennis strategy with him was to keep him running as much as possible. "And the bread, cheese, and wine are superb," he continued.

"Full credit to Mordecai," Patricia said, extending a long arm in my direction. "And he made the salad." Our guests applauded again. I stood up and took a bow. When I sat back down, I watched Rita looking around the room.

"You know," she said, "with all this beautiful furniture and all these books and albums, you'd have a hard time introducing a child to this lovely home. I can just see a little boy trying to climb up one of those tall bookcases and bringing the whole thing crashing down on top of him." The Cassidys had left their two young boys at their West End Avenue apartment with a sitter. They'd recently made an offer on a house in Montclair.

"He'd be OK. The bookcases are attached to the walls," I said glumly.

Rita appeared to notice my expression. "What I mean is, Brian and I couldn't live in a place like this, not with our boys. And we couldn't take those wonderful trips you take every year."

"I'd better clear the table for dessert," Patricia said softly. I followed her into the kitchen, forgetting to close the swinging door. I stood beside her, my arm around her shoulders. She turned and buried her face in the crook of my neck. "Oh. Mordecai, do you think we're selfish?" I felt a tear on my neck. Out of the corner of my eye, I saw Rita, her arms full of plates, take a step into the kitchen, and then back out again quickly.

"Two things I know," I said softly, but insistently to Patricia, "you're a wonderful woman and I love you desperately. And our friends should mind their own goddamn business."

She leaned back and looked at me, a hint of a mischief on her lips. "That's three things."

"Wise ass," I said, and kissed the smile on her mouth.

Our early weekday morning runs took us through Riverside Park and up into the city streets. On weekends we drove out of town – we owned a series of Volvos – and hiked in the woods. Some weekends we stayed with Patricia's mother and ventured out from there. In the winter, we did some cross country skiing. I found the time for tennis a couple of times a week. Patricia ate whatever she wanted, but little between meals. If the bathroom scale told her she'd put on a couple of pounds, she cut back for a couple of weeks until she was back where she liked. I had to be a bit more careful, and had to work hard to lose a few pounds when I had to.

Balzac went on, year after year. He remained closely attached to his mom, which, we knew, was what he called Patricia, when he stood at her feet, looked up at her, and howled. He remained an only child, as we referred to him.

We thought about having a child and didn't use protection, but Patricia never missed her period. I decided it might be me, and I went to one of those doctors who keep skin magazines in the bathroom as a masturbation aid. My sperm count was rather low. The doctor advised me to switch from briefs to boxers. I declined to tell him that he hadn't noticed that I already wore boxers.

From that moment on, Patricia and I had little additional interest in fertility clinics. We gave some thought to adoption and, from time to time, we'd discuss the pros and cons, as we saw them. But the moment would soon pass, and we would let the matter drop. We admitted to each other that perhaps we really were too selfish, too wrapped up in our own lives, to bring a child into our home.

We wondered about the wisdom of our passive attitude toward children when first my mother, then soon after her my father, and then Patricia's mother, Mary, all died within the year Patricia turned forty. We'd seen them often over the years and had gotten along with them beautifully.

After my father died, I told Patricia about the time a few years earlier when I'd caught him looking studiously away when she'd crossed her legs near him. I'd known from the first instant he'd met her that he was very happy that I'd married such a stunning woman, and I believed that his looking away meant that he was determined not to let any masculine urge get the better of him and hurt me in the slightest way. At that moment, I'd had an indescribably tender feeling toward him. We had dozens of stories like that one about the goodness of our parents, it seemed, and Patricia and I told them to each other to bring us some measure of comfort.

Two days after Mary's funeral, an exhausted Patricia and I drove out to the place in the country where we'd watched the horses playing, all those years ago, when our relationship was taking root. Now it seemed that we'd always been together - the five years we'd been apart had never happened. Horses were still there, behind the fence. Patricia and I sat side by side. I put a hand on her thigh and caressed the flesh beneath the fabric of her black trousers.

"Alone together," I said softly.

"Maybe we should join a temple," she said. "Maybe we'd find some comfort there."

"But you know how I feel about religion," I said. "It's a racket to keep people away from their normal carnal instincts and from eating what they want to when they want to."

"Then why, after anyone close to you dies, do you tear a button off your jacket at the funeral and then sit *Shiva*? Including for my Catholic mother, for goodness sakes."

"It's a religious way of mourning them, of course, but when I do it, it has nothing to do with religion." I watched Patricia roll her large gray eyes. "No, seriously," I said, "I do it because I believe that it's a practice devised by some smart people who knew a hell of a lot about human nature and the need to honor the departed, pay homage to them."

"And god? Where does he, or she, come in? Oh, wait, don't I know your position on the existence of *el supremo?*"

"Wipe that smirk off your pretty face. You know my position on *el supremo*. He, or she, doesn't exist."

"So how did we get here, you and I, on this rock, able to talk so intelligently?"

I could tell that she knew what I was about to say, but I said it anyway, for the hundredth time. "A happy accident," I said, "or unhappy, in the end, if you're the victim of some power-mad nutcase. Anyway, sometime after the big bang, natural selection took over, and after a lot of that, here we are, two intelligent people sitting on a rock, as you said."

"You have a point, Mordecai, but it's not very comforting. So no synagogue for us, is that it?"

"I couldn't stand it," I said.

There was a look of triumph on Patricia's face. "Even though you went to one for months, to say *Kaddish* for your father."

"I was in mourning, and I didn't have the imagination to express myself any other way."

"So that's what you'll do when I die – sit on a box and go to shul to say *Kaddish*."

"It's not something I'm going to have to deal with," I said. "You're going to outlive me for decades." I waited a beat. "Even though you're considerably older." At which point, Patricia hit me in my upper arm, and then, with a gesture familiar to me, took my chin in her hand, turned my face toward her lips, and kissed me.

My work continued to expand. In addition to an annual book for general audiences, I became a contributing editor on environmental issues for a national magazine. Jim Upton retired, but I still did edited books for his successor, a young woman by the name of Jane Caldwell, who, I was happy to learn, never drank at lunch. I no longer needed the engineering society and product promotion work, so I let it fall away. I made radio and TV appearances from time to time. NPR used me, I supposed, because my views came across as well balanced. Sometimes I asserted the benefits of a new technology; at other times I cautioned against going ahead with one.

TV producers called only occasionally for the same reason. Perhaps I wasn't strident enough for them. Still, I had a name.

Patricia made a huge success of the museum's publishing program. She reworked her dissertation for a university press, which sold enough copies of her book to delight her. She wrote articles for academic journals and art magazines from time to time.

When she turned forty-five, she took on additional management responsibilities at the museum for awhile, including oversight of the human resources department. She wisely left the details to the department's professionals – as long as they could explain their rationale for any difficult decision clearly, and the museum's lawyers could assure her that the law was being followed correctly.

She approached this new assignment – it ended after eighteen months, and she was happy to leave it in someone else's hands – calmly, except in one area. "I can't stand the sexual harassment cases," she told me while we walked through Riverside Park on a Sunday afternoon, after a heavy rain had ended. "The way some of these middle-aged guys, with children and a wife yet, can't control themselves and their little penises makes me want to vomit."

Funny, you'd have to say, especially if you were possessed with a rather strange sense of humor, that I didn't remember Patricia's Riverside Park rant, when she described a sexual harassment case that had become the talk of the museum – not until after my brief Washington trip in February a couple of years later. Did I not remember because my mind was elsewhere while we walked together and she delivered the rant? Was I distracted by some difficulty I was experiencing with the book I was working on back then? Was I lost in some fog over some mundane matter? Or did I listen to my wife intently, like I always tried to do, and did I simply suppress the memory of the rant? How could I explain any of these possibilities? They all seemed absurd to me, when I finally did remember it.

In any case, I wasn't thinking about the rant on that February morning when I boarded the Washington train at Penn Station. I was heading down to a publishers' meeting, where I was to join Jane Caldwell in accepting an award for one of the environmental engineering books I'd put together for her. On the schedule was a dinner, followed by an awards presentation ceremony, where my book would be one of several dozen others to receive a prize.

I'd hesitated when Jane invited me to join her in accepting the award, which would be given to the publisher, not to me, but when Patricia told me that she had to attend an important six o'clock board meeting on that day, which would be followed by a dinner that promised to go until late in the evening, I decided to go to Washington after all. Jane would pay the train fare and the tab for a night in the hotel where the publishers were holding their meeting.

I didn't want to remember the dinner, much less the woman with the mass of curly black hair, or the short skirt that rode halfway up her tempting thighs when she sat down next to me and crossed her legs, or the high heels that brought the top of her head up to my cheekbone as she stood with her back to me in my hotel room and threw her blouse on the bed, and I cupped her bare breasts in my hands.

I didn't want to remember how she and I had laughed when she'd unbuttoned her suit jacket and blouse as soon as we'd heard the lock on the room door click shut. Nor did I want to remember what the piles of our clothes looked like on the floor, how the woman with the mass of black hair tasted, how she spasmed when she came, how I groaned when I came.

I did remember that she'd told me she was married and had three children, two boys and a girl. I did remember that I'd told her that I loved my wonderful wife. I did remember that she'd explained that this wasn't the first time she'd done this sort of thing, that we were consenting adults, and that no one need find about this night. So what was the harm in a little fun?

I did remember that I'd fallen asleep briefly after the woman with the mass of curly black hair had dressed and left my room, closing the door quietly behind her. I did remember that when I'd awoken, I'd rushed into the bathroom, knelt in front of the toilet, and vomited into the bowl.

I did remember that Patricia had called me at eight the next morning, after I'd returned from a long run up through the Adams-Morgan neighborhood, that we'd talked briefly about her meeting and my receiving the award, that I'd mentioned nothing about the woman with the mass of curly black hair, and that we'd said we loved each other. I did remember - oh, how I remembered - that I'd told Patricia years ago that I'd never hurt her.

I remembered all of it, as I sat on the train speeding back up to New York, an unread Ruth Rendell novel in my lap. I remembered that near the end of our conversation Patricia had asked me if I was feeling all right.

"Just a little tired," I'd said. "I don't sleep well in strange beds."

There'd been a pause. "Get home safe," Patricia had said.

She looked at me carefully when I came in our apartment door. She unwound from the living room couch, walked over to me, and took me in her arms. I hugged her tight and buried my face in the crook of her neck. I didn't want her to scrutinize my eyes.

"I missed you," she said. "I need to wake up next to you."

"I missed you, too." I was still holding her tight, and she still couldn't see my face. I'd just told her something that was indeed true. I *had* missed her. I'd needed her in Washington, if only to keep me from doing the stupid thing I'd allowed myself to do.

"I have a nice dinner for us," Patricia said. I released her, and she pecked me on the cheek. She looked at me intently. "Why don't you relax, Mordecai? I just have a couple of last minute things to attend to in the kitchen." I watched her walk away from me, this elegant woman I loved. How could I tell her that I'd been unfaithful? How could I hurt her?

"I'll go unpack," I said. "It'll take me just a minute." When I got back to the kitchen, Patricia was pouring a California pinot noir into our glasses. There was a basket of French bread on the table.

"I got up early and put a lamb stew in the crock pot," she said. She spooned portions onto our plates. I looked down at the meal. It was one of my favorites. I took a tentative bite and slowly chewed the piece of red potato I'd speared with my fork.

"Well, let me tell you about the meeting and dinner last night," Patricia said. I let myself look at her. She was smiling at me. "What a hoot," she said. It took her forty-five minutes to tell her tale of what was really a hilarious case of mix-ups and mistaken assumptions on the part of some normally very astute people. By the time Patricia had finished her account of the previous night, I'd cleaned my plate, polished off half of the bread, and had drunk two glasses of the pinot. I had no idea how I'd managed to eat anything. I was very nervous. I couldn't understand how I was able to ask my wife for more and more details about the meeting. We even burst into helpless laughter together. But I still felt miserable. I worried that my face was betraying me.

Patricia asked me to tell her more than I had on the phone earlier about the awards ceremony and the train rides, but about nothing else that I'd done in Washington. After dinner, we went into my office and watched a movie on TV – it was *Random Harvest*, which always left us a little weepy. When it ended, I told Patricia I wanted to check my email. She said that she'd be in the living room, writing in her journal.

We'd both been keeping journals since our early thirties. We used 200-page, ruled, hard cover record books that were meant to be used for business, but suited our purpose. When we filled one, we bought another at Staples. We both wrote only on the odd-numbered, right hand pages. Each time we wrote, we filled up the page, no more, no less – although on special occasions, like a trip, we might fill more than the one page at a sitting.

We had a deal. Each of us kept our journals locked away from the other. No peeking, we agreed, until one of us died. Then the survivor could read everything the deceased had written.

I was in bed first. When Patricia got under the covers, she stretched herself out against me and put an arm over my chest. She kissed my cheek. I tried to relax. After awhile – I didn't look at the clock radio on the night table, so I didn't know how long – I sensed that she'd fallen asleep. I was awake for a long time, it seemed, before I finally fell asleep. Neither of us turned over. Patricia's arm stayed on my chest.

When I got out of bed early the next morning, she was in the kitchen, scrambling eggs. "I thought we'd skip our run this morning and drive out to Jones Beach and walk for miles instead," she said. I drove and Patricia navigated. It was a clear, cold February day, with no wind.

When we got onto the beach, we were surprised to find a large number of people there, with their faces turned toward the sun. We walked along the edge of the water, making sure the waves didn't lap over our running shoes. We talked as we walked. We held hands. I let myself look into Patricia's intelligent, kind eyes, and let her look into mine. She didn't ask me again about my trip to Washington, and I didn't tell her any more about it than I had when I'd first returned home.

CHAPTER FIVE

I watched Patricia take her vitamins and supplements – C, D, E, calcium, magnesium, and only god, or the devil, knew what else, as I was wont to say. Reminded that I believed in neither, I would shut my trap. She had a glass of water in one hand and pills in the other. She put them in her mouth one at a time, took some water, then more water, then water a third time. It took forever. For reasons related to me often, which I immediately forgot just as often, she had an awful time getting a pill down, no matter how small. In any case, I stayed clear of her while she endured her ritual.

She stood, in her stocking feet, at the sink in her mother's old house upstate. After Mary had died, Patricia and I had decided not to sell the house, but to rent it for awhile, until we had an idea about what to do with it that made sense to us. Real estate values were low in that upstate town, so even a house in as good condition as this one was wouldn't fetch enough to have spurred us on to selling it before we were good and ready. There was no mortgage, and the taxes were easily manageable, so there'd been no rush.

Just before Patricia turned fifty, she'd learned that the largest museum in the area where she'd grown up, The Museum of Art and Industry, was looking for a new director. Next thing she knew, she was being recruited. Besides her success with her publishing operation, the additional administrative duties she'd taken on and done well at had gotten her favorable notices, and museum's search committee, knowing her connection to the area, had sought her out. She'd been thrilled.

"It's so tiny compared to where I am now, but I'd be running my own show," she'd told me, excitement in her voice. She'd told me what the job entailed, and that she'd have a free hand to do whatever she wanted, even transform the place to conform to her vision of what its purpose should be and how it should serve the public.

"I'm terrifically pleased and proud of you," I'd said. I always was, wholeheartedly. "Anything you want, babe, I want." I always meant it, without reservations.

It seemed that only a few moments after we'd agreed that the job upstate would be a wonderful opportunity, there'd been a series of interviews, a job offer, Patricia's acceptance, and a rollicking going-away party at the museum in New York. It had all gone by in a flash.

We'd been concerned about potential logistical problems associated with her taking a job 150 miles away from our home, but any concerns had proved to be groundless. It seemed that there was a benevolent force field pulling us upstate, on a pathway lubricated to remove any friction that might hinder our movement.

Patricia floated the idea of driving upstate on Monday mornings and staying in a rented apartment near the museum until driving back to New York on Thursday or Friday night, but suddenly the tenants in Mary's house informed us that they'd found a home to buy and wanted to break the lease. Mary's empty home looked ideal for us. There wasn't any wallpaper to strip, so painting it would be easy. Underneath the wall-to-wall carpeting was the original oak flooring, which we knew was in terrific shape.

We found a contractor who did everything, including installing new bathroom fixtures, kitchen flooring and granite countertops. He even built bookcases to fit the walls of the living room and the bedroom I would use for my office.

We arranged the house the same way we'd arranged the New York apartment, with the TV in the office. There were a few good pieces among Mary's furniture, which fit in with the new purchases that we added.

The 20-year mortgage on the New York apartment had only a few more years until maturity, and the co-op fees weren't out of sight, so we could easily keep it for holidays and weekends when we wanted to be in the big city. We could do whatever we wished, we thought. There was no financial pressure on us.

For the first time, Patricia's salary would exceed the amount of money I was earning. "Does that bother you?" she asked me.

"Look," I said, "I married you because I knew I'd never find another chick as smart as you and with legs as long as yours. The fact that you're going to earn so much money merely confirms how astute I was about you."

"Mordecai, you're a wonderful jerk," she said. Then she put her tongue in my mouth, but had to withdraw it because she was laughing so hard.

From the first day at her new job, Patricia was the toast of the town. Before the first week was out, the area's two major newspapers asked to do feature stories on the local girl who'd returned a conquering heroine. She agreed to be interviewed and photographed on the condition that she and I were featured jointly. I told her that wasn't necessary. I argued that I was well enough known in my own right, so if they wanted to only mention my name as her husband it would be enough. Anyway, all of the focus should be on her. But she insisted, and both papers bowed to her wishes. So both of us were in all the photographs the dailies ran along with their articles.

The editor of the alternative weekly, on the other hand, would have none of Patricia's demands. He insisted on photographing her alone, and he ran a cover page showing her in high heels and a suit with a short skirt standing in front of the museum, her feet spread apart and her hands on her hips. The photographer took the shot from ground level, so that she looked about eight feet tall.

Better yet, a little of the slit in the back of her skirt could be detected. I detected it, because I examined the photograph with a magnifying glass. Then I got on the phone and asked the photographer for an oversized print, which I had framed and installed on the floor of my office, leaning against a bookcase.

"So I can make love to you while you're at work," I told Patricia. Six months later, one of the dailies returned for a follow-up interview, this time of Patricia alone, as part of a large Sunday edition story on the half dozen women who were heads of museums, universities and hospitals in the area.

Partly because I'd attended the Institute's science communications program, the local public radio station's morning show had interviewed me several times over the years, whenever I'd published a new general-interest book. They'd put me on for ten or fifteen minutes with a host who seemed to have actually read it.

Soon after Patricia took over at the museum, Martin Fantock, the head of the station, and his wife took us out for dinner. Our party sat in the back room of a little Chinese-Japanese joint near the station. The owner and the staff treated Martin royally. That night, the Hispanic guys behind the sushi counter were in great form, and the treats kept on coming.

Two days later, Martin taped an hour-long interview with Patricia that made her sound like she'd taken over the Metropolitan down in New York, rather than a much smaller museum with a tiny collection by comparison.

However small Patricia's museum might be, she had big plans for it, and the board's backing for carrying them out. Within her first week, she ordered a detailed inventory of the museum's holdings and discovered a trove of paintings of foundries and laboratories dating back to the time when the area had been a leader in American industrialization. She found the money to restore the paintings, many of which had been executed by listed artists, and cleared a room for the collection. The *Times* ran a story in the weekday Arts section on the collection, with photos of Patricia and several of the paintings.

She proposed a merger with a smaller museum just outside the area that her museum principally served, and the board eagerly approved it an hour after they were handed the financial rationale she'd put together. Several staff members in overlapping positions in the two museums were happy to take early retirement. Patricia used the savings, combined with a gift from the board chairman, to acquire additional paintings by the industrial era artists, whose work she'd unearthed. The acquisitions prompted another story in the *Times*. She was on a wonderful roll.

"A hard-driving executive and canny deal-maker by day, a ravishing vampire by night," I said to her. She pressed her teeth into my neck,

"Flattery will get you everywhere," she whispered in my ear, and then proceeded to show me where "everywhere" was. I'd never loved her more. But every now and then, when I least expected it, the memory of that awful night in Washington gripped me. At those moments, I hurt with self-loathing.

I still kept the stupid thing I'd done hidden from Patricia. Every so often, when the memory would attack me, she'd catch me with a faraway look. I'd put her off with some excuse or other, and she wouldn't pursue the matter, to my great relief. I knew I could never tell her about that night and my unfaithfulness. I only knew that I'd never done anything like that again, and I knew I never would. I had risked hurting Patricia, and I could not take that risk again.

Nearly all of the time, fortunately, the memory stayed at the back of my consciousness, and I allowed myself, without having to think about it, to fully enjoy my relationship with the wonderful woman I'd been so lucky to marry. The museum functions, with spouses invited, were a delicious treat. They reminded me in a way of the Frankfurt times, although Patricia didn't come home with me now quite as sexually charged as she had back then.

Board members and their spouses all seemed to know of my work, whether or not they'd read any of my books or magazine articles, or seen me on television, or heard me on the radio, so my ego needed no stroking. I was freed, content even, to be a "walk behind," a spouse who walks a few steps behind his executive wife, who escorts the board chairman, into a dining room or some other destination. Why should I care if I walk a few paces behind this woman, I would tell myself, it would be me she'd be sleeping with tonight, not the chairman, no matter how powerful he might be. Besides, from the back, in her long gown that brushed against her high heels as she walked ahead of me on these occasions, the view was spectacular.

I looked at Patricia as she stood at the sink, her back to me. I looked at her hair, her shoulders, her straight back, her slender hips, her long legs. I waited until I thought she'd got the last of the pills down, and then, barefoot, I stole up behind her.

She put the drinking glass in the sink, and then leaned back against me with a sigh of pleasure as I slipped my hands into her skirt pockets. I ran my hands along the valleys between her thighs and pelvis. I smelled her newly washed hair.

She was fifty-four. Her hosiery covered a few varicose veins. There were a few gray strands in her shoulder-length blonde hair. She'd finally succumbed to wearing reading glasses.

"Even *my* arms aren't long enough," she'd said, as she held the *Times* as far from her eyes as she could. None of these signs of her aging bothered me. Her maturity seemed to make her more desirable, more perfect somehow. And perfect was what I wanted her to be, even though I'd told her that I'd murder her if she ever got a face lift and destroyed the character in her intelligent face.

She slipped into her shoes and rose up before me. I lifted her hair and kissed the nape of her neck.

"I'll be a little late tonight," she said.

"OK, I won't ask you again what your meeting's about."

"You know you can't, Mordecai. I've been sworn to secrecy. No one on my staff even knows about the meeting. And if I tell you what it's about and then lie about doing so, I feel certain I'll be found out. Look, darling, what I have cooking is too important to risk losing over my being silly, even though I'm desperate to tell my handsome husband. So you'll just have to suffer in ignorance."

"OK, OK, I give up. So what time should I expect you?"

"I'll be home by nine, no later," Patricia said. She turned and smiled at me. Then she rubbed her nose against mine. "If I kiss you now, I'll smear my lipstick and I'll have to put it on all over again." She rubbed noses a second time. "There'll be plenty of kissing later," she said. "Love you, darling," she called out from the front door, a few moments later.

"Love you, too, babe," I responded. Then she was gone.

After Patricia left, the house was silent. We'd lost Balzac toward the end of our still living full-time in New York. I'd come into the kitchen early one morning, when the first light was in the sky. Our little guy was lying on the floor, curled up, shrunken to half his normal size.

We'd been faithful about his visits to the vet. He was old, the vet said, but seemingly in good shape. He'd been playful the previous night, but as soon as I saw him, I knew he was dead. I put him in his carrier and sat with him, until Patricia joined us.

She saw him lying in the carrier and knew immediately what had happened. She sat on my lap and I held her until I figured the vet's clinic would be open, and then I carried Balzac over there.

I asked that he be cremated. The next day, they gave us a small metal box. His ashes were inside, they said. We didn't dispute that. We brought the box home, Patricia made room on a bookshelf for it, and I put it there. Then she started to sob. Neither of us had touched the metal box since. We still hadn't brought another cat into our home.

I went to my desk and logged onto the Internet. I put head phones on, turned on the CD player sitting on a shelf to the right of my desk, and hit the button for a David Diamond orchestral album that I knew was in the fourth position. The music came up loud enough and clear. I was ready to work.

I had emails with lengthy attachments from a couple of Max Plank Institute professors, who'd become friendly. They were experts on the German nuclear power industry, which was looking increasingly shaky. I copied portions of the attachments and pasted them into a Word document I was working on. I was compiling material for a book on public attitudes toward nuclear power and how the industry and politicians in different countries were coping.

Then I wrote emails to several people I knew at the University of Grenoble, to ask them about the current state of nuclear power in France. I attached a questionnaire I was using and fired off the emails.

I made a quick tour through several of the political blogs I checked a couple of times a day – Duncan Black's Eschaton, Paul Krugman, Daily Kos, Talking Points Memo, Kevin Drum, and Andrew Sullivan's The Dish. By the time I'd finished, it was nearly ten-thirty.

I took a shower and got dressed in a golf shirt, sleeveless sweater, and a pair of chinos. I went back to the computer and sent emails to three British climate researchers I knew, and then I shut down the Internet, headed out the door, and got into my car.

I drove past downtown, across the river, and headed east on the highway that runs all the way to Boston. I passed the exit that would have taken me to the Inn on the Lake and took the last exit before the toll booths.

I drove on a road that had been lined with apple places years ago. All but one of them were gone now, replaced by an agglomeration of businesses and small factories. It hadn't been an improvement. Eventually, I took a left onto Main Street, where there was a restaurant I liked with no-nonsense food and very low prices. When I got there, Bill Kramer was waiting for me.

We'd met on the golf course nearby, about a year after I'd found a bag of old golf clubs in a thrift shop, where I went every so often because I'd found some great jazz and classical CDs that other people had been willing to give away. The clubs had cost ten bucks. Six months later, a few lessons under my belt, I forked over a grand for a proper set, and I was a golfer. Sort of.

One thing I found that I didn't like about golf was riding in carts. I preferred to walk golf courses, no matter how hilly. I used a pull cart that I'd found for fifteen dollars at an estate sale and didn't need to upgrade. The 18-hole course that I liked most was usually nearly empty on weekday afternoons, except close to summer holidays, and you didn't have to schedule a tee time. Better yet, it stayed open through the autumn until the first snowfall that didn't melt away immediately. When you were ready, you just walked up to the first tee, and when the fairway was clear of any golfers who had teed off ahead of you, you could hit.

Six months after I'd purchased my new clubs, I'd just put a tee in the ground at the first tee box, when a pudgy guy drove up in golf cart and asked if he could join me. I could fold up my pull cart, he said, stow it on the back of the golf cart, and ride with him. It was a hot day, with a blazing sun, and I took him up on his offer. We got to talking and by the third hole, we'd become friends, even though we disagreed sharply about politics and the value of religion. But we both knew something about French red wine and about movies. He told me about his wife, who stayed home and hated golf, and his two kids; I told him about Patricia. Then he recognized me from the newspaper articles he'd seen. And I learned about the Sanford Glickauer law firm – although I'd read about the man and some of his high-profile cases over the years. So that, Bill Kramer and I joked to our wives at dinner one night, was how we'd picked each other up.

Bill might have been pudgy, but he could easily drive a golf ball well over two hundred yards down the middle of the fairway. He'd been playing since he was a kid. He was steady and consistent, and it never looked like he was expending very much energy. When you take up the game in middle age, you never quite catch up to a guy like that, no matter how hard you try. Which seemed to be the point. You were supposed to relax, not try too hard at this strange game, where, unlike any other sport, except those where it was a race against a clock, it's low score, not high score, that wins.

Most rounds, my score was between 95 and 105. Sometimes, when I played three or four holes terribly, it ballooned higher. I'd been a fairly competent tennis player, and I could run six or eight miles at a good clip without getting exhausted. But golf, I came to understand, really was like life, just as people said. It might not humiliate you, but it could humble you. Or if you were humiliated, it was because you'd done it to yourself.

At the restaurant counter, Bill and I both had the beef-tips-over-rice special, which came with a cup of chicken soup. The special also came with dessert. Bill had chocolate pudding. I stuck with my ice water. We each gave the waitress a ten dollar bill, which included a tip of a little under two dollars.

Outside the restaurant, I tried Patricia's cell, but voicemail indicated it was off. I sent her a text, but got nothing in response. She's probably busy, as usual, I thought, so I decided not to try to reach her on her museum line. We usually talked once or twice a day when she was at work, but not always. I wasn't concerned.

Today, I'd convinced Bill to walk the course. On the front nine, I stayed out of trouble and shot a 46, pretty good for me. Going up to the 10th tee, Bill was seven strokes up. By the 17th hole, he'd increased his lead to 14 strokes. I'd slipped a bit on the back nine, and had an 86 at that point. With 17 a par 4 and 18 a par 3, I felt confident I'd break 100, no sweat.

The 17th has a large pond on the left half of the fairway, about two-thirds of the way to the hole. Usually, I get about 180 yards with my driver, so I play it safe and aim my second shot, which I hit with a fairway wood, to the right, rather than try to hit the ball straight toward the green over the pond. I can't rely on always getting enough distance to clear the water. Today was no exception.

As I walked past the edge of the pond, I noticed that the geese, who were usually walking around there, were nowhere in sight. Then I spotted a large animal standing on the far shore. From a distance, I couldn't tell what kind of an animal it was. I kept expecting it to move, but it remained still. It wasn't until I walked closer to it that I realized it was a mannequin. It had certainly looked real. Fake or not, however, it worked.

In the parking lot, after I'd congratulated Bill on beating me yet again – I'd shot a 95 to his 80 - and wished him a safe trip home, I tried Patricia's cell phone again. The same voice mail greeted me. It was after five now. I tried her office phone, but got voicemail again. When it prompted me to punch in her assistant's extension, I tried that, but got the assistant's voicemail. I felt a bit uneasy, but suppressed the feeling. Not always being able to reach your executive wife came with the territory, I rationalized.

I changed out of my golf shoes and stowed my pull cart and clubs in the back of the Volvo. The traffic was deep into rush hour by the time I crossed the river on the way home, and there was a backup at the light at the end of the short multi-lane highway that ran north-south on the western shore of the river. It was nearly six-thirty by the time I walked in the door.

Even without dessert, I'd had a hearty lunch, so a couple of slices of toasted French bread, a quartered tomato, and a cheese omelet were enough for dinner. I drank a couple of glasses of Fleurie and read more of the day's *Times* while I ate. After I cleaned up, I went upstairs and spent the remaining time until Patricia was scheduled to be home dealing with the day's emails and working on my nuclear power book.

Nine o'clock came and went. I went downstairs and poured myself another glass of the Fleurie I'd had with dinner. I tried Patricia's cell phone, but got her voicemail again. I texted her: *Trust you're OK. Love you. Call me.* There was no response.

I went back upstairs and tried to work, but I was too distracted to concentrate. I didn't feel like listening to music or reading, so I switched on the TV. Robert Osborne on Turner Classic Movies was talking about a Paul Newman film, *The Young Philadelphians*. I'd seen it before, but left it on, once it started. It's good, and I can watch something that's good multiple times. There's always something I've forgotten. Sometimes, it's the entire movie.

It was well past ten now. I tried sitting in my office chair and watching the film, but I couldn't sit still. She's only a little more than an hour late, I told myself, so calm down. I tried her cell again, but got the same results as I had earlier. I tried her museum office line again, and got voicemail. It was good to hear her voice, but I wanted to hear it live, not recorded.

I paced back and forth in my office, then sat down again and tried to focus on the movie. Then I decided to look up the home number of Patricia's assistant, Erma Tausig. I was surprised to find two Erma Tausig's on an Internet white pages. The first number I called was answered by a woman who sounded old and querulous at being disturbed at eleven at night. She turned suspicious when I asked her if she worked at the museum as Patricia Bornstein's assistant.

"Which museum is that?" she asked. I rang off. The second Erma Tausig was the right one. But she hadn't seen Patricia since mid-afternoon. When she'd left the office at five-fifteen, she'd noticed the black wool fall coat that Patricia had worn to work that morning still hanging on the coat tree. Yes, Erma Tausig told me, Patricia had had an extremely busy day, so she didn't think it odd that I hadn't been able to reach her. Had I checked with the police and hospitals? Perhaps Patricia had had an accident.

I'd met Erma Tausig, and she'd greeted me warmly and, I'd thought, respectfully. Her tone now sounded almost exasperated, as if she thought I was an idiot for not doing the obvious things. Perhaps I was, I thought, when I bid her goodbye. She said she trusted that Patricia was probably just delayed by one of the many things she had to look after as museum director – "I hope you realize what a difficult job she has, and how beautifully she performs it"– and rang off without another word.

I called the two main hospitals in town and the local EMS, but no one had anything to report about an accident involving a Patricia Bornstein. I tried her maiden name, but there was no report about a Patricia Murphy, either. Then I called the police emergency number. The youthful voice at the other end of the line advised me to relax. Two and a half hours was nothing to be terribly concerned about. Had I tried the area hospitals?

You're being ridiculous, I said to myself, you're completely overreacting. Just go to bed, and when you wake up, she'll be lying next to you, her arm over your chest, probably. I went into the bathroom, flossed and used the electric toothbrush. I peed. But I didn't go into our bedroom. I went downstairs instead.

I thought about pouring another glass of wine. Instead, I rinsed my glass and put it in the dishwasher. For the past hour, I'd been peeing every ten minutes or so. I peed again, and flushed the toilet in the downstairs bathroom. Then I threw on a jacket and walked outside.

I walked down to the end of the driveway, then up the block. It was dark, with hardly any moon. There are no streetlights on our block, and I narrowly missed walking into a large can filled with yard debris. I walked past several houses. There was an upstairs light on in one of them. I didn't know the people who lived there very well, except to say hello to and trade pleasantries with about the weather and the exploits of their very large college-age children. The other houses were dark.

I thought about Patricia's meeting, the one she wouldn't tell me, or anyone else, about. It couldn't have been dangerous. That was crazy. She was a museum director, not a CIA operative, for god's sakes. She wouldn't be dealing in stolen goods, or smuggled treasure, not Miss Goody Two-Shoes, as she often called herself, especially when she was annoyed with herself for being such a stickler about what was morally right in her mind. I would tell her I loved her for that, but she still insisted that she went overboard about ethics sometimes. Maybe that's what made her staff see her as a chief executive who did her difficult job beautifully, as Erma Tausig had put it earlier tonight.

I thought, too, about our recent conversations, and whether I could remember anything Patricia had said that might have indicated that she was fearful, or in trouble, or threatened by someone or something. But I couldn't come up with anything. She was always her loving, even-keeled self, emotional sometimes when she was hurt or someone dear to her was, but never hysterical or far out of control.

Loving. I'd just thought of that word, loving. Had she run away? Was she with someone else? Was this the Marci horror all over again? Was I reliving the nightmare I'd endured twenty-five years ago? Had she run off with the museum's elegant, powerful, filthy-rich board chairman? That old fart? I said out loud. She couldn't have. But did I know my wife as well as I thought I did?

How could I think any such thing, that Patricia could be unfaithful to me? How could you live with someone for twenty-five years and not know what she was really like, what her innermost desires were, what turned her on? And I was self-aware enough to know that I couldn't be - no, not me - one of those overweening husbands whose wives divorce them in late middle age when they've had up to here for twenty-five or thirty years.

I wasn't one of those husbands who are oblivious to their wives' needs, who ignore them, who expect them to just follow along, no matter what they might think, that they couldn't think for themselves anyway. I couldn't be. I worshipped my wife. I loved her, I respected her. I would never do anything. . . . I stopped myself. Of course, I'd done something,

something very stupid, that night in Washington. But it was a moment of madness, and it was never repeated – and never would be, as long as I lived.

Where was Patricia? I reached in my pants pocket for my cell phone to try her again. It wasn't there. I walked quickly back to the house. I saw that I hadn't closed the door. I saw my cell on the dining table. I'd no idea why it was there. I dialed Patricia's number. I got her voicemail, indicating that the phone was shut off. Then I dialed Bill Kramer's number.

He answered on the fourth ring. I apologized for waking him. There was silence on the phone. Then I heard, "Sorry, I took the phone downstairs, don't want to wake anyone. It's two o'clock in the morning. Mordecai, what's wrong?"

I told him what I'd been going through. "Have you tried Patricia's cell phone?" he asked. I said that of course I had, many times, and that it seemed to be off. "Have you called the police and the hospitals?" I told him I had, twice.

"The police don't start looking for people until three days have gone by, so unless there's been an accident, they won't do anything for awhile," Bill said. "She's never done this before, has she, Mordecai?" I told him no. "I have to ask you this," he said, "there hasn't been any trouble between you lately, has there?" I told him there hadn't been any trouble – at least nothing I knew about. "They say the husband is the last to know," Bill said. Then: "Sorry, bad joke."

"That's OK," I said. "Maybe a little humor will calm me down."

He recovered himself. "Look, Mordecai, get into bed. Close your eyes, and if you can fall asleep, that'll be good. I'm sure that when you wake up, your lovely wife will be there beside you. To be married to a terrific woman like that, you're a lucky guy and you know it."

"Thanks, Bill. Now get back to bed. Sorry I woke you, and I hope I didn't wake anyone else."

I heard a yawn. "Take care of yourself. Mordecai," Bill said, and then he broke the connection.

Perhaps Bill's advice was good, perhaps not. In any case, I didn't go to bed. Instead I peed again, grabbed my car keys and headed out to the Volvo. I let the front door swing shut behind me. I didn't care whether it was locked or not. I drove up and down the dark, winding streets of the neighborhood, my high beams on, looking for any gray Accords that might be Patricia's.

After ten minutes, I headed for the by-pass that would lead me towards the roads that would take me to the other side of the river. Suddenly I knew, I had no idea how or why, where Patricia was.

CHAPTER SIX

I drove across the river again for the third time in fifteen hours. I got off the highway at an earlier exit that the one I'd taken the previous day, and drove along a winding two-lane road. I didn't see another car. The houses, on both sides of the road, were all dark. The light at the bottom of a long hill was red, and I had to wait before making a right turn.

There was a state police car, its flashers on, at the mouth of the alley that fed into the parking lot, the one where thirty years ago, after I'd taken Patricia dancing at the Inn on the Lake - our first evening together – we'd gone parking in my car and she'd pushed my hand away when I'd tried to caress her thighs, not because she didn't want me to, I learned later, but because of a bladder infection I was too inexperienced to recognize. I'd always remembered every detail of that night. So had Patricia, I knew, because we'd talked about it over the years.

And it was the same parking lot where, five years later, after the miracle of our running into each other at the New Year's Eve party, we'd argued and worked things out and somehow made love in the back seat of the car. All of it raced through my mind as I parked the Volvo across the road from the state police car, next to a street light. I got out and walked toward the car on shaky legs.

Before I was halfway across the road, a trooper was levering himself out of the car, and then putting his hat on trooper-style – very low over his eyes in front and in back showing half an acre of close-cropped hair, in this case blond. He was big, bigger than me, with a large head and massive hands.

"Sir, you can't leave your car there," he said, in the usual ritual of insincere politesse, which I caught, even in the fragile condition I was in.

"I need to get into the parking lot," I said, making an effort to keep the hysteria out of my voice.

"Sir, you need to move along." He pointed a finger at my car, as if he wanted to be sure that I understood him.

"Please, officer," I said, "I need to get in there."

"One last time, sir: please move your car. There's police business here. It's not a place for civilians."

"I know who's in there," I said

"Excuse me?" We were only a couple of feet apart now, in the middle of the road's westbound lane.

"I said: I know who's in there."

"Be careful what you say, sir. This is a crime scene."

I started to say something else, but he put up a meaty hand to cut me off. "All right," he said. "I'll call Detective Harnett, the man in charge here, and see if he'll come out and talk to you." The trooper studied me for a moment. "Sir, for the safety of both of us, I'd like to pat you down before I get back in the car and make the call."

He had me face his car, put my hands on the edge of the roof, and spread my legs. He patted me down, hard. He wasn't nice – or careful – about it. When he seemed satisfied that I wouldn't pose any risk to him, except possibly with my fists, he took off his hat and dropped back into his car.

I didn't watch him make the call. Instead, I turned and fell back against his car's rear door. My chest hurt. I wondered for a moment if I was having a heart attack, and then I decided I didn't care. I wanted the detective to hurry up and get here, so he could tell me what was going on in the parking lot, and at the same time I wanted him to be delayed, because I didn't want to hear what he might say.

I wanted time to stop. No, I wanted time to reverse. I wanted to be standing in the kitchen, my hands in Patricia's skirt pockets, tracing the hollows of her groin. I wanted her to be turning to me, again, but now I wanted not to be nuzzled, but to taste her lipstick and then her lips.

Detective Hartnett was in his early forties. He had a full head of short grey hair, a clean-shaven face, and a toothpick in his mouth. He was a couple of inches shorter than me, and about as broad. His wool sport jacket, the same color as his hair, sagged in front. He must carry heavy things in the jacket's front pockets, I figured. He took a notebook out of one of the pockets. He spoke languidly, as if he and I were two guys talking about normal things.

"Trooper Brown here tells me you said you know who's in the parking lot." He paused. "I don't believe I got your name, sir." I told him what it was. "Mr. Bornstein," he said, after he'd written something in his notebook, "tell me who you think is back there."

I swallowed. There was phlegm in the back of my mouth. "My wife, detective. Patricia Bornstein," I said.

"And why would you think that, Mr. Bornstein?" he asked, the languid tone still in his voice.

"We came to this godforsaken place on two occasions early in our relationship."

"And when was that, Mr. Bornstein?"

"Twenty-five, thirty years ago."

"And what did you do here? Was it during the day or at night?"

I wondered if he was baiting me now. "Night," I said. "The second time we came here, it was at night. We made love in the back of her mother's car."

Hartnett looked at me with sorrow in his eyes. I knew now what he would tell me, once he felt ready to. He opened his notebook and read Patricia's plate number to me. He told me the car was a new gray Accord sedan. I nodded. There were tears in my eyes. I could taste the wine I'd had hours earlier in my mouth.

I heard Hartnett talking again: "Blonde, in her forties, wearing a black wool coat over a suit." He was reading from his notebook. He looked down at it again. "Slender. I'd guess about six feet tall."

"Six and a quarter," I blurted out. I pictured Patricia unwinding in front of me thirty years earlier. "Where will it ever end?" she'd said, the first time she'd stood in front of me, nearly as tall as I was. "She was fifty-four," I said to Hartnett. "Can you tell me where she is? Can you tell me what's happened?"

"Some kids who were going parking at around midnight spotted a body slumped against the open door of a car. They stopped, took a closer look, saw a pool of blood, and called 911 from a cell phone."

"You're sure it's Patricia, my wife?"

"Everything points to it's being her, yes."

"Was she dead when the kids first spotted her?" Hartnett nodded. He shifted the toothpick from one side of his mouth to the other. "How did she die?" I asked him.

He looked at me, assessing whether I was in any condition for him to continue. Finally, he sighed. "Your wife was stabbed to death, Mr. Bornstein. Twice, I believe, but the medical examiner will make the final determination. I believe she was stabbed first in her chest, when she was getting out of her car – that would be my assumption. I know I shouldn't make assumptions, but given that your wife was quite tall, I assume that in

order to get out of the driver's seat of her car, she would swivel around on
her hips, plant her feet on the pavement, then push herself up out of the
seat. That's how a tall woman would get out of an automobile if she was
wearing a skirt. You've seen her get out of a car that way, right?"

A movie ran through my mind, of the first time my parents had met
Patricia. I'd driven up to Mary's house, where they were having tea with
her, the day before the wedding. They'd come outside as Patricia opened
the passenger door. I'd watched her rise up to her full glorious height in
front of my parents. I'd seen my father's eyes widen, and then there'd been
a huge smile that took over his face.

"Welcome to the family," he'd said.

Now, Hartnett's voice was breaking into the movie: "Mr.
Bornstein." I looked at him and nodded.

"You said she was stabbed twice," I said.

"I did," Hartnett said. "The second time was in the back, as she
was collapsing from the first wound. I don't believe there was a struggle.
And if it's any comfort to you, I believe your wife died instantly."

"Why did this happen?" I realized I was screaming. I pounded the
sides of my fists against my temples. I did it again. And hit myself again, as
hard as I could, and yet again. Hartnett put his hands around my wrists.
My arms went slack.

"I know how upsetting this is for you, Mr. Bornstein, but you need
to stay calm." Hartnett's tone was sympathetic. He pulled out the
toothpick and threw it on the ground. I noticed that the trooper had
removed his hat. "We think it was a robbery, Mr. Bornstein. Her purse
and wallet, money, are all missing, although her watch and rings weren't
touched. Did she have a cell phone?"

"Of course she did. I tried to reach her on it all day, but it seemed
to be turned off."

"Do you know why she might have happened to be here tonight,
Mr. Bornstein?"

"She told me she had a meeting and would be home no later than
nine. She said she couldn't tell me what the meeting was about. She said
no one on the museum staff, or anyone else connected to the museum,
knew about the meeting. I don't know why she was here."

"You mentioned a museum."

"Patricia's the head of the Museum of Art and Industry – was the
head."

"Oh yeah, now I remember the stories and pictures in the papers.
A terrific woman, I told my wife, Maggie. This is such a shame." He

paused. "And you're the writer," he said after a long moment. I nodded. "Did your wife have any enemies?" Hartnett asked.

"None that I know of. Everyone at the museum here loved her. It was the same at the museum back in New York."

Hartnett looked at his notebook again. "You said before that you knew she was here. How did you know, Mr. Bornstein?"

I shrugged. "I can't tell you how I knew. I was driving around our neighborhood, looking for her car, when the idea that she was here popped into my head. I can't explain how that happened."

Hartnett asked me to take a look at the body, just to make sure the dead woman was Patricia. He walked me through the short road leading into the parking lot, and then across the tarmac. I remembered the place. On our right was the strip of storefronts that faced the lot, with the diner in the center. They all were dark, except for a dim light in the diner.

I saw a sedan ahead of us at the far edge of the lot – it looked like Patricia's Accord, but I wasn't sure from this distance. The trees behind the car were bare of leaves at this time of year, not full as they'd been the other times I'd been here, but they were where I expected them to be. The car looked pulled in tight to them, as I'd done years ago.

I pictured Patricia's profile when I'd looked over at her in the car that first night – how happy and innocent she'd seemed. I saw her long legs again, and remembered how her smooth nylons felt as I'd run my hand over them. I closed my eyes as I recalled feeling the fastener of a garter, and then the bare flesh of her thigh as my hand had gone further beneath her skirt.

The toe of my shoe caught on something, and I stumbled. I felt Hartnett's hands on my arm and shoulder, as he caught me before I fell forward. If he hadn't kept his hands there, I would have sagged to the pavement.

I tried to focus what energy remained in my body. For the moment, it seemed, I'd forgotten how to walk. It was the pressure of Hartnett's hands on my arm and shoulder that urged me slowly forward, no more than a foot at a time. I knew I had to get to Patricia, but I didn't want to.

I did no more than nod when Hartnett lifted a sheet and showed me Patricia's face. It was still beautiful, even though it was no longer filled with life, and the intelligence that had graced it had departed.

I couldn't look away from her. Was this all a bad dream? Was it possible that I would wake up now, turn to her and watch her breathing, watch her eyes slowly open, see her smile when she realized I was looking at her, as she always did?

And then the night and the lights and the cars and the voices reasserted themselves, and I knew again where I was. There was no hope. Despair seized me. Patricia was dead. I might just as well have been dead myself. No words came to mind. I couldn't speak.

He wouldn't let me touch her. I'd reached out, and he'd restrained me, gently but firmly.

Hartnett gave the keys to my car to one of the local officers, who would bring it to my home later. He put me in the front passenger seat of his car, a shiny new Dodge sedan, and said he would drive me home. Patricia's Accord was being towed to a police facility for examination.

Once I gave Hartnett the address, he seemed to know the way. As he drove across the river in the gray morning light, traffic heavier than it had been a few hours earlier, he took a call on his cell phone. The call consumed most of the trip, which was fine with me. I didn't want to talk right then.

He followed me in the front door. I noticed that I hadn't locked it. We stood in the kitchen. I could see that he wasn't ready to leave. We sat down at the kitchen table. My mind was empty. I couldn't think. I didn't know what to say.

"That call I took while I was driving you home," Hartnett said. "One of my men talked to the couple who run the diner at the strip mall where the parking lot is. They worked late, they said, until eight-thirty, or so. They were in back, cleaning the kitchen, and left by the back door. They park their car behind the diner, on a strip of cleared land, and they can drive out without going through the parking lot in front of the diner. So they wouldn't have noticed anything happening out there. But they did tell me something interesting."

There was a tooth pick in Hartnett's mouth again. He looked at me for a reaction. I stared back at him. "Your wife," Hartnett said, "ate supper at the diner last night: grilled cheese and tomato on whole wheat and a cup of decaf. Did you know about that?"

"I told you, detective, I wasn't able to reach Patricia all day. I didn't know where she was. And her assistant was no help when I talked to *her*."

"And there's something else." Hartnett rolled the toothpick across his mouth. "It seems that your wife used to have lunch at that diner a couple of days a week over the past several months. Sometimes she had the grilled cheese and tomato on whole wheat, sometimes turkey with lettuce and tomato with Russian dressing on whole wheat toast, and always with decaf. The couple who own the diner were very definite about what your wife ordered.

"She was always alone, they said. She'd talk to them a little, and then read the paper. They said she seemed to be a very nice lady, very refined. After she finished, they said, she'd go out to her car and sit for ten or fifteen minutes, until she was ready to leave." Hartnett looked at me intently. "Did you know about that, Mr. Bornstein?" I shook my head quickly, just a few inches to either side.

Hartnett got up, and then sat back down. "Mr. Bornstein," he said, in a weary tone of voice, "I have to ask you a couple of things. I'm sorry to bother you now, but I have to do my job. You do understand, I trust." I nodded. "Were you and your wife having any problems, I mean between the two of you?"

"No." I said. "Everything was fine between us. We loved each other very much."

"I'm sorry, but I have to ask this: were you both faithful in your marriage?"

I tried to keep my eyes steady on Hartnett's. "Yes," I lied quietly.

"And where were you tonight, Mr. Bornstein? I have to ask. I'm sure you understand."

"I got home around six-thirty, after playing golf with a lawyer friend of mine, Bill Kramer."

Hartnett smiled at me, for the first time. "My wife's law partner. Great guy. Sorry, you were saying?"

"Then I ate dinner, answered some emails and did some other work – I suppose you can check on the times I sent the emails. I tried to watch a Paul Newman movie on TV, and then I went crazy for several hours when my wife didn't come home."

Hartnett stood up. He held out his hand. "I'm sorry for your loss, Mr. Bernstein," he said. I thought at that moment that he was going to ask me to go to the police station with him, so he could grill me about where I'd been during the time of Patricia's murder. But he didn't. I didn't know why not.

After Detective Hartnett left, I covered all the mirrors in the house and proceeded to sit on the same kitchen chair for a week. Whoever dropped by, or brought some food, had to sit in the kitchen with me if they wanted to stay. My few visitors took me up on it.

I had a hard time focusing my attention on any of the people who sat in the kitchen with me. I sat in a fog and let the time drag, until I went up to bed and tried to sleep for a few hours. But I had a hard time getting any sleep.

The same thoughts kept racing around in my head, in a circle that I couldn't break out of. How could such an awful, terrible thing have happened to Patricia? How? She'd led such a blameless life. She'd been a loving, faithful wife; she'd been a good and caring friend. Everyone she'd worked with had respected her. Some of the people who worked for her had even loved her. She'd had no enemies – none that I knew of, at any rate. And if she'd known of any enemies, she'd have told me. She told me everything. Everything except what that meeting had been about. But it couldn't have been dangerous, no matter what it had been about. Patricia had been an intelligent, careful woman. She wouldn't have allowed herself to be lured into a life-threatening situation. Why hadn't I made her tell me what the meeting was about? Why had I let her leave home yesterday morning?

I'd known everything about her, hadn't I? Except what she'd been doing that night – that I hadn't known. And I hadn't known about the lunches she'd eaten at the diner and why she'd sat in her car in the parking lot after she'd finished eating. Had she been hiding those lunches from me? Why? She'd never mentioned them. Why not? But why would I have needed to know about them? Hadn't I trusted her? Of course, I'd trusted her. Hadn't I trusted her years ago in Frankfurt, when the blue-blazered smoothies had made so much of her?

No, no, I was the one who couldn't be trusted. I was the one who'd been unfaithful. I was the one who'd done something unbearably foolish. I was the one who'd risked hurting the person I loved more than anyone or anything in the world. Was Patricia's death some sort of cosmic payback for my transgression? Why had she been punished for what I had done? Why hadn't I been punished? Or was her death my punishment? I didn't believe in god, I wasn't spiritual even. So how, I asked myself, could I think such things?

Pictures and videos kept flashing through my mind as I sat at the kitchen table. Hartnett's description of Patricia's death played over and over in my mind. I saw her on the tarmac, the way he described it, blood oozing out of her. Had she really died instantly, as he'd told me? I prayed to the god I didn't believe in that she had.

After a week, I got the whirring to stop, if only for a brief time, every so often. Then I would grieve – for Patricia herself, the achievement denied to her, and for the lost love and the years that she and I would have shared. I grieved for the large part of my own life that was lost forever. I went over and over every detail of the pictures I had of her: the light hitting her cheekbones, her hands folded on the cushion of a wing chair, a glimpse of knee and leg emerging between the folds of a long dress.

The police had no clues, nothing. They theorized that after Patricia had finished her supper, she'd driven her car to the edge of the parking lot, where it was dark. She'd been getting out of the car at around eight o'clock, for some reason, when she'd been stabbed. Her body was found slumped against the open driver's-side door of her Accord. It might have taken Patricia a slightly longer time to get out of the car than a woman of average height would have taken, so her assailant would have had a slightly longer time to move in for the kill.

The police couldn't definitely determine how the killer, or killers, had gotten hold of Patricia's purse and cell phone. Was she taking them out with her, when she was getting out of the car, or had the killer reached over her and taken them out of the car interior? In any case, there was no murder weapon, no clothing fibers, no hair, no skin, no DNA, or anything else that could serve as a clue of some sort. No one had seen the crime being committed, apparently – no one responded to police appeals for information, even after I'd added a $75,000 reward. The cranks and crazies had a field day, but that was it.

The museum board gave Hartnett carte blanche to question staff and board members. No one knew anything about the mysterious meeting that Patricia had mentioned to me. There was only the highest praise for her accomplishments and integrity. Hartnett couldn't find a possible enemy. With Erma Tausig's assistance, he conducted a two-day search of Patricia's office. He had the best upstate forensic personnel he knew of search Patricia's computers. Nothing useful to his investigation turned up anywhere.

Erma Tausig called me when the search was over. "I have all of your wife's personal effects boxed up for you," she said. "Would you like me to have them sent to your home, or would you like to come in and take them home yourself? You could look around your wife's office to see if I've missed anything."

A day later, the week of sitting *Shiva* over, I went into the museum to have a look around Patricia's office. It had been swept clean of papers and books. There were no pictures on the walls. There was no way to tell that Patricia had ever occupied it. It sat there empty, waiting for the museum's next director.

When I got back home, I started a search of the house. There was nothing I didn't expect to find in the garage, the basement, or the first floor. Nothing on the second floor, either, until I went through the desk in the third bedroom that Patricia used when she needed to work at home. In the top right-hand drawer, I found a pile of photographs.

We had around a dozen photograph albums on book shelves between the upstate house and the New York apartment. Since we'd bought digital cameras, a few years ago, we'd stopped filling up more photograph albums, although we still had plenty of loose photographs in one place or another. So the pile was no surprise.

I spread the photographs out on Patricia's desk to look through them. I lingered over them. I'd seen all of them before, except for one – a shot of a young Patricia sitting in a sun dress on a low stone wall with a handsome man, much older than she was. She was smiling; she looked radiant. I turned the photograph over. "Edward, Carmel, 1984" was written on the back. I put the rest of the photographs back in the drawer where I'd found them. I put the photograph of Patricia and Edward in a drawer of my desk. I remembered his last name and googled him. He'd died years ago.

I invited Hartnett to bring a forensic team in. He took me up on the invitation, and a four-person team went through the house carefully, including my office, and found nothing. I thanked them for not destroying anything. They left the key to Patricia's cache of journals where she'd said I'd find it. I read back a year or so and found no mention of anything suspicious or useful to the investigation. Reading her journal was a bittersweet experience. I postponed reading back further.

The police needed Patricia's body for several weeks. The day after they released it, I buried her on a hillside with a view of trees, bare of leaves now, and the sky. During the service, I stood facing the view, but I couldn't focus on it.

The museum board chairman's wife arranged a memorial service at the museum shortly after the funeral. I asked only that the event not be blanketed in sadness. I sat in the front row and tried not to cry at the pictures and videos projected on a screen at the front of the large room. Speakers said many things about Patricia that I already knew and some things that I didn't know but was pleased to learn. The board chairman spoke last. He focused most of his remarks on the kind of person Patricia was. Toward the end, he recounted her achievements at the museum.

"We owe Patricia a great debt of gratitude for everything she did for our museum community," he said in his conclusion. "And I believe all of you will agree with me that we will owe her an even greater debt when the fundraising that she started for the addition to our museum is completed, the addition is built, and the new galleries open. I know all of you will be gratified to learn that I will be recommending to the board of trustees that we name the museum's new wing the Patricia Bornstein Gallery.'

The applause started before the chairman finished saying Patricia's full name. Afterward, people came up to me and told me how much they missed her. I agreed with them, over and over. I gave them, as well as I could, a calm face to look at. What anyone could see in my eyes – that I wasn't at all sure of. Could these people understand how terrible my pain was? Would they exert themselves to examine me for signs of it? I looked for hints of what they might be doing, but I couldn't penetrate the politeness and expressions of concern that I sensed people felt obligated to demonstrate.

"I'm giving my Irish wife a proper goddamned *Shiva*," I'd said to Bill Kramer when he'd come by on the first day. I'd watched him wince. But he put aside any differences he and I had about religion. He came by the house every day for two weeks, sometimes for an hour, twice to share a takeout meal, other days for only a few minutes. I looked forward to seeing him. He became the brother I'd never had, I suppose. In any case, I had no other family. My parents and Patricia's parents were long since buried. Her father had died before she and I had met for the first time. There were few relatives, and none that I was close to or wanted to be close to. I began to believe that I could rely on Bill to help me, sometimes with advice, other times simply by sitting quietly at the kitchen table with me or by being in a room with me and talking.

Other people made contact. Some even visited and stayed for a while, until they awkwardly told me to "take care" and got away, back to their own lives and their own troubles. Bill made me realize that I would die unless I could focus on the future as much as I dwelled, obsessed even, on the past. He helped me realize that I would do Patricia's memory no honor if I neglected my research and my writing. There was a hole in my heart. Bill knew that. But he also knew, and told me, that the rest of me was whole and could function. But he shied away from talking about my getting out. Still, he wasn't perfect.

"I can't wait for spring," he blurted out, as he was leaving one afternoon, "so I can whip your ass on the golf course." He made me smile, if only for a moment.

After the week of *Shiva*, I began to walk in the early morning again. I got back on the computer and responded to the dozens of sympathy emails from people I knew around the world. I didn't ask how so many of them in such far-flung places had learned of Patricia's death. I didn't want to prolong any discussion of it. I merely thanked these people and tried to move on. I was successful, at least in part.

I picked up where I'd left off with the nuclear power book. But I didn't have as much enthusiasm for it as I'd had before Patricia's death. I got to work on an article on carbon dioxide for the magazine where I was a contributing editor. I telephoned the museum's development director and offered to help with fund raising for the new wing to be named after Patricia.

I didn't have much to do in order to maintain the house – or myself. A nice woman came in and cleaned once a week. I found another woman who prepared several dinners for me once a week, and I found I could stretch them from one delivery to the next. Any other food I needed I brought home after a weekly excursion to the grocery store. So I exercised and I ate. I lost fifteen pounds. Loss and grief will do that to you, I guessed. I stayed away from the doctor.

I had work, and I was attending to it, but I had plenty of time on my hands. All my working life, I'd been very productive. People in the business world used to tell me that I could be so productive because meetings, report preparations, dealing with people all day long, and office politics – the foci and minutia of daily work life for most people – didn't intrude on my time.

The absence of the things I'd had with Patricia – talking over our days, sharing meals, watching movies together, making plans, and making love – left large holes in my days. Now I had a former life and a current life. I no longer spent much time with the political blogs I'd turned to enthusiastically several times a day in my former life. Too many movies bored me now, and I couldn't watch them all the way through. It was the same with novels. I did no more than skim over most articles in the *Times* and the magazines I subscribed to.

Except for my early morning walks and the grocery shopping, I didn't leave the house much. One cold, clear day in early December, I drove out to the place where Patricia and I used to watch the horses. When I got to the rock and sat down, I couldn't empty my mind of the whirring horror of the *Shiva* week. Then I started to cry. I stayed for only a few minutes.

That evening, Bill phoned and asked if it was all right if he invited me to dinner at his home on Saturday night. "Sanford and Gwennie Glickauer will be here," he said. "They're looking forward to meeting you. And you don't have to ask: it'll be just you, me, Iris and the Glickauers. Sanford's cool. He won't make you feel like a fifth wheel. But if you don't want to come, Mordecai, Iris and I will understand completely."

Iris, Bill's wife was a calm woman, who spoke thoughtfully. I liked her, and she'd sounded the right tones when she'd come by with Bill during the weeks after Patricia's death. I suspected she'd coached Bill on how to present the invitation to me, and I was grateful to her. As for the Glickauers, I didn't know what to expect. In any case, the dinner sounded like something I could handle, and I accepted the invitation.

Over the past several years, Bill had tried a couple of times to get the Glickauers together with Patricia and me, but things hadn't worked out, due to some bother or other with Gwennie Glickauer, we'd been told. Holiday parties at Sanford Glickauer's law firm were limited to partners, staff members, and spouses. Based on what Bill had told me about the Glickauers, I had a picture of them. It turned out to be off, just a little.

Sanford was an inch or two taller than me. He was lean and sharp-featured. His skin was taut, and he had a leonine mane of gray hair. Gwennie's hair was gray, as well. It was pulled back from her broad face and gathered in a ponytail that reached her waist. Her face was scrubbed clean of any makeup. She was a solid-looking five-eight or so in her low-heeled shoes. She wore a loose-fitting dress that was hemmed at mid-calf. She kept a heavy shawl around her shoulders. It looked as if the overall effect was meant to conceal a figure grown bulkier than she liked.

Of the two, Sanford did most of the talking throughout the evening. His condolences were effusive. He sounded sincere, as if he cared deeply about how I was taking my wife's death. He was a good storyteller, and he wasn't shy about regaling the rest of us with accounts of everything in his life from his legal triumphs to his Boston boyhood.

He started with lengthy descriptions of several expensive divorce cases his firm had handled years earlier. "Tales out of school," Bill murmured. "Let 'em sue me!" Sanford bellowed, and then roared with laughter. He emptied the last of the second bottle of wine into his glass. Perhaps that was just for show. I'd noticed that he hadn't been drinking much wine.

"Mordecai" he said, "I think you might be interested in how I got started collecting art. It's kind of a funny story, actually, and it begins, oddly, at the Hebrew school I went to when I was growing up in Boston. Let me put you in the picture, so to speak. For a little kid, one of the main things was, it was a terrifying place. The principal was a fierce bespectacled man, always in a rumpled suit and creased tie. He quivered with rage and shouted at the top of his lungs at the boys, never one of the girls, for any real or imaginary infraction, large or small. He loomed over us, a Goliath backing little Davids against the wall, most of us far too frightened to reach for any kind of slingshot. Except for the Kravitz twins – I'll tell you about them in a second. I was bored out of my mind in Hebrew school, and I had it in my head for a time that I would be the object of this uncontrolled wrath for nothing more than if the principle discovered how bored I was. I could see myself cringing with fear when he confronted me. So I avoided any and all contact with him.

"But one summer afternoon, in front of the small apartment building on the hill in Roxbury, just below the one where I lived, I saw the principal hunched over in the bright sunshine. He was weeping shamelessly. I was startled to discover that I was looking at a little old man. Where had the raging Goliath gone? I edged closer.

"'Mar Raskoff?' I said quietly. The old man pushed the palm of his hand past his hip, keeping his back to me, shooing me away. 'Mar Raskoff, can I help you?' I repeated. The old man snuffled. 'I don't want to die,' he wailed. I can still see myself standing silently behind him for what seemed like an eternity. There was more snuffling. The old man repeated the shooing motion with his hand, and I finally turned away, not with compassion, or pity, I realized, but with disgust directed not only at the weeping, shrunken Mar Raskoff, but at myself.

"I had the sick feeling that had this little old man raged at me and backed me against a wall, I wouldn't have had the guts of one of the Kravitz twins. When Mar Raskoff had attacked *him*, *he'd* told the old man to go fuck himself. The twins had been expelled from Hebrew school. And where was the penalty? They didn't have to endure four weekday afternoons and Sunday mornings of boredom, and because their parents believed the twins needed a lot of discipline, they secured the toughest, but the best Bar Mitzvah instructor around. Some penalty."

Sanford swallowed some water. The wine he'd poured for himself stood untouched. "But here's the punch line. I was so emboldened by my encounter with the shrunken Mar Raskoff that late one afternoon I sneaked into his office after the rest of the Hebrew school had gone home. No one was ever allowed in there except the janitor.

"As I approached his desk, I was surprised to see a picture of a nicely decorated room where two women were sitting and talking. I won't bore you with a description of every square inch of the picture. What's important is the style of painting I experienced. Every detail looked real, but at the same time, the focus was a little soft. I thought from a distance that I might be looking at a photograph taken with a patch of light gauze over the camera lens. When I got closer, it looked like a painting. But when I got the picture out of the frame, it was paper, not canvas. It was a print, of course. Whatever it was, now it was mine, I thought, so I rolled it up, put it in my book bag, where it fit nicely, and walked nonchalantly home with it. I hid it on the floor under my shoes in the back of my closet. I took it out to examine it when my parents thought I was asleep.

"I forgot about it. I don't know what became of it. But the first time I saw Sam Hudson's painting, *Morning Coffee*, which shows two women sitting in the dining room of an apartment, sun streaming through a window, the details of that picture I'd stolen years before from Mar Raskoff's Hebrew school office came back to me, and I knew I had to have Hudson's painting.

"So I paid the gallery an outrageous amount of money. Had I bought it for sentimental reasons? Perhaps. Of course, four months later, the gallery had another Hudson for sale, and, of course, they called me."

"Sanford was much too enthusiastic," Gwennie Glickauer broke in. We all turned away from Sanford and looked at her. "He should have played it cool. The gallery owner, that little Italian in the five-thousand-dollar suit, he knew that Sanford was smitten. Sanford should have told him that he was buying that first Hudson as an investment – to turn it over quickly even and make a tidy profit. Well, he didn't, so the next one was even more expensive than the first."

"It was larger," Sanford interjected.

"Sanford paid by the square foot," Gwennie said. There was an edge to her voice, but a big smile lit up her face.

"Of course," Sanford responded. "The larger the painting, the more expensive it is. That's how it works, more or less, although other factors can come into play. For example, this gallery carried pictures by an Eastern European – I forget exactly which country he lived in - who painted buildings with lots of windows with multiple panes. As a joke, I asked if he charged by the window. 'No, by the pane,' the gallery owner told me."

"By this time," Gwennie said, amidst the laughter, "Sanford and Hudson had something of an artist-patron relationship. So Hudson put Sanford in the next painting."

"*The Afternoon Party*," Sanford interjected. "It shows about twenty people gathered in the living room of Hudson's and his wife's apartment, which he used as his studio. I'm there with his friends – other painters, musicians, art dealers, and his shrink."

"*Morning Coffee, The Afternoon Party* – Hudson was working his way through the hours of the day. Anyway, several of the people in *The Afternoon Party* desired the painting," Gwennie said, her tone unmistakably sarcastic. "So Sanford, who *needed* it more than anyone else, just *had* to pay a king's ransom for it." We all watched Sanford exaggeratedly roll his eyes.

"Then," Gwennie continued, with a very slight touch of sarcasm, "Hudson told Sanford he felt guilty that he hadn't put *me* in the painting, even though I was at the party. He offered to do a portrait of Sanford and me together – if we would commission it for god knows how much. The *chutzpah* - can you imagine? In the picture he had in mind, we would be doing something, sitting somewhere – he hasn't gotten around to spelling his concept out to us."

"Why hasn't he?" I asked.

"He had the good grace," Gwennie went on, without skipping a beat, "to go onto other projects with other couples and families – other suckers. I would have let Hudson take everything Sanford owned, if push came to shove, but not a penny of mine. In any event, Sanford was put onto another two Hudsons in a private collection and bought them."

"For a total of five, three of them emphasizing nudes," Sanford said, a smirk on his face. "Hudson is a master at painting nudes, female *and* male."

"I've seen Hudsons in gallery exhibition catalogues, but never in the flesh," I said. "*The Afternoon Party* is legendary." I turned to Bill Kramer. "Have you seen Sanford's Hudsons?"

"Just once," Bill replied. "Iris and I had a private viewing. If you like realist painting, they're quite remarkable."

"I'll bet they'd look great in the new wing being named after Patricia," Iris said enthusiastically.

"I think not," Gwennie said dismissively. "Hudson was a New York City painter. I can see an exhibition in the not-too-distant future, with a catalog with essays, at someplace like the New York Historical Society. And when Sanford dies, the paintings should go to a museum in the city."

Sanford nodded. "Of course," he said.

After the Glickauers left, I stayed and talked with Bill and Iris. I didn't want to go home just yet and face Patricia's absence. "How long have they been married?" I asked idly.

"Forty years," Bill replied. "Twenty and twenty."

"I don't get it," I said.

"Wait 'til you hear this," Iris said.

"They were married for twenty years," Bill drawled, "then Sanford divorced Gwennie – it cost him a bundle – in order to marry a much younger woman named Phoebe Armstrong, a gorgeous little blonde, a Brigitte Bardot type. He'd met her at the Oyster Bar in Grand Central Station.

"Five years later, he divorces Phoebe and remarries Gwennie, becoming financially whole again in the process, although technically Gwennie now had more of their money than he did – except for the settlement with Phoebe. Why? Phoebe turned out to be a real airhead, he claimed, although why Sanford hadn't known that up front is beyond me. Anyway, the joke he used to tell about why he left Phoebe is she never learned to warm the plates in the oven before serving dinner on them."

"So does that explain the edge to Gwennie's voice? When I was listening to her talk about Sanford and his mania for Sam Hudson's paintings, I thought the edge could be attributed to the money Sanford has shelled out over the years."

"No one can know for sure what goes on in another couple's marriage," Bill said. Iris nodded affirmatively. So did I. The three of us were silent for a few seconds, and I got up to leave.

"There's one more thing I wanted to ask you," I said to Bill, as he walked me to the front door. "I'm uneasy about Maggie's husband's investigation into Patricia's murder. He seems too easily satisfied with robbery as the motive. He doesn't even give me the third degree."

"Tim Hartnett's very good at his job. He has a great reputation for not letting go of a case until he's exhausted all the logical possibilities. And I don't say that just because he's Maggie's husband."

"So you think I shouldn't hire an investigator of my own?"

"I can't tell you what to do. I wouldn't want anyone telling *me* what to do if I were in a situation similar to yours. All I can say is that Hartnett's someone you can trust. You can trust both Hartnetts, come to think of it."

Several days later, Iris called and asked me to join her and Bill for New Year's Eve. "Nothing fancy, Mordecai. We'll go to a movie and then come home for corned beef and pastrami sandwiches." I asked her to give me a couple of days to think about it.

New Year's Eve had always been special for Patricia and me, of course, ever since the party where we'd unexpectedly run into each other after having been separated by a continent for five years. People would invite us to parties, but we begged off and stayed home. We'd cook a terrific dinner, planned carefully in advance, drink a bottle of expensive French Burgundy, and slow dance to a Johnny Hartman or Dinah Washington record filled with ballads. We dressed for the occasion, Patricia in black slip and high heels, me in black dress shirt and pants, clothes we could take off each other easily. At the end of the record, I'd carry Patricia, minus the slip but not the high heels, into the bedroom, where we had champagne on ice.

I'd had two passions in my life – my work and my wife. I was passionate about my work because it was something I could leave behind to the world – we'd had no children, so the work was pretty much it, except for whatever memories of me people I'd touched would carry around with them.

And I'd lived to nurture and celebrate Patricia, body and soul, soul and body. I'd had a responsibility that I'd taken to heart, so I would earn the love and respect of the woman I doubted I'd deserved – certainly not after that night in Washington, the memory of which would always haunt me. After that, I'd tried even harder to nurture her spirit, so she would grow emotionally and intellectually and achieve whatever she'd wanted to achieve. And I'd celebrated those successes. I would do so forever. Or so I still told myself so very solemnly and ponderously, as if to demonstrate to myself how virtuous I'd been.

On those New Year's Eves, like on so many other nights, I'd laid her down on the bed, and she'd stretched her long arms over her head. And then, like on that first time we'd gone to bed, I'd crawled up her long body inch by tantalizing inch. I'd felt like a finite mortal worshiping a limitless goddess, who'd granted me her favors out of eternal goodness. When I'd finally gotten to the point where she could put her tongue in my ear, I'd let her roll me onto my back so she could straddle me and put me inside her.

Especially on those New Year's Eves, our most meaningful anniversaries, we'd made the love-making last as long as we could.

So now, it seemed ridiculous to stay home alone on New Year's with such memories in my whirring mind. I needed something to distract me from the whirring, and I knew I wouldn't find whatever might work unless I got out of the house. So I telephoned Iris and said I'd be happy to join her and Bill.

CHAPTER SEVEN

I'd read on the Internet that people have reported sensing that they'd seen a dead spouse alive again. Perhaps a husband had seen his dead wife wandering around outside the house, smiling, as if nothing had happened. Or he'd heard her speaking to him. Or he'd awakened in the dark of night and felt her presence on the other side of the bed and reached over and been certain he'd touched her.

I remembered the tall blonde I'd seen on the main floor of Saks over twenty-five years ago. I'd thought she was Patricia, until I'd gotten closer and realized she was a teenager I'd never seen before. And I remembered finding Patricia in the chaos of the halls at the Frankfurt Book Fair, being courted by a blue-blazered smoothie.

Maybe, I thought, I should go to Saks or to Frankfurt. Sooner or later, I'd spot a tall blonde, and I'd experience a moment of joy – this could be Patricia, she was still alive! So what if the moment didn't last, once I'd realized that the woman I'd spotted couldn't have been Patricia. At least I would have experienced the joy of that brief moment, when my heavy heart took flight.

I knew that this kind of thinking was mad. Hartnett had shown me Patricia's face, and I'd seen that there was no life it, and that the intelligence that had animated it was gone.

I did this thought experiment: what if Patricia and I hadn't run into each other at the New Year's Eve party twenty-five years ago? What if, instead, I'd spotted a tall blonde in Saks last week? What if this woman was Patricia, and now was the first time I'd seen her in thirty years – and we hadn't been together for the past twenty-five years? Would I trade the promise of the future with her for the time we'd been together? Would I take that deal?

My life was in transition. I went down to the New York co-op around Christmas, and rattled around the beautiful, but empty rooms. Patricia had always spared me the presence of a Christmas tree and decorations, so I didn't miss them. I only missed *her*, terribly. I missed her turning toward me as I came up behind her. I missed her taking my face in her long fingers and kissing me after she'd opened the holiday gift I'd bought for her.

I tried to read. When I looked at the novels and short story collections on the shelves, I tried to remember where and when Patricia and I had bought them. I took a collection of William Trevor's stories off a shelf. I looked at the table of contents. Some of the stories sounded familiar, but I wasn't sure whether or not I'd read any of them before. So I read them, possibly for the first time, possibly not. I couldn't tell one way or the other. No matter: the stories were very good, and I couldn't understand why I didn't remember them.

I had a brief visit from Brian and Rita Cassidy, who were empty nesters now. They told me how blissfully quiet their Montclair house had become, except for holidays, when their two boys would bring wives and grandchildren for several days at a time. The Cassidys' expressions of condolence were heartfelt, and we got along for the hour or so that they were with me - at least they didn't say that it's good that Patricia and I had had no children - but I wasn't at all sad to close the door behind them when they left.

I didn't sleep well. I got into bed well before eleven every night. Within half an hour I'd doze off, and the book I was attempting to read would slip from my grasp. I'd turn off the bedside lamp and fall asleep almost immediately. I would sleep until around three, and then my eyes would be open. I would close them again and try to get back to sleep, but to no avail.

By five, I would give up, and half an hour later I would be out on the street, walking down Broadway. (I'd recently switched from running to walking to save my aging knees for golf.) I wasn't surprised by the number of people I saw heading to subway stops and hailing taxis. This was New York, after all. But it always surprised me to see how many people were jabbering on cell phones at that hour. What on earth could so urgently require a pre-dawn phone call? Who else was up and about, wanting to talk? I felt disconnected from all the activity that swirled around me.

Towards the end of my morning walks, I stopped for breakfast and read the *Times*. Except for the co-op's doormen, a news dealer or a waitress or the person taking telephone orders at one of the Asian restaurants I called, I didn't speak to anyone most days. So I had plenty of time to think about what I should do about the apartment and the house upstate. But any thought of consolidating my possessions into either of my residences - all the choosing of what to toss or take to Goodwill and then moving and unpacking all I'd kept – exhausted me. Putting off any decisions was almost comforting. So that's what I did.

The whirring in my head didn't stop. Why hadn't I been more attuned to the possibility of Patricia's being in danger? Why hadn't I known that I should have followed her that day, when she was being so mysterious? Then I would have been in the parking lot when the murderer approached, right?

I could picture myself intercepting a shadowy figure, thwarting the planned assault. Why hadn't I seen the need to get away from my desk and abandon my golf outing? Why hadn't I devoted my day to preventing harm from coming to Patricia, instead of tending to my own inconsequential pursuits?

When I returned to the house upstate two days before New Year's I decided to plunge into a project that I'd been considering for several weeks – a memoir about Patricia's and my relationship. Writing it would be a form of therapy. I'd read that the writing would help me confront my grief. Better still, I thought, working on a memoir would bring Patricia into my days – I would be able to feel her presence in the room with me as I worked.

I'd decided that the memoir would focus as much on her life as mine. I had plenty of material to draw on for writing about Patricia's life. Mary had kept a lot of stuff from Patricia's time in school – report cards, drawings, and what appeared to be every paper she'd ever written. Patricia had saved materials from her working life. I could talk with teachers and classmates and the people she'd worked with.

There were the books and articles she'd published. And with her death I was, per our agreement, permitted to the journals she'd kept from before we'd gotten married. I counted thirty volumes, in all. I had my own journals, of course. I could compare our individual accounts of events we'd shared and get a fuller picture than my own journals and memories would otherwise provide. There were all the photographs, each of which evoked more memories.

I didn't know what the ending would be, of course. As far as I could tell, Hartnett seemed no closer to solving the mystery of her murder than he'd been at the beginning of his investigation. He stopped by the house at the end of a midweek afternoon.

"I saw your car in the driveway," he said when I let him in, "and I figured you were home."

I led him into the dining room. We sat down on opposite sides of the table. "How'd you know it was my car?" I asked. "It could have been the cleaning woman's – and she wouldn't have opened the door to you."

"I saw your Volvo on the night of the murder. Besides, it's close to six o'clock, and I figured anyone you might have working for you here would have gone home by now." He grinned at me. "That's why they pay me the big bucks – I can figure these things out."

"Can I get you something to drink?" I said.

Hartnett sighed and shifted in his chair. "No thanks, I'm not staying long. As I said, I saw your car, and then I thought I'd ring the doorbell and ask how you're doing." He leaned forward in his chair and put his forearms on the table. "So how're you doing?"

I gave my standard answer. "I'm hanging in," I said.

"Filling up the days?"

"More or less – I get some exercise, do some work, prepare meals or order out, and sleep badly. Nothing out of the ordinary for someone whose wife's been murdered."

"I don't mean to pry. I'm just concerned."

"I appreciate your interest."

"Any plans?"

"I'm taking things one day at a time. I might go over to Paris for a while – not right away, but when I feel up to it." I'd surprised myself. I hadn't thought about traveling until this moment.

"Why Paris?"

"It holds – held – special meaning for Patricia and me."

"Like that parking lot where we met that night?" Was Hartnett avoiding saying that parking lot where your wife was murdered? "You told me that night that you remembered the last time you were there – twenty-five years ago."

"That was because Patricia and I stopped the car there and told each other some important things that night, which sort of sealed the deal on our loving one another. Neither of us ever forgot that night." This time I left out the part about our making love in the back seat of her mother's car, like a pair of mad teenagers.

"It's a shame she kept returning there. She was a target for robbery: a well-dressed woman in a shiny Accord. In a dark parking lot, the temptation was too great for someone."

"You're still treating her murder as a robbery?"

"Look," Hartnett said, "I'm still treating your wife's murder as a robbery because I can't find any other motive on anyone's part for the attack. No jealousy at this museum or at the last one where she worked, no gossip about an affair, no murmurs about any unpaid gambling debts – don't look at me so incredulously, Mr. Bornstein, I'm simply telling you that I've looked at all the possibilities."

"So you're finally getting around to me, now that you've exhausted all other possibilities?" I made the sentence sound like a question, and then I leaned back in my chair and folded my arms across my chest.

"Actually no, Mr. Bornstein, even though I have nowhere else to turn. I have no reason to believe you had anything to do with your wife's murder – absolutely none. But I have to keep digging, if for no other reason than I'm sure you want me to keep working on this case." He paused, and when I didn't say anything, he said, "and I'm also sure that you want your wife's killer brought to justice."

"Of course," I said finally, my mouth dry, "but more than anything, I want my wife back – which I know is impossible. But I still want it, crazy as it may sound to you. I want you – no, I need you – to find and arrest whoever murdered my wife, but I will take no satisfaction from it, because it won't bring her back."

"Most people in your position feel differently about whether their loved one's killer is brought to justice."

"An eye-for-an-eye is not the sum total of my philosophy for dealing with this kind of horror."

"Why not, Mr. Bornstein? When you say such a thing, it makes me wonder what kind of man you are."

"The kind of man who had a terrific, loving marriage with an incredible woman. I worshiped her. Even with all I've accomplished, I believe that my life would have amounted to nothing if she hadn't been part of it – the major part of it."

"What everyone tells me, Mr. Bornstein, is that you and your wife had a wonderful marriage. So relax. You're not a suspect. I'm not going to get a warrant to search your house again – this time for evidence that you hired a hit man – or go on some other wild goose chase. Given what I've learned about you, that makes no sense."

"Thanks," I said. I didn't know what else to say. "Sure you won't have something to drink?" I asked, as Hartnett stood up.

"Thanks, but I've got to be on my way." He paused and looked at me steadily for several seconds. "Here's something that gets me," he said matter-of-factly, "I can't understand how you didn't know that your wife frequented that diner. Why wouldn't she have told you?"

"I haven't thought about it," I said to Hartnett, as we walked toward the front door. "I don't know why that is, I just haven't. Maybe I don't want to deal with the idea that you can't know everything about another person, no matter how close she is to you."

"Maybe not," Hartnett said, as he was leaving the house. He turned on the walkway. "Have a good evening, Mr. Bornstein," he said. I watched him get into his car and drive down the street.

As I got up to leave the Kramers' on New Year's Eve, I had to admit that I'd had a good time. The Kramers had managed to take me out of myself for a few hours, and I was grateful to them for that. Bill stopped me as I was heading out the door.

"Mordecai, from everything I've heard about helping a friend who's grieving, I know I shouldn't say this, but you ought to get out of that house more often." I nodded. "Look," he went on, "there's a little furnished office just down the hall from us that's going to be available as of the day after tomorrow. Why don't you rent it for a while and work there? It will get you out of the house. As Sanford says, 'it'll do you good.'" I told him I'd think about it, but three days later I signed a lease on the space.

A series of old photographs in the lower lobby depicted the groundbreaking and construction of the 1920's era office building where I began to spend my working days in January. So I skipped any research into the history of the building. Besides, I thought my stay would be temporary. I'd negotiated only a one-year lease on the furnished two-room office that Bill Kramer had told me about.

Because the office was furnished, all I needed to bring from my home office were a laptop, a printer, and a few files. The next year would be the first time I'd ever worked anywhere but at home.

The most important decision I had to make had to do with my working hours. The decision was a fairly easy one. To my mind, there had always been a direct correlation between the amount of time I spent at my desk and the volume of work I produced. I learned a long time ago that the best and perhaps only way for me to get a high volume of work done was to keep regular working habits. I worked at home my whole life, and most mornings I went to my desk right after breakfast and put in a solid three hours before lunch. I went out for a leisurely lunch most days and would be back in time for three or four solid hours before dinner. If there was anything pressing, I would work through lunch and after dinner.

In fine weather, once Patricia and I had moved upstate and I'd taken up golf, I'd play a round in the afternoon once or twice a week. And I could waste time reading the political blogs I followed. But I still managed to log large swaths of working time, despite any distractions.

I parked my car in an open lot a few blocks from my new upstate office by eight forty-five every weekday morning. The mornings were cold; the grimy snow left in the streets was taking its time melting. There were a few sunny days, but most days were overcast. When I ventured outside, there was usually no more than a weak winter sun in the white winter sky.

Except at lunch hour and when office workers gathered at the downtown bus stops at the end of their working day, the streets were nearly empty of people. Most large buildings were served by multi-level garages at the rear. So people who worked in those buildings could park their cars and get to their offices without having to walk more than few steps outside. If they wanted to, they could go to work without having to experience any contact with downtown.

From the beginning, I found the downtown streets lonely. Not only were they nearly empty of people most of the time, I didn't run into anyone I recognized when I walked through them on my way to and from the lot where I parked my car or at lunchtime, when I hit one of the Chinese places or the sandwich shop that had decent turkey and tuna salad sandwiches.

I went to the downtown's main watering hole, a clubby restaurant with dark wood, cloth napkins, white tablecloths, and waiters in black suits and white aprons. It had been in business for ages and had become *the* place to observe and be seen. I sat with my back to a wall and watched everyone talking. If anyone took any notice of me, I didn't spot it.

When I was a young man, and I wanted to make a new friend, I'd find a woman. Of course, such relationships might have delivered on sex, but they certainly didn't deliver on lasting friendship. What had I been thinking? Nevertheless, when Patricia and I had found each other at that New Year's Eve party, I knew I'd found my best friend, for life.

The truth I faced now was that when Patricia and I had each other, and our busy lives, as well, there must not have been much time for friends, even the few we had. Moving upstate when we were middle-aged hadn't helped. We didn't have the natural path to making friends that couples with children in school enjoy. We hardly knew our neighbors. Patricia had suggested our joining a synagogue to make new friends, but I'd rejected that idea on the somewhat specious grounds that I wanted to stay as far away from religion as I could. I hadn't changed my mind.

When I took up golf, I considered joining a golf club, but decided that I didn't care for the atmosphere and the political conservatives I found – perhaps because they were what I expected to find – in such places. So I hadn't done anything that might have produced new friends. Of those few friends I did have, only Bill Kramer worked here, in this downtown. But I hadn't seen him for in the two weeks I'd been going to the downtown office.

I still believed that Bill's suggestion that I rent the office – and get out of the house – was the right one. But it didn't – and couldn't – cure everything. Not that there might not be an unwanted cure available. A couple of times, women who worked in the building struck up a conversation with me while we waited for an elevator. I was polite, but reserved. If any of them was offering anything beyond a comment or two, I wasn't interested, and simply tried not to be rude. Then one of the women recognized me, and word must have gotten around. After my first few days there, all the women would offer when they looked at me was a sad smile.

I stayed in the office until quarter to six, well into the dark of winter night in that upstate city. Except for any Internet correspondence that arrived after I got home, my evenings were solitary. I didn't want to impose on the Kramers. Nor did I call anyone associated with the museum. I'd gotten to know board members during my walk-behind days, and several had even dropped by during the week I'd sat *Shiva*. But I couldn't bring myself to impose on any of them, either. Indeed, I didn't know how I would start a conversation.

I needed to find ways to fill the time on weekends. One Saturday morning, I went to my desk and tried to get some work done, but I found myself turning away from it after a short while. I packed a change of clothes, a toilet kit, a book, some magazines, and my journal, and drove west, toward the Finger Lakes. I ate dinner in an inn in downtown Skaneateles, but the place was far too bustling for me. I preferred sleeping in a nearly deserted motel on the outskirts of town.

Not that I slept well. The sleep pattern I'd experienced in New York was still with me. I could fall asleep before midnight, but within four, or even three hours, I was awake again, and unable to get back to sleep. It became a matter of waiting until five, when I would get out of bed and soon be dressed and outdoors, walking.

Now I discovered that even though I thought that I detested being alone, I was beginning to embrace my new condition. Did being alone threaten to depress me? Possibly, but I didn't shrink from it. I decided that I wanted to be alone. Moreover, even if I wanted to change my life, I wouldn't have known how to go about it. I didn't have the will to do so, in any case.

I wasn't interested in finding a new woman to share my life with. The one I'd lived with for twenty-five years was irreplaceable. I didn't feel sorry for myself. I accepted being alone. I decided that it was something I could deal with. I grieved for Patricia, and for the years she had lost. I didn't grieve for myself and for what I had lost. I thought that doing so would be self-indulgent and would reek of self-pity, and I steered clear of it.

By the beginning of my third week downtown, I began to consider selling the upstate house and moving back to New York full time. The streets were just too empty up here. There was a terrific used bookstore in a residential area just up the hill from downtown – I could walk to it at lunchtime – but I couldn't go there every day, even though I liked to talk to the proprietor. There was a small art gallery downtown, but little else of interest. I could walk to Patricia's museum, and did once, but didn't feel up to going inside. Perhaps New York would be better for me.

One problem I would have with living in New York was that I would see so many couples – in particular, so many good looking men and women doing things together. I had no way of knowing how happy these couples were, or how many problems they had. But I couldn't escape the yearning to again be part of a couple like the one that Patricia and I had been. I recognized the immense danger in this yearning. I feared that it might lead me into self-pity – and that condition, more than any other, was what I sought to avoid, at almost any cost.

Still I knew that I would have more diversions down in New York – I could join a chess club or participate in some other activity with other people – but not so many diversions that they would distract me from my work. For when it came to my work, I was extremely disciplined.

Work on the nuclear power book was going as well as I had any right to expect. I could envision finishing it within a few months – six at the very most. The memoir about Patricia could be my next project, I thought.

Still, I didn't work full time on my projects when I was in the office. Several times a day, I found myself cycling through the political bloggers I followed. I'd gotten back to them after a self-imposed hiatus. I even spent time on youtube, watching videos of jazz artists and old movies. So I had enough ways to waste time without going on such popular time-wasters as facebook in order to look up classmates or other people I'd known. Of course, the problem I could see coming at me had nothing to do with the ways I was managing to waste time. My problem was that I hadn't come up with a new book project or magazine article I wanted to propose to one of my editors.

I was feeling this uncertainty about the future when Bill Kramer finally turned up one afternoon. "You doing all right here?" he asked. He stood in the doorway to my inner office, hands in his pockets, a pudgy guy, with his shirt tails halfway out of his pants. He glanced around the office, trying to take it in without making too big a deal out of what he was doing.

"You mean the office or downtown generally?" I locked my hands behind my head, tilted my chair back, and tried to look casual.

"Either. Both." Bill grinned, trying to look casual, as well. This was just a friendly conversation about nothing much, apparently.

"I'm hanging in." I wasn't about to volunteer anything more than this tiny morsel. I didn't want to reveal too much about how I was feeling, lest anyone offer any sympathy.

"It's not New York, of course," Bill said, "not what you're used to. There's nowhere near as much action in the streets."

"They're pretty much empty," I said cautiously.

"Don't let it get to you," he said quickly, and then looked as if he regretted it.

I smiled. "You're leading the witness, counselor."

Bill laughed. "You'd make a good lawyer," he said, "or a judge. Anyway, I thought I should see if you were still here. It's after three – time when the self-employed head for home, unlike us working stiffs."

"Checking up on me?" I tried to keep my tone light.

"No, it's nothing like that." He leaned against the door jamb and folded his arms in front of his chest.

"Then what's this visit about? And what took you so long to come down the hall? I've been here for well over two weeks." I smiled and spoke softly.

"I have to apologize for not looking in on you until now, but we've been crazily busy with a huge divorce for the past month."

"Not yours, I hope, or Sanford's."

"Certainly not Sanford's – Gwennie already cleaned him out once. There'd be nothing in it for either one of them."

"Unless there was a third party that one or the other couldn't live without."

"Nah, I'd have heard."

"How so?" I asked. "You know everything about the life of Sanford Glickauer?" I turned my chair around and pretended to write in my journal, which was lying open on my desk. "The life of Sanford Glickauer," I repeated. "If anyone decides to write his biography, the title has a ring to it."

Bill smiled and nodded. "Writing Sanford's biography would be a piece of cake. He's an open book about how much money he and Gwennie have, about how it's invested, about their home life, about every sexual encounter he's ever had – about everything having to do with

Sanford. I think he talks about himself so much because he wants to keep everyone focused on him. It's like we say around the office: it's all about Sanford."

"So there's nothing about Sanford that you don't know?"

"Look, Mordecai, how could I be sure that I knew everything about Sanford? There's no way, obviously. But I can say this: if he's harboring any secrets, I'd be gob smacked."

"You haven't said anything about you and Iris. And I hope you don't."

"Me and Iris – divorce? No way – for us it's 'til death do us part." Bill saw my blank stare. "Oh, sorry, Mordecai, I need to watch what I say."

"Don't worry about it," I said, "I'm not that delicate."

"Good, because one of the reasons I came to visit you this afternoon was to invite you to join Sanford and me – and Maggie Hartnett is usually with us – whenever you're free for one of our lunches in the place downstairs. It's where Sanford likes to go some of the days when he's in town. They leave a table free for him in back."

"Before I answer, I have a couple of questions. First of all, what's my being delicate, or not delicate, have to do with joining the three of you for lunch? My second question is, why the invitation?"

"The answer to your first question is that there's a lot of no-holds-barred banter at any table where Sanford presides and he likes everyone to join in. It's not a scene for anyone with a delicate sensibility. We discussed the tragedy you've experienced, and decided to ask you if you feel up to the sort of scene I'm describing."

"I think I can handle it," I said. I was determined not to give the impression that I couldn't take some rough and tumble.

"Sanford understands that there will be limits on how hard he can push you – for the time being, at least."

"Look, Bill, I don't want to come off as some delicate flower that's been damaged and needs tender care. I hope I come across as somewhat tougher than that."

Bill hesitated before he responded. He was being careful, it seemed to me. "I didn't mean to imply any such thing," he said quietly. "I just want you to know that Sanford and I understand that your wound is still raw and that you're still grieving."

"And you need to understand that I'm grieving for Patricia, not for myself."

Bill frowned. "I understand," he said after another pause.

"I'll figure out what the atmosphere at your lunches is like quickly enough. If I can deal with it – better yet, if I like it – then I'll join your little group."

"Fair enough."

"Now answer my second question: why me?"

"The answer to your second question is that Sanford found you interesting when he met you at the dinner at my home, and he believes you'd bring an interesting perspective to the group. If he has another motive, he'll reveal it in due time."

"I thought you knew everything about Sanford."

"I know all about his past. I don't even try to divine what he's thinking about or will do in the next minute."

"He's that unpredictable?"

"Not unpredictable – more inventive, I'd say. Over the years, I've come to appreciate the distinction. As have lawyers opposing him in many of the cases he's litigated."

"You make lunch with Sanford sound like one big game," I said.

"You're definitely onto something about Sanford. He likes to play games. Games are a big part of the lunch scene, as you'll find out. And Sanford likes to win the games he plays."

"What kinds of games?"

"Some games have been in Sanford's repertoire for years. Some he makes up on the spur of the moment. A game might involve a question and an answer, and then Sanford will analyze your answer so that he can tell a story about you. Or it might involve getting the rest of us at the table to do something because Sanford's tricked us into doing it. He's always looking for whatever might tickle him and, more important, relieve the boredom that he says he's always laboring under. He needs action all the time, he needs stimulation."

"Does the game playing ever stop? Does he ever take a break?"

"Slowing down and taking a break aren't in his nature. But don't worry, it's not exhausting. It's fun – always fun."

"I'm not worried about Sanford's games tiring me out, and I could use some fun. And you make it sound like the object is to put other people on the spot and even embarrass them."

"Like I said, you have to have a thick hide if you want to be around Sanford. You also have to understand, as you'll see, that Sanford doesn't exempt himself. Sometimes he's the butt of the joke, but that's all the more fun for him. He's not cruel – he just likes to laugh and alleviate the boredom of everyday life."

"OK, but just one more question: what do Sanford's games involve?"

"They involve women and money, mostly. And sometimes a game will involve art, which, as you learned at that dinner at my house, is one of his great passions."

"Women, money, and art: what else is there in life?"

CHAPTER EIGHT

"Let's do table nine today," Sanford announced, just loud enough for the three of us – Maggie Hartnett, Bill Kramer, and me – who were sitting with him at the table, called "Sanford's table," at the back wall of the restaurant. "Here's where table nine is," Sanford said, tapping his finger on a plastic sheet on his placemat. "Angie tells me there will be a party of four arriving in just a few minutes. I asked her not to tell me who they are. She'll give me a sign when they arrive, and we'll all be able to get a look at them."

It was a simple game that we were playing. You won if you came closest to the total amount, before tip, that the party would be charged for their lunch. But Sanford made the game seem more complex. He went into action the second Angie pointed surreptitiously at an older man leading two younger men and an attractive redhead, who looked to me to be in her mid-thirties, to seats at the table. "Anyone else recognize any of them?" Sanford asked.

"That's Leo Spillane," Maggie Hartnett said in a low voice. "He has a law office down the street."

"The woman must be a client," Bill Kramer said, also in a low voice. "Leo just pulled a chair out for her."

"And they're possibly in a hurry," Sanford said. "Otherwise Leo would have taken her to lunch at the club uptown."

"Who are the other two guys?" I asked. I'd never laid eyes on any of these people.

"They're Leo's partners," Maggie said, "but Leo runs the show. Sort of like Sanford does – or thinks he does."

Maggie, Sanford, and Bill all laughed. I watched them, without laughing myself. I'd been joining them for lunch two or three times a week for a month by now, and I still wasn't able to always determine whether a comment was meant to be serious or a joke. Glamorous Maggie had told me more than once that Sanford liked to be surrounded by pretty women who gave him shit, but that still didn't help me determine how one of her comments was meant to be taken.

"So," Sanford said, "the three amigos and a fair senorita who's looking for a divorce or a personal injury claim."

"She's not that expensively dressed," Maggie said, as if on cue. "If she was looking for the really big bucks, she'd have come to us, so I'd be of the opinion that they're treating her nicely, but they don't have to pull out all the stops."

"Agreed," Bill said. "They'll keep the tab for this lunch under three figures."

"How can you be so certain," I asked, "that they're in a hurry and that she's a client and not an important one, at that? She could be a new member of their firm – or someone they're recruiting. And they're not taking her to a more expensive lunch at the club because Leo wants to show her that it's important to be frugal."

"The plot sickens," Sanford said, in a tone meant to sound approving. He smiled at Bill. "*Our* new recruit is acquitting himself quite well."

I'd learned to be suspicious of Sanford's approbation. He probably knew that the redhead wasn't being recruited to join Spillane's. So he knew that my analysis was flawed, but he wasn't about to let me know that he knew. He wanted to lull me into driving my estimate of the table nine tab to well over a hundred dollars. That's what he liked to do to you: lull you into a false sense of security, and then turn the tables on you and make you look foolish.

I'd seen him do that sort of thing to Bill, during a lunch the previous week. "You may not know this about Gwennie," Sanford had said to me, "but Maggie and Bill know very well that Gwennie's an expert in helping battered women." I'd watched the two of them nod. "She's written a book about them that's into its second printing," Sanford had continued. "No surprise, then, that's she's been asked to speak to a group at the Institute – that's where you got your master's, right Mordecai?" I'd had my chance to nod and had taken it. "I told her not to accept their invitation. Those women would find some way to take advantage of her being married to me."

"Oh please," Bill had said to Sanford, "does everything have to be about you? You testify to the fact that she's an expert. She ought to be allowed to talk about what she knows." I'd joined him and Maggie in a bit of laughter at what we'd thought would be Sanford's expense.

"You think I can be too full of myself?" he'd said to Bill, making the words sound like he was inviting an answer to a question.

Bill had laughed again. "Now why would I think that?" he'd said. I'd noticed that Maggie had remained quiet throughout this brief exchange.

Then Sanford had taken his smart phone out of his inside suit jacket pocket, swiped the screen, and tapped and swiped it several times. "Here's an email I got from the head of that women's group the very next day," Sanford had said. "I'll just read a couple of key sentences: 'Our group would be most appreciative if you would schedule meetings with the following list of state assembly persons and senators. We will provide you with talking points, if you should want them. In any case, we would expect to accompany you to the meetings.'" Sanford had shut his phone off and glanced up at the three of us. "There followed a list of no fewer than ten people I was expected – is that too strong a word? - to contact."

Bill had covered his face with his hands. Maggie had laughed. I had understood that I'd been treated to an example of the art of a master.

Recalling that bit of effortless one-upsmanship didn't help me decide how much I thought table nine's bill would be. In accordance with Sanford's rules, our estimates were to be given to Angie on slips of paper when she took our orders. I did a calculation in my head, using prices for salads, entrees, a glass of wine each, and coffee for everyone. I threw in a few extra bucks for two espressos and a cappuccino.

My three lunch time companions smiled at me as they handed their slips to Angie. As far as I could tell, everyone had done their own calculations in their head. During our lunch, none of us looked at table nine to see what its occupants were eating and drinking. Sanford asked us not to. He said that if we didn't look it would "keep the tension thick enough we could cut it with a knife."

Despite the games and all the game-playing, or perhaps because of them – I welcomed the diversion, after all – I was enjoying the lunches with Sanford and his mates. It would have been an added bonus if the food in the restaurant where we ate lunch was terrific, but it was no more than serviceable. It wasn't in the same league as food I could get for the same, or even less, money down in New York. We didn't get together to drink beer or wine or any other form of alcohol. The four of us had water and coffee or tea with our lunches. I couldn't say much for the ambiance. The restaurant was rather cave-like, and it gave the impression that had bright lighting been installed, the dirt on the carpeting, the streaks on the glassware, and the general seediness of the place would have been exposed.

No matter the restaurant's imperfections, Sanford found it and its food entirely to his liking, mainly, it seemed to me and to everyone else familiar with Sanford's predilections, because he always ate the same things – a bowl of chicken broth, a plate with only smoked salmon or grilled chicken, and a large green salad. Add to that the restaurant's convenient location: all Sanford had to do was take an elevator down to his building's lower lobby, walk through the restaurant's back door, slide into "his" place in "his" table, and he was ready for Angie's ministrations.

The restaurant's dining area narrowed at the back so much that there was just enough room for Sanford's table, which was on a small platform with subdued lighting. In the evening, the table was removed, bright lights were turned on, and the platform became a stage for musical acts.

From his lunchtime seat, Sanford could survey the entire dining area. He loved the bustling scene in front of him – the restaurant was always filled at lunch – and he loved having so many women in the crowd. Whether they knew it or not, they were there not there just to have lunch with friends and co-workers, but also to be observed by a man who seemed to want nothing more from any of them than to be the object of his attention for a brief period of time.

Sanford had numerous other enthusiasms, including art, which I knew about, politics, movies, and the fortunes of Boston's professional sports teams, particularly the Red Sox, with whom he'd been intimately involved since Enos Slaughter had made a mad dash around the bases and scored the winning run for the St. Louis Cardinals in the 1946 World Series.

Sanford seemed to be on a first-name basis with every New York artist and local politician, all of them subjects of stories which were sometimes laudatory, often times embarrassing, and which were always delivered with the admonition that they not be repeated. As for movies, Sanford could recall large swaths of dialogue from numerous favorites, dating back to the mid-1940s, when he first began going to theaters with his mother on Saturday afternoons.

The point of having lunch with Sanford and his two associates, I soon realized, was purely and simply to be in his presence. It was an opportunity for me to avail myself of an unexpected education, for Sanford had in-depth knowledge of a wide variety of subjects.

Moreover, he was a wonderful storyteller. Most of his stories had a beginning, in which characters were described and a scene was set, a middle, in which the action took place, and an end, where Sanford made clear the reason for the story. He never had to resort to the lame phrase: "you had to be there." The stories were well constructed, the building blocks firmly anchored. In someone else's telling, you would have suspected that the stories had been rehearsed. But listening to Sanford, I concluded that the effortlessly and perfectly told stories were the fruits of a natural gift.

So when Sanford held forth on his Boston boyhood, the area where he grew up – Roxbury's Elm Hill Avenue – sounded like an oversized mid-Twentieth-Century bricks and mortar *shtetl* populated with the most intriguing characters you would ever hope to come across in such a setting. How could I not play close attention to the tales of the desiccated old man in the airless apartment who taught Sanford his Bar Mitzvah reading, the fire-and-brimstone rabbi who presided over the synagogue where Sanford came of age, and the residents of the apartment building where Sanford lived as a boy, all of them, except his own parents, sitting, in those pre-air conditioning days, outside on the front steps during hot summer evenings.

I didn't worship at Sanford's feet. At no time did I allow myself to compare me with him. He was what he was, I determined, and I was what I was. I never felt inferior to him. After all, because of the articles and books I'd produced, googling my name produced dozens of pages. I felt secure in my estimation of what I'd accomplished professionally.

I wasn't drawn to Sanford entirely by what he talked about. Much of the time, what grabbed me was the *way* he talked about one of his enthusiasms. His stories were interesting and funny or poignant, but I had the impression that they would have been rather pedestrian had anyone else been telling them. This notion reinforced itself on the few occasions I tried to retell one of Sanford's stories. I would get all the particulars right, but the stories never retained their punch.

Sanford had a gift for drawing attention to himself. Everyone knew what he was up to and didn't hesitate to let him know it.

"It's all about Sanford," Maggie Hartnett said to me at the first lunch I attended, when Sanford turned a Bill Kramer comment that didn't appear to me to be related to Sanford into something about himself. What's more, he spoke seductively, drawing you toward him, flattering you for having the good taste to closely follow what he was saying. His other great talent was for showering people with praise and making them feel good for being in his presence and attending to his discourse.

"You're meant to believe that Sanford's kindly about the superiority of his knowledge," Maggie said to me. "You're meant to believe that he doesn't want you to feel bad when it becomes obvious that you don't know as much about a subject – of his choosing, of course – as he does. And haven't you noticed how he lets you off the hook when it becomes equally obvious that you can't synthesize the knowledge of the subject as well as he can, that you can't put two and two together as well? And here's where he really gets you: he shows you that you can't possibly reach a more meaningful and interesting conclusion than he can from an analysis of the same bits of information available to both of you."

"It does seem to me," I said to Maggie, "that I know more than Sanford does about many things, particularly about subjects rooted in science and engineering, but somehow the things Sanford knows more about he makes seem far more interesting than the things I know more about. And I really can't tell you how he does it."

"Does it bother you?"

"What I can tell you is that I don't care that he does it." I didn't even care that when I said something at the lunch table that I had no doubt was clever, Sanford would nod in agreement and then sit back, smile, and say, "You're not as smart as you think you are." I could only laugh, although I had to admit that on such occasions I would come close to a line across which there was exasperation. I knew that Sanford could always pull me back from that line, with little more than a disarming grin and a pat on the hand.

He possessed a magical art by which he made you want to be in his presence and made you feel that it was all right that he was superior to you. So there was nothing I could say in response that wouldn't diminish me in my own eyes, much less Sanford's - and Maggie's and Bill's, as well, although, I believed, they would understand my predicament. In any case, I couldn't keep talking. I had to cede the floor to Sanford.

Then there would be a moment went Sanford would make amends for any pain he might have caused. He would bring up some silly business about his life away from the office, which would provoke a sharp comment from some else at the table – usually Maggie – that would send everyone into prolonged, uncontrollable laughter. Sanford would laugh the hardest, slamming his open hand against the table. As long as the joke was on him, and he was the center of attention, he found it immensely funny, much funnier that when the joke was on any of the rest of us. So any discomfort, any rage, was soon put aside. But I didn't entirely dismiss it.

"Why did you ask me to join Sanford's little lunch crowd?" I asked Bill Kramer when I was in a testy mood. "Am I there to learn something from the great man? Or am I there as nothing more than an additional admirer? Or do I have something to contribute?"

"From what I've noticed, you seem to be having a good time at the lunches," Bill said, with a wide smile.

"I can't deny it," I had to admit. "The fact of the matter is that the lunches take me out of myself. Oh sure, I'm there physically, and if any of you ask me about myself, I answer, and I don't stint on details. But what the lunches do for me is they make me forget for an hour whatever it is that's troubling me, anything that makes me unhappy once it lodges in my mind. So I guess I should shut up and be grateful." Bill's smile was back, and I did shut up.

I wondered about Sanford's professional life, of course. I asked him questions about it to indicate my interest, if nothing else. Although I was interested. For one thing, I found it amazing that Sanford had managed to set up a successful firm that often dealt with high profile divorces so far upstate from Manhattan, where I would have expected such a firm to be located. And I wouldn't have minded being titillated by inside information about some of the divorces Sanford had handled.

But through it all, Sanford was careful, unlike at the Kramers' dinner, when I'd first met him. "We can't tell you anything about what goes on in our office," he said at the first lunch I attended. "No tales out of school about recent cases, either."

"I'm not interested in being titillated," I said. "I want more than that. I want to learn about human nature. You – and Maggie and Bill – don't have to tell me about who did what to whom and shouldn't have." I paused. "But I won't cover my ears if you do." Everyone laughed.

"Mordecai, you're full of crap," Maggie said.

"You're right – I am full of crap," I said, and everyone laughed again.

As I quickly learned, it was Sanford himself who was interested in being titillated. Throughout each lunch, his eyes roved the restaurant. He was looking at women - not only the young and toned, the women anyone might look at, but at all women. "I can't keep my eyes to myself," he told me, right off the bat.

"His hands are another matter," Maggie followed up immediately. "He's a dirty old man deathly afraid of putting himself in a confrontation where he might not be able to control the outcome." Sanford guffawed. I looked at Maggie and tried to raise one eyebrow. "He likes to assess the fillies," Maggie continued, "and I don't mean the four-legged critters at the racetrack."

Sanford smiled. "You know me so well, my dear," he said to Maggie. "But you will admit that you find my assessments well worth paying attention to. As a matter of fact, I've never known you to reject them.'

"Like all your assessments, no matter the topic, my dear Sanford, what you have to impart about a woman you have looked over carefully, but may never have actually met, seems always to be spot on. So naturally we mere mortals all pay close attention to the word of a god. There's always so much to learn – about the fair sex - and about you, too, my dear." These remarks, delivered in a breathy, kitten theatricality, were directed toward me, I figured. In any case, I wasn't entirely sure how I was meant to react to them, or to Sanford's volleys in this banter. It sounded good-natured, but was it?

"Such long legs on such a short woman," Sanford said suddenly. "Perhaps it's the very high heels that make this stunted creature worthy of my attention."

Without thinking, I turned around to get a look at the woman Sanford was fixated on. I spotted a well dressed middle-aged woman standing at the restaurant's entrance. She looked short, as Sanford had said, but she also looked well-put-together, which Sanford hadn't seen fit to mention. More to the point, her proportions looked perfectly normal. Then I heard his laugh. I turned back around, feeling guilty that I'd found it necessary to get a look at the woman myself.

Maggie's hand was on my arm. "It's a game," she said. "Before I even looked at the woman I could have told you that she was attractive, which is why Sanford noticed her in the first place. But she has an attribute – a lack of height – that the great appraiser could turn into an exaggeration." Maggie rolled her eyes. "But the appraisal had a purpose, which was to make you turn and look. Like I just said, it's a game."

I laughed politely, which I thought I was supposed to do. I looked at Sanford. He was smiling at me, a bit sheepishly, it seemed to me. "Can't help myself," he murmured.

I thought I knew what he was getting at. "I'm not a delicate flower," I said.

"I'm sure you're not," Sanford said.

Angie came to our table a moment after Leo Spillane's group had left the restaurant. "You came pretty darn close this time, counselor," she said to Sanford. "If the young lady had ordered two scoops instead of one, you'd have been right on the button."

I looked at Sanford in amazement. "OK," I said, "how did you figure it?"

"I figured on deli sandwiches for the three men, a Caesar salad with grilled salmon on top for the redhead, one hot coffee, and three iced teas," he said. "Then Leo wanted to make the girl happy, so he suggested she order dessert. The two younger partners ordered pie and ice cream to make her feel better about indulging herself. So she allowed herself to order a dessert. One look at that slim body of hers and I figured she'd go for an order of ice cream. I thought she'd order two scoops and leave some. She fooled me and ordered one scoop and finished it." He looked at Maggie.

"I had four salads, all with grilled salmon on top, and no desserts," she said. "A typical women's gambit, I know, but it seemed right to me. Then I piled two espressos and a cappuccino on top of four iced teas. That killed me."

"You don't want to know what I had for them," Bill Kramer said. "All my talk about it not being a celebratory lunch was an attempt to fake the rest of you out. I was way, way over the amount of their check because I had the lunch as some sort of celebration, and I was counting on Leo ordering a bottle of wine. He's done that before, and I thought I detected a celebratory mood, despite what I said." He shrugged and smiled weakly. "I faked myself out. Besides, what do I know about sizing up other people's moods and motivations?"

"More than you're letting on just now," Sanford murmured, "otherwise you wouldn't be so valuable to our firm." Bill rolled his eyes, but he was smiling broadly now. So were Maggie and I. Once I gave an accounting of my seriously flawed estimate, which was somewhat like Bill's, it was clear that Sanford had won the game rather easily. But judging by our smiles, we all seemed to be feeling good nonetheless.

A couple of months into the lunches and I was also spending some late afternoons and early evenings with Sanford. He'd come down himself to my office a month earlier at around three one afternoon. I had two small rooms, a little over three hundred square feet. The outer room had a sofa, an armchair, a couple of overflowing bookcases, and two floor lamps that were positioned for reading. The inner office, with a window on the courtyard, had two desks, a couple of swivel executive desk chairs, and three four-drawer filing cabinets. I had two computers, a printer, and a scanner.

I'd filled a CD tower with contemporary classical music discs, which I listed to on headphones. I kept all the jazz stuff at home. I couldn't put on a jazz record and get work done. Classical was better background, perhaps, I thought, because the rhythms weren't so insistent.

I'd brought the electronics, files, books, and music from home. The other stuff was there when I signed the lease for the office..

"Anybody home?" I never locked the outer door, and Sanford had entered without knocking. We sat in the outer office. He came right to the point, as always. Praise for my talents -Sanford excelled at praise - would modify his request perfectly. "I'd like you to write a profile of me, sort of a short biography," he began. "I've read a couple of the marvelous magazine profiles that you've done, and I have no doubt that with your superior talent you could do me justice, even though I'm a lawyer, not one of the scientists and engineers you usually write so well about." There was the usual challenging smile on his face. "Maybe you'll find the essential me. Who knows? " He cupped his chin in one hand. "Actually, I bet you will. You've got great insight."

I rolled my eyes, and Sanford laughed and clapped me on the shoulder. Half an hour later, we shook hands on a deal – on Sanford's terms, of course. He disdained tape recorders. Instead of talking into a machine, he needed to talk with me, in person, for two hours or so twice a week, starting at four-thirty in the afternoon. Exactly which days in any given week, he'd let me know by email on Sunday evening.

I figured I could live with it. I was beginning to feel at loose ends, anyway. No money changed hands. The deal was that we'd talk and I'd get something down on paper and we'd see what we had. Then we'd decide how to move forward. It didn't strike me as being very businesslike, but I was in no mood to make any demands.

"There's one more thing, Mordecai," Sanford said, as he was leaving my office. "I'm going to let it all hang out. I'll tell you things I've done in my life that I've never told anyone else. Not before now. But I don't care who knows what. Not anymore. I'm too old to care - or too mature." He laughed. "So make whatever you want of what I'll tell you. It'll all be up to you." I couldn't help feeling that my sessions with Sanford would be an ultimate game.

"Ever go to bed with a fat girl?" he said one day. "I don't mean just zaftig. Zaftig's fine. I mean fat."

Sanford started a lot of our early conversations that way. He wanted to talk about women and sex, and he wanted to for my jugular, as it were. At the beginning, I'd asked him to give me some juicy stuff from his years in divorce work, but he said that he'd get to the parched pussy parade, as he lovingly called his female clients, all in good time. Then he'd reassured me. They weren't all desiccated old bags, he'd said; you could still get the juices flowing in some of them. Whatever. I would have to wait for his accounts of divorces won and settlements achieved.

"I did once," I responded to his sally. I knew I sounded tentative. I couldn't help it.

"Come, come," Sanford said, cupping his hand and moving it like a traffic cop. "Give."

I didn't object to the coarse way Sanford could talk about women. And I was more than willing to talk with him about sex. I'd had enough sexual encounters with women to be able to hold my own in the face of Sanford's many tales about tail, as he sometimes put it, a tender smile on his face.

But I wasn't completely forthcoming. I'd never been with anyone, I finally had to admit to myself, not even with Patricia, despite my protestations to the contrary. Always, on reflection, I'd realized that I'd held something back. Over the years, whenever I'd thought about another of the women I'd met at the hotel out by the highway on the Saturday nights during my time at the Institute, I'd told Patricia about the sexual conquest. I hadn't bragged, I'd just told her. She'd said she wanted to know. She hadn't appeared to be judging me. But I hadn't explained to her my need to act as a loner on those nights, my activity hidden from everyone, while I sought a sexual connection with someone.

"I'm not proud of what happened," I said about the fat-girl question.

"We often aren't, especially on the morning after. But tell me about this fat girl."

"She wasn't big and fat. She was a small, round woman, with a soft bosom and round creamy thighs."

"She sounds reasonably attractive. Tell me more."

"She had a pretty face, she wore a silk dress that was flattering, and she had shiny black pumps. She smelled good. And she wanted to give herself to me. I just didn't give her enough in return."

"You have to be specific. *I* give *you* a lot during these conversations. *You* have to give *me* something in return."

Never mind that I was supposed to be gathering material for a profile. Sanford needed titillation, despite the fact that he always seemed to have more sexual exploits to recount than I did. He could go back to any stage of his life and one-up me. His prom nights, for example, had always ended with the girl he'd escorted removing her clothes and offering herself to him. Mine had ended with my date and me changing into bowling shoes.

The pretty, round little girl and I had gotten onto a large bed, with the covers thrown back. We'd been on a field of white, with no clothes on.

We left the lights on. Turning them off would have been better. I sat with my back against the headboard. She got between my legs and eagerly took me in her mouth. I'd caressed her shiny black hair. Later, I felt that I hadn't tried to give her enough pleasure and I'd felt horrible about it.

This was a couple of years before Patricia and I reconnected. I'd thought I'd seen her in Saks. She must have been on my mind. Maybe that's why the coupling with the pretty little round girl had been a failure.

There wasn't anything I wanted to admit to Sanford about that time with the pretty little round girl. I shouldn't have gotten started talking about her.

Sanford leaned back and put his hands behind his head. He flashed me his tender smile. I sensed that I was being let off the hook. Then he waxed what passed as philosophical in these back-and-forths.

"You've seen one pussy, you've seen them all," he said.

"You must tell me more about your career as a gynecologist," I drawled.

"What I mean is, it's the place to start when you're getting acquainted." He laughed. "What the woman actually looks like doesn't matter so much, although, obviously, it does matter somewhat. Down there is where there are no surprises – until you swing into action. What you do, how you perform, and how she responds, that's where the variables come into play. Looks don't matter so much, as long as she's not disgusting. If you need to, imagine the proverbial paper bag over her head."

"You're a living, breathing sex manual," I said. "I'll assume that what you've just said will go in the introduction."

Sanford ignored my sarcasm. "I've thought of writing one. If only I had the time." He sighed theatrically. "I've even thought of a title."

I braced myself.

"I'd call it *The Divorce Attorney's Guide to Making a Woman Truly Happy*. If only I had the time," he repeated.

"I'm not sure that such a title would coax buyers into looking through the book to decide whether they wanted to buy it."

"You may be right. The publisher would have to work around the title, I suppose. Whatever, I still like it. I'd like to think that if I got such a manual right, it would kind of sum me up."

"What about a woman's heart and mind? How would you deal with them?"

"That's where the game-playing would come in," Sanford said.

The tenor of the conversation was different on the afternoon when Gwennie joined us. She and Sanford were going to a dinner honoring a local prosecutor who'd made a name for herself with several celebrated battered women's cases, including one where a wife had killed her abusive husband.

Gwennie was wearing a black caftan, high heel sling-backs, and large pieces of gold jewelry. Her gray hair was pulled back from her face into a knotted arrangement at the back of her head. Patricia had sometimes worn her hair that way, when she thought an occasion called for it. She'd worn it that way on the New Year's Eve when we'd unexpectedly run into each other after five years apart. The hairdo had looked a lot more sophisticated on Patricia than it did on Gwennie, who nonetheless looked better than she had the first time I'd met her, at the Kramers'.

I hadn't expected Gwennie to be there with Sanford. He hadn't mentioned her coming along. And I hadn't expected her to be so vocal.

"I supposed Sanford's been regaling you with tales about Boston Latin School," she said as soon as she and Sanford had sat down side by side on my outer office couch, where he usually sprawled out alone. Sanford had attended Latin School, a public school down the street from the Harvard Medical School and near numerous other institutions, for six years, starting with the seventh grade, which was called Class VI, and graduating in 1955.

"I'm sure he's provided you with the hilarious tales of how the boys used to tease the teachers," Gwennie went on. She'd made air quotes around 'hilarious.' "Just to kill time, the boys made those hapless teachers provide the same Latin word derivations and explain the same German sentence structure over and over again. What a hoot!" Gwennie rolled her eyes.

"They were called masters, not teachers," Sanford interjected.

"Right, that's the thousandth time you've corrected me on that. I wouldn't be surprised if you get to two thousand."

"And they weren't hapless. They could be just as cruel as we were. They seemed to enjoy telling a boy he was fit for nothing more than bricklaying or demanding that another boy, who had stood to answer a question, but had gotten it wrong, sit down because he was confused. Or making a boy, whose stomach must have been rumbling with hunger, copy a passage out of Cicero because he'd hurried down an 'up' stairway to get to the cafeteria at lunch time. Some of us were a pre-pubescent ten or eleven when we started there. We didn't have even the vocal power to fight back."

"They needed to control you little savages."

"Is that what you would call middle class boys who grew up in the city?"

The repartee was rapid-fire. I sensed that Sanford and Gwennie had gone around this argument many times before this. I was just a new audience.

"How else would you describe a boy who kept one necktie tied in a noose in his locker and tightened the noose under the collar of whatever shirt his mother put on him —solid color, plaid, cotton, flannel, it didn't matter.

"That was why a black knit tie was best. It wasn't our fault that we were required to wear a tie."

"They tried anything they could to civilize you. It's why they made you take five or six years of Latin, and they threw in French and German, or Greek if you were so inclined, for god's sake."

Sanford had already told me about the paucity of science courses at Latin School. He'd cracked that the curriculum had barely changed since the school's founding in 1635, the year before Harvard was founded – "so Latin School boys would have a place to matriculate."

"They taught us how to think," Sanford said to Gwennie. I was sure she'd heard it many times before.

I wondered if what I was witnessing was any sort of clue to the state of their marriage. I might not have been much of an expert, but I did know how difficult it was to figure out what was going on inside a couple's marriage. So I decided to leave such questions alone.

"Did they teach you anything useful?" Gwennie snapped. "Anything that would help you make your way in the world?"

"I've told you about the career days that they had. Graduates would talk to us about their professions. I've told you about the newspaper reporter who assured us that journalism wasn't the career for making a lot of money. And about Leonard Bernstein, who showed up in a turtleneck, as I remember, and talked about playing the piano as a career."

"A lot of good that must have done," Gwennie said in triumph, and then they went on in this vein of another half hour.

The following week, Sanford, alone again, talked about his father, Gabe. "Shortly after I entered Latin School," Sanford began, "my father decided he'd had enough of working for someone else, even though the money had been very good, and he decided to strike out on his own. He'd risen to be the highest paid salesman for the carpet merchant who rented space in one of the large department stores on Washington Street downtown. He was a big man, an inch shy of six feet tall, a bit over 220 pounds, and there was great strength in his body, with his broad shoulders, barrel chest, and heavy arms and legs. But the thought of turning back someone else's rugs to show customers what lurked in the middle of a heavy pile of Orientals had begun to wear on my father. He thought the turning and the lifting would be easier if the rugs belonged to him, not to someone else."

"So he and my mother, Sophie, built a nest egg that they hoped would get a rug business started. When my mother's bachelor uncle died and left her a small pile of bonds that could be cashed in, my father saw his chance. He scouted a storefront on Blue Hill Avenue, the great thoroughfare that ran all the way from Roxbury out through Dorchester and Mattapan to the Blue Hills in the suburbs.

"The storefront was in a block opposite one of the main entrances to Franklin Park, which had a zoo and a rose garden. There was large semicircular plaza in front of the entrance, with a long arc of wooden benches at the back. On fine days, the benches were filled. The people who came to sit there couldn't help but notice the large sign that would go over the front of my father's store, and on their way home many would surely stop to look in the windows at the artfully arranged displays that he envisioned. It would be easy for neighborhood housewives to visit the store when their children were in school, and the store would stay open until nine on Monday and Thursday nights, when the women could bring their husbands in to look at the rugs they'd selected and the samples for wall-to-wall carpeting that my father intended to add to his inventory. He envisioned hiring two women who would help customers make selections in the store or would arrange for visits to customers' homes to provide on-site advice and to make any necessary measurements.

"But by the 1950s, more and more of his potential customers, Jews, who lived in apartments and two- and three-family homes in Roxbury and adjacent Dorchester, began to flee the encroachment of black families into their neighborhoods."

Sanford lifted his hands and waggled his fingers. "The schvartzes are coming, the schvartzes are coming!" he cried out in mock horror.

Then he sonded sober again. "The Jews were on the move, mainly to single-family homes in the suburbs and the more suburban parts of Boston itself, such as West Roxbury. Besides, my mother argued forcefully one night at the dinner table, the people who squatted on the Franklin Park benches were probably renters, who wouldn't be in a position to spend money on wall-to-wall carpeting for apartments they didn't own. I remember sitting at the dinner table in amazement. This was the first time I'd ever seen my small, bird-like mother criticizing my strapping father. More amazing yet, my father didn't put up any counter-arguments."

"My parents had the same dynamic," I interjected. "It was indeed surprising the power those tiny women had over their much bigger husbands."

"So with my mother urging him on," Sanford continued, " my father decided to follow his potential customers. He opened a store in the Chestnut Hill section of Brookline, on the corner of a street that fed into Route 9, a main westward artery out of Boston. The location was within easy reach of customers in West Roxbury, Brookline, and Newton, three prosperous communities. Anyone heading out Route 9 couldn't miss the large sign he put up, and there was enough time after first spotting the sign, for a motorist to turn into his parking lot.

"He'd abandoned the idea of Blue Hill Avenue store with little regret. He believed that the changes in the old neighborhoods were part of a natural flow of people of different races and religions through American cities. As far as he was concerned, there was nothing wrong or racist about his belief; in his mind, it was just the way things were, and it was perfectly natural. He reasoned that the same phenomenon would be happening in other cities where a name like Glickauer might attract customers, and he made a couple of trips in his new car to scout out potential locations in those cities' suburbs. He was looking for cities that seemed to have the same characteristics and inner migration patterns as Boston and thus offer the same opportunity.

"But let me talk about that new car. It was a Cadillac. My guess is that the business was generating enough cash so that he felt comfortable with one of General Motors' top-of-the-line models to take him from the Elm Hill Avenue apartment out to his store on Route 9. Besides, my mother loved the luxurious, roomy interior. The three of us would pile into the Caddy on Sundays for a drive out of the city to a dairy farm stand for homemade ice cream.

"My parents knew their days on Elm Hill Avenue were numbered. They planned their own move out to the suburbs, once I'd been bar mitzvahed at the familiar Mishkan Tefila. Some evenings, they would work their way out to the suburbs, to look at fine homes and neighborhoods. They took special note then they came upon a synagogue. My father called these outings "toots," and when the Caddy would glide by a particularly impressive home, he'd murmur, "that's what I'm going to give you," drawing each "that's" and "I'm" out, and the three of us would laugh with delight. When I saw a big house coming into view, I'd say, in the deepest tone I could muster, "That's what I'm going to give you." Whenever I turned to look at my mother sitting in the in the back seat, there would be a smile on her lips.

"By this time, I'd begun to see Latin School as a dingy old relic. I thought I belonged in a suburban school, where I could escape the Latin School strictures. What I was really looking forward to was having girls in my classes and going to dances with them. I had just turned thirteen, and I was beginning to get other ideas about what I might do with a girl, if only I had the chance.

"So I was delighted when I overheard my parents agreeing one night that a sprawling ranch house, with a picture window and clean lines inside large, bright, airy rooms, would be to their liking, and they were sure they could find what they were looking for in Newton's Waban section, where the better class of people they knew were settling.

"One Sunday, I remember, a realtor shepherded us through houses she said were ideal for a couple with a child nearly ready for high school – either of the two Newton high schools would be suitable and were on a par academically with Boston Latin. So I began to campaign for my parents' moving to Waban. But my dreams never materialized."

"What happened?"

"I can still remember the afternoon when I came home and saw my mother walking lightly into my parents' bedroom. She left the door half open, and I could see inside. My father was lying on his back on top of the bed. His trousers and socks were still on, but his barrel of a chest was bare. There was a man sitting on the bed next to my father. I recognized the man: he was the doctor that my parents took me to. The doctor was half-turned toward my father and was tapping his chest with one hand while the other hand pressed an instrument against the hairy skin.

"My mother turned to me. I was standing just outside the doorway. She moved toward me, a finger against her lips, and closed the door gently.

"'Your father has something called angina,' my mother told me half an hour later. 'He's resting now.' I can still remember the glass of milk she poured for me. I lost my taste for milk that day; I never drink the stuff. Breasts are another matter, of course. I remember my mother saying, 'He'll have to be careful. The doctor's prescribed nitroglycerine tablets. He'll need to take one when he feels the pain.

"'Of course, he won't be able to lift those heavy carpets anymore,' she went on, 'but it's going to be a good business, you'll see, Sanford. We'll just have to hire an extra person to do the lifting.' I learned later that she'd urged my father to shift his business away from floor coverings toward window treatments. She told me that she said to him, 'I'm much more interested in window treatments. I can help you with them.' That was her argument. But my father would have none of it, she told me. Carpets were what he knew – that was *his* argument.

"So my father did hire another person, and then another one, as his business started to grow, and they were the ones who did the heavy work of turning back carpets when customers wanted to look through a pile of them. But with the added wages, Waban became too expensive for my parents. One night at dinner, when my mother said that all of Newton was out of the question, my father hit his hand on the table, but then he quickly calmed down and murmured his agreement.

"Then, at the dinner table on another evening, as I remember it, my father mentioned that he'd had a call from his lawyer, who lived in West Roxbury, inside the Boston city limits, on the road to Providence. There was a six-room ranch, a few streets over from where the lawyer lived, that was coming up for sale. The family, who had bought the house when it had been built a few years earlier, was moving down south. The lawyer would arrange for a showing, and if my parents liked the house, he'd negotiate an attractive price for them before any realtors got involved.

"When they saw the house, they liked it, even though it fell far short of what they'd envisioned for their move to Waban. The neighborhood, full of similarly modest houses, was reasonably attractive. The street emptied onto the Veterans of Foreign Wars Parkway. Turn right and you were on your way to downtown Boston. Make a U turn a block up and you were pointed toward Providence. Gabe could find his way to and from his Route 9 store without too much trouble. Best of all, my parents reasoned, living in West Roxbury meant that I could stay in Latin School."

Sanford stopped talking abruptly, and silence filled the room. He and I sat without speaking for a long while. I closed my eyes. If I turn out the lights, I thought, Sanford and I could fall asleep together, perhaps until morning. I opened my eyes after a while – I didn't know exactly how much time had elapsed since Sanford had stopped talking. I looked over at him. His eyes were open. I couldn't tell what he was focusing on, if anything. He seemed at peace. Or had his recounting of a part of his father's life drained him?

"Was your dad's business a success?" I asked, keeping my voice low.

Sanford looked at me blankly for a moment. Then his face cracked into a smile. "Oh, sure," he said finally. "He opened a second store in Cleveland, at around the time I graduated from Latin School, and both stores prospered. 'I've become quite the carpet mogul,' he told me."

"So he had a satisfying life," I said.

Sanford looked away, as if preparing to formulate a response. "I'm not sure my father was satisfied with what he achieved with his business,"

Sanford said after a long moment. "He didn't discuss it that much at home. He preferred to talk politics at the dinner table."

"Are you trying to tell me that he didn't enjoy his success?"

"I don't know what he enjoyed. He and my mother didn't do any traveling. He just continued to go to the store almost every day. He got to the store in the early morning, and he was home by five-thirty every afternoon. He left the store closing to his employees. They were there without him on Monday and Thursday evenings, when the store stayed open late. I don't know whether he ever asked himself why he never varied his routine. He seemed devoted to my mother and me and to his business. That was his life, the sum total of it. If he wanted anymore than that, he never said so — not to me, at least, and not to my mother, as far as I could tell."

"It almost sounds like he was depressed, in spite of the material success."

"Perhaps so - I never asked him. I suppose it didn't occur to me to ask my father such a personal question, not until it was too late. And it was too late before I knew it. He lived for only ten years after I graduated from Latin School."

"Did he want you take over the business?"

"Not really." Sanford paused and smiled again. "He told me I should leave the flipping of heavy carpets to people with strong backs and weaker minds. Not that his own mind was weak, or that he thought ill of the minds of the men he employed, but I knew what he meant. He wanted something grander for me." I could see Sanford's eyes misting. He blinked. "One of my greatest regrets," he went on, "is that my father didn't live to witness some of the things that I accomplished."

We fell into silence again. After what seemed like several minutes, I said, "I know what you're talking about, although my own father did live long enough to hold some of my books and magazine articles in his hands. I still think about him whenever I publish anything new and wish he could still be there. I miss him terribly — not as much as I miss Patricia, of course. And I miss my mother, too. When it's not Patricia I see when I close my eyes, it's my father, coming home from the fish market he owned for awhile, his hands swollen from digging in the ice. He never said so, but I knew always, even when I was little, that he put himself through the long days for my mother and me. He came last."

"We owe our dads an awful lot," Sanford said quietly, and he reached out to lay his hand for a moment on top of mine.

CHAPTER NINE

It had been a relief to focus, even if only for a short time, on my father's memory, instead of Patricia's. But once I was back home an hour after listening to Sanford talk about his father, I was immersed again in thinking about her. It was hard to escape from doing so. Every piece of furniture, every picture, so many of the books and CDs contained a story involving the two of us.

We'd bought our dining room chairs at a tumble-down antique barn south of Syracuse on a cold, late-autumn afternoon. The sign on top of the gray barn read "Gramps." The proprietors were an elderly couple, who parted with the six maple chairs for seventy-five dollars apiece. As I wrote the check, I asked the old couple, "So which one of you is Gramps?" Patricia had snorted. "Pay no attention to my rude boy," she'd said, as they'd directed their attention up at this tall woman. "I'll wash his potty-mouth out with soap when I get him home." We'd all laughed.

In my study is a photograph – from the early 1900's – of a small low factory with a tall smokestack and a dog at one of the doors. We bought it at a Cape Cod flea Market during the week we shared a small cottage with the Cassidys on the Wellfleet marsh. We cooked dinners on a makeshift grill, drank wine while the sun went down, and later made love as quietly as we could next to the thin wall between the bedrooms. No matter which object my gaze fell upon in the house I now occupied alone, a motion picture starring Patricia played in my head.

I had my distractions: Turner Classic Movies, over a thousand jazz and contemporary classical CDs, even the odd basketball game or some other sports on television, although I wasn't much of a sports fan, except for baseball when I'd been growing up in Columbus and followed the Indians, who played up the road in Cleveland. Throughout the house there were shelves filled with books. Like everyone I knew who bought lots of books, I would never get around to reading everything I'd accumulated. I could put my hand almost anywhere on one of the bookcases and find something I'd always meant to read, but hadn't got around to. At least the books made no demands on me, unlike magazines, which kept coming and piling up, crying out for attention before the post office delivered another one.

I subscribed to a dozen magazines. I didn't read any of them cover to cover, of course. I read only one or two of the major articles in any issue of *The New Yorker*, for example. My selections were always suspect. A week or two after I'd finished with an issue, there would be letters about articles I hadn't read, never about one of the articles I had.

Since Patricia's death, I'd felt guilty about spending time on distractions, for there were piles of sympathy letters and cards that needed my attention. By no means was I familiar with all of the names of the people who had sent something. But no matter who had sent it, each and every expression of sympathy that landed in my mailbox deserved an answer. I had no doubt of my responsibility to respond to the avalanche of grief that had buried me.

So I dug my way out, one letter or card at a time, each with a written expression of thanks. Then I had to address an envelope, of course. It all took a lot of time. I wrote with a fountain pen – a Parker 51, which I also used for writing in my journal - so I didn't have to bear down. I thought I would have an easier time that way, but my writing hand kept cramping up anyway.

In one of my darker moments, I thought of having a photograph taken of me kneeling in mourning, my hand to my face, like a figure in a Kathe Kollwitz drawing. I would just sign the back and slip it in an envelope. Then I remembered a house Patricia and I had visited briefly in Cambridge, where the walls were lined with framed prints of Kollwitz drawings. The most mournful were in the dining room. We'd barely managed to stifle the hysterics until after we'd left.

I couldn't manage more than five to ten replies a day, even on weekends. It was taking weeks to get through them all. That evening, after Sanford I had spoken about our fathers and the sacrifices they'd made for us – which had brought us unexpectedly close to one another – I had dinner alone at my dining room table. It was a dinner I often had these days: just a bowl of pasta with one of Rao's sauces, a salad dressed with oil and vinegar, and a couple of glasses of inexpensive red wine. But I used one of the placemats that Patricia had been fond of, a matching cloth napkin, and good cutlery. I wasn't about to turn into a slob. I read the

London Review of Books while I ate. I tried to guess which articles would draw letters that would be printed in future issues.

After I cleared the table and fired up the dishwasher, I put a pile of envelopes, some stationary, and my pen on the dining table. Then I fetched half a dozen sympathy cards from the basket in the front hall where I tossed them when I retrieved the mail.

The third one I opened surprised me. It was an elegant card, purchased at a museum in Rome, I noted, when I turned it over, not a sympathy card with a canned message of condolence. The moment I saw the card, I knew the drawing on the front was of a building designed by Andrea Palladio, the great Sixteenth Century Venetian architect, whose work can seem awfully familiar. The connection I made, which I was meant to, I quickly realized, was to Patricia's museum.

The message inside the card was written in a bold hand. It was simple. "I cannot fathom your loss," it said. Then: "Call me if you wish." The card was signed by Joanna Stanton, the high school teacher Patricia had talked about on that night long ago when she'd announced she was moving to California and I'd thought I'd never see her again. A telephone number was underneath the signature.

I put the card down, got up from the dining table, and went into my study. I turned on the television. A William Powell detective movie was on. The screen flickered in front of me, but none of the action registered. My mind was elsewhere. In it, I was watching old movies of my lost wife, including the night when she talked to me about Joanna Stanton and the pass she'd made. I played them while the movie on the television played on. The movies in my head were the only way now that I could see Patricia walking toward me, hear her words, and see her smiling lips approaching mine. It helped me remember how her lipstick smelled on her.

I went to bed later than usual – a little after midnight. I picked up the Ross Macdonald novel I was reading for the second time and turned a few pages, but left the bookmark where it had been. After I put the book back on the night table and turned out the lamp, it took me an hour to fall asleep.

But I was awake at six. I sat on the edge of the bed and listened to NPR's Morning Edition for a while, then made the bed, shaved and took care of other business, put on my running clothes and went for a long walk through the neighborhood. For some reason, I didn't follow my usual morning four-mile route. By the time I finished breakfast, a little after nine, with the *Times* unread on the table, I couldn't remember where I'd walked.

I picked up the phone and dialed the number on Joanna Stanton's card. A gruff male voice answered: "Stanton residence."

"Is Joanna Stanton available?"

"Who should I say is calling?"

"Tell her it's Patricia Murphy's husband," I said.

"Just a minute."

I heard the sound of the phone being laid down on a hard surface. Several seconds later I heard a rush of labored breathing before a woman's voice said, "Thank you for calling, Mordecai. May I call you Mordecai?"

"That'll work fine," I said. I heard a murmur of assent through the breathing on the other end of the line. "I opened your card last night," I went on. I paused. Then: "I read your message, and then I played a movie in my head of the night when Patricia talked to me about you. It was a long time ago, that night: thirty years."

"Yes, it was: I was a teacher then." Joanna Stanton paused. I could hear her breathing. "I've been retired for ten years," she went on finally. "But I still remember Patricia, of course. In fact, I think of her often. She was a very special young woman. But I'm sure I'm not telling you anything you don't already know." She paused again. I stayed silent, waiting for her to continue. "I loved her," Joanna Stanton said after a long moment.

"But not as a daughter," I was about to say, but didn't. Instead, I said, "I know," and left it at that.

"I'm sure she told you everything about me," Joanna Stanton said. "You know," she went on hurriedly, catching her breath, "my husband was always aware of my feelings for Patricia. But he didn't mind. He understood that the only people in the world I loved in that way were Patricia and himself."

"Quite a guy," I blurted out.

"He would raise a glass of his best dark beer," Joanna Stanton went on, ignoring my sarcasm. "He makes his own beer, did you know that?"

"I dimly remember Patricia's mentioning it. Like I said, she told me everything."

"It's very sweet. I mean, his beer is very sweet. Well, so's the fact that he makes it. And so is he, come to think of it." I heard the labored breathing. "Anyhow, he would raise a glass of beer and say to me, 'there's enough of you for two, Joanna.'" She laughed heartily at a long-remembered joke, and then the laughter was swallowed up in a fit of coughing.

"Like I said, quite a guy," I murmured, but this time I wasn't being sarcastic. I heard Joanna Stanton struggle to suppress her coughing and catch her breath.

"Perhaps you'd like to meet him when you're over here," she said.

"Oh?"

"I have some photographs of Patricia from her high school years. I doubt that you've seen any of them. Perhaps you'd like to. I'll give you a cup of coffee and some home-made cake, and perhaps we'll get to know one another a bit. You'll find that I'm not such a bad person."

"I'd like that. I don't want you to think that I think you're a bad person. Patricia told me that she had great respect for you."

"Thank you, Mordecai. I should tell you that I followed your and Patricia's careers quite closely, so I already know a great deal about you." She giggled, and then coughed again. "In fact, I googled you just yesterday."

"When would you like me to come over?"

"How about now? It's within walking distance. I'll fire up the coffee maker with a fresh pot."

I agreed that now would be a good time, and Joanna Stanton gave me the address.

The Stantons lived in a new condo development across the by-pass from where I lived. The walk took me less than twenty minutes. They occupied one side of a double-condo unit. From left to right, there was a front door to their neighbor's condo, the neighbor's two-car garage, their own front door, and their own two-car garage.

The street was lined with similar units. They looked well-built, and each condo seemed to have almost as much privacy as the kind of free standing home that I lived in. I'd heard the development referred to as a collection of retiree storage sheds, but I'd also heard what the condo selling prices were, so I expected the interior of the Stanton home to be substantial. I wasn't disappointed in that regard.

The woman who came to the Stantons' front door looked to be in her mid-seventies. In her black pants suit, she was as big as advertised. Her bosom and hips were as broad, and her backside and thighs as large, as I'd expected from Patricia's description of long ago that I still remembered. The heavy bangs that lay across Joanna Stanton's smooth broad forehead were as expected, as well. Her hair was jet black, straight, and cut so it looked like a helmet. Her unlined face featured two large, black eyes and generous lips covered in bright red lipstick. She reached over and took my hand in hers.

"It's wonderful to finally meet you, Mordecai," she said, suppressing a cough.

"It's my pleasure, Mrs. Stanton," I said. I let her keep my hand.

"Please," she said. "Call me Joanna." She looked me over appraisingly. I ventured a smile and returned the favor, although less obviously, I hoped. She was about five-nine and weighed two-twenty, I figured, though I was a lot better at heights than weights.

"You're a handsome man," she said. "You and Patricia made a great looking couple."

"Most of the time," I said, without offering an explanation about one night thirty years ago. Just then a heavy-set, bearded man, with a prominent belly hanging over his belt, passed behind Joanna Stanton. He was carrying a tray with two large pieces of coffee cake and a large mug with steam rising from it.

He grinned and winked at me. Sauce for the goose, sauce for the gander, I thought maliciously. I couldn't help myself. I watched the man out of the corner of my eye, as he proceeded towards a distant part of the condo.

Joanna Stanton turned and pulled me gently along with her. "First coffee and cake and some conversation," she said gaily. "Then a quick tour of our home – we're rather house-proud, you know – and finally the pictures." She suppressed the cough again and smiled at me. I let myself begin to like this woman. It was an easy thing to do.

The kitchen chairs, heavy enough to hold the Stantons, were quite comfortable. The coffee cake was delicious, moist and not too sweet. No barista I'd ever come across had done better by a cup of strong black coffee. Joanna Stanton looked at me approvingly – the appraisal was over, I figured, and I could relax – while I polished off the coffee and cake.

"I like to watch a man eat what I put in front of him," she said, coughing slightly. I noticed that her eating had kept pace with mine.

We sat and talked for over an hour. She told me what she knew about an aspect of Patricia's life or, less often, even my life, and I filled in any gaps in her knowledge. She showed great delight in everything I had to say. She smiled at me with her entire face, especially her large dark eyes. She leaned forward intently when I told her at length why I had been so drawn to Patricia and how I had thrown it all away at the beginning. She took my hand in hers. It was soft and warm. It felt somehow like a hand I could trust – a motherly hand. I felt completely at ease.

Even though the reason Patricia had pulled away from Joanna Stanton abruptly, but regretfully, was never far from the forefront of my consciousness as she and I talked, I felt myself drawing ever closer to her. I wanted her to like me for myself, not only as Patricia's widower, I realized, as I tried to draw her out about her own life. It was back to my graduate school days – back to the technique I'd used to make a woman do what I wanted after I'd met her at that hotel out by the highway. Here, however, I was simply interested in making a woman like me.

I needn't have bothered. Joanna Stanton seemed utterly charmed. Besides: "I hate to dwell on the past," she said. "We have our ailments, my husband and I, otherwise we have a good life within these four walls. Knock wood. That's all that matters to me." She grinned and rapped on the table. Then the persistent cough. She stood up, and I stood up with her. "Now let me take you on a tour of our home," she announced. "It's a requirement for every first-time guest."

Joanna Stanton breathed heavily as she climbed the two sets of stairs in her home, and she coughed at the end of each climb, but she managed to show me everything on all three levels. She seemed especially proud of her husband's lair, as she called it, in the finished basement, where he kept his library of physics texts and his beer-making equipment. He didn't look up from his laptop while his wife and I roamed around his domain.

"Those are for you," I heard him say, as we started up the stairs. On the bottom step there was a canvas tote bag with four bottles of beer in it.

"Thank you," I called out. I turned to see him wave a thick arm. I still didn't know his name, I realized.

The top floor's highlight was the loft overlooking the living room. It was lined with bookshelves, which were filled with coffee-table-sized art books, DVDs, and CDs.

"My kind of room," I said, as I casually removed a volume from a shelf, wondering what the odds were that it would be that book with the pictures of nude women that Joanna Stanton had opened for what she'd hoped was Patricia's benefit. Her hopes had been dashed, as hopes so often are. Mine were, too. It was a book of Atget Paris photographs, not a collection of Helmut Newton nudes. Oh, the cruelty of chance.

"Christopher has his brewery, I have my library," Joanna Stanton said. So that was his name. She wheezed as she bent down and retrieved a photographic album from a lower shelf. There were two recliners side by side against the loft's railing. The chairs faced a large window. On this sunny morning, the skylights in the living room's cathedral ceiling behind us made it bright enough to see photographs without turning on lights.

Joanna Stanton sat down heavily and motioned me to sit down beside her. She pushed back, and the recliner flattened somewhat, but the footrest stayed down. She planted her feet solidly on the floor. The cough returned.

Then she opened the album. She let me look at each page for a few seconds, and then she turned to the next one. Neither of us spoke. I couldn't have spoken, even if I'd wanted to. Was I still breathing?

Each page contained a single enlargement of a shot of Patricia. In every one, she seemed unaware that her picture was being taken. She looked completely natural, totally unaffected. In the first one, she was standing on the steps of her house, looking down at someone or something in the driveway. In the second picture, she was sitting on the top step, her feet together on the second step down. She was absorbed in a book. In the third picture, she was walking back up the steps. In the fourth, she was opening the door.

She looked sixteen or seventeen. Her blonde hair was combed into the thick bangs I remembered so well – the bangs that Joanna Stanton still wore. I couldn't detect any makeup on Patricia's face. It looked sweet and fresh. She wore a scooped-neck red tee shirt that hugged her slender body and blue shorts of minimal length. I was startled by the outlandish black high heels. They made her impossibly long legs look impossibly longer. My heart turned over. Then I took another look at the shoes and recognized them.

In the fifth photograph, Patricia was striding up the street toward her home. She was wearing a short jacket, jeans, and running shoes. I could detect the length of her stride, the stride that easily matched mine.

I put my hand on Joanna Stanton's, to keep her from turning the page. "How were these pictures taken?" I asked her. I tried to keep my voice level. "Wait, I think I know," I said before she could respond: "a telephoto lens."

"Yes, Mordecai," she said softly. Her cough was quiet, too.

"How many pictures are in here?"

"About three dozen."

"And you took them all?"

"I took about half. Christopher took the rest."

"Jesus. This is a problem for the *New York Times* ethicist: What's worse? That I take pictures by myself of one of my students – who I have a crush on - without her knowing it, or that my enabler husband takes them? For god's sake, Joanna. What the hell were you and Christopher thinking? Were you thinking at all - about invading Patricia's privacy or about anything else? Oh, and another thing, was your enabler husband after Patricia, as well?" I took hold of the album and pulled it out of Joanna Stanton's grasp.

"Please, Mordecai, it wasn't anything sordid. You must believe that. I just wanted to have Patricia with me, always. I wanted to be able to hold her to my breast – without hurting her. Without subjecting her to me, without forcing her to do anything that she might not have wanted to do." Joanna Stanton coughed for several moments. "She wouldn't have wanted this mountain of flesh. Who would? Except Christopher, who's an even bigger mountain than I am."

"Are there any shots of Patricia without her clothes on?"

"No, none: it wouldn't have been decent."

And would have put you and your beer-bellied hubby in jail, I said to myself. Then, out loud: "I'd like to look at the rest of the pictures of my late wife alone, if you don't mind."

Joanna Stanton got up without a word and went downstairs. I heard her washing dishes, and then refilling the coffee maker. I sat with the album closed on my lap for awhile, before I opened it again. I looked at each of the pictures for several moments, before proceeding to the next one.

All of them were mesmerizing. The young, coltish Patricia was stunning. Later, as an adult, she'd also exuded an inner beauty, nourished by a good heart and keen intelligence that had been captivating. I could see that same inner beauty in these illicit pictures. So now I held a treasure – a record of her from a time years before she'd first stood up in front of me and asked me that question I can never forget: "Where will it ever end?" I put the album under my arm and walked down the stairs.

Joanna Stanton was pouring coffee into two cups. "Please sit down, Mordecai," she said.

"I'm taking this album with me," I said matter-of-factly. "I'll buy you a fresh one – empty unfortunately."

"Go ahead. Please. It belongs to you now." There was another cough. "But have another cup of coffee before you go." She slid the cup across the table. She looked miserable, defeated. She'd tried to give me a gift, and I'd taken it, but there'd been rejection of the giver in the taking. "We're not bad people, Christopher and I," she said.

"No, you and your husband aren't bad, Joanna. And, of course, I'm glad to have these wonderful – I have to say that, because they are wonderful – these pictures of a beautiful girl who became a beautiful woman. How and why they were taken is ancient history and doesn't much matter anymore. So I should say thank you and leave it at that. Thank you."

"You're welcome. Now please drink your coffee."

"Only if I can pee before I walk back home," I joked. There was no point in staying angry at these flawed people. I opened the album to one of the last pages and turned it around for Joanna Stanton to look at.

"By the way," I said, "I noticed that Patricia's face looks a little fuller in the last of the photographs."

"That's when she was pregnant, of course," Joanna Stanton said.

"What? Pregnant? What are you talking about?" I felt light-headed. It hit me, like a roaring wind in my face, that I not only had evidence of what Patricia had really looked like in high school when she hadn't been posing in front of a camera, I also was seeing through a window into a dark space where something terribly important and tragic had been hidden from me, for whatever reason, good or bad.

"Mordecai, you didn't know?" Joanna Stanton looked truly horrified. "But you said that Patricia told you everything." The cough again.

I stood up. I couldn't stay seated. "I was wrong, apparently. What happened?"

"Patricia had an abortion. We, Christopher and I, took care of it. No one else knew, not even her parents – except her friend, Mary Farley."

"The girl with the curly red hair?" I'd seen her only once - at the Inn on the Lake, the first time I'd taken Patricia out, but I'd never forgotten her. I'd never forgotten any detail of that night.

"Yes, but how do you know her?"

I didn't answer the question. I had other questions of my own. I sat down heavily and pushed the coffee away. "Jesus," I shouted, "what other mysteries are behind these photographs?"

"There are no other surprises," Joanna Stanton said miserably, and then broke into a strangled combination of sobbing and coughing.

I heard a heavy tread on the basement stairs. "Who got Patricia pregnant?" I said, my voice level again. "What's his name?" I felt pain, suddenly, that it couldn't ever have been me, not with my low sperm count. Whether we'd wanted children wasn't the point – it was a question of manhood, wasn't it?

"What does it matter? Why torture yourself with this?"

"Please tell me," I said quietly. "I need to know."

I saw Christopher come into the living room. "Mary Farley knows, of course," he said in his gruff voice. "She lives in town now. You can look her up under Howard, the name of the rat bastard who dumped her years ago, lucky for her."

I now knew the name I was looking for. I gathered up the album, buttoned my jacket, and headed out the door. I didn't shake hands. Touching the Stantons at this moment seemed somehow impertinent. When I turned out of the driveway and headed down their street, I looked back at their front door. They were standing in the doorframe, filling it with their bulk. Joanna Stanton was leaning into her husband. I could tell that she was crying. His head bowed, he had both his heavy arms around her, as if holding on to her for dear life. His or hers, I didn't know. Maybe both. I realized I was looking at a scene that I had no hope of ever truly understanding.

As I walked, I managed to pull Mary Howard's address up on my iPhone. She lived in the oldest part of town, nearly two miles from where I was now. I was in a hurry to get to her, but considering the mood I was in, I was reluctant to get behind the wheel of my car. So I kept going toward her place on foot.

I didn't attempt to find her phone number on my iPhone. You could get lucky, but that sometimes wasn't as straightforward as it had been years ago, before entrepreneurs had put in place charges for such basic information. In any case, I wasn't interested in phoning ahead, even though I was taking the risk of not finding her at home in the middle of a weekday. Walking was the thing I needed to do right now.

The day was cold and clear, and I'd dressed for it, in a light wool turtleneck and thick Harris Tweed jacket. I was warm as I walked – too warm, in fact – and by the time I stopped to pee finally at a coffee shop at the town's major intersection, I was sweating lightly. I took my jacket off and carried it folded over my arm the rest of the way. It wasn't until then that I realized that I'd forgotten the beer that Christopher Stanton had put in a tote bag for me.

I had to cross the old, no longer used rail tracks to get to Mary Howard's street. I found her address a few minutes later. She lived in a small, two-story frame house that badly needed a coat of paint. I walked up wooden steps that needed replacing onto the front porch and pushed a button next to the door. I heard a bell ring inside.

I didn't immediately recognize the face of the woman who came and opened the door without hesitation. I hadn't expected to. After all, I'd seen Mary Howard for no more than half a minute three decades ago in rather dim and haphazard light on the porch of the Inn at the Lake. Besides, I'd been focused on Patricia that night. But when the woman in the doorway now looked up at me with an expression of interest on a tired, but still pretty face, a penny dropped into the deep, dark pool of memory.

She was small woman. The red hair I summoned up from memory had turned a gray-streaked white. She wore an oversize sweatshirt over a pair of man's plaid boxer shorts. A pair of good legs ended in bare feet. I had the impression that under the sweatshirt she was thin. That said, she was attractive and had an air of nervous intelligence.

"My name's Mordecai Bornstein," I said. "I'm looking for Mary Howard."

"You've found her." A smile formed on dry lips bare of any lipstick. "I guess you don't remember me. I used to be a redhead, but that was in another life."

"Actually, I knew who it was from your expression, even though I only met you once years ago."

"At the Inn on the Lake," Mary Howard cut in. She cocked her head and pointed at me. "When you were Mike Born," she said, and then laughed. "In another life."

She'd pegged me too easily, I thought, but moved on. "I needed that alias so Irish mothers would let their daughters go out with me."

Mary Howard laughed again. "You didn't fool me. Maybe you fooled Patricia, but that was because she needed you." Her look hardened into defiance. "Don't act puzzled," she said. "I'd guess it's not your style. Besides, I'm getting cold standing out here. Come in, Born . . . stein, or whoever you say you are nowadays. Oh yeah, Born . . . stein it is. That's what you said, anyway." There'd been pauses between the syllables in my last name.

I followed Mary Howard into the living room. It smelled like the refuge of a smoker. The furniture had seen better days, but the flat panel television mounted above the fireplace looked fairly new.

"My grandkids," she said, indicating the toys scattered over the floor. "My daughter drops them off on her way to work. You just happened to show up on a day when she has to take them to the doctor. They won't go without mommy; Gran isn't good enough for them today. So I'm free to light up. She hates it if I smoke when her kids are here, so I keep the peace and let the little ones distract me from climbing the walls."

"How many grandchildren are there?"

"Two: a boy four and a girl three. Any more, and I'd be a candidate for the looney bin."

"Still, it must be nice to have the time to care for them."

"I had to switch to the late shift at the Farmer Boy. That's a diner, by the way."

"I've driven past it, but I've never gone inside."

"I figured. It's not your kind of place."

"Oh, c'mon. I like diners. I even have my favorites. I've just never been to that one."

"Whatever."

She threw herself down on a dark green couch. I sat down on a chair within reach of her. "I've just come from Joanna Stanton's," I said.

Mary Howard smiled. "I know," she said. "Joanna phoned me. I haven't heard from her in years. She told me to expect you. And she told me that she was worried about you."

"She needn't bother," I said. "I'm not out to make trouble. I just need to know some things."

"A little knowledge can be a dangerous thing."

"Please," I said. Then: "Joanna gave me this." I handed the album to Mary Howard.

She put it on her lap and reached for the pack of cigarettes on the end table next to the couch. She shook the pack and drew a cigarette out of it with her lips. She flicked a lighter, waited a moment, and then took a deep drag.

"Oh, sorry," she said, picked up the pack again, and held it towards me.

"No thanks," I said.

"I figured as much."

"Actually, I did smoke cigarettes when I was a teenager." I paused for effect. "But I didn't inhale."

Mary Howard rolled her eyes, and we both laughed. Then she took another deep drag. She coughed as she exhaled. Women had been coughing in my face all day, for one reason or another.

"So what can I do for you?" she said finally.

"Take a look at the pictures," I said. "Then I'd like to have a talk."

She opened the album and hooted. "Who took this pic?"

"Joanna Stanton herself."

"Really? Did she say anything about this outfit Patricia was wearing that day?"

"No. Why?"

"Prepare yourself for a rare treat," Mary Howard said. She leaned over and patted the couch, indicating where I should sit. Then she got up, put her cigarette out in a full ashtray on the end table, and walked across the room to a low cabinet next to the mantle. She knelt in front of the cabinet, rooted around for a few moments, and got to her feet with a DVD jewel case in her hand. When she had the DVD loaded in the player on top of the cabinet, she returned to the couch.

She threw herself down again, and then fished a remote out from under the cushion she was sitting on. The TV screen above the dead fireplace came to life. A few clicks later, and a Table of Contents appeared on the screen. Mary Howard highlighted Chapter 4: Pas de Deux, and after a moment the screen showed a doorway with a short flight of stairs behind it.

Two beats later, a teenager appeared at the top of the stairs. As he came down them, I noticed that he was wearing a unitard with a tank top. He was barefoot. He was heavily muscled, but as he passed through the doorway, he looked rather short to me. He stood against the wall to the left of the doorway.

Another two beats later, and a pair of very long legs and part of a torso appeared at the top of the stairs. I recognized the legs. I'd first seen the blue shorts and red top a couple of hours earlier. As the young woman, holding onto a railing, made her way carefully down the stairs on the black high heels I remembered so well, Patricia's entire teen-aged body came into view. She had to duck her head as she came through the doorway.

Mary Howard laughed. "We found this low doorway in the basement of the auditorium," she said. "Patricia was as tall as the opening in her bare feet. Then, in those heels, she was over a foot taller than Ted."

"*That's* Ted Howard? Jesus."

"Watch the movie."

I had to admit I found it pretty amusing, probably because Patricia played one of the starring roles. Despite the Pas de Deux title, the two participants didn't perform a dance. Instead, they played a game of keep-away with a transistor radio that started out in Ted's hands, was snatched away by Patricia, and then snatched back by Ted, and on and on.

Once they went into their routine, I noticed the music, which started out at a moderate tempo, in time with the duo's movements. As the music speeded up, Patricia and Ted moved more frantically. I smiled when Patricia draped herself over Ted, winced when he picked her up with one of his heavily muscled arms and balanced her long body on one of his shoulders, and then smiled as she reached down behind him to get at the radio in his free hand. I was relieved when he put her down gently. She rewarded his gallantry by holding the little radio aloft. He managed to snatch it away from her despite her considerable height advantage.

After three or four minutes, the music stopped, and the two performers stood on opposite sides of the doorway, looked directly at the camera, and smiled. Then the screen went black.

I applauded. It seemed the proper response.

"Glad you liked it," Mary Howard said. She'd lit another cigarette. "I did the camerawork. It was pretty good, if I say so myself. We sneaked the school's video and sound equipment down to the basement at night, when no one was around."

"Whose idea was it?"

"The three of us had heard the music during a music appreciation class, and then we had this idea for a comic pas de deux. Patricia and Ted sketched the thing out, and then they more or less winged it while I shot it. We were afraid to linger, so the first take had to do."

"Well, the three of you did a great job," I said. I coughed as Mary Howard blew smoke out of her nostrils. "When did you transfer the film to DVD?"

"Just a few years ago."

"Did you have a showing?"

"Not really. Besides the three of us, you're the only one who's ever seen it."

"Why the secrecy?"

"No secrecy – we just wanted to keep this for ourselves. We didn't want to share it. I can't tell you why."

"Do you think the pictures in the album were taken the same day as the pas de deux?"

"Probably. I never saw Patricia in those crazy shoes again. Just as well: I thought she might break her ankles in them."

No, she'd learned to walk in them, I thought. They'd been a weapon – and a lure. "What was her relationship to Ted when you shot the movie?"

"The three of us hung out together sometimes. He was *my* boyfriend."

"So what happened?"

"He wanted Patricia one time. Ted called her his number one challenge. He said that to my face."

"And what did you say to him? Did you tell him that she was a human being, not some sort of prize?"

"Look: Patricia was very smart. We all knew she would be somebody someday. She was sort of a prize. Ted made me believe that. He managed to convince me that once he'd had sex with her we'd go on just like before, and it would be even better between the two of us, because he'd have gotten Patricia out of his system. Once would be enough. He made both of us believe that. And I had to hand it to him. He did exactly what he said he would."

"But what was *she* thinking? Did you know? How the hell did he manage to get to her? She was a smart girl. Could she have been that naïve?"

"He was a fabulous con man, my Ted. I suppose he believed he had to be because he thought he was too short for a guy. Of course, his lack of height didn't matter. He was plenty big enough in the right places, if you know what I mean. But he had a high opinion of himself as a manipulator. He thought he could charm the leaves off the trees in the springtime, if he'd had to. Or charm the pants off any girl, including tall Patricia.

"She never told me how he managed to seduce her. She only told me that she thought she'd lost her mind." Mary Howard took a deep drag of her cigarette and blew smoke out through her nostrils. I didn't cough this time. Then she laughed. "I just remembered what she said. It was, 'my emotional development hasn't kept up with the length of my legs.' But if I had to guess how Ted got in her pants, I'd have to say that he managed somehow to get her to believe that it was *she* who was seducing *him*, not the other way 'round."

"And when she knew she was pregnant?"

"She panicked. She was afraid that her life would be ruined. A baby was the last thing she wanted. She ran to Joanna Stanton, who she knew would fix the problem, without telling anyone, especially not her parents." Mary Howard snorted, and then had a coughing fit.

"Except Patricia told you?"

"That's right, she did. She said that she felt dirty and guilty - both for having sex with Ted and for getting rid of the baby. You know, I even told her that if she didn't have the abortion, I'd find a way to adopt the baby and raise it as my own child. Plucky Mary. Can you imagine a sixteen-year-old saying something so incredible? How would I have pulled that off? She never questioned my motives. I couldn't have given her a sensible answer, anyway. So we didn't go down that road.

"She went ahead with the abortion. It had been legal for a few years by then, so she didn't have any trouble. I think the Stantons might have posed as her parents."

"The next time I saw her, she said she wanted to assure me that she had no intention of stealing good old Ted away from me." Mary Howard paused and lit another cigarette. "So I had him all to myself. Unfortunately." A drag on the cigarette. Then: "But I did get a wonderful daughter and two wonderful grandchildren out of him, eventually. So he was good for something."

"What happened to him? Where is he?"

"We split up twenty years ago. I threw him out. Dealing with his con jobs – he was conning me, he was conning the people he did business with, he was conning everybody, it seemed - had become just too much for me. I needed peace. And my little girl came first, before my relationship with him.

"He died of AIDS five years ago. He started up with men after I threw him out. That's what he told me, anyway. I'd had no idea he was interested in men that way. I guess they were interested in his great little body, and he reciprocated. When I found out from some mutual friends that he was sick, after I hadn't seen him for fifteen years, I brought him back here and cared for him until I couldn't keep up with it all. I felt so sorry for him. I feel so sorry for all of them. They don't deserve it."

Mary Howard stamped the cigarette into the ashtray. She bit her lip, trying to keep herself from tearing up.

I leaned over and pressed the back of my hand against her cheek. She put her hand over mine. "Thank you, Mordecai," she said. "You're a good man. I'm sorry you had to find out about all this. Joanna shouldn't have made the mistake of telling you. But once the genie's out of the bottle – well, you had to have the full story, I guess."

I got the album and my jacket and walked with Mary Howard to her front door. "Call me if you need anything," I said. "I mean it. Oh, and when you look in the phone book, it's Bornstein, not Born."

She smiled up at me. "That night at the Inn on the Lake, when I saw Patricia with a guy and then got a good look at him – you, I mean – I was so happy for her. You looked so solid. I thought, he'll help her be everything she can be. Despite her stupidity with Ted, I still cared for her. I just couldn't let her know it."

"It took me a while, but I think I eventually got it right with Patricia." I didn't know what else to say. I looked away, and my gaze fell on the toys scattered around the living room floor. "Enjoy your grandchildren," I said.

"Oh, I do." Mary Howard's smiling face seemed lit from within. "They're the greatest thing that's ever happened to me."

I bent down then, kissed her on a dry cheek that smelled of sour tobacco smoke, turned and went out the door. I thought of going back inside and demanding that she get rid of every cigarette in the house and swear off them for life. But you are the only one who can rid yourself of your demons. And maybe her love for her grandchildren would eventually do the trick. I hoped so.

CHAPTER TEN

I was numb for a couple of hours, and then the shock of learning about Patricia's teen-aged abortion slammed into me. I sat on my living-room couch and slowly turned the pages of Joanna Stanton's album. I looked at each photograph carefully, examining each long-ago expression in my dead wife's face. I tried to assess her body language. I wasn't an expert in finding meaning in a person's facial expression or her body language. I knew how to determine what words and diagrams on a printed page meant. I was good at that. I didn't think I was good at the other.

I bent the heavy album cover back and carefully removed the clear plastic sheets. Each sheet contained two photographs, placed back-to-back. I was relieved to find that they weren't glued together. I gently removed them from the plastic and spread them out on the dining table in their original sequence. How much time had elapsed between the first one and the last? I couldn't tell. I dismissed any idea of calling Joanna Stanton to ask her.

Then I wondered if the Stantons had retained negatives, or if there were more pictures that hadn't made it into the album for some reason. I'd never asked where the pictures had been printed. Had there been a darkroom in their old home, where they'd lived before they'd moved into their condo? There must have been, but I hadn't asked. That had been stupid of me. But I didn't know what to do about it. Maybe it wasn't important. I clung to that thought.

I shifted slowly down the dining table, letting my eyes drift from each photograph to the next. Except for the first four shots, where Patricia wore the provocative outfit with the tee shirt, short shorts and outrageous heels, she was dressed in everyday clothes. But no matter what she was wearing, the long-limbed, coltish sexiness never deserted her. It was obvious why the besotted Joanna Stanton had kept all the pictures.

I went back to the first shot and moved down the table slowly again. I was looking for clues – but to what? Did I expect to be able to tell which day it had been when Ted Howard had fucked Patricia? Was I looking to see whether she'd had a Mona Lisa smile of contentment, or a look of disgust, on her face?

What changes over time was I looking for, as I passed along the photographs? Was it an expression of anticipation over the days or weeks when Ted had been seducing her? Or was it fear when she must have known that she was pregnant with his baby? Except for the first group of pictures, the rest appeared to have been shot on separate days – Patricia was wearing different combinations of clothes in each of the photographs – so I could carry a sense of time elapsing as I looked through them in sequence. I tried to ferret out patterns and changes over time. But after an hour, I was getting nowhere and decided to give up.

I carefully slipped the photographs onto the plastic sleeves, stacked them up, and then secured the pile in the heavy binder. I sat back down on the couch to think. But sitting down to think has never worked for me. I think best when I'm doing something, whether it's a routine physical activity like walking, or it's listening to music, or it's even reading.

Smoking works for some people – or it used to, when people smoked. My father claimed it was the case, during the time in his life when he smoked pipes. Cleaning the pipe's bowl, loading it with tobacco, tamping it down just right, then the lighting, and finally, at long last, the puffing, and all of it leading to momentous thought. It seems silly to me now. Here's what works for me: Something occurs to me when I'm otherwise occupied, and only then is my mind off and running.

Perhaps I don't know how to think. Maybe all that I can do is come up with ideas and string them together or expand them. Maybe the reason I operate that way is because I work in technology, not in philosophy, say. I don't understand how I get anywhere. Perhaps I don't even know what thinking is. I realize that I can string sentences together in one of my technical books and build paragraphs and chapters. But I can't get my mind to work in any other way.

I got a pad of paper and a pen and made a list of the few ideas I'd generated about the photographs. Not much there, it seemed to me. Then I went through the album picture by picture and made notes about each one. I kept at this task for all three dozen pictures. No brilliant insights, I decided reluctantly. I put the pad and pen down. I had to admit, at least for the time being, that the pictures couldn't tell me anything that I hadn't already known, except for the startling piece of information about Patricia's teenage pregnancy.

I was troubled. I had little interest in getting any food down. Toast and an omelet sufficed for dinner. But why was I troubled?

Of course, the pictures didn't bother me in and of themselves. If anything, they excited me: when I looked at them, I felt I could touch, smell, and taste Patricia again. They were gifts that I knew I would treasure forever. I liked the video, even though Ted Howard was in it, and promised myself to ask Mary Howard to send it to me.

The sex I'd learned about today wasn't the problem. I felt sorry for Patricia that she'd allowed herself to be seduced by Ted Howard. But I didn't condemn her behavior. If it had been a longer-term affair than a one-night stand, I wouldn't have condemned it either. It wasn't my place to do so – or anyone else's, for that matter. Mary Howard, who turned out be a generous person, didn't either, apparently.

Was it any different than the serious affair Patricia had during her time in California – the one she told me about when she and I got back together for life? We'd been able to put that affair in its proper context, which was that it would never stand in the way of our happiness. None of my own flings and affairs before we'd committed to each other stood in our way, including my three-week idyll with Lisa after my first date with Patricia had ended so strangely.

I didn't care about the abortion. Patricia's body and her life were hers to do with as she needed to. That was her right. Oh sure, the liberal pro-choice pieties could dribble out of my mouth without my giving them a second thought. But that didn't mean I believed them any less. Why would I change my belief in Patricia's case?

What bothered me, of course, as I lay in bed around midnight, unable to sleep, was that Patricia had never told me about her pregnancy and abortion. We'd said we would tell each other everything. As far as I knew, that included everything from the time before we'd ever met, in addition to everything after that. I'd always thought that was the deal we'd struck. I'd honored the deal. Well, almost. In any case, I'd believed that she'd honored it - especially about things as important as pregnancy and abortion. Had I been wrong about that?

I thought back to that night thirty years ago – the Night of the Shoes. That was the name Patricia and I had given that night whenever we'd reminisced about it, which we'd done many times over the years. We'd talk about how easily she'd told me the intimate story of her broken relationship with Joanna Stanton and how it hadn't dawned on us that night that there was chemistry between the two of *us* – so much chemistry that when we met five years later, there was enough to instantly spark the flame of a life-long romance. But now I knew that Patricia hadn't told me everything about her relationship with Joanna Stanton. Patricia hadn't mentioned the help in getting an abortion.

The sequence of events was another mystery I couldn't solve without questioning Joanna Stanton. Had she made the pass at Patricia before or after the abortion? Where did the pass fit into the photograph sequence in the album now in my possession? And if Joanna Stanton had made the pass after the abortion, had the reason that Patricia hadn't reported the pass been that she feared her teacher's revealing the abortion?

And there was something else: Was I overreacting? Was I going mad again, as I had in the days after Patricia's murder?

Patricia was no longer here to defend herself. I couldn't ask her: "Why didn't you tell me? Was there something about my behavior that inhibited you? Didn't you trust me to deal with you sensibly and without rancor? Have I seemed so intolerant? I can't remember a time when I've said anything to give you such an impression."

Then, as I continued to lie awake, Patricia's image, the Patricia I'd just been talking to - out loud, for all I knew - faded from my mind. I tried to conjure her up again. I wanted her to be in this room again, alive again. I wanted so desperately to tell her about that one-night stand in Washington – the awful thing I'd done that I'd never been able to tell her about. But why now? I asked myself. Do you want to get back at her for what she didn't tell you?

And then, as sleep still wouldn't release me from my torment, I realized, to my chagrin, that there was another thing, and that it was the most important thing. Why hadn't it struck me first? I felt guilty that I'd focused on Patricia's not having told me about her high-school pregnancy and abortion. Was I so self-absorbed?

Why wasn't I asking myself how she might have felt when she'd learned she was pregnant and when – right away? later? - she'd decided to have the abortion? Had she been the calm, cool Patricia I'd known? Or had she been depressed, frantic, had she been out of her mind with worry, had she been forced to admit to herself, let alone anyone else, that she was frightened? There'd been so many things to be scared about. The school authorities finding out, her parents finding out, and the medical risks must have been just the beginnings of her fears.

I thought about the Stantons' photographs again. I didn't remember any expression of worry or fear on Patricia's young face in the latter photographs. She must have known she was pregnant. Had she come to any conclusion about what she planned to do about her pregnancy?

I got out of bed, went downstairs, and took the album out of the bookcase, where I'd made room for it earlier. I looked at the last few pictures again. I could see no worry on Patricia's young face, no fear. It meant nothing, I decided. Maybe the Stantons had thrown away any pictures that showed worry or fear on Patricia's face. I put the album back, went upstairs, and got back into bed.

As I pulled the covers back over me, I felt suddenly that I was finally coming to my senses. All during the long day I'd just lived through, I'd attempted to direct my feelings outward - to sometimes condemn the Stantons, to sometimes try to understand them, and to sympathize with Mary Howard. I'd tried to keep my focus on these other people, not on myself. I hadn't been entirely successful, of course, but I hadn't done too badly. I knew that. Until now. I knew that, too.

For my efforts were all entirely misdirected. Why should I care about the Stantons? They were damaged goods. Why waste a moment's thought on them? It was all right to have sympathy for Mary Howard, but she'd manage without it. She'd weathered some awful things in her life. She was a strong woman; she didn't need my sympathy. And why focus on myself? I wasn't the one who'd gone through anything as bad as Patricia had – except for her murder, of course. But that had happened to her, not me.

Why wasn't I focused on the fact that I couldn't have been there for her when she might have needed me? OK, I knew that wasn't possible when she was in high school here and I was in Columbus, Ohio, five hundred or so miles away. But wasn't that the question I should have been asking myself? So what if she'd never told me everything? That wasn't what was important. What she'd had to cope with and how she'd managed, what fears she'd faced and how she endured them – *that* was what was important. The pictures of a vulnerable young woman – vulnerable, no matter how calm and cool she looked, I insisted to myself – stayed in my mind through the night.

I was eating myself up inside. I was enmeshed in the now familiar cycle of obsessive internal talking. Things whirred around in my head, like they had when I'd suffered with guilt feelings in the days after Patricia's murder. I lay awake, deep into the night, alone in the dark, quiet house. Sleep wouldn't come. I couldn't focus elsewhere, to get the whirring to stop.

I was tired and irritable the next afternoon, when I sat down with Sanford for one of our sessions. I'd skipped lunch. I'd ducked him and his sidekicks. I hadn't trusted myself to be sociable.

"Mordecai, you look like shit," he said.

"You're very observant," I blurted out.

"That's quite true." He tried a small smile. "Look, I can tell there's something the matter. Why don't you tell me what's bothering you?"

Had Sanford and I forged a strong enough bond in what was, after all, a very short time, so that I could confide in him? Could I trust him not to betray me? I didn't know. I knew he loved to play games. Would he treat my confidences as fodder for one of his games? But given how tightly wound I was, and given the trouble I was having stopping the whirring in my head, I decided that I should try to talk with him about my troubles – the troubles that had assaulted me through the previous day and night.

Sanford looked at me sympathetically. I'd been told how seductive he could be when he wanted you to open up to him. That was how he made his living: he got people in divorce case depositions to talk, and when they talked, they revealed things. Well, here he was in action. But I didn't resist. I didn't want to. This wasn't the time to worry about how Sanford, once he knew what was troubling me, might handle me and any information I might give him.

So I talked, while Sanford continued to look sympathetic. I went back over the events of the previous day – the walking I did, where I went, who I talked with. I talked about the Stantons, my feelings toward them, and about Mary Howard.

After I finished a description of the contents of the Stantons' photograph album and a run-down of the pas de deux video, I said: "What I don't get is how Patricia let Ted Howard, a guy half her size, have his way with her. I know about the body-building and all that, so I guess he didn't look that small to a lanky teenager. And I know it was just the one time. Or so I've been told. And she was just seventeen or so. But in the photographs, she looks so cool and in control of herself. And, mind, those pictures are an accurate record, at least in my view. Patricia had no idea her picture was being taken, so she wasn't posing. Those pictures captured the real Patricia – like I say, cool and in control."

Sanford had listened to me without speaking. Now he smiled tenderly. "C'mon Mordecai, you know very well that people can manipulate other people. Men manipulate women; women manipulate men. It goes on all the time. I imagine that you've played the game yourself."

A picture of an older woman in my arms on a hotel lounge dance floor, years ago, when I was in my twenties, flashed in front of my mind's eye. "Yes I've been there."

"Do you really think a teenage boy couldn't have manipulated a teenaged Patricia? I don't care how cool and collected you think she looked. He probed for an insecurity here, another one there – I don't care how small they might have been – and then he was soothing her, telling her that nothing mattered to him, that he wanted her despite any of her faults. And then he was in . . . well, I don't want to get too graphic here."

"His widow did say that he could charm the leaves off the trees in the springtime."

"I rest my case, even though I haven't even gotten warmed up. But let me make sure that you've gotten the point. Let me tell you a story."

I switched the little tape recorder in my head on. I was going to wait before I brought up any more of what was troubling me. It was all about Sanford, of course.

"I went to an elementary school, the William Lloyd Garrison, about ten or fifteen minutes walk from where I lived on Elm Hill Avenue in Roxbury."

I nodded. We'd talked about the Boston neighborhood where Sanford had grown up in our last session.

"The Garrison is a tall, forbidding, U-shaped brick building. It's still there, by the way. Every morning, back in the day, pupils pledged allegiance, and teachers read the twenty-third psalm. Everything was always in order.

"Nearly all of the teachers were women. Teaching was one of the few professions open to smart women in those days – the Nineteen Forties. Were they dissatisfied with what they could achieve professionally? Who knows? Did they subliminally take out their frustrations on their pupils? Again, who knows? In any case, a lot of them – most, as I remember - were very strict, no-nonsense types. They saw to it that misbehavior earned punishment. The most severe punishment was meted out by the sole male teacher, a tall, handsome man, who occupied a first-floor classroom at the front of building. He kept a rattan, which he used to strike wayward pupils' open palms."

Sanford paused and leaned forward. I settled back. "Enjoy the show," I said to myself.

Sanford continued: "I was eager to please my teachers, not because I feared punishment, except for the rattan, which everyone feared, but because I wanted my capabilities recognized. I certainly wanted to please my second-grade teacher, who had straight dark hair and the best figure in the whole school. So I was the first to learn the multiplication tables, through twelve times twelve.

"Then I took a test or something and became a member of the second-grade elite, thirty-six pupils who were chosen to make up a full classroom of overachievers who would take the third and fourth grades in a single year. Because my birthday's in March, I'd entered grammar school a little early. The double promotion meant I would finish sixth grade a few months after my tenth birthday and would graduate from high school a few months after I'd turned sixteen. My parents talked it over with me, and we decided to go ahead. They must have reasoned that anything that would push a Jewish boy ahead was a good thing.

"By fifth grade, I was ready for more than classroom activities. I persuaded my homeroom teacher to let me become the school's milk monitor. I was responsible for dividing the half-pint milk cartons that were delivered in heavy wood and wire crates into the number of cartons required for each classroom. I held the job for two years. The best part of the job was that I was allowed to do it without supervision, and I could roam the halls at will. As far as I can recall, I never made a mistake. But I did make a mistake elsewhere. Luckily, I was able to correct it.

"The place to go for a striving Boston boy after grammar school was Boston Latin School, which you could attend from seventh grade through senior year in high school. I've talked about it with you earlier. It was boys only back then, not co-ed, like it is now. In those days, you qualified for admittance just by having good grades. You have to take a test now to get accepted, but not back then. One warm, sunny morning, toward the end of sixth grade, the boys who had qualified to enter seventh grade at Latin School were invited to attend an orientation in the large assembly hall there. I took public transportation – it was safer back then, I guess – to get there.

"It was the largest auditorium I'd ever sat in. The ceiling had row after row of bright bulbs. I remember looking forward to a time when I'd be able to count them. The headmaster tried to impress on us the difficulties that lay ahead. 'Look to right of you and look to the left of you,' he said. 'Only one of you will still be here at graduation.' I thought that with all the studying I'd have to do that there might not be time in the coming years to count the bulbs on the ceiling.

"After the orientation, I found that I was in no mood to go back to the Garrison for the rest of the school day, as all the boys had been instructed to do. Instead – well, I don't remember what I did - I might have wandered aimlessly in Latin School's neighborhood. Finally, I went home, instead of going back to the Garrison. My mother, who was home, was none the wiser.

"When I got to school the following morning, I was told to report to the principal's office, which was in a quiet corner on the top floor. The office seemed isolated. When I arrived, I was told to go in and take a seat next to two other boys, in front of the principal's desk. She sat behind it, looking from one of us boys to the other. She was tough Irish lady. There was probably a severe expression on her face. I do remember that she dressed in sort of a dark, old-fashioned way, and that she wore her iron-gray hair pulled back from her smoothed, scrubbed face – a face like the ones I'd seen on nuns in the streets of Boston.

"After a few moments of silence, she came around the desk and stood in front of the three of us. She ordered us to stand. Then she asked each of us in turn why we hadn't gone from the orientation directly to the Garrison, as instructed. I was asked last. I listened as the other two boys give lengthy excuses. The principal said nothing in response to either boy's drawn-out plea for forgiveness. She turned to me and waited.

"'I know what I did was wrong,' I said as clearly as I could, "and I'm prepared to accept any punishment you think I deserve.'

"I remember that she looked right at me for a second or so. Then she said: 'Thank you, Mr. Glickauer. You may go back to your classroom.' As I turned to leave, I heard her say to the other two boys, 'You two stay.' I don't remember what punishment she gave them. Maybe the rattan!"

Sanford laughed and clapped his hands together once, the triumph still fresh in his mind. "A master manipulator of women at ten!" he exclaimed.

"Next thing, you'll be telling me you were in the principal's pants before the end of the school year," I drawled.

"Well, I *was* a precocious ten-year-old," Sanford said. He caught the sardonic look in my eye. "Just kidding," he said.

"Do you remember *All the King's Men*?" I asked.

"I remember the movie. Broderick Crawford played Willie Stark, the Huey Long character."

"That's right. There's this scene where Willie's drinking heavily in the governor's mansion. His son, a star football player, has just had a bad automobile accident. The girl who was in the car with him is at death's door. Her father shows up at the mansion. Willie, who's pretty far gone, tries to buy the guy off with a state contract.

"Willie's always pushed the kid too hard, and the kid drinks too much. Earlier in the movie, we saw him drinking in the car when he crashed it. The kid's up in his bedroom when the girl's father shows up.

Despite Willie's protestations, his wife – the kid's mother – brings the kid downstairs to face the girl's father.

"The kid basically tells the father what you told the principal: I did wrong and I'll accept whatever punishment you think I deserve. The kid's not cynically manipulating the girl's father. He's saying what he honestly believes - just as you did, Sanford. The story sounds better with the ending you gave it, I guess, because you wanted to prove a point with it. But I don't think it rings true."

Sanford smiled. "You're probably right," he said. Then: "No, you are right, Mordecai. I *have* twisted the ending of the story to suit my purposes." I could tell he was comfortable with my challenging him.

"It's still a good story," I said.

"I just have to forget my personal feelings about the story, and tell it like it really was. Is that what you're saying?"

"I suppose so."

"That sounds healthy, all right. Thanks for the advice. But look at yourself, Mordecai. You've got to divorce yourself from your personal feelings, too." There was a hint of triumph on Sanford's face. The lawyer in him was turning the conversation back to his advantage. "You've got to hand it to that Ted Howard guy who got your Patricia into the sack. He went after a girl he had no business going after and he succeeded. Congratulate him and be done with it. It happened long before you came on the scene. Don't tear yourself apart over it."

"I wish it were that easy," I said.

"I know, I know. She was your wife, she's gone, and the circumstances were tragic. Actually, they would have been tragic, no matter what they were. Still, you need to force yourself to take a broad perspective."

Sanford got to his feet and began pacing back and forth. Then he started to talk again. "The first girl I really went after was somebody else's girlfriend. It was my senior year at MIT, and one afternoon I ran into a guy I knew, Jack Carmichael. He had this beautiful girl with him. The first thing out of Jack's mouth was that his girlfriend was a model. I remember that, and I remember that I could tell that he was really proud of it. And she looked like a model - tall and slim and very pretty. She smiled at me, held out her hand for me to shake, and said her name, Gretchen Kauffmann. Two f's and two n's, she said, without my asking. I guess it was sort of a tic with her.

"Anyway, remember that, Mordecai. It's important. I must have asked her where she did her modeling, because I remember her laughing and saying, 'oh, here and there, no place in particular.' I must have said

something clever, like 'oh?' Because then she said, 'I only do it part time.'
I'll bet that the next thing I asked was 'what do you do the rest of the time?'
Because I'm pretty sure that it was right away, at the end of our little
conversation, when she said she went to Wellesley. Then Jack probably
said they were in a hurry, because I remember that the next thing the girl
and I said to each other was 'nice meeting you.' I'm pretty sure that was
the last thing we said to each other on that first meeting – it was fifty years
ago, after all. Anyway, that was supposed to be that.

"Only it wasn't. I thought that physically Gretchen was the girl I'd
always dreamed about. There she'd been right there in front of me, and
there hadn't been a damn thing I could do about getting her phone number
or asking her out. Jack had made it clear that she was his girlfriend. The
implication was: hands off.

"But I couldn't get Gretchen out of my mind. I wanted to see her
again, very badly. I thought of calling Wellesley and trying to get them to
connect me to her dorm room, but I was afraid that approach would
backfire. In any case, I didn't have the nerve. But I was ahead of the game
in one respect: I hadn't had to ask Jack how I might find her. And then I
decided that she'd told me she went to Wellesley for a reason: she *wanted*
me to find her.

"When I thought about it, that idea was preposterous. Jack was this
six-foot-five fraternity jock. I tried to play sports, but I was a lousy athlete.
He came from a wealthy family in Virginia. I was a commuter. I dressed
like a shlubby MIT student. Some guy wrote a column in the *Atlantic
Monthly* about how shlubby we all were. Well we really weren't a lot of the
time, but I guess the guy had space to fill. Anyway, Jack dressed that way,
too, some of the time. But he also owned clothes where the jackets and
pants matched - you know, *suits*. He was probably wearing one, with a
white shirt, when he ran into me with Gretchen on his arm. And I must
have been in a sweatshirt, because that's how I usually was dressed, unless I
was going to a mixer or a meeting that was important.

"So why would this gorgeous girl prefer me to Jack? Unless she got
to know me better - that was my only hope, and it was a pretty slender one,
at best. Maybe I could show her I was a really smart guy, and maybe she
liked smart guys, though it wouldn't have surprised me to learn that Jack
was not only bigger and better built and better dressed than I was, and his
parents were wealthier than mine, but he was also smarter. Even back then,
when I was only twenty, I knew that life was unfair."

Sanford arched his back and stretched. I stayed quiet, waiting for
him to continue. He started pacing again. "A few days later, I borrowed
my mother's car and drove the twelve or fifteen miles out to Wellesley. I

found a parking space on one of the shopping streets near the campus. As I was locking the car, I saw Gretchen walk out of a delicatessen, wave to a couple of other girls, and cross the street. I caught up to her on the sidewalk."

"She was all dressed up, in a sweater and a skirt, with heels. I'd had the good sense to put a sport jacket on over a shirt and tie." Sanford stopped pacing again. He sat back down opposite me, crossed his legs, and got comfortable.

"What happened next?" I said.

"Give me a minute," Sanford said.

"OK, I don't want to rush you."

"It's just that I'm working on remembering the whole conversation again."

"You must have a very good memory. It was fifty years ago."

"As it happens, it was a short conversation. But the reason I can recall it in detail is that Gretchen talked about it a lot over the next few years."

"Patricia and I used to do the same thing. We liked going over momentous times that we'd lived through together – the good *and* the bad."

"A lot of couples do that, I think. It draws them closer together." Sanford stood up again and went over and leaned against one of the bookcases. "So I put my hand lightly on her arm," he went on, "and she stopped and turned to me. 'Hi,' I said. She tried to look at me as if she didn't know who the hell I was, but it seemed to me that she knew damn well, but was trying not to let on that she did. I remember thinking she might start screaming for a cop. She told me later that the thought had never crossed her mind and that she'd been playing the little game I'd guessed she'd been playing.

"'Sanford Glickauer,' I said. 'I met you the other day at MIT.' She let a look of recognition light up her pretty face. 'Oh, right,' she said, 'I remember now. What are you doing way out here?' I'd prepared what I was going to say next. I think my lines must have come from some B movie or other that I'd seen – not a first-run movie like *All the King's Men*. 'I was hoping I might run into you,' I said. Before she had a chance to respond to that, I said 'Is there somewhere we can talk?' She looked at me speculatively then and said, "let's go across the street and have a cup of coffee.'"

"That qualifies as getting to first base," I said.

"I hit a single that day, not a home run. Gretchen was committed to Jack, you see, so she thought she had to get rid of me. And the best way to do that, she figured, was to talk me out of pursuing her, and to let me off easy while she did so. So she didn't get all huffy and offended that I'd come out to Wellesley to put a move on her. Of course, she insisted on paying for her own coffee and sat as far away from me as she could, but we did talk for a long time. I guess we got to know each other a bit. But she didn't give me her phone number, and I didn't ask for it. I let her believe that, once again, that was that."

"Patricia and I had a long conversation like that, too, at the start of our relationship, but then we didn't see each other for five years. And I'm not sure I would have played it as cool as you did."

Sanford laughed. "It didn't take anywhere near as long as five years for Gretchen and me to get together again," he said. "It was only a few weeks, in fact, right after MIT graduation. Jack went back down to Virginia, because he had a construction job waiting for him. I had a summer job working for a professor at MIT, so I was still around. Gretchen, who was going into her junior year, lived on the North Shore. I drove up there, went in a public library, and looked through the phone books. There weren't that many Kauffmanns who spelled their name the way her family did. I got lucky. The first number I tried, she picked up the phone herself.

"I talked to her about herself. I asked her how she'd done on her finals, what her plans for the summer were, etc., etc. I worked hard at getting her to recognize how interested I was in her as a person, which I was. She ate it up, of course. It worked. It always does."

"I know," I said.

"I'm sure you do, Mordecai. Well, to make a long story short, which I hate to do, but it's getting late, Gretchen and I began meeting several times a week. In addition to a few modeling jobs that summer, she had a job teaching a couple of hours a day at a modeling school for high school girls near Copley Square in Boston. Miss Allen's, I think it was called. Anyway, Gretchen had plenty of free time during the week. My job didn't have any fixed hours, so I had some free time during the week, as well."

"What about weekends?"

"No could do. Jack drove up from Virginia two or three times a month, and otherwise her family made her go with them on their long summer weekends."

"So you had to move fast is what you're saying."

"The first time we fucked, it was on the grass under some bushes at the side of a restaurant where we'd had dinner. It was dark and humid, and I got bug bites all over my ass. Towards the end of the summer, I rented a crummy apartment out near Worcester Polytechnic Institute, where I was getting my master's in mechanical engineering. That became our love nest for most of the next two school years. Gretchen drove out there a couple of times a week. Not enough for my tastes, but it had to do."

"Summers?"

"The next summer went just like the first one."

"And where was Jack all this time?"

"Jack was out at Stanford, getting his master's in metallurgy. He flew back east on school breaks. Otherwise I had Gretchen all to myself – unless there was a third guy, of course." Sanford looked at me deadpan.

"You're kidding."

"I'm kidding."

"So it's graduation time again."

"Right you are. Well, MIT's a land grant college and has ROTC. Jack and I were both commissioned officers when we graduated. We could put off starting our two-year service obligations by attending grad school. When we got our master's, we both went on active duty. Jack went off to Germany for a year. I went down to Aberdeen Proving Ground in Maryland and stayed there for my whole two-year stint, in pretty much an engineering job, even though I was an Army officer."

"What about Gretchen?"

"Gretchen moved down to Washington, about seventy miles south of where I was stationed. She and Jack had decided to get married, but she wanted to be on her own for a year. That's what she told everyone, at any rate. She found a great job at Garfinckel's department store downtown. She did some informal modeling, but most of the time she was a trainee in the advertising department. She lived in a tiny apartment in DC. I had weekends free, so I could join her on Saturdays and Sundays. Our hangout was the old Bassin's restaurant, a block from Garfinckel's, on Pennsylvania Avenue, at the foot of Fourteenth Street. They had tables out on the sidewalk. We loved that place."

I thought back to my horrible relationship with Marci Treadwell, who'd cheated on me, just as Gretchen had cheated on Jack. But Gretchen had been only in her late teens when the affair with Sanford had started. I couldn't imagine a woman that young being so duplicitous.

"I know you were the beneficiary of Gretchen's behavior, but did it bother you?" I asked Sanford.

"It was *exciting*. I didn't stop to think about it. Perhaps it was wrong – cowardly, even. Worse yet, I suppose, I didn't give Jack a moment's thought. Instead, I thought it was stupid of him to keep putting himself thousands of miles away from the gorgeous girl he said he loved."

"Was *she* in love with *him*? She must have been; she married him."

"The subject was off limits. We were both very clear about that."

"So you never knew for sure. That was clever of her, I guess, because she didn't have to risk your ending the affair if you knew there was no long term future. On the other hand, did you want a long-term future? Were *you* in love with her?"

"I asked myself that very question, lots of times. And if you have to ask, well, forget about it. Jack came back to the States after a while and was stationed at Picatinny Arsenal in New Jersey. Before I knew it, Gretchen was gone and the two of them were married. And in case you're wondering, they'd already had sex while they were still in college, so Jack didn't unexpectedly find a girl who wasn't a virgin underneath him in bed on their wedding night."

"So you didn't fight for her."

"No, I didn't. When I saw *The Graduate* years later, I did wonder why I hadn't driven up to the church and spirited Gretchen away – but only for a moment."

"Another movie allusion," I said. "But mentioning *The Graduate* doesn't answer this question: Why'd you give Gretchen up so easily? The other thing I don't understand is: why do you sound so blasé about losing Gretchen – your ideal woman, you said earlier – even all these years later?"

Sanford laughed and clapped his hands together. "You're missing the point," he said. "The thing with Gretchen had become a game. I felt I could win it whenever I wanted to. I just got tired of it."

"So you never saw Gretchen again?"

"Never," Sanford said. "I let Jack have her. Pretty soon I was involved with Gwennie – the name starts with another G, doesn't it? - so in the end I wasn't sorry I'd let Gretchen go so easily."

CHAPTER ELEVEN

"**I**'m worried about you," Bob Steinberg said. He leaned back in his chair and belched softly. He did that a lot. Then he lifted his glass of expensive Burgundy and took a hearty swallow. "Let's get another," he said, as he put his glass down. He signaled to our waiter and pointed to the nearly empty bottle in the middle of the white tablecloth.

I kept silent and let my gaze wash over Steinberg. He was my third editor at the firm where I'd first started publishing. There'd been Jim Upton, the major league drinker, Jane Caldwell, the teetotaler, and for last ten years, Steinberg, who liked good wine, but always stopped before things got out of hand.

He wore good clothes, but they were always in need of a bit of pressing. His shoes were usually scuffed beyond redemption. He once told me that he never had his shoes polished. He just threw them out, right after he'd bought a fresh pair in the same color and style. He was my age, give or take a year or two, an inch or two shorter, twenty pounds heavier, and none of his pounds were muscle. He had most of his hair, which he wore brushed back over his scalp. His bespectacled, smoothly shaven face seemed always slightly tanned. He was in awful shape athletically, but he didn't seem to have any health problems beyond the soft eruptions from his belly and, on occasion , his behind.

He had a cute little wife, in her mid-forties, and two polite teenagers. The Steinberg family had stopped once at our house for dinner on their way to Lake Placid. They hadn't, not one of them, been able to take their eyes off Patricia.   In addition to the soft belching and farting, Steinberg had a habit of, or was it a weakness for, quoting English writers and other personages – accurately, for all I knew, but incessantly. Now he was at it again: "'No man but a blockhead ever wrote, except for money.' Samuel Johnson was right when Boswell said he said it, and it's still right today."

"I couldn't agree more," I said.

"None of this save-the-world bullshit impels you. Am I right, Mordecai?"

I nodded.

"So why is this nuclear power book so fucking turgid?" He didn't shout. Instead, he spoke as if the judgment was the saddest he'd ever had to deliver to one of his authors. That was Steinberg the editor – a gentle, albeit scatological, soul nearly all of the time, except when he acted like the fencer in the Thurber cartoon, who says *'Touché!'* as he lops off his opponent's head.

The second bottle of Burgundy had appeared on the table. Steinberg belched softly again and took a sip of wine from a fresh glass. He swirled the wine around his mouth and swallowed. After a moment, he smiled at the waiter. "That's fine," he said. He took another swallow, put his glass down, and belched again. He would have farted, as well, but today he was polite enough to wait until we were out on the sidewalk, heading back to his office. Unlike the unsanitized version of LBJ's depiction of Gerald Ford, Steinberg could fart and chew gum – or walk – at the same time. Whoops, I thought, you're doing it yourself – throwing off one of those venerable old quotations.

The main course had appeared along with the second bottle of wine. I cut off a piece of rotisserie chicken and put it in my mouth together with a perfect specimen from a generous pile of salted *pommes frites.* I let Steinberg hold the floor. My sessions with Sanford had gotten me accustomed to remaining silent for longer periods than usual.

"The book has your usual intellectual heft," Steinberg, went on, "and the arguments are rigorous. There's even what that guy who used to edit *Scientific American* called intellectual tension. But the fucking prose has no snap." He chewed on his bloody steak and several quick forkfuls of *pommes frites* from his own pile and swallowed. I thought I might have to put my forearm around my plate to block an attack on my own pile.

"Look," he went on, "I can only imagine what you've been going through, Mordecai. So I don't want to burden you with any heavy editing, or god forbid, rewriting bullshit. But we're interested in money here, just like Doctor Johnson was."

I nodded. Steinberg continued again: "The book's for a multiplicity of audiences – if the marketing assholes can somehow figure out how to get more than one audience interested – and I don't think there'll be any trouble with your old, standby technically minded readers. They won't care about the prose. It's the general readers I'm concerned about. If Dwight Garner or the fearsome Japanese chick in the *Times* – we should be so lucky if either one even picks it up, let alone reviews it - calls the book earnest, but dull, the public won't pay any attention to it, and we won't be able to maximize sales. *Capisce, boychick?*"

"So what do you want me to do about the book?"

"Nothing about this book – it's already on the spring list and there isn't any time anyway." More steak and wine disappeared down Steinberg's throat. I kept pace with my own meal. It was a treat, and once I started, I felt like eating it. Steinberg cut another piece of steak and put down his fork. He gestured at me with the point of his knife. I held my ground and chewed as nonchalantly as I dared.

"I'm feeding you this fancy lunch with good plonk because of the next book, not the one you've just finished," Steinberg said.

"Thanks for keeping the faith."

"There's a slight twist however." He twisted the knife he was pointing at me. I tried not to cringe. Who was this tough new Steinberg? The old one seemed to have disappeared into a witness protection program in some far-off region of the country. He went back to his steak and *pommes frites* and chewed energetically. After another swallow of wine, he put his knife and fork down on a suddenly empty plate.

"I've been looking through the old Jim Upton files," Steinberg said. "Back in the day, you were damn good at putting edited books together. They sold pretty well. Today, with the Internet, we can do even better with those tomes, with all their nuggets of information useful to scientists and engineers. Or so I've been told."

"I'm not sure I can go home again, so to speak."

"I'll make it really easy for you. I've got this terrific new assistant. Rachel Gormsby. She's a graduate of that same Institute program that you attended years ago, so she's very well qualified for what I have in mind."

"I vaguely remember the program," I said with a laugh, "although it did make me everything I am today." I rolled my eyes.

"Like I say," Steinberg went on, undeterred by any sarcasm on my part, "you were damn good at what I have in mind. Besides, I'll arrange things so this new project will be a piece of cake. Speaking of which, how about some cheesecake? The chocolate chip version they make here is wonderful."

"Sounds perfect," I said, "it'll help counteract the effects of the wine." I noticed that we hadn't drunk half of the second bottle. I felt relieved. I was seeing the Cassidys in a few hours, and I didn't want to appear plastered. "But make mine plain," I said, I'm a purist at heart."

After ordering dessert and coffee, Steinberg got back to business. "All you have to do is come up with the idea for a new reference work – a handbook or an encyclopedia, it doesn't matter to us. Then suggest a table of contents and some potential contributors, and Rachel will start to put things together. You'll work out a collaborative arrangement with her, I'm sure."

"And by the time the project's finished, Rachel will have learned how to develop the next one and it's bye, bye, Mordecai." I smiled at Steinberg.

"You're such a suspicious prick," he said, and smiled back at me. "But to prove to you that I really do have your welfare at heart, I've also asked Rachel to recommend to me which of your old reference works should be considered for new editions. We'll take care of getting outside reviewers to comment on her recommendations, and whichever books we decide to move ahead with, she'll contact the original contributors and recruit any replacements, under your direction. The final tables of contents for any new editions will be up to you, of course. You'll propose new chapters and delete old topics as you see fit." Steinberg beamed. "I should think that this plan must sound like it's to your advantage, Mr. Suspicious Prick," he said, looking quite fond of his new name for me.

"By which time you'll be able to remove this Rachel's training wheels," I said.

Steinberg put his large head in his hands and groaned theatrically. "You'll find that she's terrific to work with," he said. "In fact, I see you assuming the role of her mentor before too long."

"Don't make any assumptions," I said with a smile that I left on my face for several seconds. "Just kidding," I finally went on. "Let me mull things over for a few days and I'll get back to you."

"I couldn't ask for anything more."

"Don't. The lunch was terrific, but not *that* terrific."

A few minutes later, Steinberg, who'd been silent while he'd been contemplating ordering a second dessert, I guessed, pushed his plate to the side and folded his hands on the table. "There's one other thing, Mordecai," he said. He looked at me intently, his brown eyes tinged with sadness behind his small spectacles. "It's a rather strange bit of business. You know, the firm sent a twenty-thousand-dollar check to your wife's museum as our contribution toward the building of the new wing that they were going to put her name on."

"No, I didn't know about the donation. It's a generous gesture. Thank you. But what do you mean by '*going* to put your wife's name on?' I haven't heard about any change in plans."

"That's the thing. We hadn't heard of any change in plans until yesterday afternoon, when the museum's new chair – it's a woman by the name of Helene Finckel – called our chairman and told him that the museum was returning the check and asking that we put our gift on hold while they went through the process of determining what they were going to do about naming the new wing."

I felt lightheaded suddenly. "I don't know what you're talking about," I said. "No one from the museum has contacted me."

"Maybe a big donor has come forward, and they're looking for some other way to honor Patricia."

"I'll have to see this Helene Finckel when I get back upstate. You're just full of surprises today, aren't you Steinberg."

"Easy, Mordecai," he said, and reached across the table to pat my hand. "I'm sure things will get sorted out when you get back up there."

The Cassidys weren't due at my apartment for a drink until late afternoon, so I had enough time to walk home from the restaurant. On the way, I stopped at Fairway to buy some fruit and at Zabar's for bread, cheese, and some cold cuts and smoked salmon. The cleaning service had been at the apartment just the day before, so I expected it to smell sweet, not as if it had been shut up for some time.

I arrived with a few minutes to spare. I put the food in the kitchen and walked into the living room. I stood in front of the bookcases where Patricia had shelved the books that she and I had written and edited over the years. Hers were on the left. My eyes fell on those first. I smiled as I read each of the titles. In my mind's eye, I could see Patricia working deep into the night in her robe, heedless of the lateness of the hour.

My books took up a lot of shelf space. As I surveyed them, a feeling came over me that was certainly not associated with pride of accomplishment, the feeling I normally had at such moments. Now I felt disgust, which quickly gave way to a wan hopelessness.

I used to take pride in my technical, and even general-interest, books residing in public, academic, and other libraries all over the world, which was the case. But would the books still be in those libraries in the future? The last time I'd wandered into the stacks in the Institute's main library, I'd seen that they were filled with old tomes that I doubted more than a very few students and faculty members looked at anymore. It was only a matter of time, I reckoned, before those volumes were deaccessioned, which was library- and museum-speak for getting rid of. It was profoundly silly of me to imagine that my own books would enjoy a better fate.

Oh sure, my books could stay alive on the Internet for a longer period of time. Electronic storage is cheap, after all. But who would read them, yet alone find much useful in them, a hundred years from now? Technical information can have a short shelf life. Maybe fifty years of useful life was all I could hope for – or forty, or thirty. One of the reasons I'd kept throwing myself into the books was the thought that they would be a lasting legacy. Right now, the thought struck me as absurd.

And there was another thing: to whom would I leave these books – in fact, any of the books in the apartment and in my house upstate? There were no children or children's children. After me, there was no one.

As I stood in my silent living room, I contemplated pulling the books I'd published off the shelves onto the floor – all of them, every single last one. I wanted to kick them from one end of the apartment to the other. I wanted to tear them apart. All that stopped me was the ringing of the doorbell. I took a moment to calm myself down before admitting my guests.

I suppose I let my hair down too much with the Cassidys. While I didn't tell them anything about the boy who had gotten Patricia pregnant, which was information I'd given Sanford, I did tell them about the abortion, which I'd also told Sanford about. And while I told the Cassidys my acute discomfort at not having known about the abortion until I'd learned about it almost by chance only a couple of days before – in fact, Joanna Stanton had been surprised by my astonished reaction – the discomfort was something I hadn't told Sanford about. Also, I told the Cassidys about my having become upset with myself when I'd realized that I should have been more concerned about what Patricia had had to cope with after she'd learned she was pregnant than about my not having ever been told that she'd had a teenaged abortion – another thing I hadn't discussed with Sanford.

"Sooner or later, Mordecai, you're going to have to move on," Brian said. Even while I was talking, I'd become worried that I'd somehow been disloyal to Patricia by confiding so much in the Cassidys, our mutual friends, after all. Now I was getting confirmation that my concerns might not have been misplaced.

"You see, Mordecai?" Rita said. "If I died tomorrow, Brian would be out looking for a hottie before I was even cold in the grave. In fact wouldn't put it past him if he started looking while I was lying in a hospital bed dying of some dreaded disease."

"Now, Rita," Brian said. "Where's all this coming from?" His voice had a slightly higher pitch than I was used to hearing.

"It comes from your telling Mordecai to suck it up and move on. Can't you see how much he's suffering? Can't you see that he's still grieving, like a husband who really loved his wife should? You don't understand anything about people, Brian. You never have."

"I understand people perfectly well, Rita. I'm just trying to trying to give Mordecai encouragement, so he can get on with his life."

"Next thing I know, you'll be pushing me onto him."

"Oh, Rita, have some more cheese." Brian reached over and attempted to put a small piece of bread with cheese on it into Rita's mouth. She snatched the morsel away from him and put it in her mouth herself. Brian looked at me and winked. Rita made a prune face at him.

The Cassidys had been in the apartment for nearly an hour by the time their spat had erupted. Before I'd begun to talk seriously about my current concerns, we'd spent the time on everyday chit-chat – stuff about their kids, plays and movies we'd seen, New York, the weather. The kids were out of the house now. Perhaps Rita and Brian were spending too much time together without enough to distract them from attacking each other.

We'd had just a little wine; after the wine at lunch, I was going pretty slowly. After the cheesecake, I was steering clear of the cheese, as well. But the Cassidys were doing damage to the wedge of Brillat-Savarin I'd put on the coffee table. Rita pointed to the meager amount that was left on the plate. "Any more of that?" she said. "It's super!" Brian nodded in agreement.

"Sure, I said. "There's more in the kitchen. You'll have to excuse me, though. I put it in the fridge, so it might be a bit too chilled."

"We're not fussy," Brian said, "just starved, I guess. We have a reservation for an after-theater supper, but that's hours away, so we're chowing down now." He leaned his head back and laughed.

When I closed the refrigerator, I heard the swinging door behind me. I turned, and Rita was standing a few feet away. She said, "Patricia should have told you."

"It doesn't matter anymore," I said.

"Of course, it does. She was unfaithful to you."

I winced and then hoped Rita hadn't noticed. "That's ridiculous. She had the pregnancy years before we first met."

"That doesn't make your finding out about it any less painful, it seems to me. You're just like Brian, Mordecai. You don't understand anything. You don't even understand your own emotions, or lack of them."

"Oh, come on, Rita. I've just told you and Brian how much this ancient history has been eating me up inside."

"Whatever. I'm just telling you what I know about men. You're not the most self-aware creatures on god's green earth." Rita folded her arms in front of her chest. Then she seemed to shift gears. "So I don't understand why it is that you're so bothered about how she felt after the abortion."

"Isn't that a normal reaction when you love someone?"

"The point is, she never got pregnant with you, Mordecai."

"You really don't know anything about Patricia and me, Rita. You don't know how we lived our lives. You don't know why we didn't have children." I felt Rita picking at the scab of an old wound she'd inflicted.

"I know how much she cared about her precious career. She wouldn't have let herself get pregnant."

"Enough, Rita," I said. "You know, it crossed my mind over the years that you never liked Patricia. In fact, you might have even hated her. But I always told myself that I was mistaken. Anyway, Patricia and I never talked about it, so I don't know how she felt."

Rita paid no attention to me. "Oh, I know things," she said, folding her arms in front of her chest. "I know that her meeting you by chance at that New Year's Eve party was nothing of the sort."

"Where'd you get that idiotic idea?"

"I knew it the moment I heard that fairy story about how you two met after not having seen each other for years. It was too much of a coincidence. New York's too big a place for such a thing to happen."

"How much have you had to drink? You're not making any sense."

"Only this makes sense." She stepped forward and put her arms around me. She pressed her face against my chest.

"Rita, please." I said her name as gently as I could. I wondered what Brian was doing. I reached behind me, took her wrists, and extricated myself from his wife. "Go back to Brian," I said to her.

"Oh, fuck Brian," Rita snarled. "And fuck you, too, Mordecai."

Rita preceded me back into the living room. She took my chair, opposite Brian, who'd been leafing through a catalogue of a Jewish Museum exhibition of paintings by Max Liebermann. If Brian had heard any of the kitchen conversation, it wasn't apparent to me. Rita planted her high heels a few inches apart on the Persian rug, hiked her dress halfway up her thighs, and lifted one leg over the other high and slowly enough so that Brian could get a good look at what could be on offer in the wee hours.

"You want to come with us?" he said to me, acting oblivious of the tease his wife was performing in front of him. "I can call the box office and see if they've had a cancellation."

"Thanks," I said, "but I've got some follow-up work to do after this afternoon's lunch with my publisher." Besides, there was enough theater going on in my apartment to last me awhile.

I didn't want to throw the Cassidys out. I didn't want to have to put up with another outburst from Rita. So the three of us continued to talk for another half hour or so. There was more chit-chat, and even a few laughs. An air of forced gaiety pervaded the room. I couldn't tell whether or not Brian noticed.

Mercifully, he and Rita were finally gone, and the living room was silent again. I picked up the Liebermann catalogue and leafed through it. I found the paintings of pre-Holocaust Jewish life in Germany restful, even though unspeakable tragedy was around the corner. I shouldn't have invited the Cassidys, I thought, when I got up to put the book back in the bookcase. Their visits are fraught with despair. I'm better off alone.

And alone I remained for several more days in the New York apartment. I fell willingly into my recent routine, with my solitary walks and infrequent brushes with other city inhabitants. And then it was time to take the train upstate and meet with the new museum chairwoman.

I was somewhat taken aback when I arrived at the museum and someone I was unfamiliar with ushered me into Patricia's old office for my meeting with Helene Finckel. The new chairwoman came out from behind Patricia's old desk, a slim, cool hand extended in front of her.

"Helene Finckel," she said. She must have taken note of the expression on my face, for the next words out of her mouth were "I'm doing a second job as museum director until we find a suitable replacement for your late wife." Then she smiled and revealed brilliant white and rather small teeth. "I'd say that the new director will have a large pair of shoes to fill, but that's impolitic if the shoes belonged to a woman."

It was my turn to smile, I surmised, so I managed one. "Nine," I said. I looked down at the desk. The nameplate read "Dr. Helene Finckel."

"Excuse me?" Dr. Finckel said.

"That was her shoe size: nine. Not all that large for a six-footer. Patricia used to say that she wasn't really that tall for her height." You're trying too hard to be funny and charming, I said to myself. I tried to relax.

The hint of a smile on Dr. Finckel's face was frozen in place. She indicated that I take a seat in one of two facing armchairs on the far side of the office from the desk. There was small, low table between the two chairs. Dr. Finckel arranged herself on about half of the seat of her chair and crossed a pair of elegant legs. She was a trim woman of medium height. Her straight, jet-black hair framed a rather attractive face. Her brown eyes looked calm, intelligent, and a bit wary, I thought. I put her age at sixty, although she looked younger. She was wearing a yellow-mustard Chanel suit with black piping and black pumps. It was hard to miss the large gold rings on her left hand. The pearls at her throat looked real. The outfit set off her skin, which was the color of black coffee.

"I'm sorry for your loss," she said. The smile had faded, and the eyes had a look of concern.

"Thank you," I said. "Everyone at the museum has been most kind."

"Everyone here has the deepest sympathy for you, Dr. Bornstein."

"Yes, I know. Thank you. And by the way, it's mister, not doctor. Unlike Patricia, I never got a PhD. In any case, just call me Mordecai."

"I'll be glad to. Would you care for some coffee?"

"Thank you," I said, for the third time. I was beginning to wonder whether I'd be able to be forceful enough when it came time to confront this woman. That was the point of her little game with the Dr. Bornstein business, I figured. She had to have known that I didn't have a doctorate.

She leaned forward and poured coffee from a silver pitcher into a China cup. Cream and sugar resided in silver serving containers. There was a small pair of silver tongs next to the sugar. She poured herself coffee and sat straight with the cup and saucer just above her lap. Neither of us had touched the cream and sugar.

The office was very quiet. I looked at Dr. Finckel. She looked back at me. She didn't speak. She was used to waiting people out, I surmised. "What happened to your predecessor – the chairman, I mean."

She sipped her coffee. "He was elected to the board of a museum down in New York," she said. "He preferred that position over the one he had here."

"And he recommended you as his successor?"

"He knew I was about to retire from my day job. I'd been a hospital CEO for fourteen years, seven-year stints in two places. After seven years in one place, it's time to move on, give someone else a turn.

This time, I wasn't interested in starting at a third hospital. I'd done two partial turnarounds, and that was enough.

"On the other hand, I wasn't about to sit around the house and watch the soaps, and I wasn't interested in consulting. I never listened to consultants and I didn't expect other hospital administrators would listen to me. My husband's still the chief of cardiology at the last place I worked, and he doesn't want to retire just yet, even though he's sixty-seven. So traveling the world wasn't in the cards. When the former chairman approached me – I've known him and his wife for years, by the way – he convinced me that I would find the museum an interesting and fulfilling challenge."

This little speech sounded to my ears like a canned recitation of recent details of Dr. Finckel's resume. You were meant to think that she'd given you intimate revelations about her life, but she'd done nothing of the sort, of course. She was a guarded woman who wanted you to think she thought nothing of spilling her guts out to you.

She put her cup and saucer on the little coffee table and looked at me. She's waiting for my next move, I thought.

"You mentioned the word challenge," I said finally. It was a place to start, I figured, better than the silence. "Is the museum living up to it?"

"Picking up where Patricia was interrupted hasn't been easy. Your late wife involved herself in many things. But she ran a tight ship, and for that I'm very thankful. So she made a difficult job easier"

"Yes, she really threw herself into things here. She didn't bring her work home with her, but she did tell me about some of the more interesting things she was doing. I guess there's pillow talk in every marriage."

Dr. Finckel let my remarks sail right past her, like a fastball six inches off the plate. I had the sense she was waiting for a hanging curve that she could wail. "I'm very happy to be here," she said. "It's been a wonderful change for me. I'm tremendously appreciative of the opportunity to be able to continue to serve the community. Making a difference, that's what motivates me, makes me get out of bed in the morning."

The platitudes were piling up. Pretty soon I wouldn't be able to see over the top. Obviously, Dr. Finckel was expert in this sort of Q and A. I needed to find another way to ease into the questions I really wanted to confront her with. So I tried to outflank her.

"How long have you and your husband been married?" I said.

She shifted a couple of inches in her chair. "It will be four years next month."

"It's the first marriage for both of you?" I had no idea whether my guess was correct or not. In any case, my asking the question surprised me. Without intending to, I'd just thrown a nasty slider, low and just on the outside edge of the strike zone. I tried not to show it.

Dr. Finckel took the question – and what I'd thought was an unhittable strike - in stride. "It's my first and Stephen's second. He has two grown children and a grandchild. I got an instant family."

"That's nice for you," I said. I put my cup and saucer on the table in front of me. I thought about asking about the first Mrs. Finckel, but decided I'd gone far enough with being snarky. Besides, I could already tell that my attempt to get to this woman was decidedly amateurish. I was sure she'd come up against much nastier customers than me in her career and hadn't been flummoxed. She was undoubtedly a lot tougher than I was. And then she showed that she was a jump or two ahead of me.

"Stephen's first wife died ten years ago," Dr. Finckel said. "Stephen was very much in love with her. She was a wonderful woman, and she raised two marvelous sons. Much of the time, she had to cope by herself. Stephen was there for her, but not at home, because he was always so terribly busy. Then he almost gave everything up to help her when she battled her cancer. They were very much together when she died. It took Stephen quite some time before he was ready for love again, but when he was ready, so was I. He's a wonderful man. I'm truly blessed."

Another well-rehearsed little speech, I thought. Stephen must love it nonetheless. I wondered if I should ask Dr. Finckel to record it for Rita Cassidy. I decided to leave the question of how Helene and Stephen actually got together for another day. It was best I get to the point. But, again, Dr. Finckel got where I wanted to go before I did.

"So what brings you here today, Mr. Bornstein?" she asked. "I'm sure it isn't to poke around in my married life." She gave me another sweet smile. I doubted it was sincere.

"I don't mean to pry," I said, then went on before she had a chance to interject a response: "I want to ask you about something that came up during a lunch I had with one of my publishers several days ago. It concerned a donation they'd made to the museum in support of the new wing, the wing that they – and I – thought was going to be named for my late wife. I was told the check had been returned - for the time being, at least. Things seem to be on hold, as far as naming the wing after Patricia's concerned. I'd like to know what's going on."

"I can't tell you. It's an internal matter."

"No announcement's been made about the museum's not naming the wing after Patricia. Look, Dr. Finckel, I really need to know what's going on." I kept my voice level. It wasn't easy.

She looked down at her hands folded in her lap. When she looked up at me after several seconds, she said, "We're trying to sort out our concerns."

"What concerns are those?"

"I really should have legal and HR here, but considering your relationship with Patricia, I'll try to be as candid as I can be without them. There are two issues. The first involves the car that the museum put at Patricia's disposal. It was supposed to be used for business purposes, including travel between your home and the museum."

"That's what she used it for."

"Not entirely. There's the matter of her travel to the diner out of town for lunches." I was about to interrupt, but Dr. Finckel held up a hand, which stopped me. "The police have told us about those trips," she went on. "They wondered if we might be able to shed any light on them. We weren't, and I've been told that you weren't either. Then, of course, there's her use of the car on the night she was slain." Dr. Finckel's voice had softened considerably as she spoke that last sentence.

"That's so much Mickey Mouse," I said. I tried to keep my voice calm. It was getting harder to do so. "Figure out the mileage and I'll reimburse the museum, if you're so worried about every nickel and dime."

"It isn't the money, believe me."

"What is it, then?"

"It's the bad publicity, which the museum can't stand. The right-wing radio stations in town would like nothing better than to take down any institution that smacks of elitism. A museum qualifies in that regard in their opinion." She uncrossed her legs and leaned forward, her forearms on her thighs. "Fortunately, the radio stations have been slow off the mark. But several of the anonymous local bloggers who specialize in venom have started attacking the museum. Their audiences are small, which I'm very thankful for, but influential people do read them. So I expect the radio outlets to join the vigilante posse soon. Then it will be only a matter of time before the television stations and newspapers run stories about what they'll call the developing controversy."

I shook my head. "In the old days," I said, "you would have told me that you'd received several letters accusing Patricia of wrongdoing. Then I would have said, 'Do you know who sent them?' 'They weren't signed, of course,' you would have said. You would have told me, 'we turned them over to the police, but they haven't gotten anywhere either.' It would have been like something out of a third-rate detective novel."

"Perhaps art did a better job of imitating life in the old days." She smiled, but the smile quickly faded. "There's also the matter of the ninety thousand dollars," she said.

"What ninety thousand?" I tried to envision recent online bank statements. Had Patricia opened a new Swiss account before she'd been murdered? "You think she stole it?" I said.

"It doesn't involve stealing. What happened was this: Patricia convinced the board to allow her to set up an account that she would control. The board agreed to put ninety thousand into the fund during the first year of its existence."

"That doesn't sound so strange."

"No, it doesn't, except that in this small museum such a fund is unprecedented."

"What was the money supposed to be used for?"

"No one seems to know."

"Not even your predecessor?"

"I've asked him, of course. But he's told me that the board gave Patricia discretion to spend the fund as she saw fit, with no strings attached."

"It could have been used for a temporary hire – a consultant, say – or a small capital improvement, or even a small acquisition, or the down payment on a larger one."

"As I say, no one knows what your late wife might have used the money for, although not for an acquisition. Everything we own has come to us through a bequest. We've never had to purchase any of our works of art. We've never had the money in our operating budget, and we husband our small endowment against a rainy day."

"So it's a mystery. But the money wasn't embezzled."

"Of course, it wasn't. The money's all there, in an account in the museum's name. But I still fear the bloggers' getting wind of the whole business and railing on about what would have happened to the money if Patricia's life hadn't been interrupted. Besides, my predecessor has informed me that Patricia told him that she intended to add to the fund in future years."

"So in your mind, this unexplained fund and the unauthorized but minor use of the museum's car are enough to derail the naming of the new wing in Patricia's name?"

"In this age of malicious bloggers, we have to be careful, Mr. Bornstein. *I* have to be careful." Dr. Finckel stood and smoothed her skirt over slender thighs. She put out her hand for me to shake. "I'll do a better job of keeping you informed," she said. Then she smiled, and I knew I'd been dismissed.

CHAPTER TWELVE

We were driving out to what Sanford called his summer home. He was behind the wheel. He'd promised me a good dinner. "Don't worry, Mordecai," he'd said, "Gwennie will have made sure the plates are nice and warm." He'd laughed then. He knew that everyone was acquainted with the story of why he'd left his second wife and gone back to Gwennie, his first. She'd always warmed the dinner plates; the second wife hadn't.

The familiar urban street, lined with stores, a movie theater, and mainly wooden two-families, turned into a long suburban shopping strip with one bank after another. After passing through the edge of the neighborhood of twisty streets where Patricia had grown up and I lived now, and then past the high school she'd attended, we were on a rural two-lane highway that kept rising toward the distant hills. Sanford hadn't turned the radio on. It was quiet in the big new silver Lincoln sedan. I settled into the plush leather seat and shut my eyes, even though I knew that sleep wouldn't come.

"When I was a little kid," Sanford said, as the heavy Lincoln eased smoothly up the rising road, "a long hallway ran along one side of our six-room apartment. I could ride my tricycle from the vestibule in a circle through the living room and a room my mother called 'the alcove' in front, then I would ride through the vestibule and head toward the back of the apartment. I'd go past a bedroom door, the bathroom door, another bedroom door, and a dining room door, to a space next to the kitchen, where the ice box, eventually replaced by a refrigerator, stood. Then I'd turn into the dining room, go through it and out its other door back into the hallway. I'd turn left and race back down to the front of the apartment, completing the circuit, which had missed the kitchen and pantry only because there wasn't enough space to turn around in them without backing

up. The hallway was wide enough so I could speed past the telephone
table, which was positioned at a bend opposite the door to the second
bedroom - as long as no one was sitting there, that is. I loved that ride.
I've never forgotten it."

A few more minutes, and we were up into the hills. The big car
shouldered around a corner and stopped. We were on a narrow dirt road.
Sanford shifted into neutral and gunned the engine.

"When I found this road, I knew I wanted to own it. It reminded
me of the hallway I'd raced my tricycle on when I was a kid on Elm Hill
Avenue." Sanford laughed and threw the car into drive. We shot forward.

The dirt road was narrow. There was a steep wooded hill on the
right. When I looked left, all I saw was gray sky.

"What's on the left?" I kept my voice under control. I wasn't
about to let Sanford think he could frighten me.

"Nothing," Sanford said. "It drops off immediately. How far
down, I don't know - hundreds of feet, I'd guess. If you look over there,
you can see the downtown we left behind." He turned to me, while he was
pointing with his right hand to the vast open space to his left.

I refused to look where he was pointing. I thought that if I did,
we'd fly into the void. "Watch the road, pal," I said matter-of-factly.

"Calm down, Mordecai. I've driven down this road a million
times."

I grinned at Sanford, although all I could see ahead now was gray
sky. The road had disappeared.

Sanford turned the wheel to the right, and the big car made a
smooth turn without complaint. There was road ahead of us again. I
realized that I was pressed against the passenger door. I looked back and
saw the air was filled with light brown dust. Then I looked at Sanford. He
was grinning at me contentedly.

"Don't you drive with your eyes on the road?" I asked him. "What
if a car was coming the other way? You know, like right at us."

The big Lincoln was slowing down. "I have a sixth sense," Sanford
said, "and the brakes on this baby are terrific."

I ignored him. "What if Gwennie had decided to drive out just as
you were starting down this dirt road?"

"But she's not here."

"You know that for sure?"

"She did tell me that she wouldn't be coming out here today. She'd
be staying in town. She has a major errand to run, she told me. She'll be
here tomorrow. I'll come out again late in the day, like we did today."

"What about warming the dinner plates?"

"The housekeeper always follows Gwennie's instructions to the letter."

"Glad to hear it. And remind me to take my own car next time I come out here," I said with a laugh, "but not before I make sure you're either not here, or if you are, you're not planning to go out."

"I never would have guessed you're such a wuss."

"Does Gwennie drive this road like you do?"

"Of course not – she's much too sensible. And if you want to know, she hates the way I drive on it."

"She's not rooting for widowhood, then."

Sanford threw his head back and laughed. "She already has most of the money." He maneuvered the car around a pond and stopped in front of a large wood and stone house. "Need a change of underwear?"

I flipped him the bird. He roared with laughter again and killed the engine. The silver beast seemed to settle with a sigh of relief.

"It was great ride," I said. "I haven't had this much fun for ages." I wasn't going to give Sanford any satisfaction in yet another game.

A minute later, Sanford closed the double front door behind us, and we walked up a short flight of wide steps from the foyer into a large room. Beyond the opposite wall, which consisted entirely of large panes of glass and two sets of French doors, I could make out only shadowy shapes in the late afternoon gloom. The room was dark. My eyes were slow to adjust. When I glanced to my right, I could see light leaking around an edge and the bottom of a door. I turned back to the outside view. Then suddenly the room was brilliantly lit, and the glass wall in front of me was black.

In front of me there was a large white couch facing the glass wall. I looked around. All the chairs on the room were white. The chests and tables were all light-colored wood. The bare wood floor looked bleached. There were no lamps. All the light in the room came from overhead. I realized that the room had a very high ceiling.

"Enjoy," Sanford said, from somewhere behind me. He must have stopped to turn on the lights. He didn't say anything more. He knew that he didn't need to. He could allow me to let my curiosity guide me, and I would do what he wanted me to do – which was to experience the three bold and very large paintings that dominated the huge room.

As I'd mentioned to the Glickauers when I'd first met them at the Kramers', I'd seen reproductions of many of Sam Hudson's paintings in an exhibition catalogue of a retrospective held at a gallery five or six years ago. But I'd never had the privilege of seeing any of them in the flesh, so to speak, although the catalogue had drawn me to Hudson's work. Patricia had liked them, as well, I remembered.

Now here were three of them. I didn't move, except to turn my body. The paintings were so large that I needed to experience them from the center of the room. No matter – even from twenty feet, their heightened realism easily pulled me into Hudson's world. I could almost step inside the daily life of a working artist.

On the side walls, opposite one another, were paintings of two of the artist's models, beautiful long-limbed women relaxing during a break or after a session had ended. In one painting, which I'd never seen before, either in a catalogue or in the flesh, the model was seated on a couch, talking into a telephone. She hadn't bothered to cover herself. Perhaps the call had interrupted a session. She sat unselfconsciously, her legs splayed, seemingly unaware that there would be anyone looking at her.

She wasn't alone. To the left of the couch, you could see the artist. He was sitting with his back to the woman – and to the viewer. He seemed to be fiddling with a brush. I could see the backs of an easel and a canvas behind him. There was no hint of the painting he might have been working on, except it must have included the nude woman. Dark shades were drawn over a group of windows in the wall behind the couch. I would have expected that. Some artists needed light to remain constant, so they used artificial light, not the changing light from outside.

In the painting on the opposite wall, a woman sat on the end of a day bed, her legs apart and crossed at her ankles. I had seen this painting in the gallery's catalogue. There was a pair of blue high heeled shoes next to her feet. She had put a blouse on, but hadn't buttoned it over her bare breasts. She had nothing else on. She was making no effort to look seductive, even with the cigarette in the hand that rested on the bed cover next to an ashtray. She looked relaxed, perhaps gathering herself before she got dressed and left the painter's studio.

You could tell that's where she was because the painter was in the picture, as well. You could see him through an open door, holding a cup and saucer, the backs of an easel and a canvas behind him. Again, the woman's presence was the only hint as to what the artist might have been putting on the canvas.

You want to keep looking at these paintings, I thought. It wasn't because of the beauty of the two women and the sexual frankness with which they had been posed. It was because of the artist's ability to render the female form with sensitivity that bordered on reverence.

The two paintings were like a pair of bookends. The theme in the paintings was similar. It was the same artist in both paintings, although the women were different. The paintings, both very large, looked to be similar in size. They were large enough so that the women appeared to be almost life-size.

I turned to Sanford. He was beaming with pride of ownership. "I remember your telling me that Hudson is very good at painting women," I said. "You were right."

"He's good at men, too," Sanford said, "as you will soon see."

"So what did he call these two paintings?" I waved a hand at the paintings on the side walls.

"*Blue Shoes* and *A Telephone Call*. That's Sam Hudson for you – a bit of a comedian."

"When were they completed, and how did you come to own them? Did you buy them from Hudson directly, through a gallery, or from another collector?"

"The two nudes were bought from a gallery on the Upper East Side by a rich Baltimore socialite. She befriended Sam, just like I have. I think she was attempting to emulate the Cone sisters, who also lived in Baltimore, and who befriended Matisse decades ago. Their Matisses are at the Baltimore museum now."

"I know. Patricia and I made a special trip to see them a few years ago. It was worth it."

"I agree. But to get back to *my* Baltimore woman: she bought these two paintings twenty years ago. She lived in a massive stone townhouse in the downtown, and she hung the paintings in her living room. It must have cost her a fortune to light them properly in that dark old mausoleum. Her family hated the electric bills – and they hated the paintings. They thought they were vulgar. They had to put up with them for fifteen long years, until the old lady suddenly dropped dead of a coronary.

"It was well know in gallery circles that I already owned three of Sam's paintings, so I was among the initial bidders – although the paintings never went to auction. I simply offered enough so the family was advised not to even bother to haggle."

Sanford smiled with satisfaction – more than I'd ever seen him exhibit, even when he'd triumphed in one of the games he'd devised. "Of course," he went on, "my other major coup was not just buying Sam's most famous painting, *The Afternoon Party*, but getting myself in it."

"I remember your talking about being in it when I met you and Gwennie at the Kramers. And now here it is, isn't it?"

Sanford was standing next to the massive painting, which must have measured nearly eight by over twelve feet. He was smiling at me. I found him in the painting almost immediately. He was third person in, as I scanned the painting from left to right. He was in profile, sitting on chair with a drink in his hand and talking to a person sitting a few feet away.

I noticed a framed drawing hung just below the lower left-hand corner of the painting's ornate frame. When I got closer, I saw that it was guide to the identities of the twenty-three people in the painting. I studied the legend of names. I was surprised to find that Hudson's name was among them.

"The party was in Sam and Deborah's apartment on the Upper East Side," Sanford explained, when I looked at him quizzically. "It's where he has his studio, where he paints all of his pictures."

"How did he execute this one?"

"He won't tell me – or anyone else – how he makes any of his paintings. He won't own up to exactly what technique he uses – whether it involves photography or not, for example, or projection."

"Now I remember reading about his refusal to discuss his technique in the gallery exhibition catalogue," I said. "It was a minor scandal for a while."

Sanford smiled and shrugged his shoulders. 'What can you do?" he said. "These artists make their own rules."

I shrugged. "Show me the other two Hudsons," I said.

One of them was in the dining room. It was *Morning Coffee*, the painting I'd heard about at that first meeting with the Glickauers. The two women in the painting were bathed in a warm, golden light. And they were wearing clothes.

We walked back through the living room. A large library was on the far side. It was furnished with a desk at one end and elsewhere several chairs arranged under reading lamps. On the largest wall there was a painting with a man and a woman, nude, lying on top of an unmade bed.

The man was lying on his back, his head propped on a pillow, and one bent leg drawn up. He was reading a newspaper. The woman was propped up on one elbow, her head on her hand. She was on the far side of the man and was turned toward him and the viewer. The bodies, as usual with Hudson, were very well executed. The couple's faces were in slightly soft focus. The scene was lit by a lamp; an edge of the shade was just visible. The newspaper covered their private parts.

"My guess is, at least one of these two is married to someone else," I said, as I stood in front of the painting with Sanford. "I imagine that you've hung it over here so you can see it when you're working at your desk on your latest divorce case– for inspiration."

"The title gives no hint of anything of the sort. The painting is called *The Newspaper.*"

"Oh, *there* it is." I pointed at the newspaper.

I got the laugh I'd hoped for, but it wasn't genuine. When I looked at Sanford, he was rolling his eyes. "I thought you'd find it sooner or later," he said. "You have a nasty mind, Mordecai, unlike me." It was my turn to roll my eyes, but I relegated myself to smiling as insincerely as I could manage.

A few minutes later, Sanford and I were back in the living room. He sat on the oversized couch and drank the white wine he'd brought in from the kitchen while I wandered around with a glass of wine and looked at the three large paintings again. There were cheese and crackers on a glass coffee table in front of us when I finally sat down. The food and drink were rather ordinary, not as expensive as I'd imagined.

Sanford got up, dimmed the living room light, and turned on outdoor flood lamps. They lit a patio with outdoor furniture made of glass and gray metal. The chairs had gray pillows on the seats and backs. There was shrubbery on the far side of the patio. I could see more tables and chairs beyond the shrubbery.

"There's a swimming pool on the other side of the patio," Sanford said. "We leave the furniture out year-round. Our handyman covers it when the weatherman hints there might be snow in the forecast." He took a tiny sip of wine and turned to face me. "Tell me the truth, Mordecai. What do you think of what Gwennie likes to call 'Sanford's ladies?' When we have people over, Gwennie always says, 'He likes to show them off, don't you darling?' And believe me, I can't detect even a trace of irony in her voice."

"I find them very impressive," I said. "I like them, but I can't imagine they're to everyone's taste. Some people might even find them offensive. We don't live in sophisticated, albeit decadent Europe, after all." I made air quotes when I said the word decadent. "Here in America, mothers can't even breast-feed their babies in public without people freaking out. What do you do when you're having guests who might be made uncomfortable by the nudes, or guests are coming with children?"

"We have tapestries on stretchers that fit over the paintings with my ladies. If you don't already know there are paintings underneath, you're none the wiser."

"You're not afraid you'll damage the paintings? What about a fire? And what about all that weight hanging on the walls? The frames look very heavy."

"When Gwennie and I built this house a couple of years ago, we had the first floor built with steel beams so the walls could take all the weight. But here's the thing, Mordecai: These aren't the original paintings."

"Excuse me?"

"They're exact copies of the originals. I found an outfit that could make the copies for a reasonable price, so I had them do it. You can't tell the difference even if you put the original and the copy next to one another."

"I'm sorry I asked. I so enjoyed looking at Sam Hudson's work in the flesh, as I said earlier." I went with a small smile and a lift of my eyebrows. "So where are the originals?"

"They're safely locked away in a fireproof storage vault," Sanford said. "They tell me there's nothing that can harm those paintings, short of a nuclear attack."

"Does Sam Hudson know about this?"

"He got wind of it, we don't know how. And he's quite pissed about it. He says we've violated his copyright – his moral right. But I assured him that we've made the copies only for our own, temporary use, and that we'll eventually destroy them. I told him that I should know, because I used to be an intellectual property lawyer before I became active in big-time divorce work. It mollified him enough so that he didn't get his own lawyer involved, but he's still pissed. Besides, this isn't the end of the story."

"There's more?"

"You don't think that Sam would have been satisfied with my verbal assurances, do you?"

"No, I suppose not. Something else must have convinced him, then."

"Of course it did. Sam insisted on seeing originals and copies side by side. So I had the originals brought here from the vault. I had a couple of the originals hung, and stood up a couple of the copies on the floor, a mix and match, to make it harder for Sam to figure out which was which."

"So how did he do?"

"He couldn't tell his own canvases from the copies. I hadn't expected him to be able to. I just sat in a chair and watched him. First he was calm, then he got panicky, and finally he flew into a rage. He swore at me. He was quite inventive, I must say. When he threatened to put a knife into every painting in the house, all the originals and all the copies - he was screaming that he no longer cared about them and wanted to destroy them - I immediately turned out the lights."

"And you subdued him?"

"No, it was nothing like that. What happened was, he could see a couple of luminescent dots in each of the copies. He knew he hadn't put them in any of the originals."

"I don't recall seeing any glow-in-the-dark dots when I came in."

"It wasn't quite dark enough. I'd drawn the drapes before Sam arrived. And it was after dark when I put on the show."

"So that mollified him?"

"Not completely. I could see that he was still seething with suspicion. So I produced an affidavit from an auditor at an accounting firm here in town. It testifies to the truthfulness of my story about the copiers I'd hired putting tiny luminescent dots onto their paintings. Sam finally gave in, but not before he accused me of plotting to create entirely new paintings in his style and sell them. These copies were just practice, he raved, and wasn't I pleased that he hadn't been able to distinguish between copies and originals."

"I've heard of that being done, but only after an artist has died."

"That's just it! According to him, I was going to murder him and his wife Deborah, wait awhile, and then put the fraudulent paintings on the market."

"How did you finally calm him down?"

"I had my cell phone in my pocket. All I had to do was tap the send button. The call was a signal to the crew who were returning the original canvases to the vault. Once four large, beefy men were in the living room with Sam and me, he became quite reasonable. He even began to laugh about the ordeal he said that I'd just put him through."

"You make it sound like just another one of your games."

"You could look at it that way, I suppose."

Sanford had the self-satisfied smile that I'd come to recognize on his face. I remembered seeing that smile during the conversation at the Kramers' dinner party. "Maybe that's why he won't paint a picture of you and Gwennie," I said.

"Could be," Sanford said.

We ate dinner in the brightly lit, very large, and well-appointed kitchen, at a sturdy farmhouse table. The same white wine we'd had with cheese accompanied dinner. We both drank sparingly – I wasn't about to encourage imbibing on Sanford's part. I wanted him sober on the ride back, and I doubted he'd surrender the keys if he wasn't.

Sanford served the meal. It had been prepared by the housekeeper, who was the handyman's wife. Sanford had made sure before we'd left town, in response to my question as we ate, that she'd already left the house, lest he run into her on his dirt speedway.

The food, some of it warming in the oven, along with the dinner plates, of course, and the rest of it chilling in the refrigerator was plentiful – a large tossed salad with a selection of bottled dressings, a hefty portion of veal ptarmigan with ziti in a bland marinara sauce, and vanilla ice cream with a full package's worth of Pepperidge Farm Milano cookies. Besides quantity, the main requirement placed on the housekeeper, it appeared, was that the food not be too adventurous. The meal harkened back to Betty Crocker's heyday. Sanford concentrated on the veal and the salad and barely touched anything else.

He piled the dishes in the sink.

"Let me take care of them," I said.

"Marta will take care of them in the morning," Sanford said, "but thanks just the same. Besides, by viewing Hudson's paintings and waxing enthusiastic about them, you've already sung for your supper." He poured a couple of mugs of coffee – decaf, he announced – and we settled back into the padded kitchen chairs.

"So how did you and Gwennie meet?" I asked. The time seemed right for this conversation.

"We met during the second year I was stationed at Aberdeen Proving Ground. Gwennie Harper was a junior at Goucher College, which is in the Baltimore suburbs, not that far from Aberdeen."

"Gretchen had already left Washington," I interjected.

"Just about," Sanford drawled vaguely. "Anyway, Goucher was a women's college back then, in the early Nineteen Sixties. Someone had the bright idea to hold a mixer after spring break with Goucher girls and single officers from Aberdeen. They took us at our word that we weren't philandering husbands, but we were officers in the United States Army, so I suppose we could be trusted. Besides, it probably meant a court martial if you were accused of hanky-panky, I kid you not.

"I met Gwennie at that mixer. I was attracted to her at first sight. She was, of course, a younger version of the woman she is now: a strapping girl, athletic, a blonde thoroughbred, although she's gray now. I knew right away that she was intelligent, and shrewd, as well. I thought she liked me. We hit it off well enough that I got her to go out with me every weekend until she had to barricade herself in her dorm to study for finals. I saw her one more time, and only briefly, until she left for Connecticut for the summer." Sanford noticed the quizzical expression on my face. "No," he went on, "I hadn't slept with her. She made it clear that wasn't in the cards.

"Once she was away, I began to write long letters to her. They weren't love letters, exactly, but they did mention the possibility of our having a future together. I was able tell her that I missed her, but I was afraid to tell her that I loved her. I was afraid to phone her. I thought she might reject me if I showed my hand too soon.

"It was entirely different than it had been with Gretchen. I can't tell you why. She and Gwennie came from similar, tony backgrounds. Both were well educated, beautiful, and intelligent. But whereas I'd been willing to risk rejection in hotly pursuing Gretchen, when it came to Gwennie, I had the sense that I was better off hanging back and letting her come to me, as it were, rather than vice-versa. Did I put her on some sort of pedestal? Perhaps – or maybe I knew this wasn't a game.

"I wondered, however, whether *she* was playing a game. I waited for what seemed like an eternity for her first reply. I must have sent three or four long letters before I heard back. Waiting was agony. At the end of each workday, I'd rush back to the apartment I shared in the BOQ – that's Bachelor Officers Quarters, for you civilians – to see if a letter had come from Gwennie.

"I was crushed when there was nothing from her. I couldn't understand myself. I'd just had a long affair with a very desirable woman. Gwennie was desirable, too, but my acting like a love-sick puppy seemed bizarre to me. Yet I was trapped in that behavior by a young woman who was getting the better of me – by a long shot.

"I finally did get a letter – the first of just two that summer. I was disappointed at how impersonal it was. It was little more than a recounting of the highlights of Gwennie's Westport summer. Did she miss me, like I missed her? The letter provided no clue. You couldn't read anything into the bland prose.

"The second letter was similar to the first one, except for one thing: it contained an invitation to come for a Saturday lunch in the middle of August. Gwennie would be available for dates in New York with me after lunch and on Sunday afternoon.

"I drove up to Westport in my MG Midget. It was a hot, sunny day, and I had the top down. Gwennie's mother was nice to me, in an offhand, WASPy sort of way. She served me roast beef sandwiches with tomato and mayonnaise. I didn't expect Dottie Harper to know that Jews were supposed to eat roast beef with mustard, not mayo, so I kept my mouth shut.

"Gwennie looked terrific in a green and blue summer dress that day, with white sandals. I packed her into the MG's passenger seat and we drove into the city. I kept the top down, and she let her hair blow in the wind. She combed it out when we got to the Village.

"I took her to Chumley's, that place with the hidden door in Barrow Street and the book jackets on the walls. I loved the beef and

Indonesian rice dish they served there. Too bad I can't abide spicy food like that anymore. Later, we drank beer and listened to Dixieland. Then we took a cab up to Grand Central. Gwennie kissed me in the taxi, but kept my hands from roaming up her leg or around her breasts. She'd insisted on taking the train back to Connecticut, and I didn't argue with her.

"I stayed at the YMCA on West Thirty-Fourth Street. I liked the Y because it was clean and cheap, and you never seemed to need a reservation. In those days, you didn't have to go far before you could find an overnight parking spot on the street.

"Gwennie took the train back into the city on Sunday afternoon. We went to the Museum of Modern Art – the Gauguin's were what turned me on back then. And they still had Guernica, which everyone had to genuflect in front of. Afterwards, we walked up Fifth Avenue to Reuben's on Fifty-Eighth Street, where the Cole slaw was made with vinegar, and the apple pancake was to die for. Gwennie agreed with me about the apple pancake, but she made a face after a bite of the slaw. I loved it, though. We walked on Madison down to Grand Central, and I put her back on the train around seven. I'd barely gotten a quick kiss during the entire afternoon. I learned why the next day.

"I spent a second night at the Y. I put the car in a lot early on Monday morning. Gwennie's father, who I hadn't met yet, had summoned me through Gwennie to an eleven o'clock meeting at his office. He hadn't mentioned an agenda to her, and I hadn't asked her what might be on his mind. I had my suspicions, but I thought it wise to keep them to myself. All in good time, I tried to tell myself, but the truth was, I was bursting with anxiety and impatience.

"I was a few minutes early for my appointment with David Harper. A nicely dressed middle-aged woman, who introduced herself not with her own name but as Mr. Harper's secretary, deposited me in a small, windowless room that might have been a storeroom or the office of some junior person at one time. Now it was decorated with four metal chairs and a low table on which sat a pile of out-of-date business and legal magazines.

For the next quarter-hour I shared the room with a fellow, about my age, who looked like he was dressed for an interview. He was wearing a blue suit and a red striped tie. His white shirt looked heavily starched. I caught him looking at me with some amusement, as if he'd surmised that I was there to interview for the same position, but hadn't dressed appropriately. He'd have been correct, if that was why I was there. I had a sport jacket on over a khaki shirt with two breast pockets that had flaps that buttoned. My shoes were better shined than this other fellow's, however. Why not? I was in the army, after all.

"David Harper's secretary opened the door to the small room and asked me to follow her. As I got up, she said to the possible interviewee, 'Mr. Harper will be with you in just a few minutes. I'll come for you when he's ready.' I remember thinking that my time with David Harper would be measured by how quickly his desire to be rid of me grew to the point where he could no longer resist it.

"When I was ushered into his large office, he was standing behind his desk, with his hands on the top of his leather chair. Beyond him, I could see other tall buildings and the East River. He was a barrel-chested, handsome man with close-cropped hair and a tanned face. While I was eating lunch at his house on Saturday, I'd been told that he was out on the golf course. Now he was in shirtsleeves, the top button undone, his expensive-looking tie pulled down. He was much taller than his wife. She'd married him because she wanted tall children, I thought.

"I couldn't help noticing how large his hand was when I shook it. I could tell that he enjoyed the power of his grip. When he finally released me and indicated that I should sit in one of the leather armchairs facing his desk, he wasted no time in telling me that he had an important interview scheduled in a few minutes, so our time together would be brief. Mercifully brief, I remember thinking. Gwennie had not prepared me fully; this large, powerful looking man was more than I'd bargained for.

"Gwennie had told me that her father was a partner in a law firm with a thriving corporate practice. When I met him that day, it seemed obvious to me that his clear blue eyes and square jaw gave David Harper an air of solidity and reliability that any corporate president would find reassuring. When the blue eyes bore into me, however, I was hardly reassured.

"David Harper was too well-practiced a lawyer to be obvious. I was prepared for the age-old question about what my intentions toward his daughter were. But no, he didn't ask me such a simple, old-fashioned question, one that I would have had an answer to. I remember thinking as I left him that I wished he had.

"Instead he affected a rather gentle manner as he probed in another direction, one that I should have expected, but hadn't prepared for. The moment came back to me years later, when I watched Teddy Kennedy fail to provide a coherent answer to Roger Mudd's straightforward query, 'Why do you want to be President?' I mean, there I was, face to face with the father of the woman I was pursuing, and when he asked me what I wanted to do professionally, the answer I gave him was this: 'I want to spend my career solving interesting engineering problems.' The moment I gave that answer, I realized that David Harper surmised that I meant that the problems would be *academically* interesting.

"I suppose that at that time in my life what I said amounted to what it really was that I wanted to do with my professional life, but it was a damn stupid thing to say to a man like Gwennie's father. I've thought about that conversation a great many times over the years, and I can't fathom my obliviousness to the situation at hand that morning. I must have sounded very immature to the big-time corporate lawyer I was hoping to win over. Later, I wondered whether the attitude I exhibited was a result of my having had the double promotion at the William Lloyd Garrison School that I told you about. As a result of it, had my emotional development lagged my intellectual development as I'd progressed through my academic career?

"David Harper must have taken pity on me. He didn't dismiss me immediately. Instead, he asked me several more questions that gave me the opportunity to indicate that I might someday see something more on the horizon than a stack of academically interesting engineering problems I might want to solve. Did I want to join a corporation and work my way up the ladder to a management position someday? Or did I want to start my own business? Did I understand what I might have to sacrifice to pursue such objectives?

"He listened to me without interrupting, but he didn't seem interested in my answers. To be perfectly honest with you, I'm sure I didn't find my answers to his questions particularly interesting myself. And then, almost before our little talk had gotten started, he was on an intercom, asking his secretary – Miss Schuppert was her name, I finally learned – to take me to the elevator. I rose and we shook hands with perfunctory goodbyes.

"As I've indicated, Gwennie's father and I weren't together very long that day. After I departed the midtown building where he had his big office, it seemed to me that he had disposed of me rather gently. But dispose of me, he had. I hadn't been worth the trouble of a more intense cross examination than the one I'd received. I doubted that David Harper expected to see any of me in the future. It had been a satisfying morning's work for him. At the same time, I knew beyond any doubt that wanting and getting the woman that Jack Carmichael had was a walk in the park compared to wanting and having the daughter that David Harper had."

Sanford stood up and went to a cabinet near the sink. He took a glass down and ran water into it. As he was drinking, I heard a horn toot outside. Sanford looked down at his watch. "That will be the car service, right on time," he said. "I hope you don't think it's rude of me not to drive you home myself." He gave me the tender smile I was becoming used to.

"That's fine," I said. "There's just one more thing."

The horn sounded again. "Make it quick. They get antsy."

"I know you're a great storyteller, but it's remarkable nevertheless that you remember everything so clearly. These events took place half a century ago, after all. Or is all of what you told me part of the lore that you and Gwennie have talked about down through the years?"

"A little of this, a little of that – I leave the presentation up to you ultimately." The tender smile reappeared on Sanford's lips. He took another sip of water. The horn sounded for a third time.

"They really are antsy," I said, as I quickly shook Sanford's hand.

I settled into the back seat of another Lincoln, this one a comfortable late-model Town Car. The driver had no difficulty with the dirt road out of Sanford's property, although he did navigate it much more deliberately than Sanford had.

"Not my cup of tea, this road," the driver said out loud in an Irish brogue. He kept his eyes on the road, unlike Sanford. This time, it did seem a bit wider to me, but I kept a grip on the door handle, in case the car started to veer off the road toward the drop-off and I had to tumble out the door.

Once we were back on the paved two-lane county roads, I relaxed. I leaned back against the headrest. As the big car eased its way down the hillside, I noticed only one other car on the road. It sped past us, climbing in the opposite direction. I watched its taillights for a second or two, and then I dozed off.

CHAPTER THIRTEEN

I slept for only a very brief time in the Town Car. I was in bed soon after I came in the front door, and a few minutes later, when *The New Yorker* slid out of my hands, I rolled over, turned off the lamp, and fell back into delicious, dreamless oblivion. But sleep didn't last long enough. At two-thirty, I woke to the sound of Sanford's voice in my ears and a vision of his tender smile in my mind's eye. As the hours of sleeplessness rolled by, I couldn't keep his stories from rushing through my mind. All the while, I kept asking myself: how much of what Sanford told me should I take at face value?

The stories dealt with events that had transpired many years ago. Some people he talked about - David and Dottie Harper, for instance - were no longer living. They couldn't dispute Sanford's version of events, of course. But how should I deal with any discrepancies I might uncover between his stories and the accounts I intended to obtain from Gwennie, or Gretchen, or Phoebe Armstrong, Sanford's wife in the interval between his two marriages to Gwennie?

I had to talk with Sanford's women. I would need to fill in details of his portrait, after all. How would he react to my bringing up any discrepancies? Would a different version of any of his stories wipe the tender smile off his face? At this point in my relationship with him, I had no idea.

At mid-morning, I was still at home. I read through recent posts on the blog that was the leader of the pack making trouble over Patricia's tenure at the Museum of Art and Industry. I was dismayed to see that the anonymous blogger had something new to report. He – or was the he a she? – had gotten wind of the ninety-thousand-dollar fund over which the board of trustees had given Patricia sole discretion.

Here was a new charge to add to the litany of charges the blogger kept hammering and inflating, insinuating that they were only the tip of an iceberg of possible wrongdoing that a complaisant board of trustees had neglected to pay sufficient attention to. Now there was more ammunition for the blogger to use in demanding that the board of trustees accept a boatload of recommendations about museum governance. Everything was echoed by readers in the comments section. There was no discernible dissent.

After a dispiriting twenty minutes, I picked up the phone. The first call I made was to Helene Finckel at the museum. When I punched in her extension, I was pleased to find Erma Tausig, Patricia's former assistant, answering my call.

"It's nice to hear your voice, Mr. Bornstein," she said. She didn't allow time for me to respond, but quickly continued, "Let me see if Dr. Finckel is free. It's been a very busy morning already."

A few seconds later, Helene Finckel was on the line, exchanging pleasantries with me, but cautioning me that she had only a couple of minutes to talk. She and Erma Tausig knew how to keep a story straight.

I came directly to the point. "I'm calling to see if there's been any movement in putting Patricia's name back on the museum's planned new wing," I said.

"As I indicated the last time we spoke about this issue, which I understand is of the utmost importance to you, we're not yet in a position to make any final determination," Dr. Finckel said.

"I see that the blogger leading the pack of hyenas is screaming about a new charge. The blogger's going crazy over the discretionary fund the board gave Patricia. Have you seen the blog today? Now the bloggers can push harder for action on the museum's part. If the blogger gets what he wants, which, among other things, is for the museum to not put Patricia's name on the new wing, it would deeply outrage and sadden me. I can barely stomach reading through the blog, but I forced myself to just before I picked up the phone to call you. "

"I do more than you just did – I read through the lot of these blogs every day. I have seen the report on the new revelation, as one of the bloggers puts it. And yes, I see that they'll use the information about the discretionary fund as another reason to push their demands that the board of trustees, and me personally, address, without further ado, the alleged fiduciary irresponsibility that the museum allowed to take place when your late wife was director.

"So keeping your late wife's name off the new wing – the demand that is extremely important to you - is only one of the demands we're being bombarded with. The bottom line is, the board of trustees and I are being accused of not exercising due diligence over your late wife's activities and their aftermath, a charge I find personally repugnant. I've always taken pride in the care and seriousness with which I approach my job – or any task I undertake, in fact."

"I did see the demands for greater transparency and for expanding the board of trustees to include what the blogger calls non-elite members of the public. They sound like demands that someone with your executive experience can deal with. I'm sure you've been under pressure more intense than this in your professional life. Isn't there something you've learned to do that will bring this nonsense to a satisfactory conclusion?"

"Well, I can't very well confront the bloggers directly and tell them to desist. If I did, charges of censorship would engulf the museum. My concern now is how to deal with mainstream press outlets, who are about to start reporting on what they will deem a controversy. They don't have to acquiesce to the charges while informing the general public they exist – which gives them a measure of legitimacy, unfortunately. And I can't ask the newspapers and the radio and television stations not to act like journalists. The right wing radio stations would be apoplectic."

"So what can you do about this mess? Surely there must be ways for you to deal with it."

"I haven't found a satisfactory way to deal with this particular mess yet. Let me be as candid as I can be. I believe you deserve that consideration. Let me tell you what I intend to say in the one-on-one press briefings I'll be holding this afternoon. I'll say that the museum has hired a consultant to perform an internal investigation and I'll say, further, that I believe the best strategy is to let things play themselves out.

"To be perfectly honest with you, I can't personally be seen by the press as pushing back against the charges too hard. I can't be seen as an advocate for keeping your late wife's name on the new wing. I have to be seen to be above the fray. I have to take the position that I will look at the results of the consultant's ongoing investigation and make a dispassionate decision based on the facts. And there's one more thing: I must ask you to keep this conversation confidential. Promise me that."

"I appreciate the candor, and I will keep this conversation between us only. But I also have to say that I'm disappointed by what you've told me."

"You have to trust in the process."

It sounded like consultant- or CEO-speak. The word trust was still buzzing in my ear as I put in a call to Detective Hartnett. "I haven't heard

from you in a while," I said, as soon as he picked up and we exchanged
perfunctory greetings. "Is my wife's murder case still open?"

"It seems like only a few days since we talked."

"And is anything new?"

"Nothing is new, Mr. Bornstein."

"So you still consider the murder collateral damage, so to speak,
from a robbery?"

"That's an interesting way of putting the matter, but the answer is
still yes."

"You haven't found any of the personal belongings that were taken
from the murder scene?"

"We haven't found a thing. No one has reported usage of any of
her credit cards, for example. There's been no cell phone usage, to take
another example. We can't locate the phone. It must have been destroyed.
Whoever took her belongings – her killer most likely – has left no traces."

"And that still points only to robbery as the motive for her
murder?"

"Do you have another theory? You're free to hire your own
investigator to pursue it, if you're not satisfied with our progress."

Bill Kramer had dissuaded me from doing so. "I've discussed it
with someone I respect," I said, "but he told me that you do a thorough
job, detective. So I don't see any point to undertaking my own
investigation. But I'm still uneasy about your conclusion that robbery was
the motive for my wife's murder."

"If we discover a reason to change our opinion, we'll let you know.
You can trust us to do that."

I wasn't about to admit to Hartnett that I was getting sick of my
second-guessing Worse yet, I was feeling more and more isolated by my
lack of trust. But at the same time, no one was providing satisfactory
answers to any of my questions.

There was one more place I wanted to go before I hung up with
Harnett, at least for now: "You've heard about the malicious bloggers who
seem to be taking great joy in attacking my late wife and her tenure at the
museum?"

"I've heard about that bunch from Dr. Finckel, the new
chairwoman of the board of trustees. You've met with her yourself, I take
it." I murmured affirmatively, and then Hartnett continued: "If these
bloggers engaged in physical violence, then we could go after them. But the
violence they perpetrate is verbal, and it would be improper for the police
to go after them for it. They're exercising their right of free speech, which
the government should not even attempt to stop. They're not a threat to

the government or the citizenry, after all." Notions of civil liberties protections seemed to wafting though the ether.

"I know that. But my problem is that these bloggers aren't exercising their freedom to speak in the abstract; they're defaming my wife's memory with their protected speech."

"So take them to court. That's your remedy. My wife Maggie tells me that you've become friendly with Sanford Glickauer, and that you're working on a writing project with him. Why don't you ask him to look at what the bloggers are saying about your late wife? Let the lawyer decide whether it's libelous."

"The problem is that the information they've uncovered – or that's been fed to them – is true. It's the spin they put on the information that makes them so annoying."

"There you are, then. It's better to let their craziness – their obsessive behavior – run its course. I wouldn't be surprised if that's what Dr. Finckel's been telling you. You have to trust me, and her, to do the right things in the end."

I had come full circle. It was time to end the phone calls, at least for one day.

I decided not to go into the office. I was expecting a call from Rachel Gormsby, my upstart editorial assistant, and I was in no mood to talk with her. Just to make sure, I turned my cell phone off. I drove across the river to a place I knew where I could walk down a long country road. I put in half a dozen miles.

I started under a milky white sky, but the cloud cover grew progressively darker as I walked. A light rain started when I was a half mile or so from the car. The rain was coming down heavily as I drove toward the village that I'd passed on my way to the country road. I didn't go home directly. Instead, I lingered in one of the village bookstores for nearly an hour, while it continued to rain steadily. I stopped to buy groceries on my drive home.

The phone was ringing as I came in the door. I answered it, hoping it wasn't Ms. Gormsby, in hot pursuit. Instead, it was Bill Kramer's voice I recognized.

"Sanford's dead" were the first words out of his mouth.

"Good lord – I was with him last night."

"He died in a car crash this afternoon."

The memory of yesterday's wild ride flooded my brain. "Did he lose control of his car on that dirt road, the one into his summer house? He drove me down it yesterday afternoon, and he was going too damn fast."

"The road slicked up in that cold rain this afternoon, and he probably was going too fast. Apparently, his car slid off the road at the bend and plunged hundreds of feet down the hillside. Tim Hartnett called me with the details as soon as they got down to the wreck with a helicopter, which couldn't have been easy."

"How did the police know he'd gone off the road?"

"Gwennie heard a tremendous noise, ran down the road, and called 911 on her cell phone. They scrambled the chopper immediately."

"I'm shocked, but I'm not surprised. He told me that he took pride in driving dangerously on that narrow road. The sheer drop-off was like a dare. But that's neither here nor there. It's just a terrible thing. It shouldn't have happened. I'm terribly sorry for Gwennie and all the rest of you."

"Thanks, Mordecai. I want you to know that I'm sorry for you, too. In fact, I wanted you to learn about the accident from me personally. You and Sanford were spending a lot of time together, weren't you?"

"We were having some interesting sessions."

"So a relationship was developing."

"I think so." I wasn't entirely sure, but I answered somewhat affirmatively. The issue of Sanford's game playing had always been at the back of my mind whenever I was with him.

"That's good, very good," Bill said vaguely. His mind was already elsewhere, I could tell.

Sanford's fatal accident was the lead story on the local television and radio news, and it was on the front pages of the local morning papers. The *Times* obituary, which must have been written sometime earlier - except for details about Sanford's actual death - was rolled out in time for the following day's editions. By all accounts, Sanford had died in a car crash caused by a sudden storm that had made the road he was driving on unexpectedly and dangerously slippery. Of course, no mention was made of the way he challenged himself on that road.

There was no mention of Gretchen Carmichael in any of Sanford's obituaries that were published over the next two days. There was only a single sentence in the *Times* about Phoebe Armstrong, Sanford's second wife for a few years. Her name did not appear in the local papers' obituaries. Gwennie appeared in every obituary, of course. In the *Times*, her marriages to Sanford were covered in the final paragraph. No other survivors were mentioned in any of the obituaries.

The *Times* used Sanford's love of games as the springboard for its obituary. It put forth the idea that his success as a divorce lawyer flowed from the way he treated his adversaries. They were nothing more than opponents in games that he would devise to suit particular situations. This technique allowed Sanford to remain dispassionate in situations that were fraught with emotion.

In addition to a review of Sanford's entire legal career, which had started in the intellectual property area – defending his corporate clients' patents and trademarks – the *Times*' main story concerned the case that had made Sanford's reputation as a top-tier divorce lawyer: the notorious Alice Burns' split from her husband Harlan, the celebrated CEO of American Tractor, the farm equipment behemoth that he had parlayed into a hugely profitable global powerhouse with major forays into pharmaceuticals and financial services.

Before Burns retired, the business and the popular press both touted AT as one of the world's most profitable and admired companies, and every commentator gave him full credit for the company's successful transformation and expansion. Books touted the genius of his management style.

Sanford's obituary was filled with juicy details of the fight he and Burns got into over Sanford's handling of the copyright case that AT lost to publishers of scientific journals. There were more juicy details about the divorce and the settlement Sanford had won for Alice Burns, after Harlan became romantically entangled with Bethia Davenport, the founder and CEO of a major women's personal care products company. The lovers married soon after the divorce became final.

Sanford and I hadn't gotten to this part of his life's story, and I wondered how much more there was to it than the *Times* had seen fit to print. I couldn't interview the Burnses about it, unfortunately. They'd been killed two years earlier, when their private plane crashed on a night flight to their Montana ranch.

I put the obituary clippings into a manila folder that I tossed on the car's front seat. Sanford's memorial service was being held at the large synagogue located next to the city's leading private school. It was cool and sunny. A wind from the north had cleared out the unsettled weather of the past several days. I had to wait at a light at the school before I could continue toward a parking spot near the synagogue.

Groups of students crossed in front of the car, the boys in chinos, the girls in absurdly short pleated skirts. I wondered idly what Sanford would have had to say about the parade of youthful thighs and knees. He wouldn't have let it pass him by without a comment – I was sure of that. I was already missing him, I realized.

The synagogue auditorium was filled with light and well dressed people. I stood on the side, about halfway down the aisle. I spotted

Gwennie first, and then Bill and Iris Kramer. Not far from them were
Maggie and Tim Hartnett. I recognized other men and women from
Sanford's firm; I'd seen them in elevators and corridors of the office
building where the firm had its offices and where I'd perched for the last
several months. I recognized some politicians and even a couple of media
personalities. I spotted Martin Fantock, the head of the local public radio
station, who had dined with Patricia and me one night.

Except for these few people, I didn't know anyone in the big crowd
that had gathered to pay homage to Sanford. It came home to me, yet
again, that I wasn't really part of the place where I mostly lived now. The
cashiers at the store where I bought newspapers knew me as a regular
customer. My doctor seemed to remember me from one year to the next.
The hygienist who scraped my gums called me by name as soon as she
spotted me in the waiting area, and the periodontist knew me by more than
the condition of my mouth. I could name a few more people I did business
of one sort or another with. But with only a few more exceptions, such as
the Stantons and Mary Howard, I was still an outsider in Patricia's old
home town.

The eulogy was given by a pale, chunky man in a blue suit, white
shirt, and dark tie, who introduced himself as the temple's chief rabbi. He
was quick to admit that he and Sanford had never been close. He'd tried to
engage Sanford whenever they'd met, but Sanford stopped in at the temple
only once a year, when he handed over a substantial check in support of the
religious school, "probably to atone for his misbehavior when he was an
unwilling Hebrew school student," the rabbi said in as mischievous a tone
as he could muster. There was a release of laughter in the audience. They
don't know the half of it, I thought, as I recalled the story of the purloined
print from the Hebrew school's principal's office.

Buoyed by the laughter, the rabbi warmed to his task. He might not
have known Sanford very well, but he'd read the obituaries and he'd spoken
with Sanford's many colleagues and friends, so he had plenty of material for
a eulogy. He told stories, many of which I'd already heard from Sanford
himself or at my lunches with him, Bill, and Maggie. The rabbi spoke about
Sanford's love of games – he gave the example of estimating the amount of
the check at another table – and how he treated his legal skirmishes as
games.

He didn't let on as to whether or not he'd heard about Stanford's
penchant for commenting about the physical appearance of any woman
who happened to be in his line of sight. He stuck to stories that were
funny and poignant and showed Sanford in a good light. The rabbi used
them to embellish a practiced eulogy that could fit any successful and

recently deceased man or woman – "so much accomplished, so much still left to do" was no doubt a stock phrase. At the end, there were affectionate anecdotes that the rabbi credited to Sanford's most intimate colleagues and friends. I didn't hear Gwennie's name, but put any thoughts about its absence aside.

As the crowd shuffled past me on the way to the exits, I heard murmurs of approval for the job the rabbi had done. He'd given the crowd what they'd come to expect from him, and they were satisfied. Sanford's sendoff had been up to the rabbi's usual standard, I heard an older man whisper to a henna-haired woman, who nodded affirmatively. Perhaps they were hoping that the rabbi would do as well for them when their time came.

I caught Bill Kramer's eye and nodded to him. He and Iris waved back, the smiles on their faces tempered by the sadness that was expected of them and I had no reason to doubt was genuine. I made eye contact with no one else. I got into my car and drove toward home. The funeral procession went off in a different direction.

I hadn't decided against going to the cemetery until the end of the pale rabbi's eulogy. It was then that I thought that I had said my last goodbye to Sanford. I was done with him, to be blunt and unsentimental about it. There would be no more sessions, no more reckless rides with him down the dirt road to his summer house, and no more stories from his lips. I wouldn't write a magazine profile, or a biography, or whatever our collaboration would have produced. The obituaries and perhaps even the eulogy would have to be, as far as I was concerned, the final formal words about Sanford.

I met Bill and Maggie Hartnett for lunch the next day. We went to our usual restaurant, off the lower lobby of the building where Sanford's firm had its offices and where I was still perched, although for how long I hadn't decided. We sat at Sanford's table in the back on the raised platform. From there, I could see everything and everyone in the entire restaurant, just as Sanford had. From the moment we sat down, I missed his running commentary, as obnoxious as it sometimes was, about the women in the place.

After Angie took our order, I followed Bill's gaze to the entrance. With Sanford gone, there were no more gotcha moments, and it was safe to look around. Or so I thought. A large young woman had just come through the front door. Even from a distance, I could tell that she was attractive, with dirty blonde hair pulled back from a pretty face. Below the waist, she was big. Her heavy thighs filled out her jeans.

I can only imagine what Sanford would have had to say about that one," Bill said. "I'm not going to even try. What about you, Mordecai, or you, Maggie? Channel your best Sanford."

"Oh, please," Maggie said emphatically. "Who gives a shit what nasty comments Sanford would have made about those big thighs that draw your attention away from that pretty face. There, I'm channeling him, whether I want to or not."

"Take it easy, Maggie," Bill said. He put a hand over hers. She moved her hand a few inches, out from under his. "She won't hear any comments, nasty or otherwise, and neither will anyone else. Whatever we say about her, it won't hurt her."

"You don't understand," Maggie said. The light reflected on her oversized glasses such that I couldn't see her eyes.

"It's just a game, like it always was," Bill said.

"It's a game, is that what it is?" Maggie folded her arms across her breasts. "Then what are the rules? Who keeps score? How would we know when someone's won and the rest of us have lost?"

"Sanford made the rules and kept score, of course," Bill answered. "In this case, he would have said that we had to guess whether the young woman was eating alone or meeting someone, whether that someone was a man or a woman, and we'd have to guess some stuff about that person. We'd have to turn our backs so we couldn't see who she was meeting – or whether she was going to eat alone."

"After toting up the score, Sanford would tell us that the pretty face and the big thighs had led him to an inescapable conclusion," I said.

"Which would have been that one, I suppose," Maggie said scornfully. A bearded young man, tall and slender, wearing jeans and a sweater, moved to stand next to the young woman. He'd been waiting for her at the bar. He took her hand and guided her to a table in the middle of the restaurant.

"Boyfriend or husband?" I said.

"Sanford would have figured it out," Bill said, laughing. "Angie would have confirmed it with a few clever questions when she took their order."

"Oh, for shit's sake," Maggie said. She threw her hands in the air, and then she got up from the table. Bill and I looked up at her. "I can't stand this," she said. "Sanford's not here. He's never going to be here – or anywhere else, except six feet underground in that cemetery. I hate that. And I hate that we're pretending that it's acceptable, and that we can somehow make up for it." She turned and snatched her handbag off the table. "I'm going," she said.

"Don't leave," Bill said. "We'll find other things to talk about."

"There isn't anything else to talk about – not for awhile, at least." Bill reached out for her. "Have your lunch," Maggie went on. "I'll be all right. I'll pick up a sandwich and eat at my desk. God knows, we have plenty of work up there."

I watched Maggie walk stiffly, her back arched, head held high. A big man ducked back to let her go past him, as she made her way swiftly out of the restaurant's rear door. There had been no point in trying to stop her, if it indeed had been possible. Now the table seemed too large for just Bill and me. "What was that all about?"

"That was Maggie being Maggie. I've seen her do that when she's pissed. So I'm not surprised. The thing is, she and Sanford had a special relationship. They worked together beautifully. Sometimes, she could even anticipate what he wanted to do."

"I saw her give him a lot of shit, but she wasn't mean about it, as far as I could tell."

"You're quite right. It was all part of the game."

"What game was that?"

"The game of winning the case, I should think."

"Of course – I should know that."

Angie brought us coffee and sandwiches – turkey club, my old standby, for me, and a grilled chicken wrap for Bill. We told Angie to leave the salad Maggie had ordered and to bring an extra plate. We ate silently for a couple of minutes.

"I'm thinking," I said finally, "that with Sanford gone, it doesn't make much sense for me to continue with the project he and I were working on."

Bill put his wrap down on his plate and looked at me intently. "Don't give up on the project just because of what happened to Sanford. You can continue without him."

"What would I accomplish? The *Times'* obit covered the high points of his life pretty thoroughly, it seems to me. I'm afraid there's not much left for me to do but fill out the story with more details."

"C'mon, Mordecai, you'd be doing a lot more than that. I'm surprised at you."

"Of course, I know the difference between an obit and a profile or a full-fledged biography. There's more to it than density of detail. But Sanford's gone, and he was the main source of material."

"But he was hardly going to be the only source. Who else have you talked with?"

"Well, I haven't talked to anyone besides Sanford, actually – unless you were to count yourself and Maggie, although we haven't done anything formally yet, of course."

"I don't understand this reluctance to proceed. I'll bet you've started and finished other projects with a lot less to go on at the start. I'm sure you must have a lot more on your plate right now, but you did put some time and energy in with Sanford, and it would be a shame to toss it all away."

"Actually, I'm not all that busy. I've toyed with writing a memoir about Patricia, but I haven't gotten very far. And one of my publishers is hounding me about an edited reference book that he wants me to dream up and about some possible revisions of the edited books I completed years ago. He's even foisted a young woman on me to help get the project off the ground. I've told him that he wants me to teach her everything I know about getting these books done so she can carry on without me."

Bill ignored my diatribe. "Look, Mordecai, why don't you see some of the people in Sanford's life? Talk to them, see what you come up with, and then decide about the project."

"You sound like you badly want me to see it through."

"One, I cared for Sanford." Bill was using his thumb andfingers to count off the points he was making. "Two, you're curious about Sanford, aren't you?" I nodded my head in agreement. Bill went back to his fingers. "Three. I think know a bit about your work." He went on. "Four, I have no doubt you'll dig up everything and put it in whatever you decide to do, warts and all, as they say. So five, I believe that Sanford's legacy will be burnished by your writing about him, no matter what you write."

Bill had run out of digits, and I'd run out of excuses. No matter, I was back in the Sanford Glickauer biography business, for better or worse.

Bill and I agreed that it would be a good idea for me to bring Gwennie up to date on the Sanford project, and he arranged for a meeting. A few days after he convinced me to continue with the project, I drove out to the house in the hills.

It was a sunny afternoon, and the dirt road into the property was dry. The car sent up a dust cloud, even at the slow pace I maintained. When I pulled up to the front of the house, I was greeted by a large animal. It remained motionless, and after I got out of my car, I realized that the animal wasn't alive.

"I put it there to keep unwanted critters, human and otherwise, away from the house." Gwennie was standing in the open doorway, a smile on her face.

"It looks like the one at the golf course where Bill and I play sometimes."

"It's a carbon copy. A woman I know who plays golf there told me about it. Perhaps you've run into her there." Gwennie said a name I was unfamiliar with, like most names from around here.

"Sorry, I don't know her. When did you install the animal, if I can call it that?"

"Not that long ago." Gwennie's tone was vague. "Tell me," she said, after a beat, "how do you find the road in here? I mean, what's your opinion of it?"

"It's all right, if you don't go too fast." Our eyes locked for an uncomfortable moment of silence. "I'm sorry about Sanford," I continued finally. I didn't know where else to take the conversation. "He must not have realized how dangerous the road was, although he could have read the outside temperature on his instrument panel, and he must have known that the potential for icing was present."

"He always drove the road much too fast, no matter what condition it was in. I warned him over and over about the danger he was putting himself in. But he kept telling me about the hallway he used to speed up and down in his tricycle when he was a kid. He said the road reminded him of the hallway."

"He told me all that."

"As if riding a tricycle indoors is equivalent to driving a four-thousand-pound automobile with a million horsepower in bad weather." Gwennie shook her head and put her hands on her broad hips. She was dressed in loose-fitting bleu de travail. I was reminded of the woman in the restaurant that Bill had pointed out. I watched Gwennie silently. "You should come in," she said after a few seconds.

We walked up the stairs into the living room. I looked at the life-size Sam Hudson nude on my right, and then turned and looked at the one to my left. The paintings, and the women in them, were as remarkable now as they had been the first time I'd ever seen them. I felt Gwennie's eyes on me.

"I'm having some people over," she said, "so I can't give you much time. And I hope you don't find me rude, but I'm not going to offer you anything to drink. I thought you might want another look at the ladies, though, to make your trip out here worth your while."

"Thanks – they're quite magnificent." We nodded simultaneously, as if in mutual satisfaction about the quality of our judgment. "I won't take up much time. I just came out here to ask you formally if you had any objections to my continuing with the project Sanford and I started. Bill filled you in on it, didn't he?"

"He told me about the project so far. My question is, how do you plan to proceed, now that my husband is no longer available to talk with you?"

"I plan to talk with the people who were important in his life."

"That would include me, I take it."

"It would, of course. I can't imagine drawing a complete picture of Sanford's life without talking with you."

"That's certainly appropriate, but I'd like you to talk with the other people in his life before we talk."

"You're not concerned that I might form wrong impressions?"

"There's a very good reason for my request. I want to do everything I can to make sure that what you write about my late husband is the truth. As I see it, the best way for me to accomplish this is to be the last person you talk to about him."

I didn't see her point, but I decided not to dispute it. Instead, I said, "I can't give you the final say on what I write about Sanford, if that's what you're getting at."

"That's not how such projects work, is that what you're telling me?"

"That's correct, but you will have your say – and you can be the last person I talk with."

"So that's the best you can offer me?"

"I think you can trust me to portray Sanford truthfully. I don't have any axe to grind. I have no need to portray him in any particular way."

Gwennie looked directly into my eyes and held the look. "So we'll see him warts and all, with nothing airbrushed out of your portrait of him."

"Whatever I see is what you'll get." I turned around and found Sanford's profile in *The Afternoon Party*. "I want to write about Sanford more precisely than the way Sam Hudson painted him. Is that possible? It seems to me that Hudson takes some license. He's a painter, not a photographer, after all. Nevertheless he still captures the essence of the man, I believe. Well, that's what happens when an artist portrays another man, or a biographer writes about his life. The artist, or the biographer, is a filter. Can you live with the truth as I see it, which may not be the truth that you see, or anyone else you know sees?"

"I suppose I'll have to, unless I resort to taking legal action to ward you off the project. I've talked to Bill about doing so, and he's advised me not to take that route. I've agreed with him, because I respect his judgment, as my late husband did. But here's a question: You won't try to spice up the story, if it turns out to be too dull for your purposes, will you?"

"I think I'll get what I expect." I didn't know what that was, but the words, meant to mollify Gwennie, sounded right to me nonetheless.

"I hope you do," she said, "and nothing more. Or less."

CHAPTER FOURTEEN

I wanted to make finding an authoritative account of Sanford's imbroglio with Harlan Burns as simple a matter as possible, so I put in a call to Bob Steinberg to ask for help. Before I said anything, he snarled, "You haven't responded to Rachel Gormsby."

"You must have caller ID."

"Actually, I'm psychic, if that means anything to you science types."

"I'll get back to Rachel, I promise. Right now, I need your help with something else."

"You want to talk to Gilbert Ryden," Bob said in response, when I'd spelled out my request. "He spearheaded the publishers' association's efforts in the American Tractor case, even though his firm doesn't publish scientific journals and didn't stand to make a dime from the case."

"You make him sound selfless."

"Trust me, Gilbert's never even been accused of being selfless, although he might be the most courtly man you'll ever come across. The point is, he did understand then, as he no doubt does now, that if one group of publishers is getting ripped off by anyone who steals their content, all publishers, no matter what markets they serve, need to get involved in stopping the intellectual property theft. He worked very hard to keep all of the publishers committed to seeing the case through to its conclusion. He had to, because some of them got cold feet as Harlan Burns put up more and more of a fight and the litigation expense threatened to mount up."

"It sounds like Ryden's the person I should talk to."

"Definitely: his is an eyewitness account. I'll be glad to set up a meeting with him. Just make sure that you're up to speed about the case. You know, google the fucking thing. My fee is your promise that you'll return Rachel's phone calls."

I promised. I already knew what the outlines of the case were. It dated back to pre-Internet times, when the photocopier was king. AT, a large company active in several scientific, technical, and medical fields, had numerous researchers on the payroll. Many of them used learned journals in their daily work.

The journals were big, in terms of the number of articles and pages published annually, and subscriptions were very expensive. AT's management, ever cost conscious, in response to Harlan Burns' continual hectoring, permitted company librarians to maintain only a single subscription to each journal, no matter how many researchers used it.

Researchers didn't go to the company library to read journals of interest. Instead, librarians circulated a journal issue to any researcher who indicated that he or she routinely read that particular journal. Researchers would make copies of any articles of interest and retain them for future use.

That was a problem, if not downright illegal. Under United States copyright law, as I understood it, just because you buy a publication, you don't really own it. You can't make copies of all or a substantial part of a publication, unless it's for some purpose defined by the law as "fair use." Making copies of journal articles at American Tractor, a profit-making company, where the articles were used for commercial purposes, didn't qualify as fair use, and the copyright law required the company to pay fees for any article copying. This wasn't a hardship. The publishers had set up an organization, called the Copyright Clearance Center, where AT could remit any copying fees without much fuss.

So the publishers' trade association sued American Tractor, on the grounds that the company was using a scheme that circumvented the need to purchase multiple copies of journals and then wasn't compensating journal publishers for large numbers of copies of articles that the company made. The publishers asserted that the numbers of copies had to be large because American Tractor employed lots of researchers who needed to use journal articles in their daily work.

It wasn't a trivial case, or an arcane point of law that only a lawyer, or a law school professor, could love. Quite the contrary: if the publishers won the case, then a principle would be established under which substantial amounts of revenues would be realized.

"Bob tells me you're here for an eyewitness account of the great confrontation," Gilbert Ryden said to me. "I'll endeavor not to disappoint." He was a handsome man, in his early seventies, I guessed, although he looked younger. The gravitas gave away his age. His manners, I surmised after about eleven seconds, were impeccable, as were his clothes – a lightweight tweed suit, a pale pink Oxford cloth shirt, the button down collar rolled just right, and a regimental striped tie.

He sat on a wing chair, across a glass coffee table from the sofa where Bob and I were perched. The book-lined office was furnished in mahogany and dark leather. Persian carpets covered the floor. I'd hesitated in the doorway, wondering whether I should remove my shoes, ala *Mad Men*, until I noticed that Ryden's gleaming brogues were still on his feet.

"The fact of the matter was," Ryden continued, "that even before we publishers sued American Tractor, my colleagues and I were concerned with the extreme disparity between their resources and ours. Their annual sales were not only greater than those of any single publisher, they easily exceeded those of all publishers combined. My colleagues and I feared that if Harlan Burns directed AT's lawyers to drag the case out, which the company could easily afford to do, the publishers association would panic at the amounts of money being spent and would throw in the towel.

"Now, if you were American Tractor's legal counsel, how would you go about forcing the publishers to spend the maximum amount of money on the case?" Ryden's smile as he asked me the question indicated his confidence that I knew the answer.

I tried not to disappoint him. "They would have demanded that lawyers from both sides go through every researcher's office in every American Tractor location, in order to count every photocopied journal article...."

"Plus the number of pages in each one," Bob interjected, "because the amount of a copyright fee for a journal article depends on the number of pages in the article." A soft belch made him pause.

"It would have been a time-consuming process, of course," Ryden said. "The longer it lasted, the more money it would have cost. And as the costs mounted up, a split would have developed in our association between the publishers who would have been willing to spend whatever it took to fight to the end of the case and the publishers who would have said that the price of an uncertain victory was becoming much too high."

"Fortunately, however," Bob murmured.

"Fortunately, perhaps," Ryden continued, "but a great deal of credit should be shared between counsel for both sides and the judge who presided over the case. As you know, our counsel floated the idea that instead of both sides having to go through every researcher's office, they would select one researcher, go through his office, tabulate the number of photocopied articles and pages, and apply those numbers across the entire company.

"The judge bought the idea – and so did AT's legal counsel, who was Sanford Glickauer, their outside patent attorney, who'd been retained by the company to litigate the copyright suit we publishers had brought. Deriving the numbers at issue in this fashion would save a lot of time and money – and keep the playing field level, despite AT's financial advantage over all of the publishers put together.

"Everyone knows about the idea and the fact that it was adopted. But what everyone doesn't know is what happened at the meeting between my publishing colleagues and I and several of American Tractor's senior managers, including Harlan Burns, when the idea was put forward for final approval between the contending parties. Now that both Glickauer and Burns are dead, I doubt that their reputations will suffer any harm from any revelations from that meeting, which, to my knowledge, has never been publicly discussed. I believe I have the liberty to be just a little bit indiscreet, if you will."

I caught a slight smile on Bob's face and ventured one of my own. Ryden uncrossed his legs, adjusted his trousers so they didn't strain at his knees, and leaned forward. When he continued, the volume of his voice was a little lower than it had been. "We met in the board room at American Tractor's headquarters in Stamford."

"Michael Fletcher and Nigel Fisher, the F-boys as they're called tongue-in-cheek, were there with you," Bob interjected. He burped softly when he was finished.

"That's right. Our legal counsel, John Gardner, was there, of course, as was Ted Jenkins, the head of the publisher's association. We all sat in very comfortable leather swivel chairs on one side of a large, beautiful table, which looked like it had been made from a single piece of wood from an enormous, very old tree. On the other side was the American Tractor team – just four people, including the chief librarian, the vice president for research, and of course, their chief outside legal counsel, Sanford Glickauer, plus Harlan Burns himself.

"I'd met Sanford many times before, but I'd never been in close proximity to Harlan. He was much smaller than I'd guessed from the photographs I'd seen, – although hardly a bantam weight. I couldn't help but notice how elegantly and crisply turned out he was."

"He was famous for his tailoring," I remarked.

"Saville Row from head to toe," Bob cracked.

Ryden smiled. "We thought the meeting was just a formality, where we would lay out our proposal and everyone would sign off on it. It was a done deal, we thought. The two lawyers did the talking, but it was Harlan who drew my attention. As the main points were set forth, his smooth, tanned face became deep red. He looked like his blood vessels were ready to burst.

"Now, our side had been given to understand that Sanford had *carte blanche* to negotiate the deal. We surmised that his authority came from the highest levels at American Tractor. Of course, one should assume nothing in this world. And as I observed Harlan, I wasn't at all sure what to believe. Had Harlan not been apprised of the deal? Or did he know full well what the deal consisted of, and was he play-acting for some purpose?"

"Did anyone else notice Harlan's behavior?" I said.

"It was impossible not to, especially when Harlan stood up, shaking with rage and started bawling – a world-class, Steve-Jobs-level tantrum. Then, as he tried to catch his breath in the midst of racking sobbing, he started shouting. 'If you publisher bastards want to find out how many copies of your shitty journal articles my researchers have made, then you'll have to go through every desk and every file cabinet in every one of their offices! You can't rely on fucking sampling!' I may not be giving you what he said word for word, but I can vouch for the profanity. 'And you'll have to foot the bill, you cheap cocksuckers,' he screamed. He was spitting the words out, and mucous was coming out of his nose. He was a sight to behold."

Gilbert Ryden sat back in his upholstered chair, legs crossed, hands folded in his lap. He was consulting his memory, I guessed, making sure he got the details of the story right. I picked up from his last sentence and looked at this erudite and cultivated man carefully. He was unlike anyone I'd ever met in my writing and editing career. None of the editors or other publishing people I'd worked with had his aura of respectability and authority. I shouldn't have expected them to, of course. They didn't own a company, after all.

Ryden seemed like a throwback to an earlier era, when publishing was known as "a gentleman's profession," not an "accidental" one. He acted like he'd been born to the role he was playing, simply because publishing was in his blood. No wonder he felt obligated – I was sure he did, because of his eminence - to represent a segment of the industry he had no part of in the negotiations with American Tractor.

After a few moments Bob broke the silence. "I would have been laughing," he said, as he emitted a gentle fart.

"It was certainly undignified, but it wasn't funny. No one was laughing, to be sure. Then Harlan was yelling at Sanford. 'Why did you agree to make things easy for these goddamn thieves? Don't you know who your client is? These bloodsuckers want to steal money from my company. We bought their fucking journals, with all that useless research crap in them. We own them. They can't tell me what I can and can't do with something I fucking own, I don't care what the fuck it is. And this prick of a judge: just who the fuck does he think he is, siding with the bloodsuckers against my great company? Who? Who?'"

Gilbert's voice had risen, as if he was speaking in tongues. He looked uncomfortable. Repeating the f-bombs must have been unsettling. He looked down at the carpet, and then back up at Bob and me. "No one on the American Tractor side of the table made any effort to restrain Harlan. I had no doubt that they'd seen such performances before, and there was no point in intervening. Harlan was a brilliant executive in some sense, but in this instance he was out of control. My colleagues and I were stunned by his display of vituperation. And then, once Harlan stopped screaming at Sanford, the board room became eerily quiet.

"Harlan stood behind his chair, breathing heavily. He glared at Sanford. I could see that Sanford was seething. But he controlled himself. As did I, as I remember. Without saying a word, I pushed my chair back, got up, and my colleagues followed me out of the room. In fact, none of us spoke until we had exited the building and were safely back out in the street.

"As I was leaving the board room, I looked back. Harlan was shooting his French cuffs. The redness on his face was fading. Sanford, his face set in stone, was standing. His briefcase was on the table, and he was stuffing papers into it. Neither man was looking at the other."

"Now that you've gone through the episode again," Bob said, suppressing a slight belch, "do you think it was an act on Harlan's part – to gain some sort of an advantage – or was it for real? He didn't pull his expensive suit jacket off, throw it on the floor, and jump up and down on it, after all. Or did you leave that detail out?"

Gilbert smiled shyly. "No, I wouldn't leave a detail like that out. In any case, Sanford thought the tantrum was for real. I'm quite certain about that. His body language was unmistakable."

"In the end, of course, the tantrum had no effect on the proceedings."

"Correct, Bob: two days later, the judge ordered American Tractor to comply with our discovery process. We didn't hear another word from Harlan personally. Why should we have? After all, the company's annual report made the eventual settlement sound like a rounding error on the bottom line."

"Let me guess," I said. "Sanford and Harlan didn't kiss and make up."

"Correct, Mordecai. Sanford, we learned, was off the case immediately after the abortive meeting, which didn't surprise anyone. A week later, he called me. 'Good luck,' he said.

"I'm sorry that things went awry for you, I told him, or something to that effect. I didn't know what else to say.

"I remember his exact words in response: 'It's nothing more than a game,' he said. Then I remember a pause, which must have lasted several seconds. I sensed he would add something, so I remained silent. 'And it's far from over,' he said finally."

A few days later, I was playing detective and on the move. I drove a rental car from the Charleston airport to the Hominy Grill, which was in a neighborhood on the upper part of downtown. I was seated in the main dining room. The wooden tables were covered with sheets of craft paper. Ceiling fans revolved slowly. The wrought iron wall sconces sported burgundy shades.

Another room, another solitary meal, I thought. It no longer mattered where I was: I was, yet again, eating alone at a small table in a restaurant crowded with people smiling and talking to each other. My companion, as usual, was the *Times*, the Gray Lady she used to be called even after the advent of color in the paper.

The wait staff wore street clothes. A young man brought a paper bowl of boiled peanuts, meant to be eaten in the shell, I figured. I ate several, and then tucked into a delightful plate of Red Snapper, a helping from a squash casserole, and some lima beans cooked with shitake mushrooms. I'd expected artery clogging, Southern food, and it was present on the menu, but my meal seemed surprisingly benign from a health standpoint. Too healthful, it seemed to me, because there wasn't quite enough food on the plate. So I ordered a piece of cornbread, which didn't come with the meal, to go.

It was about a twenty mile drive to Kiawah Island, where Alice Burns lived. The road took me over a drawbridge that spanned the Intracoastal Waterway and then a high fixed bridge over more water and a huge expanse of marsh. For half the journey, however, much of the landscape was suburban. I passed half a dozen shopping plazas, a rather shabby looking golf course, small churches, restaurants, medical offices in small one-story buildings, construction businesses, and several places that sold fireworks. It looked messy - sometimes prosperous, sometimes down at the heels.

After a sharp left, there were intermittent long stretches of overhanging live oaks that darkened the atmosphere and might have provided a Southern Gothic element, had it not been for the steady stream of two-way traffic and the back and yellow striped warning signs in front of trees growing dangerously close to the edges of the narrow road. Then there was a last stretch of several miles where there were two lanes in either direction, with a wide grass median.

A roundabout shot me out past a Kiawah Island sign and soon onto a causeway bordered with tall grass. Marsh extended out from both sides of the road. There were trees ahead and in the distance on both left and right. The landscape was completely flat. The blue sky above, which seemed free of pollution, looked immense. There were white and blue-gray birds everywhere, large creatures, some of them standing at attention, others soaring through the clear air.

I had to stop at a gatehouse. "Bornstein visiting Mrs. Burns on Flyway," I said to a guard who looked down at me from a window above the car. She gave me a large pass, which I put on the dash, as she instructed.

Once I was inside the gate, the world changed. It wasn't messy any more, and by no stretch of the imagination could a single square inch of it be called down at the heels. I passed a green bordered by bunkers and a water hazard, and then the road cut through trees. There were openings in the woods where I could see lush fairways and some houses beyond. I passed a fire station and large wood signs for markets, golf clubs, and a park. There was a sign for The Sanctuary, the island's sole hotel. Except for a few golfers and some people on bicycles, the place seemed very quiet. There was landscaping at the sides of the road, but the effect was natural, not fussy.

The road rose up a short hill, and then there was a second gate. The guard peered at the windshield, and as he waved me through, he indicated that I should make an immediate right turn.

Now there were houses lining the road on both sides. All of them were large. Each had a flight of steps leading up to the front door. I found Flyway, Alice Burns' street, after a few minutes. Her house number was on the right, after another few minutes.

I eased the car up onto a brick apron and proceeded slowly down a long drive. I parked in front of a set of garage doors. The house, which had not been visible from the road, was four stories tall. There was a pond in front. An alligator was lying at the edge of it. I could hear the ocean off to my right, but I couldn't see it. A mound of dunes blocked the view.

The property looked carefully landscaped, but there was no grass to mow. The gravel crunched underfoot as I made my way to the wide stairs leading to the front door, which was flanked by pairs of large windows.

A middle-aged Hispanic woman, with a pleasant face, answered the door chime. She was dressed in crisply pressed black slacks and a black tunic. She turned without a word, and I crossed the threshold. I closed the door behind me and followed her through a wide foyer into the edge of a very large room with a floor-to-ceiling glass wall opposite. It was filled with sky.

We turned left into a large library. Three walls were completely covered by bookcases filled to capacity. The fourth wall had a large window, flanked by groupings of pictures.

I was going from one library to the next, I thought. But this one was different than the last, for there was no desk. Instead, the center of the room was dominated by a large white sofa, which faced two wing chairs. There was a coffee table, with a pile of books on it, between the sofa and chairs. Four floor lamps were arranged for reading.

As I approached the sofa, a slender blonde of medium height and indeterminate age got gracefully to her feet and put out her hand in greeting. She was a beautiful woman, with a scrubbed face, clear blue eyes, and short hair that looked like it needed little attention beyond washing. She was dressed identically to the woman who'd ushered me into the library, except that her outfit was white, and there was a heavy gold chain at her throat.

I heard the door click shut softly behind me.

"Alice Burns," the blonde said. She shook my hand quickly and with hardly any pressure. "Am I correct, Mr. Bornstein, that this is your first time on Kiawah?" She'd asked the question before I'd had the chance to introduce myself. Her crystalline diction testified to her years on the stage, although she hadn't acted since her divorce from Harlan. I'd read her Wikipedia pages, and I knew this much about her.

"Please call me Mordecai."

"If you'll call me Alice."

"It's a deal. As for Kiawah, you're correct. I did read up on it, though – origins as a plantation, development by the Kuwaitis in the Seventies, and all the rest. It's mentioned in *Porgy and Bess*, I believe. From the little I've seen of it, I can tell that it's quite beautiful. Is that what brought you here – the beauty of the landscape?"

"That, of course, and the solitude I found here, which was something I craved after I divorced Harlan." She paused. "And after I got rid of Sanford Glickauer." Her eyes roamed over the bookshelves.

"Now, I have my books. I can get to the beach on my boardwalk over the dunes. I get up for the sunrise every day and jog by the ocean. I can ride my bike or play golf most days. It rarely gets very cold here. Carmela sees to my needs. She does all of the grocery shopping for the two of us. I've even taught her how to buy good wine. She cooks our meals. Some nights, when what's on Turner Classic Movies pleases both of us, we watch it together."

She sat down on the sofa and crossed her legs. I sat down on one of the wing chairs. I didn't ask any questions – not yet.

"Except for Carmela, I don't need anyone," Alice continued. "She goes home to her family two or three nights during the week, and she has Sundays off. It's not far for her. I bought a small house for her and her family in a convenient location a few months after she came to work for me."

I idly wondered whether Alice missed the applause she'd received when was on the stage, but I didn't mention it. "You must have interesting neighbors," I said instead.

"The people who own these enormous houses spend only a few weeks of the year in them." She smiled for the first time since I'd been with her, but the smile didn't reach her eyes. Her acting skills are in mothballs, I thought. "Welcome to the beach mansions of the one percent." She snorted mirthlessly.

"I know what it's like to be alone most of the time. . . ." Alice seemed to be looking through me, and I finished the rest of the thought in my head: "although it's not by choice in my case." If she was giving any indication that she had any interest in my life, I was missing it. It's probably the case, I thought, that the lives she encounters in books are the only ones she has any desire to deal with.

"Perhaps I was alone even when I was married to Harlan. I didn't realize it at the time. We were always so busy, always on the go. He was often away on business; I was in one play after the other, it seemed. Sometimes we traveled together, and we went to parties together. There were even evenings at home, with just the two of us.

"But we never really talked. Harlan was always occupied with some business matter; I was always learning my lines. I could always get his full attention in bed, but only for a short time – too short a time." Alice snorted again and stifled a laugh that didn't reach her eyes.

I pretended to ignore the joke about Harlan's sexual prowess. "There must have been some exciting times. You both performed at such a high level."

She abruptly changed the subject. "Did anyone ever tell you that it was Sanford who introduced Harlan to Bethia Davenport?"

"I hadn't heard that." I tried to keep any surprise out of my voice.

"Oh yes, he orchestrated a meaningful encounter, in his own inimitable way. The encounter, which I'll get to in a minute, was a key part of a complicated game of revenge that Sanford concocted to pay Harlan back for his humiliation. Game was the word Sanford used when he eventually told me what he'd done."

"The word game always fit Sanford."

"And the angrier Sanford was about something, the more patient – and the better at playing the game – he became. He liked to take his revenge cold, and that made it all the more total.

"The first part of the game involved the setup. Sanford needed to find someone who would be irresistible to Harlan. Then he had to arrange an encounter that would force Harlan to throw caution to the winds in his pursuit of that someone."

"He needed an irresistible woman."

"Not exactly: he needed a woman who he could make irresistible to Harlan. You understand the difference?"

"Of course."

"Sanford set his sights on Bethia Davenport not only because she was beautiful – she reminded everyone of Elizabeth Taylor – but also because she was a great business success. But those attributes weren't enough for Sanford's purposes in and of themselves. There was still work to be done.

"The place to start was with Bethia herself, of course. Now, even though she was filthy rich, she didn't need to surround herself with a retinue of people whose job it was to shield her from the public. She had an aura that shielded her, I think. Selling women the means to preserve their beauty and allure might have been a key to people's respecting her privacy."

"You mean that women, especially, didn't want to distract her from her purpose."

"I think that's right. Additionally, she hired other women – ageing but still glamorous supermodels, for example – to be the public faces and bodies for her products, so her own face and figure weren't always on view.

"Of course, Sanford knew exactly what she looked like, and it didn't take him long to engineer an encounter on the street that looked entirely serendipitous. He walked up to her outside a restaurant where she'd had lunch with a couple of other women and he picked her up. Just like that." Alice snapped her fingers.

"He'd done the same thing years before with another woman he wanted," I said.

Alice gave no indication that she'd heard me and continued with her story. "Right at the beginning, he made it clear to Bethia that he picked her up because he wanted to fuck her, and not just once." Alice bit down hard on her lower lip as she uttered *fuck*.

"He was a married man. Wasn't he concerned about being found out?"

"He was married to Gwennie at the time. He told me later that she wasn't paying much attention to what he was doing, and with whom."

"But whether Gwennie bothered to suspect anything or not, there was the rest of the world to consider, wasn't there?"

"Sanford took care of the rest of the world when he and Bethia concocted a cover story to explain why they were spending so much time with each other and were often seen in public together. So when the premier gossip mongers from the *New York Post's Page Six* asked them about their relationship, they said that Sanford was working on patent and trademark issues for Bethia's product lines. *Page Six* reported the story with a straight face. They weren't sure whether they'd be sued for libel if they even so much as winked at the story."

"This is getting convoluted."

"The setup for Sanford's game was to toss a raft of questions in the air. Was his and Bethia's relationship strictly business? Or were they lovers? Were they being discreet about the relationship? Or were they flaunting a romance? What did it mean when they were seen in public together? There were scads of rumors, people certainly had their opinions, but no one knew anything for sure. This went on for a couple of months. Then Sanford decided it was time to bring Harlan into the game."

"I'm sorry, Alice, but I need to stop you here. Now, I don't read *Page Six*, or any other gossip columns. I don't watch much TV, either. So I wasn't aware at the time of this part of the story. In any case, what you're saying is that Sanford gave his relationship with Bethia an air of mystery. My question is, why?"

"He wanted two contradictory things: He wanted Harlan to believe there was sexual congress between himself and Bethia. And, when he got around to me, he wanted me to doubt that there had been any such congress."

"I'm sorry to keep asking, but why?"

"Sanford wanted to convince Harlan that he was taking Bethia away from her lover – Sanford himself - who Harlan loathed. And Sanford wanted me to believe that his primary motive in representing me in my divorce action against Harlan was to help a woman who'd been wronged, not to gain revenge against Harlan."

"And you and Harlan were both convinced about opposing – I don't know what to call them – OK, theories?"

"Crazy as it sounds – yes."

"Sanford trusted that you and Harlan wouldn't compare your ideas about whether or not he and Bethia were lovers."

"He took that risk, and it worked out."

"What about Bethia?"

"I doubt she cared that Sanford was playing a game with people's lives. Once he delivered the great Harlan Burns to her, she had what she thought was the grand prize, and everything else was immaterial, as far as she was concerned."

"How did Sanford pull this whole thing off?"

"I was there when Sanford got Harlan to take the bait. This is twenty-five years ago. There was at an enormous birthday party for one of those obscenely rich mutual fund chieftains. He rented the Rainbow Room at the top of Rockefeller Center – I think the room was still operating as a restaurant with dancing back then, but you could rent it for a private party - and installed for the night several celebrity chefs, a couple of famous bartenders, and half-a-dozen musical acts that nobody paid much attention to. The entire extravaganza must have cost millions."

"I would have loved to have been there." With Patricia, I thought. She would have loved it, too, no matter how foolishly extravagant we both would have found it.

"I'm sure you would have. The room was teeming with rich men smoking cigars – you could smoke anywhere in those days, of course – and startlingly beautiful women, scads of them. Nevertheless, Harlan and I were recognized, and homage was paid to us – the mogul and his actress wife. Harlan, bless his dear soul, had eyes for only one of the many beauties there – and it wasn't me, in case you haven't already guessed." Alice smiled again, and again the smile didn't touch her eyes.

"It was Bethia, of course."

"Although Harlan managed to hide it that night, he was mesmerized by her – not because she was the most beautiful or the wealthiest woman in the room, although she certainly was beautiful and very rich in her own right, but because she was on Sanford's arm. From the first instant, I later realized, Harlan was determined to do whatever it would take to possess her. He was mad – madder about getting her, and getting her away from Sanford, than mad about her as a woman. I don't think that he realized just how mad he was, and in what ways. He would became like a snorting, stamping bull, blind to everything but the objects of his desire and his wrath, and to his need to wrest Bethia away from Sanford. They were lovers, Harlan was certain of it, and it only increased his need and his desire for her."

"I've heard about how carried away Harlan could get. But how did he treat you at that time?"

"He ignored me."

"That must have been difficult to deal with."

"I was used to his ignoring me. It was nothing new. Soon, his behavior would be appalling."

"What was Sanford doing?"

"As far as I can tell, now that I've had time to think about it, Sanford was interested in only one thing: that he had Harlan where he wanted him. He must have been ecstatic once he determined beyond any doubt how the game he had set in motion would play out. Harlan would single-mindedly pursue Bethia. Sanford would act as if Harlan had forced him out of his relationship with Bethia. I would turn to Sanford, who would help me get a divorce that would cost Harlan half his fortune. During the divorce proceedings, unsavory details about Harlan's professional and personal lives would emerge, and his reputation would suffer." The unhappy smile took over Alice's face again.

"Good lord. It's as if Sanford was treating you as so much collateral damage in his war with Harlan."

"That's easy to understand now. But at the time, I didn't have a complete picture of Sanford's game. I blamed everything on Harlan, who deserved plenty of blame. But he hardly deserved all of it. What I think now is that he probably deserved less than Sanford did."

I was about to say something to the effect that the Sanford Alice was portraying sounded nothing like the Sanford I'd come to know in the weeks before his death, but I stopped myself. After all, Sanford had told me how calculating he could be. And the way he talked about women at the lunch table hadn't been particularly attractive. I had to admit to myself that Sanford had surely been capable of acting in the ways that Alice described. And the game she was recounting certainly sounded like one that Sanford would have enjoyed. I had the feeling that she would need no prodding to describe how the game played out.

"So now that Sanford had set the game in motion," I said.

"Oh, yes, and once he had Harlan hooked, he turned his attention to another cog in the machine – me."

There was soft knock on the door. Without waiting, Carmela entered the library with a tray. On it were two glasses of iced tea, two cloth napkins, and a plate of what looked like lemon squares – which they were. Alice nodded, and Carmela withdrew without a sound until the door lock clicked closed. Alice sipped from her glass, put it down on the tray, and settled back in the sofa.

"I've never told anyone this part of the story," she said, but there's no point in keeping it in any longer. The truth can't hurt Sanford now – although I wish it could."

"What about his widow? Can the truth hurt her?"

"He never cared about her. Why should I?"

"Do you mean that what you're about to tell me could do her harm?"

"I'll tell you what happened. You can decide what to do with the information." Alice leaned forward and sipped more iced tea. "Sanford insinuated – I don't have a better word for what he managed to do – he insinuated his way into my life. A week or so after the party, he pulled his old trick of casually running into me on the street after I'd had lunch with some friends. It had been a very long lunch, and it was late afternoon. He asked me if I'd like to have tea. I knew who he was, of course, and I agreed.

"He was very attentive. I thought he might be taking steps to seduce me. But instead of seduction, he offered friendship. Sanford lived and worked in New York then, and we met for tea or coffee every few days, it seemed, and we talked on the phone frequently."

"What did you talk about?"

"We became friends, and we talked about everything – books, the theater, politics, even sports – everything but my troubled personal life. Thinking back, it was if he consciously avoided the topic. I was taking time off from my career and spending a lot of time in the Upper East Side apartment that Harlan and I had. He and I didn't see much of each other. I thought he was busy with running American Tractor, until I learned that what I'd sensed might be happening between Harlan and Bethia at the Rainbow Room party had metastasized into a full-blown affair. He was fucking her every day and night, actually." Alice turned away from me, as if to hide any raw emotion that might invade her visage.

"How did you find out?"

"I think, now, that Sanford led me to my suspicions. And when they were finally aroused. . . ."

"Sorry to interrupt, but when were they aroused?"

"Two months after the party – what took so bloody long is beyond me - I asked Sanford for his help."

"Why did you go to him specifically?"

"Well there he was, wasn't he? Little old Johnny on the Spot, just here to help. He'd planned it that way – it was all part of his game – but I didn't realize it at the time."

"What did he do when you asked for his help?"

"At first he consoled me, told me what a wonderful woman I was and that he couldn't fathom – that was his word, fathom – how Harlan could even be interested in anyone else. I remember quite clearly that Sanford never said that Harlan had abandoned me. Sanford was very careful about not letting me get the idea that he was leading me on."

"Did his compliments comfort you?"

"I wasn't looking for comfort. I wanted revenge – as Sanford suspected I would."

"And he was able to provide revenge."

"He was in perfect position to do so, as I well knew. He knew about many American Tractor employees' negative feelings toward Harlan, and he'd got some of them to talk about him. Sanford had managed to learn what Harlan's retirement package might contain – which I didn't."

"I've never read about any employee ill will toward Harlan."

"Oh, it was there – for example, among the engineers who were left out in the cold – many of them were let go - when Harlan shifted the company's emphasis away from machinery to pharmaceuticals and finance."

"The business press didn't say much, if anything, about any negative results of that part of Harlan's stewardship. The emphasis in Harlan stories was relegated to the financial benefits of his requiring that AT focus only on businesses that could achieve and hold the number one or two rankings among their competitors."

Alice nodded. "You can add to that the matter of AT's testing laboratories."

"At one time AT published these wonderful books filled with information about materials properties that the testing labs had measured – and gave them away."

"Giving them away – that broke Harlan's heart."

"It must have. He did away with those books."

"And once the lawyers gave their blessings, he did away with testing labs, and then destroyed the reports with all the test results. One evening, when Harlan and the help were all out, I answered the phone. When I told the gentleman at the other end of the line that he couldn't speak with Harlan at that moment, he ignored me and launched into a rant about how Harlan had destroyed AT's premier collection of test specimens. The collection, the man on the line said, was priceless to universities, but no one had been able to persuade Harlan to donate it, even though there might have been a tax write-off of some sort. The man on the phone, who wouldn't give me his name, was sobbing, literally. He called Harlan a stubborn, vengeful bastard."

"Did you mention the call to Harlan?"

"It wouldn't have done any good."

"Then there was the retirement package."

"All those past and present AT employees, with an axe to grind as far as Harlan was concerned, became my allies. The things Sanford found out! All those guaranteed retirement perks were amazing – all the wine and brandy, all the vacations, the use of a private plane, and on and on. Harlan wasn't going to tell me about them. They amounted to a small fortune, over and above everything that Harlan already had and that we hadn't shared jointly." Alice paused, leaned forward, and sipped more iced tea. "It all came out in the divorce proceedings, which I'm sure you're familiar with."

"Yes, I've read the accounts in the newspapers."

"Then I think we're finished here." She picked up the book on top of the pile on the low table in front of her. "And I have to read the last three chapters before dinner."

I was being dismissed. "Thank you for your time and for your candor. But please, just one more question."

"All right, but I do have to get to my book,"

"You said earlier that you got rid of Sanford. Could you elaborate just a bit?"

"After the divorce proceedings concluded, Sanford and I became very close – very close, indeed. One night, before he went back to that Gwennie of his, he had a moment of hubris. Perhaps he was too relaxed. I don't know the reason, but he sat holding my hand, while he told me how he'd set up his little game and nudged it here and there until it played out so beautifully. I sat quietly until I'd heard every smarmy detail. I let him kiss me for just a moment, and then I walked him to the door of the apartment.

"When he turned to me for a last kiss and to say good night, I said, 'Goodbye, Sanford. Never contact me again directly, for any reason whatsoever. You have served your purpose, as I have served mine.' I closed the door after him and never did see him or speak to him again."

I didn't realize that Carmela had come into the library until she was standing nearly in front of me. "Carmela will show you to the boardwalk," Alice said. "It's windy on the beach this afternoon, but very beautiful. Take a drive around the island before you leave. You should see some of our wonderful wildlife. We have birds, a colony of bobcats, deer, and, of course, a great many alligators."

"I'll do my best."

"I trust you got what you came here for," Alice Burns said, and then looked down at her book.

Outside, Carmela pointed me toward the house's long boardwalk, which ran out over the dunes. I walked across it to the beach. The sun, still fairly high in the sky, was to my right. I could see a couple of large buildings far down the beach. One of them had to be The Sanctuary. The other way, to my left, I could make out only a smaller building. I turned around. Behind the dunes, there was a line of large houses, with little space between them.

I turned back to the ocean. Gulls were everywhere, looking busy. Armies of sandpipers were scurrying at the edge of the shoreline. It was their place, not mine. I felt like an intruder.

I didn't see any ships in the water. There was nothing on the horizon. Europe was out there, over there, somewhere.

The beach was nearly empty. There was only one other person on it besides me – an older man, it looked like, wearing a felt hat and street clothes that looked too heavy for the beach, and out of place on it. Just like me, another fish out of water, I thought.

CHAPTER FIFTEEN

"What did you think? That Sanford was a saint – a Jewish saint, no less? Well, we don't have them!"

"Take it easy, Bill," I said into the phone. I thought a chuckle might calm him down, so I tried one. You can be such a *putz*, I thought about myself.

"OK, I've never heard the entirety of this story about Sanford, Harlan and Alice Burns, and Bethia Davenport before. Did Sanford never tell it to me because he was somehow embarrassed about it, or thought it demonstrated that he was a conniving son of a bitch who got revenge against Harlan no matter how much it hurt several innocent women? Did he hide this episode from me because it was so sordid?"

"I didn't say any of those things."

"But the way you told it, the tone of your voice, gives away your disapproval."

"I think you're hearing something that's not there."

"It sounded to me as if you feel that somehow Sanford had duped you into thinking he was this gentle soul, and now you've found out that he was nothing of the kind."

"I don't have any illusions about Sanford. I don't think I ever did. For example, there's his marriage history."

"It's unusual, and you could say that it's somewhat brutal."

"Precisely. And then there are his comments about any woman who passed through his line of vision, and the fact that he didn't seem to care who heard him - not that Maggie, for instance, seemed at all fazed by his comments, no matter how crude they were."

"A lot of men make crude comments about women. Our gender is full of shits – discerning shits, of course, as Sanford would say if he were still around." Bill chuckled. He did a better job of chuckling than I did, it seemed to me.

"I'll admit that there were times during my conversations with Sanford when I felt close to him – like the time we talked about our fathers and what their selflessness and hard work meant to us."

"And you were thinking that you and Sanford were alike, brothers under the skin, so to speak? Are you shocked that Sanford was capable of concocting, setting up, and playing to his satisfaction a nasty revenge game? After all, it's the sort of behavior that you couldn't even contemplate, right?"

"I hope that I'm not that naïve. Like I said, I have no illusions about Sanford. Maybe I sound naive because I'm amazed at how Sanford was playing chess while the other three people in the story, all smart and successful, were playing checkers."

"There you go – it was nothing more than a game to him. And nobody got killed – not right away, that is, not until Harlan and Bethia were killed when their plane crashed."

"But did Sanford win or lose in the end? That's my question. Did he get his full measure of revenge on Harlan, who, after all, ended up married to the beautiful and rich Bethia?"

"You have to look at the whole picture. After all, Harlan's reputation took a major hit when disgruntled former AT employees got to air their grievances against him in the press, and the revelations about his retirement package came out. Plus the divorce from Alice cost him a bundle."

"I'll grant you that. Then there's Bethia. She got the famous and still rich Harlan, with his retirement package still intact, minus the hefty monthly payments to Alice. Better than being collateral damage, I suppose, like Alice was."

"You got sucked in by Alice. For one thing, how was she able to tell you such a detailed and compelling story about events that happened twenty-five years ago? Did she remember every detail, or did she make stuff up to make herself look like so much collateral damage from Sanford's nefarious game?"

"Well, she was an actress. So you're saying that she was playing a part in a drama she had written for my benefit."

"That would be another game, but I'm not accusing the woman of anything, although by your description of her current life, she does seem to be doing what she wants to with her days. Maybe that Carmela services her sexually, so she's got that area covered, as well."

"I can imagine Sanford coming up with that last thought. See, I don't have any illusions about him. And maybe he didn't win the game. After all, Alice sent him packing when hubris tripped him up and he told her everything he'd done."

"How do you know that slipup wasn't Sanford's way of getting out of any entanglement with Alice that would have jeopardized his relationship with Gwennie and made it more difficult for him to get back with her – if he'd even left off with her while the game was playing out? I wasn't acquainted with Sanford and Gwennie at that time, so I don't know for sure, but letting himself be tripped up by speaking out of turn does sound like a Sanfordian method of putting an end to something he wanted ended."

"So it was a kind way of disengaging from Alice – letting her feel superior, not abandoned again. Then he had to deal with Gwennie. We can only wonder what that must have been like – unless one of us has the balls to ask her."

"You'll probably have to, in order to get the full picture of Sanford." With that, Bill hung up on me, without any goodbye.

He called back a few minutes later. "Look, I cared very deeply about Sanford. I told you that when I convinced you to keep going with the biography or the profile or whatever the hell you're calling the project. And I told you that I expected you would find some warts. So maybe you found a big wart – if you believe Alice Burns, that is. Let me ask you this: Do you think she's lying for some reason?"

"I think she was telling the truth – or what she believes to be the truth. But why do you ask?"

"I'm a divorce lawyer. On my bad days I assume everyone is lying."

"Don't tell me that on your good days you assume everyone is telling the truth. Or at least some people are."

"Nah, on my good days I give a few people the courtesy of asking them whether they're telling the truth before I go to the default position – that everyone lies."

"So you think Alice Burns might be lying because what her story says about Sanford's character doesn't square with your picture of him."

"I'm a little surprised, that's all. I saw Sanford in action many times when we were interviewing people during divorce depositions."

"When people were under a great deal of stress."

"Exactly."

"And he could be tough, I'm assuming. I wouldn't be shocked to hear that he could bring people to tears – or to a screaming rage."

"He could do both, and did both. But it was part of the job. When you're a lawyer, withering examination comes with the territory."

"It's play-acting, then, isn't it? I wonder if he prevailed on Alice to teach him a few things about acting."

"That would have been another way for him to use her."

"So you acknowledge that Sanford could be cold-blooded."

"Of course. He wasn't always a warm, fuzzy teddy bear. When he knew what he wanted, he went and got it, no matter what obstacles might be in his path."

"It sounds to me like the tables are turned now – that you're the one who's shocked by the picture of Sanford that Alice Burns' story paints."

"I'm not shocked."

"Then why do you ask whether I think that Alice Burns is lying?"

"Maybe it's because the story lifts a curtain, and I can see what Sanford is like when one of his games involves him in such a deep, personal way."

"I didn't participate in very many of his games, so I don't have that big a sample. But come to think of it, the games of his that I did witness didn't touch him personally, although they could be intrusive when it came to other people."

"I'm not sure that's true. I'll have to think about it."

"How well did you really know Sanford?"

"Pretty well, I think. I mean, I worked with him for twenty years, and there were times when I was around him when we weren't actually working on something."

"Yes, I know that. But how much can you know about another man's life? You can't observe him twenty-four hours a day. You can't see what he does in bed – alone or with someone else – when he's not sleeping. Of course, you probably don't want to observe him having sex with his wife, or god forbid, with himself, unless you have unsavory tastes. You can't see what he does when he's alone in the bathroom. More to the point, you can't be inside his head every moment. You can't know what he thinks, can't see what he sees, can't hear what he hears, etc., etc. Even if a person is an open book, or wears his heart on his sleeve – we all know those clichés – you can't know every aspect of how he reacts inside himself to anything that happens to him or he sees happening to anyone else. So you can see expressions on a person's face of joy or sadness, to mention the easiest facial expressions to perceive, but how can you know the totality of what they really mean?"

"I hope you're not saying that your project is a waste of time."

"Not at all. What I'm saying is that you and I know some things about Sanford – you know many more things than I do – but we don't know everything. My talking with people who were in his life is filling out the picture because they had their own interactions with him and therefore see him differently than either of us."

"That's the way anyone investigating anything has to work. We lawyers know that. And what I also realize is that you and I should both be prepared to be surprised by what people tell you about Sanford."

"Shocked, even?"

I left the house at around eight, so I would miss the morning rush around New York and could have an early lunch at Teddy's Restaurant on Main Street in Cranbury, New Jersey. There was hardly any traffic on the Thruway and on the 287 loop that passed by Morristown and took me to the Jersey Turnpike. I got off at the Cranbury exit and found Teddy's without any trouble. The roast turkey in the club sandwich was real. I didn't care for the fries, but you can't have everything be to your liking in this world. Maybe the next one, if you believe in such things. After lunch, I got back on the Turnpike and made just one stop, in Maryland, before I had to fight the ridiculous non-rush-hour traffic crush on the Washington Beltway, which took me to Rockville, where Phoebe Armstrong lived.

There was still plenty of the afternoon left as the navigation system took me into her neighborhood of single-family homes, which had been there long enough for the trees at the curbs to have grown tall and full enough to provide shade over the sidewalks and half of the front lawns. Her house was standard issue, two-story suburban. It sat back from the curb on a cul-de-sac. I pulled into the driveway, and before I could get out of the car, I saw her in the front doorway. She must have been waiting for me.

She was dressed in a loose-fitting jogging outfit, as if she'd put on a little weight and was trying to hide it. "I googled you," she said. "I found pictures of you, some of them with your wife. She was beautiful. I'm so sorry about what happened to her."

"That's kind of you."

Phoebe looked like she was thinking hard about something. "Of course," she said, "it isn't true that a man who had a wife who looked like that can't be bad. I should know. Anyway, I'm good with faces, and you have one I can trust. So I guess that letting you in the house isn't dangerous."

I followed Phoebe into the living room. "Thanks for letting me come and see you." We sat down, and I put a small tape recorder on the table that was between us. "Do you mind?" I asked. I'd mentioned on the phone that I'd be recording the conversation, but it was prudent to check again, it seemed to me.

"That's fine. You can tape our conversation. Your project sounds very interesting. I'm sure people will want to read whatever you write about Sanford. Even me." She giggled lightly. "So we could have talked on the phone for as long as you wanted."

"I like to talk to the people in Sanford's life face to face."

"You just want to check some of them out, I bet." Phoebe giggled lightly again. I saw a mouth full of flawless white teeth. And from what I could see of the rest of her, she was worth checking out, even if she might be carrying a few pounds too many for her own taste. She had blonde hair brushed back from a round, beautiful, unblemished face. She wore lipstick, and she was made up around her brown eyes, but she looked healthy and natural. "Anyway, it was a long way for you to come," she said.

"The drive down here wasn't bad, and I got to have lunch at a place that serves a terrific turkey club. And then, as you say, I get to check you out."

"That's what Sanford was doing when he met me: checking me out." Phoebe smiled. The memory wasn't all that horrible, if I had to guess.

"Tell me about it. That's why I came down here, for you to tell me about things like how you and Sanford first met."

"Well, I was working for a guy who published paperback books. He was a dirty old man. My first day on the job I ran into the old man in the hallway. He stopped to shake my hand and welcome me aboard, and then he dropped his pen on the floor a couple of feet in front of me. He bent down to pick up the pen, and when I looked down at his large bald spot, I could see that he was trying to look up my skirt and was studying my legs as he straightened up. He wasn't very coy about it - that was for sure." Phoebe laughed lightly, and I smiled at her.

"You must have been fresh out of college."

"I'd just graduated from Fairleigh Dickinson. Fairly Ridiculous some people call it, even though it's a very good school. Maybe it's because it's in New Jersey."

"Maybe. But it is a good school."

Phoebe and I were sitting opposite each other on a sectional sofa that formed three sides of a rectangle. One long wall of the living room was three-quarters filled with bookshelves that were nearly empty of books. The shelves held a collection of small objects and framed photographs of Phoebe, her husband, and two sons – she'd told me about them when I'd phoned to ask if I could come down and talk with her. Home-theater speakers were arranged on the shelves, which were cut out in the center to accommodate a large flat-screen television set. There was an electronic reader on top of a pile of magazines on the low table between Phoebe and me.

"I used to walk up Madison Avenue and then over to Grand Central at lunchtime," Phoebe went on. "I loved that walk. I used to wear suits and dresses with pantyhose and high heels, and I looked terrific. I could make heads really turn in those days."

"Where did you go in Grand Central?"

"The Oyster Bar - I liked the Manhattan clam chowder."

"Me, too."

"It's good, isn't it? They give you a biscuit – a hot cross bun around Easter - and you can eat all the crackers you want. I used to sit at the counter, where they have bowls of them. I poured them into the soup, and they nearly filled me up. But I still had room for dessert. The Irish ladies who worked at the counter would give me the largest portions they could manage."

"Betty and May," I said. "Betty had dark hair and May was a redhead. They had wonderful brogues."

"They always looked out for me, those two. One day, while Betty was serving me dessert, she kept flicked her head to her left."

"That was Betty – always circumspect. So she wanted you to look at something or someone, I would guess."

"That's right. I didn't want to attract any attention to myself, either, so I reached down the counter for a bowl of the crackers, even though my dessert was sitting in front of me. It must have looked obvious, but I managed to steal a look at the gentleman who was sitting three or four seats away from me."

"Sanford, unless I miss my guess."

"I didn't know who the gentleman was, but I could see that he was well-dressed in a suit and tie and that he had a mane of blond hair combed back from his face. He looked a lot older than me, in his forties, maybe."

"Was he looking back at you?"

"Yes, and there was a slight smile on his face."

"What did you do next?"

"I finished my dessert, of course. Nothing would keep me from doing *that*. The Oyster Bar desserts were wonderful." Phoebe sighed with pleasure at the fond memory. "But I should have stayed away from them. They got me into a bad habit."

I sat quietly and waited for Phoebe to continue. In a second or two, she said, "when Betty brought me my check, I asked her how long the man had been staring at me. 'He's been doing it for the past few days,' Betty told me."

"How did that make you feel? Do you remember?"

"Probably a little creepy, but I don't remember exactly."

"Did you get up and run?"

"No, I didn't. I sat there and asked Betty if she knew who the guy was. 'His name is Sanford Glickauer,' she said, and then added something about his being a big-time attorney. Then I looked over at him again. There weren't any dishes in front of him, just a newspaper. I remember that because he told me later that he'd finished his lunch that day and was waiting, just like he had been doing for the past few days, ever since he'd started looking at me."

"He was waiting for you to stand up."

"Yes, he told me that. How do you know?"

"Because years later he told me that he loved to see a woman get up from a chair because then he got to see what she really looked like."

"That sounds like Sanford, all right."

"You had to get back to the office, I suppose, so sooner or later you had to get up and leave the Oyster Bar and walk up that incline to get to an exit to Forty-Second Street. Were you scared by this time?"

"Betty asked me if I wanted company when I left the restaurant. When I told her that I didn't, she asked me if I wanted her to call a cop. When I told her that I didn't want her to do that either, she asked me if I wanted her to get one of the big guys in the kitchen to come out and speak to Sanford, but I told her that wasn't necessary."

"What was Sanford doing while you and Betty were talking?"

"He got up when we finished, came over to me, and said something like, 'It's a beautiful day, miss. I'd love to walk you back to your office.' Then he told me his name and said that he had an office in a building at the southwest corner of Lex and 42nd."

"I know that address. It's called the Chanin Building. I got to know the woman who ran the bookstore on the ground floor, before she moved it to Scarsdale, down the block from Zachy's wine store."

"I didn't know her."

"I got along great with her, but other people thought she was a crazy woman who shouldn't be allowed near a potential customer. I haven't seen her for a long time. I wonder if she's still there."

"Maybe you should go and see."

"Maybe I should, but enough of my memories. Let's get back to yours. Did you take Sanford up on his offer that day?"

"Once he spoke to me, I wasn't afraid of him. It was curious. From the first moment he was by my side, I had the idea that there was nothing to be frightened of. Instead, I fell in love with him."

"So he swept you off your feet, as they say."

"He was very handsome – tall and fit, and, as I said before, very well dressed. I loved walking back to the office with him that first day. I had the sense that when people on the street looked at me, they were envious that I was a head-turner who had captured this older, elegant man just because I looked so great. I was living proof that life is unfair, and I gloried in that."

"When did you find out that Sanford was married?"

"Almost from the first moment. He made no effort to hide the fact."

"Did it make you uncomfortable?"

"Strangely no, although I wasn't brought up that way."

"What do you mean?"

"I mean that I was brought up to be a good girl, to get married some day to a nice young man, not to get involved with a married man twenty-five years older than me."

"Well, you were young, and Sanford had to have been very hard to resist."

"Sanford was very kind to me right from the beginning."

"So he didn't force himself on you."

"No, not at all. That first time he walked with me, he didn't touch me. In fact, he let me initiate physical contact between us – when I took his arm when we were crossing the street. But that didn't happen right away."

"What did happen right away?"

"We started to meet for lunch at the counter at the Oyster Bar."

"Did he invite you?"

"No, we just seemed to arrive at two empty seats next to one another at about the same time. Betty even got used to it. 'You two again,' she always said."

"So you were friends."

"I could see that we were becoming more than just friends, but the progression from one kind of relationship to another seemed like the most natural thing in the world."

"So did you have the feeling that things were progressing at the pace you wanted?"

"Oh, yes – that was Sanford's genius, you could say. He let me think I was in control of when we became lovers."

"But you weren't really in control."

"I know that now. I didn't know it then."

"Did you keep your job at the dirty old man's place?"

"Phoebe giggled. "Once I made Harry – that was the dirty old man's name, by the way – understand that he had to stop looking up my skirt and make sure to never put his hands on me, the job was a lot of fun, actually."

"Did you keep your own place, as well?"

"No: once Sanford and I became involved, I moved from a small apartment I had in Brooklyn, on the less yuppie part of Park Slope, to a one-bedroom in Murray Hill."

"He wanted you to be closer to him, that's why you moved. Sanford must have paid for part of the new place."

"He paid for all of it, actually. He wanted me to use all of my salary for clothes and cosmetics and a hair salon, things like that. He wanted me to look great when we went out together."

"So you didn't just see each other at the Oyster Bar and at the apartment. You were a couple, and you went places together."

"As time went on, we began to go out more and more together, and Sanford began to spend the night at the apartment. He kept some of his clothes and toiletries there."

"What about Gwennie? They were still married."

"They still were, but Sanford told me that their relationship had turned cold, that Gwennie no longer cared what Sanford did or where he was."

"I heard that from someone else recently." Phoebe looked at me quizzically. "Alice Burns, whose divorce Sanford handled not too long before he met you, told me the same thing about his relationship with Gwennie."

"In fact, we didn't speak about her and the marriage very much at all. Sanford told me exactly how he would end his marriage to Gwennie, and I believed him. I had the sense at the time that he was devoted to me and would do whatever I wanted." Phoebe paused for a moment. Then: "But some time later, when I thought back to that period, I had this strange sense that the whole affair, even our marriage, was some sort of game with Sanford. Right from the beginning. He had given himself so many points for picking me up, so many points for getting me to agree to let him walk me back to my office, so many for each lunch with me, and on and on. I had the sick feeling that sex was part of the game, too. I'm not sure the game ever stopped, not until we were divorced and he went back to his wife – I mean Gwennie, his other wife."

"You make him sound so juvenile."

"He was even worse than juvenile. But like I said, I didn't think this way about our relationship until later."

"I'm sorry to ask you this: do you think he loved you?"

"I was never sure, one way or the other. But he certainly made me feel that he wanted me."

"Was that just at the beginning? Or did that feeling that he wanted you wear off, do you think?"

"No, it didn't. I kept my figure all through the years we were married, and I never stopped being attractive for Sanford. The trouble was, that was all he seemed to care about: how I looked. He loved me in really high heels. He told me he always wanted me to be taller than average, which is what I am, after all. He didn't care about me as a person."

"Do you mind talking about these intimate things with me? If you do, I'll stop."

"It feels good to talk about the time I had with Sanford – and what we did with that time."

"So it was sex and not love that the two of you shared?"

"That's the way I thought of it."

"Did the fact that he was twenty-five years older have something to do with how he handled the relationship between the two of you?"

"It's funny that you ask that, because despite the age difference between us, I never treated Sanford as a much older man."

"That must have fed his ego."

"No, you're getting the wrong idea. The thing was, he never weaned himself away from Gwennie."

"But he married you, and you were together for five years."

"Yes, but during all those years, there were many times when I caught him drifting off, as if he was still with her in his mind, while his body was with me."

"Maybe he was thinking about the fortune he'd given Gwennie in their divorce settlement."

"Well, she did take him to the cleaners, although he still earned and kept enough money for the two of us to have a good life. But what I meant was that he was tied to Gwennie almost as if it was a mother-son relationship, although I was pretty sure it wasn't that. But I began to think there had been a kind of dependency in their relationship that I don't think Sanford was aware of."

"Why did you feel that way?"

"It was because Sanford didn't want to have children and he couldn't give an adequate reason why not."

"Maybe he thought he was too old, although fifty-some-year-old fathers aren't that unusual in the tony parts of New York, like the Upper East Side especially, where guys have the money to start families at any advanced age."

"No, it wasn't that – or at least he never said it was that. He just kept putting off any discussion about having kids. It seemed to me that his reluctance had to have something to do with Gwennie – that he was never really free of her, or even that he always intended to go back to her."

"What finally ended your marriage to Sanford? I've heard that the reason Sanford went back to Gwennie was that you didn't heat the plates before you served dinner on them."

Phoebe looked at me sharply. "I've heard that nonsense, and no, it wasn't that."

"Did Gwennie end it? Was she able to reel in the cord that bound Sanford to her?" Phoebe continued to look at me without blinking. "Do you mind if I ask you these questions?"

"No, I don't mind, and it wasn't Gwennie who end the marriage. It was me."

"Why? Were you just so unhappy with the way Sanford treated you – as an object, not as a person?"

"It wasn't that. I could have lived with that." Phoebe stopped and stared through me.

"Do you want to tell me? It's all right if you don't."

"I'll tell you. It's all right now. It's just that the memory of all the lies and manipulations that Sanford tried to put over on me was so painful for so long. You see, I found out that Sanford was having an affair. And it wasn't just that Sanford was having the affair – and he was having it all the time we were married, I was pretty sure – it's the way he tried to get around it. He made me feel that he'd left Gwennie and married me so it would be easier for him to carry on his illicit fucking. Because I didn't know all his tricks the way she did." A blush suffused Phoebe's pretty face.

"So the affair wasn't with Gwennie."

Phoebe laughed. It came out like a dog's bark. "I never found out who it was, but I knew he was having an affair with someone."

"How did you find out? And what did Sanford do when you found out?"

"He didn't seem to care that I'd found out."

"It's like he wanted you to find out."

"It was all so transparent. I didn't have to do anything to find out that he was screwing around. That made it harder to take in a way. I couldn't understand how he could take me for the sort of person who would ignore something like her husband's affair. I still can't."

"Do you think Gwennie knew about the affair when she took Sanford back? Do you think the affair ended then?

"I really don't give a shit." Phoebe laughed and rolled her eyes.

"Did you make any effort to find out who the woman was?"

"You mean, hire a private detective? No, not really."

"So it didn't make any difference who it was?"

"Not to me. The fact that Sanford was stepping out on me, as they used to say, caused enough pain. I didn't need to know who he was stepping out with."

"Why do you think Sanford felt he had to see someone else?"

"That's a stupid question." Phoebe folded her arms across her chest. "I'm sorry, I don't mean to be harsh. It's just that's what you men are like. Or some of you, at least. A good-looking wife isn't enough for some men. They have to have something on the side."

"I know what we're like. But as you say, you were beautiful – and young."

"But he wanted something more didn't he?"

"I suppose so, but most of the time what a guy is looking for in a mate is youth and beauty. That's what the biological need to reproduce drives guys toward."

"But Sanford wasn't interested in reproducing. He didn't want kids."

"So he was looking for something in addition to what the biological imperative dictates."

"Something he couldn't get from me."

"And something he couldn't get from Gwennie either."

Suddenly, Phoebe's face crumpled, and tears started to flow. She'd indicated earlier that bringing the memories of her time with Sanford was no longer painful, but now she wasn't acting that way at all.

"I'm sorry," I said.

"Please go. I can't talk about this – I can't talk to you – anymore."

"I'm sorry," I said sheepishly. "I shouldn't have come here and made you relive painful memories. I shouldn't have bothered you."

"Why did you come here and lull me into talking to you about a period in my life that ended so painfully? Why do you want to know about my marriage to Sanford?"

"I told you on the phone. I'm writing about him, about his life. You're part of it. I'm sorry you're feeling pain."

"You're not answering my question. Why are you writing about Sanford?" She took a wad of paper tissue out of her pants pocket and blew her nose. She looked up at me, her composure returned. "What's so damn interesting about Sanford? All I saw was a lousy husband who wasn't interested in becoming a father and who cheated on one wife after another." This wasn't what she'd said about the project when we'd first sat down. The pain of her memories had altered her opinion, evidently.

"He built a lucrative law practice, but a lot of attorneys do that", I said. "He had magnetism, though. I had to pay attention when he told his stories, and the stories seemed interesting to me. Although I have to admit that I'm an outsider, I'm an observer. I'm not in your position. Sanford didn't do anything that affected me personally. On the other hand, I saw some similarities between certain aspects of his life and mine.

"When my wife died, I was lost. So much had been cut out of my life. I didn't see any point to my work.

"I was friends with the number two man in Sanford's firm, and he helped me get back to work. I had always worked at home, and he convinced me I needed to get out more – the standard self-help for the bereaved. So I rented a small office in the building where Sanford's law offices are, and the next thing I knew I was invited to join the lunch table that Sanford shared with my friend and another lawyer from the firm – a woman.

"I'd met Sanford once before, at a dinner at my friend's house, not too long after my wife died. I guess I thought he was a bit of a character, although the long story he told that night wasn't particularly outlandish. It involved a bit of boyhood daring, and it focused on Sanford's love of art - painting specifically.

"After I got to know him a little better during those lunches, he came to me and asked me to work on a profile – a sort of biographical sketch – or even a full-fledged biography, if that's how the project worked out.

"He died before I got very far, but my friend convinced me to keep going with the project. So that's why I'm here. I think I'll keep the project going, but I have no idea where it's leading. Maybe it's living a life of its own."

"I think I understand a little better now," Phoebe said. We were standing near the front door. I'd been talking as we'd moved from the living room into the small foyer. A figure moved toward us from a short hall that led to the back of the house.

"I'm Phoebe's husband. I just got home, and I didn't want to disturb you." He was a thin, bald, bespectacled man of medium height. I put him in his late forties, about Phoebe's age. He held out a hand, and I shook it. His eyes locked onto mine. His face betrayed no emotion.

"This is Don, my real husband," Phoebe said. "That's what I call him – my real husband." She moved next to him and clasped his left arm in her hands.

"I apologize for our lack of hospitality," Don said. "We should have offered you something."

Phoebe's hands flew up to her blushing face. "I completely forgot. There's a plate of cheese and crackers on the counter in the kitchen. And I have some white wine in the fridge."

"That's all right. I need to be pushing off. I need to get back up to New York. I have some things to attend to over the next couple of days." That was true, but more than anything, I felt an urgent need to leave.

"At least stay and have something." There was a tinge of pleading in Phoebe's voice.

"Really, it's OK. I'll get something on the way back. Maybe I'll get off I95 at Aberdeen and find a restaurant." I knew immediately that I shouldn't have mentioned Aberdeen. That was where Sanford had spent his tour of army duty. But when I looked at Phoebe, no emotion registered on her face.

"Thanks for your time, Phoebe," I said. I shook her hand.

"Good luck with the project," Don said. He seemed oblivious to any pain publication of details of Sanford's life might cause Phoebe. Perhaps he trusts me, I thought, although for the life of me I couldn't imagine why.

CHAPTER SIXTEEN

Now that I'd turned down the Armstrongs' cheese and crackers and was back in the car, I was suddenly starving. I'd never had much luck finding good places to eat off the route between New York and Washington, except for Teddy's, which required a substantial detour, and was too far up the road from where I was anyway. There were a few acceptable places off one of the low-number Jersey Turnpike exits, but they weren't much closer than Teddy's. There was a place with diner food that some fellow working at the information counter at a Maryland Welcome Center had glommed Patricia and me onto one time. But I couldn't remember where it was, and I didn't feel like searching the web for it. Besides, even though I'd found the food decent, Patricia hadn't, so it had lost any appeal it might have had. What's more, I needed a crowd. That is to say, I needed a loud room filled with people having a good time who would be oblivious to my presence, and I could remain alone in their midst. So instead of heading to the Beltway and back to I95, I found the Rockville Metro station and parked the car. I knew it was straight shot to DuPont Circle on the Red Line, so I wouldn't have to go through the time killer of changing from one line to another, and it wouldn't take much time to get there.

I got off at the north end of the DuPont Circle station and made a U-turn to Second Story Books, the used book and CD store, which is on street level, despite its name. I didn't want to take the time to hunt through the couple of hundred classical CDs - most of them containing versions of the standard repertory that I'd heard too many times in my life – in the hope that I might stumble across music by a Twentieth Century composer I hadn't heard before. There were a lot fewer jazz CDs, so I spent a few minutes going through the jewel case spines until I spotted a couple of recordings by big bands I'd never heard of. I was always looking for big bands that can swing hard, and I hoped these would make me happy. Then I walked over to the fiction section. I picked out a fairly clean copy of a Rachel Cusk novel, *The Country Life*, which I figured would brighten my spirits. The English do great send-ups of life on farms and estates in the boondocks, and this one looked like it would work for me. Or maybe I'd picked it up because the author's first name reminded me of Rachel Gormsby, who I still hadn't called. In any case, I bought the book along with the big band recordings.

I walked back up Connecticut Avenue, which was crowded with attractive, nicely turned out girls and boys, most of whom looked like they'd be carded anyplace where the drinking age was twenty-one. Or so they looked to me, who was headed to geezerhood, with a dirt nap not all that far in the future. I passed half a dozen restaurants that were doing fairly good business. But when I got to Bistro du Coin, the big Belgian eatery I knew from previous visits to Washington, the place was jammed, as I'd expected,. And it was satisfyingly loud.

A dozen people were waiting to be seated. They were standing in the narrow entrance area, with a wall filled with snapshots and a coat rack on one side, and a partition on the other. A pretty blonde in her late twenties, I guessed, wearing a gray jacket and black slacks and acting like the hostess, came over to me.

"I like your style," she said. "What's the jacket made of?" Her English sounded French-accented.

I was wearing a light brown tweed jacket with a blue thread running through it here and there. I'd stuffed a pale blue pocket square halfway down into the breast pocket. I opened the jacket and showed the hostess the label sewed into the lining. "The material's called Donegal Tweed," I said. "It's woven in Ireland."

I smiled down into her laughing, intelligent eyes. She smiled back. "What time do you get off work?" I said and laughed. She laughed back at me.

"I'll find you a seat at the bar," she said, without having acknowledged my question with anything more than a pleasant laugh.

The bread was as good as I remembered, and the Cote du Rhone was dry and pleasant. The woman to my right was sitting with her legs crossed. There wasn't much room between our stools, and the toe of her right shoe – it had to be a high heel, I thought - kept making contact with my trousers. A sidelong glance or two confirmed that she was young and seemed to be alone, but I didn't dwell on whether the footsie was an amateur's accident or a signal from a pro. I read Rachel Cusk, which started well. When the rotisserie chicken, crisp and salted *pommes frites*, and the side of firm and garlicky *haricots vert* came, I put the book down and tucked in. The young woman got up and left. I had a second glass of wine.

I stopped by the hostess on the way out. "I'm sure you won't be here the next time I'm in Washington," I said. "You'll have your PhD in French literature by then, and you'll be teaching somewhere."

"Actually, I have my master's and I'm getting an MBA," she said.

I smiled into her laughing eyes, and then I kissed her on the cheek, which felt cool and dry. I brushed past people waiting for tables and headed toward the front door. I thought fleetingly about going back to the bar, getting a drink, and milling around. I'd have the chance to exchange more banter with the hostess with the laughing eyes. Who knew where that would lead? I'd have to find out what time she got off work – for real. Was there a husband in the picture? I hadn't looked for any rings yet. Or would a boyfriend be picking her up when she left the restaurant? Or was there one waiting at home? As I gently but steadily probed, she'd certainly get the idea about what I was after.

I hesitated momentarily in the doorway. How hard would it be to get in her pants tonight? She'd made the first move, after all – if her I-like-your-style remark could be considered a move, or a come-on, in the first place. Maybe she did such things to relieve any tedium in an exhausting job. I was reading too much into innocent acts, like the tip of the young woman's high heel making contact with the leg of my trousers.

I emerged onto the sidewalk and looked up at the sky. It was cool, clear night. The fresh air felt bracing. Should I take a page out of Sanford's playbook, go back in, and brazen it out? "You'll never know if you don't try." I pictured him saying that to me, the tender smile on his lips. Hell, I could take a page out of my own playbook of thirty-some years ago, when I used to pick up women at that hotel lounge near the Institute.

I started down Connecticut Avenue, toward the DuPont Circle Metro stop. I thought about turning around and going back to the bar again. So what if the hostess with the laughing and intelligent eyes was half my age? She said she liked my style, hadn't she? But those women I picked up in the hotel lounge were there because they were looking for love, or sex, or just a good time in some guy's arms on the dance floor. And what this young woman had done was probably nothing more than making a customer feel good enough to spend a few extra bucks on a second glass of wine and decide that he had to come back again.

I remembered an aphorism I used to repeat to myself. It went like this: you should live a life without illusions. I hadn't thought of those words for a long time, even though I'd considered them important in the past. Well, here I was, embracing a fantasy born of an illusion that a pretty, spirited and ambitious young woman would find a much older loner, enmeshed in research into another man's life, irresistible, the Irish tweed jacket with the pocket square notwithstanding. There, that was the problem: how could I know whether I was living up to the adage I used to find so important? Without Patricia, I recognized, there was no one to keep score.

I focused on Rachel Cusk on the Metro ride back up to Rockville. In the car, I turned up the volume on the Real Jazz channel on satellite radio. At night, I liked it better than my own CDs. No matter how good the music was, and how loud I played it, it was the occasional chatter that kept me awake.

The beltway was still jammed, although it was well after rush hour. It would be jammed at two in the morning, I thought. Then I95 was filled with cars and trucks, but the traffic moved swiftly. I was able to keep the Camry at a steady seventy-five. This was my first long trip with it. I'd bought it a month earlier. It had a navigation system, a six-cylinder engine with about two hundred and seventy horsepower, and twin exhausts. Behind the wheel, I felt like a slightly racier version of my old man.

I didn't think about Sanford until I saw the Aberdeen exit sign. The sign for the Proving Ground brought back Sanford's story about the long-term relationship he'd had with Gretchen Carmichael. Part of it had occurred while he was stationed here and she was working in Washington.

Then the conversations with Alice Burns and Phoebe Armstrong washed over me, like a tide of memory that I couldn't hold back. I could see them in my mind's eye – Alice cool and unperturbed, Phoebe overcome for a moment or two with emotion. I could hear their voices in my head.

Both Alice and Phoebe had told me a similar version of how their relationships with Sanford had ended. In both cases, the women had supposedly found Sanford out. He'd inadvertently told Alice about the game he'd played to get revenge on Harlan Burns, and Alice had realized that she'd been collateral damage. My suspicion now was that he'd told Alice because he wanted to break off their relationship – and he wanted to go back to Gwennie. Phoebe had discovered that Sanford was cheating on her. My suspicion was he'd let her because he wanted to break off the relationship – and, as with Alice before, he wanted to go back to Gwennie. Perhaps Sanford and Gwennie had let the story about Phoebe not warming the dinner plates gain currency because they wanted to deflect attention from the real reason his marriage to Phoebe had ended.

Had Sanford changed in the years between the end of his relationship with Gretchen and his relationships with Bethia, Alice, and

Phoebe? I didn't know – not yet, at least. Perhaps Gretchen would enlighten me. I hadn't taken the time to find her yet, but I had the sense that it wouldn't be particularly difficult, providing she was still alive.

One thing that hadn't changed was Sanford's technique for picking up a woman. He picked up Gretchen, Bethia, and Alice on the street, just after they'd had lunch and presumably had full stomachs and were feeling content, although possibly guilty for having overindulged. But it was safe to disregard any remorse on their part for having overeaten. They were all trim. He contrived picking up Phoebe while she was actually eating lunch, which he could easily see that she enjoyed. Only Gwennie was different. Sanford had met her at a mixer.

For many years, he'd found a woman whenever he'd needed one. The relationships with Bethia and Alice had been powered by a desire for revenge. I wasn't sure what had powered the relationship with Phoebe. Was he so attracted to her that he paid whatever price he had to – and it was considerable – to get her? Or was it simply a need to play a game with the affections of a much younger woman?

Was everything nothing more than a game to Sanford? Were women – with the possible exception of Gwennie, and I wasn't at all sure about that relationship – nothing more than collateral damage while he played his games? That ugly phrase – collateral damage – kept sliding back into my consciousness. I didn't have an answer to the question – not yet, at least.

Was the relationship with Phoebe the last one, except for the life-long bonding with Gwennie? Sanford had been a prominent divorce attorney for over two decades. He'd met many attractive and vulnerable women – and plenty of attractive and voracious ones, as well. Obviously, he'd had plenty of opportunities, if he'd cared to seize them. Or had he been faithful to Gwennie during their second twenty-year marriage?

I had plenty of other unanswered questions. Who was the woman Sanford had been cheating on Phoebe with? Phoebe didn't know. Did Gwennie? How had he gotten back together with her? It was hard to imagine him crawling back to her.

I wasn't at all sure where the research into Sanford's life was taking me. I didn't have a sense yet of what the shape of his story would look like. But I wasn't stopping.

Nevertheless, there was an overriding issue that I still hadn't worked out. Would I have taken on the project in the first place if I'd known then what I'd be hearing about him from Alice and Phoebe? Would Sanford have seduced me no matter what I already knew? And why hadn't I been able to see him for what he apparently was? All those cracks about women and their appearance, and all those games he was so fond of. Bill hadn't been any help. He was prepared to take Sanford any way he found him. I hadn't had to get sucked in. Still, there'd been something about Sanford that had brought me into orbit around him. He was the sun, and I was a willing satellite. I hadn't thought I'd been warmed by his glow, but maybe I had been.

I stopped for gas in Delaware. I remembered Sanford's story about a trip he'd made from Aberdeen up to Boston, back in the days before I95 had been built through Delaware. He'd stopped at a diner that was in the median on Route 40 - about where I was now, possibly. He ordered cherry pie – the only time he'd had it, ever. He'd claimed he could still taste the cold cherry sweetness years later. I remembered him telling me about the signs he'd seen in restaurants on his first trip through Maryland to reach Aberdeen: "We reserve the right to refuse service to anyone." It had been during the civil rights era. I wondered if the Delaware restaurant had been too far north for the nefarious separate-but-equal sensibility to have had a foothold.

I got back in the car. I picked up one of my new big band CDs. The band was called the Danjam Orchestra. The leader was Daniel Jamieson. On the album cover, he looked young. I thought about my walks earlier up and down Connecticut Avenue and decided I was getting sick of anyone and everything that could be called young. But when I started the car up, I slid the album into the CD player. I glanced at the notes. The kid had done all the arrangements. He'd composed all the music except for two standards, *Alone Together* and *Smile*.

The music was complex without being at all fussy, there were plenty of surprises, and the band could swing. I was happy. I'd gotten my five bucks worth. I forgave Jamieson his age – that was big of me, wasn't it? I said to myself - and promised that I'd buy his next CD new so he'd get royalties.

I got over the Delaware Memorial Bridge, and in a few minutes I was past the concrete no man's land that leads to the Jersey Turnpike, a fairly straight and flat road, which can seem endless or can go by quickly, depending on how you're feeling and what's on the radio. After the CD ended, I went back to jazz on the satellite. It kept me awake, and the checkpoints came up quickly. The Philly area, and then Trenton, and then the Cranbury exit, and then Newark Airport, and eventually the Holland Tunnel, and I was in Manhattan before I'd yawned for the first time. I found Eighth Avenue and headed up to Columbus Circle. It was well after midnight, but there were still people on the streets. I took Broadway up to the Seventies, and then cut over to West End Avenue, to enjoy the rhythm of the light changes. Small pleasures in the small hours, I thought. It had been a very long day. A few minutes later, I pulled into the garage, left the car, and headed to my apartment, which was filled with everything but what I wanted most but couldn't have - Patricia.

I needed to sleep off the eleven or so hours of driving, and I didn't get up until past noon. I made a small pot of the decaf that I kept frozen and toasted half of a plain bagel, also from the freezer. The butter in the refrigerator was still good. After my meager breakfast, I went out for a brisk walk. I crossed the Drive to Riverside Park and went north for awhile, and then I turned around. When I got down to Seventy-Second Street, I went over to West End Avenue and headed north again. I had to slow down on the big hill above Ninety-Sixth, but I managed to stagger back to my neighborhood. I bought a copy of the *Times* and read it with lunch at Le Monde, where I had a *Croque monsieur* with mesclun salad, two glasses of water, and a decaf espresso. I bought a couple of oranges and a few pieces of other fruit on Broadway, and then I walked back to the apartment.

I took a shower, and then I sat down at the kitchen table. I ate one of the peaches I'd bought, put the pit in a napkin, balled the napkin, and threw it into the garbage. Then I sat quietly, without moving, and stared out the window at the trees for a very long time.

While I sat and stared, my mind kept working. I'd already begun to worry about money. I no longer believed that the part of the publishing business that I'd been involved in for twenty-five years could possibly guarantee me as good a livelihood as I'd enjoyed in the past, especially when Patricia and I had pooled our earnings. I doubted that I had a best-selling environmental book for general readers in me anymore. As for the reference works with multiple contributors for the professional and library markets, such books faced increasing competition from free information sources on the Internet. I'd already had several potential contributors tell me that they couldn't write a chapter that would be any better than what anyone could find in Wikipedia on the same subject.

I still had Patricia's insurance money. I'd invested it cautiously. I'd never dabbled in the stock market to good effect, and I didn't feel that it was a good time to take risks. Besides, I doubted that I or the money manager Bob Steinberg had recommended would parlay the money into a fortune. So I'd asked the money manager to put me into a few supposedly safe blue-chip stocks and mutual funds, which he did, repeating all the while the bromide that past performance is no guarantee of future results -

while I kept repeating my hope that there would be enough money for me to live on in my fast-approaching old age.

Sitting at the kitchen table, as the afternoon wore on, I thought about whether I should sell the New York apartment and commit myself to living full-time in the house upstate. Or should I do the reverse? Or should I sell both places and move somewhere else? In any case, it seemed to me that I couldn't properly afford to live in two places. Besides, I had an awful lot of space for just one person, I wasn't having any overnight guests, and another relationship didn't seem to be in the cards.

I couldn't help thinking about all the furniture, all the books and recordings, and all the artwork that Patricia and I had accumulated throughout our years together. And I was still adding to the pile, for god's sake. It was all mine now, of course, to keep or dispose of as I saw fit after careful consideration or as whims came over me. Did I really want, or need, all this stuff? A used bookstore owner I knew once told me that getting rid of books could be liberating.

But liberated from what? After all, Patricia was a vital part of all the stuff I now had. She'd bought some of it herself; we'd acquired some of it together. Even for the stuff I'd bought myself, Patricia had very often been a presence in the background. She'd been with me one way or the other. So the more stuff I disposed of, the more of Patricia I would lose. I feared I was losing more and more of her with each passing day, anyway, and I didn't want to hasten the process. I needed to hold onto as much of her as I could for as long as I could.

Nevertheless, taking all those books wherever I went seemed like an awful physical undertaking. Of course, I could have someone pack them and the recordings and all the paintings into heavy cartons, but when they arrived at their destinations, I would have to have shelves and cabinets and wall space ready for the contents – the books and recordings, etc. – and it would fall to me to unpack them and put them away or hang them up. And this was a task that involved more than brute strength. For all the books and recordings would have to be shelved and stored in some kind of order so I could find whatever I wanted quickly and easily. In other words, the stuff amounted to a gigantic, exhausting pain in the ass.

I sat at the kitchen table for over an hour, thinking some of the time, and otherwise trying to empty my mind. I still needed rest. Around five-thirty the buzzer in the foyer sounded with a call from the building's lobby. I recognized the voice. It belonged to Gus, the doorman who came on duty at four.

"There's a Ms. Cassidy here. Should I send her up?"

Good old Gus, giving me the option of going down to the lobby to meet with Rita. I passed on the opportunity and told him to send her up.

I opened the apartment door to a chic-looking Rita. Her hair was swept to the side in a new bob. She was wearing a blue dress that flowed smoothly over her slim body. She'd always kept her figure, even after giving birth to a couple of boys twenty years ago. I heard the clack of high heels as she sauntered past me into the tiled foyer. Then she turned and faced me. She smiled at me. I smiled back at her. "Brian downstairs parking the car?" I said. I had my hopes that she wasn't alone.

"I've left Brian." She said it quickly, as if speed would give the act finality.

"I didn't know that."

"It's true. Oh, we still live in the same house, the two of us, but we don't live together, if you get my drift."

"I get your drift. It seems rather sudden. You and Brian were here together not that long ago."

I walked Rita into the kitchen. I'd gotten used to Patricia's height, and Rita, who wasn't particularly short, especially in heels, seemed small next to me. We sat at the corner of the table where I'd been sitting only a few minutes earlier. Rita crossed her legs. The silky fabric of her dress slid back, exposing a good deal of thigh. She made no effort to rearrange herself. Sanford's crack about a woman showing some leg when she was sitting down came into my head unbidden. The rest of the crack, about cleavage, arrived when Rita leaned forward and extracted a pack of cigarettes and a silver lighter from her handbag.

She straightened up. "Mind?" she asked. She already held a cigarette between her index and middle fingers. She looked at me with a dare in her eyes.

"I won't clutch my pearls and faint." I got up and brought a saucer over to the table. "You can use this for an ashtray."

"That'll work." She put a cigarette between her lips and flicked the lighter. "Excuse me," she said, after inhaling. "Want one?"

"I'll just say no," I said with a smile. "I don't remember ever seeing you smoke."

"I smoked in college. Brian made me quit when we started dating. But now Brian doesn't have any say in what I do." She blew a smoke ring, expertly. "Not anymore."

"When did you two decide to split?"

"I was the one who decided, not Brian. He would have gone on the way we were going until one of us was dead. Which would have been me. I would have died of boredom."

"Had you two been talking about separating when you were here last? I realized that things weren't perfect between the two of you, but I'm still surprised at what you're telling me now."

"I'm glad you could at least recognize something about the way things were between Brian and me." Rita blew another smoke ring and uncrossed her legs. She crossed them the other way. The dress slid further up her thighs. I looked away, out the window. The afternoon light was golden.

"You men. It takes you forever to catch onto anything that doesn't involve sports or war, or maybe science and math. I threw myself at you the last time I was here, with Brian in the next room, for Christ sakes. You do remember that, don't you?"

"Of course I remember. I didn't take what happened seriously. I passed it off as your having had too much to drink." It seemed like the safest way out. But what did I know? I was a clueless male.

"I was looking for a quick way out of my marriage to Brian."

"And I was handy.'

"No, you were more than that."

"I'm still not sure I want to go there."

"Then let's not. Let's just talk about me." Rita laughed, leaned back, drew on her cigarette, and blew another smoke ring.

"OK, sure. What is it that you want?"

"I want to live my own life," she said vehemently. "And I certainly don't want to live it with Brian."

"So Brian will be moving out? Once he catches on, that is."

Rita smiled at me, but not with her lips, just with her eyes. "You're so cute," she said. "No, Mordecai, I'm the one who's moving out. So I can move on. Brian can have the goddamn house. I'm sick of cleaning it and cooking in it."

"Where do you intend to live?"

"How about right here? I'm a pretty good cook." She laughed. I laughed back at her.

"I've been thinking this afternoon that I might sell the place. Want to buy it?"

"It's out of my price range – unless you'd be willing to give me a friendship discount. It's a real shame, though." She stubbed her cigarette into the saucer, leaned forward again, and dropped the pack and lighter back in her handbag. I looked at the trees through the kitchen window again.

"What about your job? This place wouldn't be that convenient." Rita was the office manager for a large medical practice in Morristown.

"They're moving me into their new office in the city, on the Upper East Side." She could take the same bus, I thought, that Patricia had taken when she'd worked at her museum job on the East Side, but I didn't mention it.

"So living here would be perfect," Rita went on. She grinned at me. "Oh, don't worry, Mordecai, I'll give up smoking again. The place won't stink."

I needed to change the subject. "How's Brian taking this? I haven't heard from him."

"He doesn't believe what's happening before his own eyes. That's why you haven't heard from him. It hasn't hit him yet, that I'm actually leaving him. But it will. Then he'll be on the phone, boohooing to everyone he knows. Oh, you'll hear from him, all right. Trust me."

"Are you angry with Brian? You make it sound like you might be."

"I'm not angry with him. There's no point. He is what and who he is. No more and no less - I guess that's the problem I have with him. Look, he's a good provider. He always has been. And he's a good father, as well. The boys still come to him for advice. But there's something missing. I didn't realize that for a very long time. I thought I had the perfect marriage to a strong and steady man. But I need more than that. I need some excitement. I need to live a life with some risk. Brian shies away from taking risks. Living that way is just too dull for me."

"Is there anything else besides boredom? Don't mind my saying, but are you involved with anyone else?"

"Not yet, anyway." Rita laughed. I smiled in response. "But isn't boredom enough? I need stimulation in my life, goddamnit. I need a man I want to be running toward all the time, not someone I can take or leave when we're together in the same room - or in the same bed, for that matter."

Rita threw her head back and laughed again. I laughed with her. Then she leaned forward again and took a roll of Clorets out of her handbag. I looked away from her again, and then I watched her put one of the little green wafers in her mouth. She offered the roll to me. I flicked my head no again.

"What about your two boys? How do they feel about your leaving their father? Or aren't they aware of what's going on?"

"Oh, they're aware. They understand what I'm feeling – what I have been feeling for a very long time, actually. But they won't blame either Brian or me, and they won't favor one of us over the other. I'm glad of that."

"I'm glad of that, too, for your sake, and for Brian's sake, as well."

"I hope your reaction is a sign that our friends won't be taking sides – that Brian and I will both be able to keep the friends we've made over the years. It's a terrible blow when you lose a friend. Brian and I both grieved over losing Patricia – not as much as you did, of course, no one could feel as deeply as you did."

I looked away again. The room was quiet, so quiet that I could hear the rumble of a bus going by on Riverside Drive. "You took a chance coming here," I said finally. "I spend most of my time upstate these days. I'm here today because I had to go down to Maryland yesterday and I have a couple of people to see in the city tomorrow. So there was no point driving back up to the house upstate and taking the train down tomorrow morning. Besides, I have someone to see in Providence the day after tomorrow, and I'll need to drive there. Then I'll be going back upstate. So you got lucky."

"I can't claim that I just knew you'd be here." Rita spoke with a stock Southern Belle inflection. She batted her eyes. Then the real Rita spoke. "I can't say that some sixth sense, or women's intuition, whatever that is, told me that you'd be here. All I can say is that I took a chance. Which is what I do these days: I take chances."

"Your gamble paid off, in defiance of the odds. Here I am, in living color."

We fell silent again. Rita sat still. Then she turned and looked out the window with me. Another bus trundled by. I wondered if Rita was waiting me out, until I made a move of some kind. I thought back again to the last time she'd been here and the scene with her and me in the kitchen, with Brian in another room.

"You're frowning," she said. "Is there something the matter?" She didn't ask whether I wanted her to go. I had to admit to myself that I didn't know whether I wanted her to go or not. So I let my rusty hospitality take over.

"How about a glass of wine?" I asked. "I can offer you some crackers with it. But that's it. I don't keep much food in the apartment. Like I said, I'm not here that often nowadays." I got out of my chair and looked down at Rita. "Unless there's someplace you have to be," I said, even though I knew she wasn't going anywhere for the time being.

Rita looked up at me and smiled slowly. "There's nowhere I need to be. I came here to see if I could find you at home. And here you are, in living color, as you aptly put it. That's as far as I've gotten today."

I decided not to inquire about her expectations for the rest of the day. "I'll get the wine," I said.

"Save the wine for later. Please sit down."

"Sure," I said, and sat back down.

Rita kept her eyes on my face as she slowly uncrossed her legs. I was reminded of the provocative way I'd seen in her uncross her legs in front of Brian the last time they were here. I didn't look away from her while I wondered what had happened when they'd gotten home. She got up and stood in front of me, very close, her legs apart. "Give me your hands," she said.

She placed my hands on the backs of her thighs. "Do you think I have nice legs, Mordecai?"

"You have very nice legs." I looked up at her smiling face.

"I have other nice things." She took hold of my wrists and moved my hands up to her ass. She pushed my legs apart and moved in closer. Her breasts pressed against my face. I pushed my tongue into her décolletage. My hands were kneading her buttocks. I was getting hard. Rita took my face in her hands, bent down, and kissed me. Our tongues probed each other's mouth. She tasted of chlorophyll with an edge of tobacco induced sourness. Rita Cassidy, the 2012 vintage, I thought. But I got more tumescent.

Rita pulled her mouth away from mine. "Take my clothes off," she said. "Now."

I did as I was asked, or ordered. I didn't stop to care which it was. I reached up and unzipped her dress. It fell down and pooled around her feet. She stepped to the side and kicked the dress away from her. Then she was back in front of me. I unhooked her bra and pulled it away. She pressed her breasts against me. I took one of her nipples between my lips and ran my tongue over it. I heard her murmur with pleasure. I hooked my fingers around the waistband of her panties. She put her legs together, and I pulled the panties down. She stepped out of them. She bent down and kissed me again. I put my fingers in the crack of her ass and pulled her against me. I kept caressing her nipples with my tongue. They were hard. Then I bent forward and tasted her lower down.

After a few moments, Rita leaned back. "Stand up, Mordecai."

I struggled to my feet. Rita took the waistband of my jogging pants and pushed them down over my hips. I reached down and pulled the pants off me, and then I straightened up and pulled my tee shirt over my head. I threw the tee shirt on top of Rita's dress.

Rita started to pull my boxers down.

"Careful," I said. I hadn't had sex for a long time, and I wasn't taking any chances with Rita pulling the boxers' fabric over my hard penis.

She pulled the waistband toward her and eased it over and down. I stepped out of the boxers.

"Let's find a bed," she said. She walked ahead of me, still in her heels. She reached back for me, and I put her hand on my penis. "I'm pleased. I have your full attention," she said, her voice soft and deep.

"Second door past the living room." My own voice sounded hoarse to me. The words seemed to have jagged edges.

The drapes on the living room windows were open, so there was light in the hall. But the heavy bedroom drapes, which had been drawn against daylight, were still closed, so it was fairly dark when Rita opened the door and we went in. But I could still see Patricia's black and white photograph in the silver frame on top of one of the night tables. I tried not to look at it. And I didn't want Rita to see me going over to the picture and removing it or laying it face down.

Rita mounted the bed on her knees. She crawled forward, got down on her elbows and offered herself to me from the rear. I mounted the bed behind her.

"I've wanted you for so long," she said.

But the instant I penetrated her, the tumescence retreated, and my prick softened. I sat back on my haunches.

"What's the matter?"

"It's not working. I'm sorry."

Rita sat back and reached around for me. She touched my flaccid penis. "I see what you mean," she said. She crawled around and sat with her back against the headboard. She still had her heels on.

I sat on the side of the bed, with my right profile to her. I turned my head to look at her. "I'm sorry," I said.

"You already said that, Mordecai."

"I know. I'm sorry."

"That's a trifecta."

We both laughed a little. I took a deep breath. Patricia's photograph was behind me. I couldn't see it. Thank heaven for small favors, I said to myself.

"Would you prefer the missionary position? I didn't think Jewish guys were squeamish about sex, but you're my first one, so what do I know?"

I put my head in my hands. "Don't embarrass me, please."

"You're not suddenly worried about AIDS, are you? I'm clean, in case you're asking. I had a blood test after I decided to leave Brian. Of course, I would have killed him if they'd found I was HIV-positive." Rita snorted a laugh. "Not that I thought it likely that Brian would ever do anything that would expose him to AIDS. But like they say, better to be safe than sorry." She laughed again.

I could see her shape in the dim light, but not her features. She raised herself up, removed her shoes, and drew her legs under her in the lotus position. "Whether you were HIV-positive, or even had AIDS, didn't cross my mind,' I said.

"By the way, have you been tested? Not that we got far enough so it would make any difference."

"It was only Patricia and me for twenty-five years, so, no, I haven't been tested."

"Wait a minute. Maybe you should take your Viagra, although you did get it up to start with."

"I don't have any. I've never had to get a prescription for it."

"Oh, OK, so is this when you say, 'it's not you, it's me?'"

"The cliché happens to be the truth. You're a very attractive woman, Rita. I never noticed how attractive. In any case, you're not the problem here."

"But I don't measure up, do I?" She reached over and held Patricia's photograph up. "Who has legs as long as she did, for god's sake?" She put the photograph back on the night table and laughed. "It's the first time you've been with anyone since Patricia, isn't it?"

"Yes, you're the first. Unfortunately, I guess. For both of us. It's not fair to you. That's for sure."

"I thought I could bring you out of your funk. I gave myself too much credit."

"Don't blame yourself, Rita. Blame me."

"Christ, you sound more Jewish by the minute."

"Of course, I do. The only people who have bigger guilt trips than you Irish are us Jews. Now you know that empirically."

Rita lifted the bedspread and pushed her legs under it. She wriggled down the bed until the bedspread covered her shoulders. "Do you mind if I sleep for awhile?" she said. "I'm very tired. And I'm sick to death of consciousness."

"Go ahead. I'll go into the living room and read." I got up, picked a bathrobe off a chair, and left the bedroom.

After a little more than an hour, Rita came into the living room. She was dressed. Her lipstick looked refreshed in the only light in the room, from my reading lamp. It had gone dark outside some time ago.

"You must have sneaked back into the kitchen to get your clothes," I said.

"You looked like you were sleeping, so I was very quiet." She stood straight, with her feet close together. Her handbag was tucked under her arm.

"I did doze off for a couple of minutes." I looked at her carefully. "I guess you're leaving." I got up and drew the robe more tightly around myself.

"You're very observant." She smiled. The smile looked genuine. "Thanks for the effort." She smiled again. "Please sit, Mordecai. You must be tired."

"I'm glad you're not angry. Don't be. I'm not worth your anger." I sat down on an arm of the sofa.

"Now you're sounding ridiculous. Stop the self pity, Mordecai. It doesn't become you."

"You're right. The problem is, I'm just not ready yet."

"No, you're not. And I don't know when you will be, and neither do you, unless I miss my guess."

"Maybe soon, maybe never, I don't know. You're right about that, too."

"Sooner rather than never, I would hope."

"Go back to Brian. He's a good man."

"I told you, Mordecai, that's ended. I came here looking for a beginning. Unfortunately, I didn't find one."

Rita walked over to me, bent down, and her lips touched my forehead. I put my hand on her hip. She let the hand rest there for a moment, and then she turned and walked away from me. I didn't hear her heels clacking on the foyer's tile floor. She must have been walking tip-toe. And she was very quiet with the front door, as if she was leaving me with doubt that she'd actually been here.

CHAPTER SEVENTEEN

The publishing company where Jim Upton, and now Bob Steinberg worked had offices in a large, rectilinear steel and glass building in midtown. The architectural style, it always seemed to me, suited the firm's output, which had started with reference books in engineering, expanded to include chemistry and environmental science (where I'd first come in), and later included non-fiction titles for general readers willing to make their way through discussions of complex technical subjects (and where I'd also come in).

The firm's founder was an entrepreneurial West Point graduate. A few years after the end of World War II, he'd decided that being tired of reporting up an endless chain of command and wanting instead to run his own show wasn't unpatriotic. He saw the wave of university research and corporate R&D that was building, and he had the wit to ride it. He'd been a benevolent dictator for a quarter of a century until, riddled with the cancer that claimed him after his final battle, he'd turned the place over to professional managers. With his blessing, they'd taken the company public.

The professionals were split into two armed camps. In one were the publishing types – editors, production people, marketers, and the sales staff. In the other camp were the green eyeshade wearers – the hard-money men and women, who, anytime there was a bad quarter, no matter the reason, pounced on the publishing operation and laid waste to it in obeisance to the gods of fiscal austerity – until the publishing people found a way to dig themselves out.

Or so Steinberg told the tale.

When I first started visiting the publisher back in the Eighties, I would cross the building lobby, where no one paid any attention to me, take an elevator up to the floor where the publisher's reception area was, and walk in through the heavy glass door, which was unlocked. Usually, I'd wait there until someone the receptionist had called came out to fetch me. Once or twice, when there'd been a receptionist who'd recognized me by sight or by name, I'd been allowed to go through the door to the offices while the receptionist placed her call, and I'd walked without an escort to my editor's office. No one had seemed to mind very much.

Everything changed as a result of 9/11, of course. Now, there was a security desk in the lobby, with four uniformed guards in attendance. There was a sign-in sheet in a loose-leaf binder. One of the guards, a tall, heavy-set black man in his sixties, handed me a thin ballpoint and pointed with a fingernail clipped into a triangular shape to a box on the top sheet.

"Write today's date here, sir, and then the time. Print your name and company below where you see the other names and companies, and then sign your name in the next box. Then print the name of the person you're visiting and the name of their company. You can give me their phone number when you're finished." His voice was surprisingly sweet and high-pitched.

I wrote everything down, including Bob Steinberg's name and the publisher's name. The guard turned the book around. "What company are you with, sir?"

"I work for myself."

The guard wrote the word self down next to my printed name and turned the book around. "What company are you visiting, sir?"

I looked down at the boxes I'd filled out. I'd printed the publisher's name clearly. I looked up. The guard had a placid expression on his face. Behind him, three other guards, another large black man, a shorter, beefy white man, and a slender Hispanic, were talking amongst themselves and smiling. I wondered if one of them was telling a joke about three security guards going into a bar. There was a line of several people to my right. I said the publisher's name out loud, and then, like I usually did with my own name, I spelled it. The guard picked up a booklet and began turning the pages. He stopped after several pages and stared down at the booklet. "What name was that?" he asked me.

"They're on eight, nine, and ten," one of the other guards said.

The guard I was dealing with turned another page in the booklet. "The name of the person you're visiting, sir?" he asked me.

"Steinberg."

"Here he is. Robert?"

"Yes, he's the one." I felt like the host of Jeopardy.

The guard picked up a phone. He looked down at the booklet. Then he dialed. He waited for some time before he spoke into the phone. "This is security downstairs. You have a visitor." The guard paused and looked up at me. I said my name, and he repeated it into the telephone. Then he gave a number and hung up. "I left a voicemail," he said to me.

"Why don't you try his assistant? Her name is Rachel Gormsby." I gave him the number. He picked up the phone again.

"I can only make two calls, sir. There are people waiting behind you." None of the other guards made a move to help anyone in line. My guard dialed and waited. Then he went through the procedure I was fast becoming familiar with. He put the phone down. "You'll have to step aside and wait, sir," he said, "until one of the parties calls down here."

I was used to getting voicemail whenever I called anyone at the publisher. I had it on Steinberg's authority that ever since the day telephones with caller ID had been installed, no one ever answered his phone unless it was some internal person of higher authority, and not always even then. But I had an appointment today, so I would have expected either Bob or Rachel to have answered the phone. Bob's voicemail did give callers the option of dialing another extension for someone else, but the guard hadn't availed himself of that option.

I stood by the security desk and looked at the *Times* for several minutes. I had an old habit of never going anywhere without reading material. Nowadays, a smart phone would provide profitable diversion, but I still preferred print. I noticed the other black guard sizing me up.

"What floor is your party on?" he said.

"Eight."

"Why don't you go on up? There'll be someone to take care of you." He handed me a badge on a lanyard. I thanked him, put the lanyard on over my head, and headed for the elevator bank.

When I got to the eighth floor, the glass door at the reception area was locked. There was a security pad to the left of the door for employees to scan their badges or key cards. I had to push a buzzer and wait for the receptionist to buzz me in. Today there was a problem. No one was sitting behind the reception desk. I walked back past the elevators and tried the glass door on the other side. It was locked, as well. There was a high partition several feet behind the door, so I couldn't see anyone inside. I knocked on the door, but no one appeared.

I walked back to the reception area door. I took out my phone and called Steinberg's number. His voicemail came on. When I heard the tone, I snarled into the phone, "Jesus, Bob, where the fuck are you? I can't get into the reception area."

There was a loud click in the plate glass door. A moment later, a middle-aged man with a cherubic face, horn-rimmed glasses, and a shock of wavy gray hair held the door open for me. "Who are you meeting with?" he asked as I walked in past him.

"Bob Steinberg."

"And you are?"

I said my name.

"Hey, I used to sell your books out of our Far East office before the company moved me back to the States." He put out a hand. "Artie Gross." We shook hands.

"Any relation to Werner Grosz?" I'd never forgotten the blue-blazered smoothie from the first Frankfurt trip. I spelled his last name.

"Nope, wrong spelling."

"Just thought I'd ask."

"That's OK. You probably know the way from here." I nodded and smiled. Artie Gross smiled back. "Well, pleased to meet you," he said. "And keep the books coming. I love to sell them."

When I arrived at the threshold of Steinberg's office, he was talking on the telephone. He waved me inside, then swiveled around and faced the window. I opened the *Times* again and listened with half an ear to the usual burping and farting while he talked. He ended the call about ten minutes after I'd sat down.

"My mother," he said to the world at large. He swiveled around to face me. "That's why Florida was invented. It's the staging area for Jewish parents before the final resting place. My father loved it, actually – all the cigars and card games – but he died four years ago. 'Why now, when he was finally enjoying life?' my mother said, five hundred times, maybe. As luck would have it, my accountant brother-in-law's firm opened a Miami office and he signed on as managing partner. So now my baby sister Susie and her two kids are a stone's throw from mother's condo. Free babysitting, if you can stand the kvetching. From the kids, not from my mother. She won't let them do anything. She's afraid of any normal activity. And I have to hear about how Susie lets the kids do anything they want, no matter how dangerous it is. My mother keeps me on the phone for an hour twice a week, no matter what urgent business is on my plate." Steinberg farted gently. "I have to take her calls because she knows I have call waiting on every available device, and then I can't get her off the phone."

"I can understand why I couldn't get through to you. But why doesn't your voicemail give me an assistant's extension, someone besides Rachel?"

"Funny you should say that." Steinberg half-swallowed a burp. 'We don't have many people who are called assistants anymore." He leaned back in his chair and looked at me over his belly. "Remember Jim Upton?"

"I'll never forget him."

"Remember his secretary, Estelle?"

"I do, as a matter of fact."

"She was a great old battleaxe. She had something on everyone in the company. At her retirement party, I held up the biggest computer printout I could find and said, 'Well, here's Estelle's exit interview.' It brought the house down." Steinberg farted gently in appreciation of his remembered gag.

"Anyhow, the phone on Estelle's desk had a row of buttons. When the phone rang, she'd answer it and ask who was calling. If the call was for Jim, she'd put the caller on hold, buzz Jim with another one of the buttons, tell him who was on the line, and if he told her to put the call through, she'd do so by pressing the original button. If another call came in while Jim was speaking with the first caller, Estelle would answer her phone with another button. If the second caller wanted to wait for Jim to finish his current call, Estelle would put him on hold, and the button would keep flashing. If the second caller wanted to leave a message and a call-back number, she'd write them down on a pink message pad. I don't know how many callers she could keep on hold at any one time. I never bothered to ask her or figure it out for myself.

"OK, so along comes caller ID and call waiting and message machines, and poof! Jim can handle the telephone traffic by himself. No need for a secretary to have a phone with a row of buttons, no need for pink message pads, and away goes that part of Estelle's job."

"And no need for either Jim or Estelle to actually answer the phone."

"They no longer had time for the phone. Let me explain. Estelle took shorthand, so back in the day Jim used to dictate letters, which she typed on a typewriter. She was a crack typist, but she did make a mistake occasionally. Back in the Fifties, long before you came on the publishing scene, the company typewriters were old-fashioned, so she'd have to paint over a mistake with white gunk, which she could type over when it dried.

"By the time you first met Upton, secretaries had IBM Selectrics, which I guess enabled them to type over mistakes, essentially. Something like that. Anyhow, sometime in the late Eighties, secretaries were given word processors, and you know how easy it is to correct mistakes when you're using word processing, instead of a typewriter. By the way, upper management had required elaborate productivity and cost-benefit analyses before the word processors could be purchased. What a waste of time. Unfortunately, the end result really was that everyone did become a lot of more efficient."

"You're about to tell me that increased productivity wasn't a good thing, aren't you?"

"Naturally. The argument goes as follows. Over time, of course, secretaries became so efficient that they had time for other duties, so they were assigned the task of preparing manuscripts for production. This required a change in their title, so they were called editorial assistants. I mean who wanted to be a secretary, anyway? It became such a demeaning title, a relic of the *Mad Men* era. A secretary had little upward mobility if she stayed a secretary, no matter who she slept with." Steinberg chortled and burped. "And then we had male assistants and female editors, and then sexual harassment, and the whole sex business became way too complicated. But I digress.

"To get back to the main argument: with the advent of email, editors and everyone else in the food chain no longer had to write so many formal letters to authors. So nobody needed editorial assistants for that task, either. And now editors could – on their own, because they had computers, too - put together reports. This enabled upper management to demand more reports more frequently, which left editors with less time for their basic jobs - so editorial assistants had to take on more and more of the editorial work that editors no longer had time to do. This created the need for another title change, and editorial assistants could become assistant editors.

"*Et voila!* No more secretaries, fewer editorial assistants, and no one to answer the phone when I'm busy with my fearful mother. *Capisce, boychick?* I simplify, but you get the point, I trust."

"And as a result of all this, there's no one at the reception desk."

"Oh, people are assigned to it for an hour or two, but no one has the time to wrestle with an extra job, because the mere existence of computers has convinced upper management that we can do the same amount of work – or even more work – with fewer people. Lean and mean is the watchword around here." Steinberg broke wind softly. "As a result, we're very busy, but we don't have enough time to do our real work, which is publishing and selling books. Instead, we write reports, which I think I've mentioned already." Steinberg rolled his eyes.

There was a knocking sound behind me. I turned and watched a pretty, slender redhead in her mid- to late-twenties walk into Steinberg's office. She was wearing an emerald green lightweight sweater, beige slacks and low-heeled shoes. Her hair, parted on the side, and with a bit of a wave, fell to her shoulders.

"Mordecai, let me introduce you to Rachel Gormsby. Rachel, Mordecai Bornstein."

I stood up. Rachel smiled at me. She was on the tall side, about five-seven. I shook another warm, dry female hand. Before we had a chance to speak, however, Steinberg clapped his hands together. "No time for chitchat" he said, and swallowed a burp. "Let's go to lunch, such as it is." He put on his jacket and shooed us out of his office.

On the way to the elevators, I did get to ask Rachel where she'd gone to school (Barnard), what she'd majored in (English), how long she'd been working for Steinberg (two years), and how many editors she'd assisted on finding chapter contributors, which was the way she was meant to assist me. I was the first, she admitted.

As we approached the elevators, Steinberg waved his arms and cried out, "abracadabra!" The doors of one of the elevators parted open. "Works every time," a beaming Steinberg said.

I saw Rachel roll her eyes. Steinberg noticed it, too. "You're a tough sell, young lady."

"My boyfriend thinks so, too," she said firmly.

The three of us laughed as Steinberg put his arms behind Rachel and me and swept us through the elevator's open doors. Before I had a chance to turn around, he hit a button on the control panel. I expected the elevator to descend to street level, but it shot up instead. The elevator stopped almost immediately, and the doors opened again. I noticed that we were on ten.

"Follow me, my dears," Steinberg announced with a wave forward.

We walked into a large, brightly lit room that was filled with what looked like an upscale combination of cafeteria steam tables and bar mitzvah buffet. I half-expected to see a giant chopped liver sculpture that would make a thirteen-year-old boy's parents glow with satisfaction over their achievement at bringing their son to the threshold of manhood.

"Fill up your plates," Steinberg sang out, as he grabbed a tray, set a dinner plate on top, and wheeled around to a carving station presided over by an ascetic-looking black man in crisp white chef's toque and tunic. "I'll pay," Steinberg called over his shoulder.

After Steinberg paid for us at a register station, we found a table in the far corner of the dining area, between two windows. We weren't high up enough for a spectacular Manhattan view, but there was sufficient space between our building and its neighbors for the corner to be bright.

Rachel's hair and facial coloring were transformed by the natural light. I noticed a few freckles for the first time. She looked wonderfully healthy. Her plate was heaped predictably with fruit and vegetables resting on a bed of lettuce. As I expected, Steinberg's plate indicated that he'd hogged the carving station long enough to earn a reprimand from his fearful mother, had she only known. I made do with a turkey sandwich and a side of pasta salad.

"Ever since the first quarter results came in below forecast – but above last year's results for the same period, I should note – we've been on a contingency budget. The way that works is that we cut expenses, including what we would be spending to wine and dine our authors – people like Mordecai – in expensive New York *boites.*" Steinberg had turned his head toward Rachel.

"Doesn't this operation cost a bundle?" she asked.

"The company leases this operation to a caterer and makes money on the deal. And the more the employees eat here, the more cash the company pockets, all of which drops to the bottom line."

"These expense reductions would make some sense," I said. "But there's more to the cost cutting, isn't there? Now tell me about where the big reductions are, which is where they usually are."

"Mordecai's seen this sort of nonsense before," Steinberg said to Rachel. She looked at Steinberg and me without saying anything. "Mordecai knows exactly what upper management and their accounting minions are capable of. He knows that we achieve our biggest expense reductions by eating our seed corn."

"You let people go and you cut editorial, production, and marketing costs," I said. "You don't sign up as many books as you would have, you don't bring as many books to market, and you don't sell as many copies of the books you've already published as you would have if you'd kept spending on marketing, but you might still hit your profit target."

"Thereby saving the current quarter, but sacrificing the long term. But who cares about the long term? That'll be somebody else's problem."

"Well, the two of you must be safe," I said.

Steinberg laughed and swallowed a burp. "Rachel's safer that I am. I make the big bucks, after all." He patted Rachel's hand. "Don't worry, kid. They'll lay you off over my dead body."

I watched her wince. I wondered whether she accepted Steinberg's assurances – and whether he believed them himself.

"What's wrong with sales?" I asked. "Is the economy having an effect?"

"You know, in the old days, publishers figured that the economy and our part of the book business were counter-cyclical. In a crummy economy, people would buy more books so they could learn how to improve their livelihoods. But that theory hasn't held for a long time, and especially now, when people turn to the Internet before they turn to books."

"We've talked about that," I said to Steinberg. "Haven't you guys figured out how to deal with it?"

"We have all these high-priced people with fancy titles, whose jobs appear to be safe, by the way, studying and strategizing about how to sell books, or even little pieces of books, in electronic formats. But they can't seem to find a way to make enough money to make up for the loss of print sales. They talk a great game, however, so we – me and my fellow editors – set sales expectations too high, which was what upper management wanted us to do anyway."

"The bottom line for me is that my next royalty check, and probably the one after that, and on and on, will be smaller."

"See, Rachel? All you hear from authors is complaints about how much money *they're* losing, when *we're* the ones who are really hurting." Steinberg glanced at me, and I rolled my eyes for his and Rachel's benefit. "I hate to say this, but there are times when I have to agree that the only good author is a dead author." He chortled merrily, signaling this was all in good fun. I thought I detected a quiet fart from his direction, but it could have been my imagination. "I forget," Steinberg continued, "who it was who was quoted in the *Times* unburdening himself of such a dastardly sentiment. And he didn't mention that dealing with a surviving spouse is no picnic either."

Rachel's green eyes met mine for an instant, and then she smiled shyly and looked away. Steinberg's told her my sad story, I thought.

"I must have known that the reference book business was going to hell. I've already been thinking about selling my apartment."

"You can't be serious. You have a beautiful place. Where would you go?"

"I have the place upstate. It's perfectly adequate for my needs."

"I can't imagine you not being in New York. How will you manage without everything that's available here?"

"I lead a rich inner life." I glanced at Rachel, and she looked away quickly, as if she'd been staring at me. "With smaller royalty checks, I'll have to cut my expenses. Just like you guys." I tried out my warmest smile.

Rachel looked down at her plate. Steinberg showed his teeth in what could pass for a smile if you didn't know him as well as I thought I did. "Reality bites, as they say," he said. Then he lined up his knife and fork on his plate, signaling he was finished eating. I wasn't sure about whether or not he could sympathize with anyone. But this time I was certain that I did hear him break wind softly, in appreciation, I presumed, of his high-fat lunch.

Rachel and I found a conference table in an unoccupied corner room on the eighth floor, where we could work for a couple of hours. The room's two outer walls were covered with windows. One inner wall had a large white board. The other inner wall was taken up by a large bookcase filled with the publisher's general-audience books. I took a few minutes to look at them.

"I can't find anything I want to steal," I said. Rachel shrugged.

I told her that I wanted to do a reference book covering environmental damage to materials, and we worked on a proposal. We identified sources of damage, including sunlight, precipitation, and seawater, and then we branched out somewhat with fire. We decided to include all classes of materials, both metallic and non-metallic, such as plastics and wood, as well as so-called composite materials, like reinforced concrete, which contain both metallic and non-metallic materials.

In order for the book to be useful to working scientists and engineers, it would have to cover protection methods, so we had to have chapters on preventing corrosion, paints and coatings, and on fire and flame retardants. We made lists in three columns on the whiteboard, and then I used the lists to put together an outline for the book and a preliminary list of chapters that the book would contain.

I'd been trained as a chemical engineer, and I'd been working on this type of reference book for so long that outlining it and deriving a table of contents came fairly easily to me. I was pleased when it became clear that Rachel could keep up with me, and I complimented her.

"You're a good teacher," she said. "You set things out in an orderly way, which helps me understand where you're heading."

"Bob must do that for you, too."

"With all the reports he has to write, he doesn't have time. In addition, so many things go wrong around here because we don't really have enough people to prevent mistakes from being made, that he's always busy putting out fires. Besides, he has so many books in his program, and so many authors to deal with, that he's spread too thin to be able to devote a block of time to any one project."

"It's amazing he's has time for lunch."

"Oh, he never misses lunch." Rachel giggled and shot me a dazzling smile.

"It sounds like he's been successful in teaching you how to describe a problem in his inimitable style. You sound just like him."

"Yeah, I guess he has taught me a lot."

We finished up at that point. It was nearly four by the time I got to a block lined with apartment buildings, near the East River. The street was quiet and empty, except for a woman in a broad-brimmed hat on the opposite sidewalk. I walked into a pre-war building at the end of the block. When I gave the doorman my name, he told me that I was expected and I should take the elevator to sixteen.

I stepped off the elevator directly into a large square foyer, which was dominated by an impressive chandelier that gave off a pale glow. There were glass shelves mounted in insets on opposite walls to my left and right. The shelves contained a spare selection of glass and ceramic objects, including what looked like a small collection of martini glasses.

"Come in," a male voice called out.

I walked into a living room that I recognized from Sam Hudson's most famous painting, *The Afternoon Party*, which I'd seen in Sanford Glickauer's house. Or I'd seen a precisely executed copy, if Sanford was to be believed. A handsome young couple – both tall and well-dressed, and both with Indian complexions and large manes of wavy jet-black hair – made their way past me.

"Hi," the young woman said to me. I nodded in response.

"Same time tomorrow," the male voice I'd heard before called out.

"With pleasure, of course," the young man replied over his shoulder.

"I know that what you do here is hard work, and I'm very grateful for it," the disembodied male voice called out. I heard the elevator doors slide shut behind me as the owner of the voice came into the living room. He put out his hand for me to shake. We exchanged names. Sam Hudson looked a little older than the last picture I'd seen of him - he was seventy now - but his main features hadn't changed much. He had only a fringe of sandy hair around his ears, and he had a small, pointed goatee the same color. I could see that there were heavy bags under the eyes behind aviator glasses. He was almost my height and fairly trim, except for a small, but noticeable paunch. He was wearing a white Oxford cloth shirt with the sleeves rolled up past his elbows, gray slacks, and brown leather street shoes. There were smears of paint on everything, including his glasses.

"I googled you last night," he said. "You're having a rather nice run with all of your books. I checked some of them out on Amazon."

"I hope you bought them. I can use all the sales I can get."

"Can't we all," Hudson said dryly. There was a smile on his lips, which were pressed together.

"I learned at lunch today that my publisher's having Internet-induced competition that they're having difficulty overcoming. So my long run may be petering out."

"Don't be so glum. I've been painting the same way for forty-five years and all the new styles and fashion and what-have-you haven't put a noticeable dent in my income. My advice is, stick to what you know how to do well. It takes time for the world to pass you by. I'll bet your book sales overseas are still pottering along."

"You know, that's the message I got out of my last royalty statement. And I ran into some fellow this morning who's been selling my books in the Far East, and he told me to keep them coming."

"The world isn't as flat as some people would have you believe – maybe it will be soon, but it isn't yet. So I wouldn't be surprised to learn that print sales of your books were doing better in some foreign markets than here in the US. As a painter, I've had to come to terms with a similar reality."

"You mean, your paintings are selling better overseas than they are here?"

"Look, we all follow the money. Right now, I'm doing a painting commissioned by an Indian dot-com zillionaire. He and I have made a pretty good deal. He's paying me very well and he's made only one demand on me. He wanted the painting to be of a handsome couple with particular physical characteristics. Otherwise, I would have complete artistic freedom. My patron doesn't give a hoot about what the couple is actually doing in the painting. Of course, he knows my work, so he expects the two people to be nude and the scene to be intimate, although probably not one involving sexual congress. Whatever, before we signed a contract, my Indian patron wouldn't agree to proceed unless I sent him pictures of the two people who would pose for the painting. The two people who were leaving when you arrived had the right characteristics for this commission, so they're the ones I'm working with."

"You have to understand that it's a bit different with my reference books. I don't have to tailor them for any peculiarities in any specific foreign market. In fact, overseas readers want to learn how we do things in the US, rather than elsewhere, even in such advanced industrial powerhouses as Germany and Japan."

"So it should be relatively easy to sell your books overseas."

"The main problems don't involve content. They involve royalties instead."

"Royalties on copies sold overseas are lower than they are for copies sold here, I'd guess."

"Precisely. And there's another problem: piracy. My books are expensive. They cost several hundred dollars a copy here. And if an expensive book gets popular in an overseas market, people make unauthorized copies of it and undercut the genuine article."

"Ah, copying," Hudson said. He laughed. "I suppose that before he died Sanford told you about the dustup we had over his having had copies made of my paintings that he owned."

"He did try to convey to me how upset you were when you learned about what he'd done."

Hudson laughed again. "He dined out on that story for months after we had our little contretemps."

"The story is true, isn't it?"

"Look, I wasn't as exercised over the copying as Sanford made out."

"But you were upset, weren't you? It seems to me you had every right to be."

"Of course. But I wasn't upset about the mere fact of the copying. I was mainly concerned about Sanford keeping the real paintings and the fakes straight."

"He explained to me that he had a system for distinguishing between the originals and the copies worked out, and that it was foolproof."

"Foolproof according to him." Despite his protestation to the contrary, Hudson didn't seem to me to be easy with Sanford's action.

I felt that I needed to change the subject, but still bring the conversation back to Sanford. "It's interesting to actually be in the room which is the scene of your most famous painting," I said.

"Deborah and I haven't changed anything in the room since that afternoon."

"Surely you didn't paint *The Afternoon Party* in a single sitting." I looked around. "You would have had to work at impossibly breakneck speed. And where would you have set up your easel and canvas to get the perspective that's in the painting?"

"Not in here," Hudson said vaguely.

I didn't know what to make of that comment. "As I remember the painting," I said, "Sanford was sitting pretty much where I'm sitting now."

"Your memory is entirely accurate." Hudson looked at me coolly.

"I wonder how many people there are – friends of yours, I mean – who could name all of the people in the painting and could point to where in this room they're depicted."

"I've never asked."

"I wonder if anyone who was actually here that day could pass a quiz with such questions. Where were you sitting? Where was so and so? It sounds like the sort of game Sanford liked to invent."

"Why are you asking me? I'm not sure what you're driving at." He was looking directly into my eyes.

"Now that I see the room where the party took place, I'm just trying to figure out how you executed the painting."

"I'm sure Sanford never told you."

"As a matter of fact, he said he didn't know – not for sure, anyway." I kept my tone as light as I could. I hadn't expected the conversation to be quite as confrontational as it appeared to be, and I didn't want to get into an argument.

"He wouldn't have told you. I have everyone who works with me on a painting sign a release that they won't discuss my methods with anyone."

"Well, I guess the releases have accomplished what you intended. I surfed the Web to see if I could find anything about how you work. Has anyone even asked you about it?"

"Everyone in the art world knows that I never reveal my work methods," Hudson said. "If you've seen the *Art in America* article on my work and all the gallery catalogues, then you should have noticed the absolute lack of even any reported attempt to get anything out of me."

"Why so secretive?"

"I'm not so much secretive as realistic. People can guess at how I paint, but they don't know for sure, which is a competitive advantage in this day and age. There are plenty of people with talent, but it takes vision to accomplish what I do."

"So what you're saying is that executing something like *The Afternoon Party* must require more than taking a series of photographs, photoshopping them on a computer screen, and projecting the result onto a canvas that you can paint over, doesn't it?"

"It seems to me that you're on a fishing expedition, Mr. Bornstein," Hudson said. He gave me a satisfied smile. His message was clear: I wasn't going to get anything out of him.

I watched a pleasant looking woman in a white caftan glide into the living room. She looked to be about Hudson's age, possibly a little older.

Her gray hair was cut in a page boy. She moved very quietly. She was carrying a tray that she set down on a sideboard.

"My wife, Deborah, has decided to join us, I believe. Deborah, meet Mordecai Bornstein, the famous writer and editor, whose foreign sales may have already eclipsed his sales in these United States."

Hudson and I were already standing as he held forth about me with an amused look on his face. I shook hands with his wife.

"How do you take your tea, Mr. Bornstein?" she asked. Her voice was as rich as I'd imagined from Hudson's paintings of her singing.

"Black, no sugar will be fine," I said. I waited while she poured from a flowered porcelain teapot. I took a cup and saucer from her.

"Please sit down." She poured tea for herself and her husband, and then sat down beside him.

"We were discussing my techniques and methodologies," Hudson said to her. He grinned mischievously.

"It must have been a very brief discussion, indeed," Deborah said to neither Hudson nor me. Her grin was a mischievous as her husband's. "I have some angel food cake, if you'd like," she said to me. "Please pardon my oversight. I'm used to not bringing any baked goods out for Sam. He doesn't eat sugar during the day."

"The tea will do fine."

"I'm sorry about your wife. She was such a beautiful and vital woman. Such a great loss, to her family and to the art world."

The *Times'* obituary, with the great photograph, had made all that plain, I thought. "I miss her every day," I said. I looked around the room again. "I'm very pleased to be here. It's a treat to see the room which is the scene of your husband's celebrated painting. I wish Patricia was here with me. She would have enjoyed the experience as much as I have."

"But she was here," Deborah said. "Didn't you know that?"

"My wife?" I put my teacup and saucer on the floor. There was a rattling as they settled in place. "No, Patricia never mentioned a visit to your apartment. And Sam, you didn't say anything about Patricia's ever having been here."

"I wasn't here, actually." He looked at me calmly over the rim of his teacup.

"Sam's jaw swelled up suddenly, and he had to rush to the dentist." Deborah's look was as calm as her husband's.

"When was this?"

"About two weeks before she died," Deborah said matter-of-factly.

Patricia didn't *die*, she was *murdered*, I thought. "Had she made an appointment?" I said. "Of course, she did. I mean, when did she tell you she wanted to visit?"

"She called that same morning. She said she was in New York for the day and wanted to come over and talk with Sam," Deborah said.

I remembered the day. Patricia had taken the train down to have lunch with her old boss and, presumably, to tell him how things were going at her museum upstate. "Did she say why she wanted to come over?"

"No, she didn't, but I knew who she was, so I said it would be fine." Deborah sipped her tea.

"Had you run into her at some function?"

Deborah and Hudson exchanged glances. "I don't remember how I learned who she was," Deborah said.

"Did you know that she'd written a journal article once on projection techniques that painters had used?"

"I don't recall that. Really," Deborah said in a strong voice.

"And Sam had to rush off to the dentist just before Patricia arrived," I said, somewhat sarcastically.

"It was an emergency," Deborah said firmly. Hudson remained quiet throughout this exchange.

"What did you two talk about?" I said.

"We had tea and talked about her work at the museum upstate and my music. After about an hour, the dentist called and said that Sam would have to be there for several more hours. When I told your wife that, she said that she had better be going in that case, and she left – for the train, I presume."

"Did you tell anyone about my wife's visit?"

"Only Sanford Glickauer, who was here a week later."

"Why was *he* here?"

"He came down to discuss a commission," Hudson said.

"May I ask what he said he had in mind?"

"No, that's fine. We talked about my painting Sanford with a woman."

"Did you discuss what these two people would be depicted doing?"

"Sure. Something along the lines of one of the paintings of mine that Sanford owns, *The Newspaper*, but we didn't settle on anything in particular. At the end, Sanford said he'd leave that detail – that was the word he used - up to me. Like my Indian patron has done."

"Did he say who the woman was going to be? Or was it understood that he was talking about himself and Gwennie?"

"No, I got the distinct impression that it wasn't Gwennie who we were talking about."

"Did Sanford give you any idea at all who the woman might be?"

"None at all."

"What happened next with this proposed commission?"

"Nothing. I never heard from Sanford about it again."

At the door, Deborah gave me her cool hand. Something about it looked familiar, possibly the long fingers and the nails with clear polish, the way Patricia did her nails, except on special occasions.

CHAPTER EIGHTEEN

I got into bed at a normal hour for me, but I couldn't get to sleep. When I finally dared to roll over and lift my head so I could see the time on the digital clock-radio, it read 1:00. The apartment was silent. The temperature in the bedroom seemed to be conducive to sleep – a little cool, so I had pulled a sheet and a light blanket over me, which was the way I liked the bedclothes to be arranged.

I got up and peed. When I got back into bed, sleep still wouldn't come. I turned on the bedside lamp and began to read – my usually successful method for getting back to sleep – and I did doze off when the Rachel Cusk novel fell from my grasp. But when I reached over to turn out the light, I was awake again. It was the same story I'd been living through since Patricia's death. Revelations about Patricia – in both the distant and recent past – kept whirring around in my brain, accompanied by fear that there were more things I was going to learn about her, and I was prevented from sleeping. I tried to focus on other things, like the new project with Rachel, in the hope that I could calm the whirring. Fat chance.

I propped the pillows against the headboard, sat up, and went back to the Rachel Cusk novel. This time I didn't doze off and try to get to sleep, and I finished the book. Now there weren't enough hours left for a decent amount of sleep before the alarm clicked onto the NPR morning hosts announcing the teasers before the six o'clock newscast. I lay back down in acceptance that for the remaining hours I was in bed, the same revelations and fears would keep resurfacing, over and over. And now here they came, again and again.

As I lay exhausted, trying to keep the hours from rolling on, even though I knew I wasn't going to get any sleep, I couldn't help but be reminded of the anguish I'd suffered when I learned of Patricia's high-school abortion.   How could I not remember the awful night after the Stantons and Mary Howard had given me the details of that episode in Patricia's life? And now it came back to me again, as intractable as it had been at first.

Had Patricia decided not to tell me about the abortion because we had decided, finally, not to have any children, after years of ambivalence? My low sperm count had been part of the problem. Still, I had trouble seeing how one decision fit with the other.

By not telling me about the abortion, she hadn't needed to tell me about the help and protection the Stantons had provided. And she also hadn't needed to tell me about Ted Howard, the well-muscled guy so much shorter than she was who'd gotten her pregnant. So of course, she'd never mentioned the little comedy they acted out in front of the camera operated by Mary Howard. The film was harmless. Had Patricia simply forgotten about it? Or had she not considered it worth ever describing to me? Possibly not, for if she had, I'd have asked questions about who her little fellow actor was, and the questions might have made her uncomfortable.

Paranoia conjures up strange possibilities, of course. There was Rita Cassidy's odd comment that Patricia's running into me at Karen Kolter's New Year's Eve Party hadn't been an accident. Was I now supposed to doubt Patricia's story that she'd been invited as catnip for that obnoxious seven-footer she'd made a show of dismissing? Patricia's story had made sense. Rita's assertion years later seemed preposterous. I'd dismissed it out of hand, without bothering to ask where it had come from. But I'd never bothered to check with Karen Kolter, because I remembered that she'd seemed surprised that Patricia and I had known each other.

I wondered why I'd never checked into Patricia's California history. She'd talked about an involvement with a much older man. When she was alive, and I was ignorant of some of the details of her life, I'd had no reason not to believe her. Did I have a reason to doubt her, now that there were some mysteries?

I couldn't stop myself from conjuring up the first Frankfurt Book Fair trip, when Patricia had disappeared into the private rooms at the backs of stands presided over by a series of men I'd dubbed the blue-blazered smoothies. I remembered that I'd accepted Patricia's accounts of having been required to cozy up to the old boys in order to acquire the rights to their books on the most favorable terms. I also remembered how flushed and happy she'd been when she'd emerged from those encounters.

Had there been things that I'd missed during our marriage? We'd been completely open with each other, hadn't we? I wasn't wrong about that now, was I? What else would I discover if I embarked on a project like

Sanford's biography, but with Patricia as my research subject? I'd thought about that memoir I'd been considering about Patricia and my life with her. Was that a dangerous idea? Did I need to continue with the Sanford project as a distraction from my looking for answers to questions that might occur to me about Patricia's past?

There was that strange business involving the out-of-the-way diner, where Patricia ate solitary meals occasionally. Only the diner's owners knew she was there, although they didn't know who she was, and apparently had never asked. Hartnett had brought this inexplicable behavior up again during our last conversation. He'd answered my call a few days ago. I'd been surprised. I'd expected voicemail. There'd been weariness mingled with testiness in his voice when he'd launched into his own questions before I'd had the chance to ask any of my own.

"We haven't been able to come up with an answer to this question: why did your wife have numerous meals alone at a nondescript diner nowhere near either her workplace or her home? I've asked you about this odd circumstance before. Have you been able to think of an answer to the question?"

"I've thought about it, and I haven't been able to come up with anything, I'm sorry to say."

"Call me if you can think of any reason your wife might have frequented the place."

"So you believe her going to the diner might be the key to a motive for her murder?"

"Don't put words in my mouth, please, Mr. Bornstein. I just want to know the reason why your wife happened to be in the wrong place at the wrong time, nothing more than that."

"Maybe her presence there had something to do with the meeting that she mentioned to me but never gave me any information about."

"The meeting that no one seems to know anything about." I'd thought I heard a derisive laugh at the other end of the line, but I wasn't positive. "In any case, it doesn't matter what the meeting was about, who your wife was supposed to be meeting, or even if there was a meeting in the first place."

"Oh, there was going to be a meeting, I'm sure of that. Given that, what about the person or persons Patricia was going to meet with? Isn't it curious, to say the least, that no one's come forward?"

"No, I don't think so. If the people your wife was going to meet with didn't want news of the meeting to get out, there's no reason they would come forward."

"That would certainly be the case if they, or he, or she, had a hand in Patricia's murder, wouldn't it?"

"As I've explained, we explored that angle. Everyone loved your wife. There was no jealousy on the part of anyone she worked with or did business with. We found no evidence of any affair. There's absolutely no indication that she ever got herself into any trouble of that or any other kind. The wrong people never took any interest in her. She had no gambling debts, for example."

"But you still want to know why she ate at that diner every so often, including that night."

"I've tried to be clear. I've tried to be straight with you. I very much doubt that discovering why she was there will change my conclusion about why she was murdered. It was a robbery gone wrong. But it does help if any loose ends are tied up when we catch whoever committed a crime. Then there can't be any distractions from our theories and conclusion."

"So no matter what else you may learn, your conclusion won't change, as far as why my wife was murdered is concerned. It was robbery, pure and simple."

"I doubt I'll find anything that will make me change my mind, because I haven't yet."

"So was it the perfect crime?" I'd asked. "Don't you people always find something that gives the criminal away?"

"That's generally true," Hartnett had responded.

"But not always, I take it."

"This was a robbery gone wrong." I'd heard the weary, we've-gone-over-this-more-than-once tone in his voice, and I'd begun to wonder if he was losing patience with me. "The robber killed his victim, which wasn't supposed to happen. The robber got lucky and got away with murder – at least so far. Sad to say, and I mean this sincerely, your wife didn't get lucky. That's all that went down."

"So when luck intervenes, the police are stymied. Is that what generally happens when someone is murdered in your jurisdiction?"

"There aren't that many murders out here in the 'burbs."

"I don't know what that means, exactly. Does it indicate that you and the department don't have enough experience in murder cases, no matter what the motive was?" I'd tried to keep the testiness out of my voice – how successfully I hadn't been able to tell right away. But it had immediately become evident that I hadn't been particularly successful.

"What it indicates is that everyone who's worked on this case has busted butt to get somewhere. That includes me, as I'm sure you know.

I've pulled out all the stops. So I trust that I'm mistaken if I'm hearing more than disappointment in your voice. I'd be the one who's disappointed if I was hearing an accusation that we, me in particular, haven't been trying hard enough to find your wife's killer."

The tone had become pure aggrieved cop, a man who saw himself as a barely tolerated public servant who did the things he had to do to serve uncaring civilians, who didn't understand or respect him, who would never appreciate how heavy his burdens were. If I were killed in the line of duty, the tone of Hartnett's voice had implied, the citizenry would cluck in sympathy that would dissipate at the first mention of any police excess. I hadn't felt one way or another about Hartnett, I'd thought, but I was beginning to not like him very much. Of course, I'd also thought, it could well have been my fault that Hartnett had begun to react to me with a tinge of annoyance. Had he detected a lack of respect for authority that I hadn't realized I possessed?

Now, days later, I was unsettled by the news that Patricia had visited Sam Hudson's apartment and studio, been told that he'd been called away unavoidably, according to the Hudsons' account, and talked only with his wife Deborah. I tried to conjure up the day she'd gone down to New York. She hadn't told me about the trip until the prior night. I'd had a deadline on the preface for the nuclear power book, which I was being careful with, so I hadn't any intention of taking the train down to New York with her. But she hadn't asked me to come along, had she? I couldn't remember. I also couldn't remember whether there'd been a major issue that we needed to deal with that might have sidetracked her from telling me about the Hudson visit. Why in god's name hadn't she told me about it? What could possibly have prevented her from doing so?

What else would I learn that Patricia had never told me? Was there a child from her years in California, whose existence she'd hidden from me? Had there been an affair while we were married? Had there been multiple affairs? Was she carrying on an affair when she was murdered? Had it provided the motive? No, no, it was a robbery, Hartnett kept insisting whenever he and I talked. I had to put the notion of an affair out of my mind, I told myself as I turned over in bed, too exhausted to go back to reading, and not relaxed enough to be able to get back to sleep.

I propped the pillows against the headboard again and sat up. The clock-radio said 5:30. I checked the outside temperature on my iPhone and looked to see if I'd received any emails overnight. I scrolled quickly through the junk that had accumulated, and then I put the phone back on the night table and swung my legs over the side of the bed.

I was outside by six, walking tiredly down Riverside Drive. I felt like hell. I got through the walk, and had breakfast at a diner out on Broadway. I dawdled through showering and getting dressed, and it took awhile to close up the apartment. I made sure there was nothing in the refrigerator that might spoil if left there too long. I didn't know when I'd be back.

It was mid-afternoon when the navigation system took me off I95 at what looked to be the southern edge of downtown Providence and onto a smaller arterial highway. The exit onto local streets came up almost immediately. I took a left and a right, and then I was driving through a non-descript neighborhood with unprepossessing residential structures and a scattering of stores.

After several blocks, however, the housing stock became much more substantial. When I turned right onto the top of the street where my destination was, the mostly brick houses looked like they had been built in the boom years before the Great Depression. They weren't set back very far from the street, and there wasn't a great deal of space between them, but they were decidedly grand nonetheless.

The neighborhood had an air of graciousness. The sidewalks were wide enough for grass plots and mature shade trees. Stop signs at nearly every intersection slowed the sparse traffic, which was just as well, for the pavement wasn't in the best of condition. There were only a few people on the streets - a trim youngish woman walking a pack of dogs, several other women pushing baby carriages and strollers, and a couple of joggers. The sky had clouded over. It looked like it might start to rain soon.

The navigation system announced my arrival at my destination in front of the most modest house I'd seen on the street – a two-story stucco number behind a small plot of grass and hedges of medium height. The front door was on the left, up a short flight of concrete steps. As I went up them, I noticed the wide uncovered porch, with two sets of tables and chairs, hidden by the hedges.

I watched the red front door swing open behind the screen in an aluminum storm door, and then I had my first glimpse of Gretchen Carmichael in the flesh. When I'd googled her, I'd found her photographed in newspaper articles reporting on her interior design business. She'd always been sitting down next to a client, she'd had oversized glasses on, and her hair had been pulled back from her face. But now, as Sanford would have noted had he been standing next to me, was like a moment when she'd just gotten up from a chair and I could see what she really looked like. In addition, she wasn't wearing glasses, and her hair was down.

The woman holding the door open for me looked a little over sixty, but I knew from Sanford's account that she was older, in her early seventies. Had she not been casually beautiful still, the afternoon light, still bright despite the cloud cover, would have been unkind to her. But it wasn't. Her looks were admirable and didn't need soft light to be alluring. But the mere fact of her attractiveness wasn't what made my heart thump in the upper part of my chest.

For an instant, I thought it might be Patricia who was standing there, a step above me. Was this actually Patricia, returned to life, but fifteen or twenty years older? This older woman's hair, gray with a few remaining traces of blonde, was arranged in a style Patricia favored. I looked up into her widespread eyes, I let my gaze travel down to her cheekbones, prominent like Patricia's, and then I looked at the rest of her.

The width of her shoulders, and her long and slender body all seemed familiar, as did her outfit – a lightweight turtleneck, slim slacks, and running shoes, all of them black. Patricia had often dressed that way. My mouth went dry.

I nearly fell forward when I tripped on the step as I barged into the small foyer. Gretchen moved back slightly. I righted myself and turned to face her. She was standing straight, the way Patricia always had. I was startled by Gretchen's height. She was as tall as Patricia. Her large, pale blue eyes, were looking straight back at me questioningly. I expected her to say "six and a quarter," the words Patricia had used to announce herself the first time she'd stood up in front of me. Instead, she put out a cool, dry hand and said, "Is everything all right? You look discombobulated. Perhaps it was the long drive."

"I'm fine," I said. "It was a long drive, and there were a lot of trucks on the road, so it was a bit wearing."

"Why don't you take a seat in the living room and relax? There's some bread and cheese. I'll serve you when I bring in the wine."

The living room was to the right. The food was on a low table in front of a red couch. Gretchen went past the living room toward the back of the house.

I walked past the low table and sat down on the sofa. My mind was racing. As far as I knew, Sanford had never met Patricia, but her picture had been all over the news, so he must have known what she looked like. Was the tender smile on his face when he pictured me here meeting Gretchen Carmichael for the first time - as he must have known I would do at some point? Had he started to laugh when he pictured what he must have known my startled reaction to her physical presence would be? Would he have thrown his head back with even greater amusement if he'd lived to hear me tell him what the sight of her had done to my heart? Was this visit to have been part of a game he'd set up? Had he been that much of a son of a bitch?

I realized that my teeth were gritted in fury when I heard Gretchen call from the kitchen. "Red or white?"

I managed to sound out "red" loud enough for her to hear me.

She came into the living room holding an opened bottle of wine and two large glasses. She sat down on the sofa a couple of feet from me and poured a finger of wine into one of the glasses. She swirled the wine in the glass and lifted the rim to her nose. She sniffed, took a swallow, and waited. Then she smiled at me over the rim of the glass. "I'm a wine snob," she said. "It's a Chassagne Montrachet from a good producer. "I think you'll like it."

She poured the wine, and then she turned her attention to the spread on the low table in front of her. There were three cheeses on a wood cutting board. Gretchen began to cut small portions and put them on a small plate. I watched her long slender fingers at work. The nails were cut fairly short, and they were covered with a clear polish. Patricia had worn her nails that same way.

"This is a blue cheese washed in wine," Gretchen said as she cut into a blue-veined slab. "It's from Italy. I prefer it to a French Roquefort, which I find too salty." She moved on to the next wedge. "This is an Irish Gouda. Farmstead, my local cheese monger doesn't get it year-round, so it's a treat. And this," she went on, as she cut a third small piece and placed it artfully on the small plate, "is raw cow's milk. Not to worry. As long as it's been aged for sixty days, it's safe to eat. That's the law." She smiled at me, and then she arranged three pieces cut from a baguette on the plate's circumference. She handed the plate to me. I put it down on the table next to a small knife and fork that were resting on a white cloth napkin.

"I've been called a sybarite," Gretchen said, as she repeated the cheese cutting, which had begun to look to me like a ritual. "Possibly the kindest thing anyone's ever said about me." She laughed softly. I took a sip of wine. I didn't know what to say.

Gretchen crossed her long legs, spread the napkin over her lap, cut a small piece of the Gouda, and put it in her mouth. Her eyes half-closed with pleasure. She tore off a tiny piece of bread and chewed thoughtfully.

"A Frenchman I knew – Jean Louis, who was Algerian by birth, actually – always admonished me to have bread with cheese, not cheese with bread. It's good advice." Gretchen lifted the wine to her lips and drank a little. She looked at me intently.

I bit into a piece of the bread. "Terrific," I said.

"It's from Seven Stars Bakery. I get it at the Eastside Market. The wine shop is next door."

"Is that far from here?"

"Not very. I rode my bike today, and stopped at the cheese store on the way back."

"You make Providence sound like a great place to live."

"It's a foodies' paradise." Gretchen put another piece of cheese in her mouth, followed by the bread chaser. She sipped some wine. She looked at me intently again. "You didn't drive all this way for cheese and wine, however. You're here to talk about Sanford." She sipped more wine and continued looking at me with undisguised intensity. "But let's talk about you before we turn our attention to a man I haven't seen for many years."

"I'm not important."

"I hate false modesty, Mordecai. I've googled you. I have a good sense of all that you've accomplished in a fine career that's far from over."

"If you've googled me, you've seen pictures of my wife."

"Yes, I have. I'm very sorry about what happened to her."

"Thank you."

"It must have been very hard for you to deal with."

"You have no idea how hard it's been. And there seems to be no end to it."

"As far as I could tell from searching the Internet, the police haven't caught your wife's killer. Is that what you mean when you say there seems to be no end to it?"

"That's only part of the reason I said that."

"What else could there be?"

"You must have seen pictures of Patricia during your search. Did anything strike you about the way she looked?"

"She was a beautiful woman, who exuded strength and intelligence." Gretchen had put her knife and fork down. She uncrossed her legs and sat facing me, her hands folded in her lap.

"Nothing else?" I said.

"I don't know what you want me to say about her."

"Didn't you notice the strong similarity between your looks and Patricia's?"

"I'd have to look at her pictures again, but now that you mention it, I suppose there were some similarities. She was tall and slender, like me, wasn't she?"

"The two of you are, were, exactly the same size and shape, the same height, same figure, same bone structure. Your faces match. At the same age, you could pass for each other. I've never seen two women from different families who looked so much alike. I can't believe you didn't notice the similarities." I noticed that I'd raised my voice somewhat.

"Calm down, Mordecai. This seems to mean a great deal to you. I don't know why, and I'm going to wait to ask. First, eat some cheese and drink a little wine – the whole bottle if it will relax you. I'll get a laptop and some old pictures, and we'll have a look at the evidence."

We ate and drank in silence for several minutes. Gretchen poured more wine, and then she uncoiled from the sofa – it was like watching Patricia – and left the living room. I watched her walk up the stairs and heard her tread on the second floor, above me. When she returned, she was carrying a laptop and a couple of framed pictures.

"Let's set up on the dining table where we'll be more comfortable," Gretchen said.

I got up and followed her into the dining room. For the first time since I'd been in the house, I took my eyes off Gretchen long enough to notice the Persian carpets and the gleaming wood floors.

While the laptop was booting up on the dining table, I looked at the two photographs that Gretchen had placed next to the machine. One showed her standing at the front door, her hand on the doorknob. Her face was turned to the photographer, and she was smiling. She was wearing shorts and sandals. The picture reminded me of the shots of the teen-aged Patricia that the Stantons had taken with their telephoto lens. The other picture showed Gretchen sitting in a wing chair, with her hands in her lap. She wasn't smiling, but her face was relaxed. She was wearing a blue polka-dot dress and heels. Her long legs were together and at an angle to the floor. I had taken similar pictures of Patricia at various times.

"I'm guessing these were taken about twenty years ago," I said.

"A little more than that. I'd just turned fifty." Gretchen turned the laptop so I could use the keyboard.

For my money, the photographs could have been of Patricia just before she died. I stayed silent while I brought up the newspaper cover picture taken when she'd become head of the Museum of Art and Industry. I turned the laptop so Gretchen could see the screen.

"Leave the machine in front of you," she said. "I'll stand behind you, so we don't have to keep moving it."

I felt Gretchen's presence behind my head and shoulders as I went from one publicly available Patricia picture to the next. The pictures weren't more than a few years old, but they seemed to me to be from a very different lifetime, whose happiness and gayety were beginning to fade from memory. Nevertheless, the pictures were clear and large enough to show exactly what Patricia had looked like. And I could see the strength and intelligence that Gretchen had mentioned and that I knew so well.

"There's warmth that I didn't mention earlier," Gretchen said, as if she were reading my mind. "She must have been a remarkable woman."

"Don't you see the unmistakable resemblance between the two of you? That's also remarkable."

"I do observe some similarities. But we're not exact replicas. No, I don't see that at all." She sat down and turned to look at me. I met her unflinching gaze. "I wonder why you're so adamant about this idea, Mordecai. "There has to be something behind it. What is it?"

"When Sanford talked about you, he never described what you looked like. He talked about what you were wearing at various times, but not about your hair, or your figure, or your height."

"Didn't you ask him? I thought that how we girls look is one of the main things men care about." Gretchen laughed. "Often, it's the *only* thing they care about."

"He said you were a model. That seemed to cover it, I guess. So I had a standard picture of a model in my mind whenever Sanford talked about you, and that was enough."

"Why is the fact that Sanford never described me so important now?"

"Because withholding a description of your looks was part of a game Sanford had decided he was playing with me."

"What the hell are you talking about, Mordecai?"

"You do remember Sanford's game playing, don't you? It was one of the things – perhaps the main thing - that drove him."

Gretchen looked at me reflectively. "I never thought about Sanford that way. I simply thought that he was determined to get whatever it was that he wanted, no matter what it cost – him or anyone else, when all was said and done."

"Can't you see him laughing at me when he thought about my meeting you for the first time and my being shocked at how you looked like an older version of my wife? I can picture his reaction to my surprise. I was thinking about it when you were in the kitchen opening the wine. And now he's having his moment from the grave. I can't even confront him."

"Well, he did get your reaction right. But why would he do such a thing? You and he couldn't have been enemies. If that had been the case, he wouldn't have asked you to write about him."

"Maybe the offer he made to me was all part of an elaborate joke."

"Please, Mordecai. That's incredibly paranoid. Besides, despite your protestations, your Patricia and I really don't look all that much alike. There are similarities, I grant you, but you shouldn't go beyond them."

"I can't help it." I rubbed my forehead with the tips of the fingers on my left hand.

"Tell me about Patricia," Gretchen said. She took my right hand in hers. "I think that talking about her will make you feel better."

At first, I tried to tell Gretchen what Patricia had been like as a person, and as a wife and life partner. I felt unsure of my ability to describe her accurately and wondered how well I was portraying the essence of the woman I'd professed to love so deeply. I felt that I was on firmer ground when I told Gretchen about Patricia's career, about her successes, and about the adulation she received from anyone who came in contact with her. Now I spoke with uninhibited pride in Patricia's achievements.

I also told Gretchen about my life with Patricia, and for the first time, with anyone, including Patricia herself in one key instance, I held nothing back. I told the truth, which I hadn't always done, although sometimes by leaving things out, rather than by telling lies. I told Gretchen about the three-week affair with Lisa, which began immediately after my first date with Patricia, and led to our five-year separation. I told Gretchen about the one-night stand at the Washington publishing conference that had almost destroyed me and could have destroyed my marriage. I still didn't understand why it hadn't done so.

In order to be completely honest, I told Gretchen, I would have to admit that although Patricia and I had both said that we would always be totally open with each other, I hadn't lived up to my side of the bargain. After Patricia died, I was disheartened to learn that she hadn't been entirely open either. I told Gretchen about my obsession with things Patricia hadn't told me about – her high-school abortion, the movie she made with her seducer, the questions raised about things she'd done at the museum, her solitary meals at the out-of-the-way diner, the strange visit to Sam Hudson's studio.

I'd gone over these things in my mind so much that I couldn't tell whether my concerns about them sounded silly or not. I told Gretchen about it. She took my hand in hers and looked at me, without saying anything. Then I told her about the Frankfurt trips and the private rooms and the blue-blazered smoothies and the flushed and ecstatic looks on Patricia's face when she emerged from those rooms. Gretchen laughed.

"Now, *that's* over the top," she said. Then she stopped laughing and looked at me sympathetically. "Look, Mordecai, I can appreciate how you must feel. Discovering things in a deceased partner's past has to be unsettling. I haven't had that experience – my late husband was a blameless soul apparently – but I can understand it. In any case, perhaps writing all of this down will help you deal with it. Whoops." She laughed again, "You're a writer. So you've already thought of writing this all down."

"Yes, I have. I keep a journal. Everything I've told you is in there."

"Did Patricia also keep a journal?"

"As a matter of fact, she did."

"Have you read it?"

"The deal we had was that the surviving spouse could read the other spouse's journals."

"So none of this 'destroy upon my death' stuff?"

"No, none of that.

"So please answer my question, Mordecai. Have you read your wife's journals?"

"I have looked at some of her journals, but so far I've only read back a year or so. There must be thirty of them."

"Will you read the rest of them?"

"I don't know."

"It sounds to me like you can't bring yourself to read them. Why can't you? Are you afraid of what you might find there?"

"I hate to admit it, but the answer to your question is, Yes, I'm afraid."

"I believe you loved her very deeply. You believe in that love. And why not? It still has great power over you. Why should you risk destroying it?"

When I finished talking about Patricia with Gretchen, I felt somewhat calmer than I had when I'd first seen her at her front door. I still thought that the two women looked exactly alike. Gretchen remained unconvinced, however, which left me far from certain that Sanford had imagined that my meeting her would be the high point of some sort of cruel joke. Still, when I told her about Sanford's revenge on Harlan Burns, she had to admit, she said, that there appeared to be aspects of Sanford's character that could lead one to believe that he might have been pretty much capable of anything short of murder. But when I told her about other conversations I'd had with Sanford, she used them in arguing persuasively that Sanford had liked me and would have had no reason to hurt or embarrass me.

Talking with Gretchen seemed different that talking with anyone else I knew. I found something comforting about her. She listened to me sympathetically and without criticizing me. Her analyses were precise but not harsh. She brought me to her point of view with a gentle persuasion that wouldn't have been out of place in a venerable English novel.

I was close to five when we finished the last of the wine, which had gotten better and better though the afternoon. The cheese and bread were long gone. Gretchen uncrossed her long legs and stood up. She reached down for my hand.

"How about a walk?" she said. "I can show you where some of my clients live." She turned and looked out at the street. "I'll take a quick peek at the weather. I think it may have started to rain lightly."

It was misting. I retrieved the Aussie hat and light waterproof jacket I kept in the car. Gretchen put on a red slicker. She pulled the slicker's hood over a Red Sox cap. Out on the sidewalk, she linked her arm in mine and shoulder to shoulder we set off.

Almost immediately, we stopped in front of a substantial brick house on a corner lot. The house was much larger than Gretchen's. When I looked back at her house, I noticed that from there you could see the back of this house.

Gretchen followed my gaze. "I woke up one morning a few months after my husband died and saw from my bedroom window a for-sale sign on my current home. I seized the opportunity to downsize. It was a no-brainer. I can still accommodate both of my sons and their families when they visit on holidays. Besides, I welcomed the decorating challenge the new home presented. The bonus was, I sold my old home near the top of the real-estate market. It was a gift from the gods." Gretchen's eyes danced with pleasure at her good fortune. Her face was close enough to mine that I could smell the lipstick she'd applied before we'd left her house.

We walked past block after block of large single-family homes. Most of them looked like they'd been built in the Nineteen Twenties. Gretchen pointed to each house where she'd taken the owners on buying trips to France – for a dining table and chairs here, living room pieces there, library bookcases and a desk in this one, draperies in that one.

"I love taking clients to Provence, especially L'Isle-sur-la-Sorgue," Gretchen said as we walked past a mock Tudor house with a blue Sotheby's for-sale sign in front. "I took the current owners there to find bedroom furniture. Have you been there?"

"We went to other places in Provence, but not that one."

"It's a remarkable town, with three hundred antique dealers. There's a wonderful restaurant where you can dine outdoors in a garden with animals that are free to roam. It's quintessentially French. Some of my clients have been a bit squeamish about sharing their tables with cats, however. I tell these clients that I let my cat sit on the table when I'm eating – she was sleeping upstairs this afternoon, by the way – and all they do is shudder. I can't understand why." Gretchen laughed merrily. She seemed to be enjoying herself.

After several additional client houses, she suggested that we walk on Blackstone Boulevard, which turned out to be a broad thoroughfare with a substantial median strip that contained a wide walking path. The mist had become a light rain, but it didn't seem to be deterring any of the joggers and walkers, some of who had dogs on leashes. Gretchen stopped to pet all of the larger dogs.

"I lost my last sweet boy three years ago," she remarked after she reluctantly stopped scratching a large black Labrador under the chin and around the ears. "I can't bring myself to get another one. My daughter-in-law asked if I wanted a kitten from a litter, and I agreed, reluctantly. But now Mathilda and I are great pals. She's named after a character Fanny Ardant played in that Truffaut movie, *The Woman Next Door*. Have you seen it?"

"Yes. It combines terrible tragedy with high comedy. And it has a beautiful woman and haunting music."

"By George De La Rue."

I thought fleetingly about Patricia's discussing female jazz singers with me when we first danced together, and I turned away from Gretchen for a moment.

It was close to six when we turned off Blackstone Boulevard onto Angell Street. "There's a good restaurant not far from here, in Wayland Square," Gretchen said. "How about an early dinner? I'm famished. The cheese and bread are a distant memory. It must be the walk in this cool, damp air."

The place was called Red Stripe. It was noisy and crowded. When we were seated at a small table, Gretchen removed her Red sox cap and played with her hair. It resumed its original shape. She saw me watching her and smiled. "I have it done in a town nearby called East Greenwich. I can wear down to my shoulders, and it's still easy to take care of. Quite marvelous, don't you agree?"

I nodded and grinned at her. She looked at me with mischief in her eyes.

In the dim restaurant light, we could have been any prosperous couple out for a casual dinner – possibly a banker and his wife, a professor at Brown. The fact that Gretchen was more than fifteen years older than I was wouldn't have been apparent to any restaurant patron who happened to look our way. I always looked my age, and Gretchen could have easily passed for at least ten years younger than she was, so when our harried waiter asked me through the din whether my wife and I would care to order wine, I wasn't surprised. Gretchen had managed to hear the question, as well.

"Why don't you pick a nice Italian red, dear," she said, and we both laughed. I pointed to a selection on the wine list, and the waiter wheeled around and hurried off. Then we both started to talk at once.

"Go ahead," Gretchen said.

"Please, you go ahead. I've been talking about nothing but my own life. I haven't had the good grace to ask you about yours."

"Don't apologize, Mordecai. You've been in a great deal of pain. You had to let it out."

"Look, Gretchen, I know when I've been rude. Tell me about your sons. Why don't you start there?"

"All right. They both went to Wheeler, a private school up on College Hill. They both were accepted at Brown, but they chose MIT, where my husband went to school, as Sanford must have told you. They graduated a year apart."

"So are they engineers?"

"One's a lawyer and the other's a psychiatrist. They've both done extraordinarily well for themselves."

"Ah, but have they given you grandchildren?"

Gretchen laughed. "You do know how to cut to the chase."

"Well?"

"Well, Charles – he's the lawyer – has four children, two each from his two marriages. The second marriage is working better than the first, if you want to know."

"Glad to hear it. Now how about your other son?"

"Richard and his partner Damian, who's also a shrink, managed to adopt the boy born to the woman to whom they paid a small fortune to be impregnated with Damian's sperm. She's a volleyball player who needed the money. Anyway, the adoption turned out to be a complicated legal business, which would have cost Richard and Damian another fortune, except that Charles handled it. They paid him handsomely, but he didn't charge them anywhere near as much as an outsider would have."

When we started on the wine, Gretchen went back in time to the years when she had a relationship with Sanford. She didn't airbrush any part of it, and her account seemed to track Sanford's closely. She didn't skim over any details. Her memory of them seemed to be the equal of Sanford's.

When I told her that remembering so much about a relationship years in the past meant that it must have had great significance for her, she said, "I suppose so. But I was young, and I think that youthful experiences can stay with you throughout your life. But I have a question for you, Mordecai. Does my moral relativism disturb you? Oh hell, I was a practicing moral nihilist, when you come right down to it. I mean, I had promised myself to Jack at the same time I was carrying on an affair with Sanford. Who, by the way, was perfectly happy with the way things were."

"I don't judge people," I said. "And I don't have scruples that are dictated by religion."

"Oh goody. We can leave religion out of this. But come on, Mordecai. You've written books about environmental issues. I haven't read them – sorry about that – but I did read the summaries that came up when I googled you. You make judgments about people all the time."

"That's true, but I don't get into the personal lives of polluters. I've always been leery of doing so. I'd vitiate an argument if I wrote that a toxic waste dumper was good to his wife and kids and never kicked the dog. And if I found that some horrible polluter was a wife-beater and I wrote about it, then I'd have to include positive family stories when I found them. In my business, you have to compartmentalize and deal only with certain parts of the life of a person you're shining a bright light on, not with all the aspects."

"So you'll allow me to compartmentalize my life, I take it. Is that what you're trying to say? It seems to me that the analogy is imprecise, but still. Are you trying to say that you'll let me put my relationship with Sanford in one box and my relationship with Jack in another box?"

"I can't agree with that. One relationship can be corrosive to the other one."

"I don't think I let that happen."

"Then you're better at compartmentalization than most people. That's my take, at any rate."

"I've never studied the issue. I suppose I didn't have to. After I married Jack, I remained faithful." Gretchen smiled. "But why bother telling you so? After all, you're not judging me."

"When it comes to someone's private life, I'm not in that business,"
I said, and smiled at Gretchen. She smiled back at me with her eyes, as well
as with her lips.

By the time we'd polished off salads and bowls of Portuguese stew,
I'd had Gretchen talking about herself for over an hour. I realized, without
having planned to do so, that I was employing the tactic I'd used when I
was in my twenties. Get a woman talking about herself and you'll lead her
to believe that you're interested in her as a person – which will make it
easier for you to get in her pants. I'd convinced myself back then that the
tactic could be successful. I'd never taken the time to honestly determine
whether there was any validity to my theory. In any case, the difference
between this time and my cynical youth was that I was discovering that I
was actually interested in Gretchen for herself. Was that because she
reminded me so strongly of Patricia, despite the protestations to the
contrary?

Gretchen was waving a hand in front of my face. "Earth to
Mordecai," she said. "What planet are you on?"

"Oh, sorry."

"I'm not Patricia, you know. I can't be."

"I know that. I'm sorry. Actually, I wasn't thinking about her."

Gretchen looked at me skeptically. I poured the last of the wine.
The waiter moved in to clear the plates. "Shall I show you the dessert
menu?" he said.

"We're having dessert at home," Gretchen said. Her smile had a
hint of surprise at herself.

"The lady has spoken," I said to the waiter.

Gretchen tried to pick up the leatherette folder with the bill, but I
snatched it away from her. I stopped the waiter and handing him the folder
with my credit card before Gretchen had a chance to produce her own.

"Please, it's my treat," I said.

"You don't have to."

"But I want to."

It had stopped raining when we left the restaurant. Gretchen linked
her arm with mine again, and we walked silently and companionably for
about twenty minutes, until we were back at her house. She guided me
through a low wrought iron gate to a side door. Once inside the house, we
went up several steps to the first floor hallway.

"Make yourself comfortable on the sofa," Gretchen said. Her face
was close to mine, and I could smell the lipstick she'd freshened in the
ladies room before we left the restaurant. "Unless you're in a hurry."

"I'm in no rush."

"Great. I'll be down in a little while."

She didn't turn on any lights, but I could see the shapes and positions of the furniture well enough to make my way across the living room. I pulled my shoes off and fell asleep as soon as I settled down on the sofa. It had been a long day.

I woke up and heard a tread on the stairs. It sounded like someone coming down in high heels. Then I heard "shit!" and the sound of someone falling down. I looked toward the stairs. Even in the near darkness, I could see that Gretchen was on the floor at the foot of the stairs.

I rushed over and began helping her up. She had changed into some sort of lightweight dressing gown and very high heels that stayed on as I got her to her feet. She draped herself over me and talked into my ear.

"I should never have put these fuck-me shoes on," she said. I could feel her breath against the side of my face. "I haven't worn them for awhile, and they can be dangerous." She took a couple of steps back from me. "But they have their uses," she said.

In the semi-darkness, I could have mistaken the rangy creature with her legs apart and her hands on her hips for Patricia. But I knew better. Oh, sure.

I put my arms around Gretchen, lifted her off the floor, and brought her a few feet until her back was against the wall that formed one side of the arch that led into the living room. I put her down and pushed my right hand through the opening in her dressing gown and between her legs. She wasn't wearing anything under her dressing gown. I put my left hand behind her head, found the place where her neck met her shoulder, and began to slowly kiss and lick her skin. This was what I'd done with Patricia in the dark of many nights, but I knew that the woman whose thighs were squeezing my hand wasn't her. Oh, sure.

"I feel that I know you, Mordecai," Gretchen said. I could feel her breath on me, but her voice seemed to come from far away. "I know you better than you know yourself. I want you. I want you deep inside me."

I bent down and picked Gretchen up. She pulled my collar and kissed me in the place where I'd been kissing her. "Take me upstairs," she said.

All of the doors off the upstairs hallway, except one, were closed. I heard a cat meow from behind the door at the far end of the hall. I carried Gretchen into the second floor bedroom whose door was open. She hadn't drawn down the shade on the front window, so the room wasn't in total darkness. I'd carried Patricia into rooms like this, where there was just enough light so we could see each other when we made love. But I knew the woman I'd carried into this bedroom wasn't Patricia. Oh, sure.

I put Gretchen down on her back. She pulled me down on top of her. I let her roll me onto my back. She undid my belt buckle, and I arched my back and raised my buttocks so she could pull my trousers and shorts down. She positioned herself so she could take me in her mouth. She didn't take her dressing gown off until we woke in the middle of the night and made love for the second time - and I was freed, at least for awhile, from any images of my dead wife.

CHAPTER NINETEEN

When I woke again, there was a little light in the room, the dawn of a new day. If I was to begin to free myself from my troubles and live in the present, not in the past, this was as good a time as any. I picked my wristwatch up from the night table. It was a little before seven.

I watched Gretchen slide out of bed. She bent and picked some clothes up off the floor. She waved her free hand in the air as she padded softly toward the bedroom door. When a tall woman waves her arm over her head, she can look impossibly taller. I also noticed that Gretchen, who was naked, had a firm, well-shaped ass. I heard her go click-click with her mouth as she left the room. If she'd said, 'not bad for an old lady,' I wouldn't have hesitated for as much as a nanosecond to say, 'not bad, full stop.' I was a gentleman, after all.

I heard a door open, and a few seconds later a cat jumped up on the bed. She was gray and black and not very big, which was fine by me when she climbed onto my chest and assumed the Sphinx position, her behind pointed at my chin. "Morning, Mathilde," I said. "Nice to meet you, at last."

Gretchen was back in ten minutes or so. When she slipped back under the sheet, Mathilde got up, stretched, and jumped off the bed. "Evidently three's a crowd," I said.

"I'm glad to see that you and she got to know one another."

"In a manner of speaking."

Gretchen reached down. "Ready for action, I see. I like that in a man."

"The Kathleen Turner line in *Body Heat* goes something like, 'You're not too smart. I like that in a man.'"

"So it does. Well, to each her own."

We took our time, and then we held each other for awhile. It was past eight when I went under the shower in the bathroom across the hall. A razor, a can of shaving cream, a deodorant stick, and a toothbrush still in the packaging were laid out on the sink. There was a man's bathrobe hanging on the inside of the bathroom door. I wondered for a moment if the bathrobe had belonged to Gretchen's late husband, but there was no monogram to enlighten me, so I dismissed the thought.

I put the bathrobe on and looked around for Gretchen. There were four rooms, plus the bathroom I'd used, on the second floor. The doors were all open now. I quietly took a tour. There was a room with a double bed, a night table, and a small dresser, which added up to a guest room. There was an office, with a built in desk and bookshelves filled with reference books and catalogues related to Gretchen's design business, and there was a large table supporting a pile of books with swatches of wallpaper and other materials. Two laptops, a printer, and a scanner were on the desk. And there was Gretchen's bedroom, which had its own bathroom. I knew that room quite well.

The fourth room was a reading and media room. There were two Eames-style chairs, with reading lamps set up behind them. They faced a flat screen television mounted on a wall. There were bookcases. They were small. I looked at the spines of the books. There was some poetry, there was a collection of pop-up books, and there were some old books that looked to be in good condition. I pulled one out. It was a child's history of England. The illustrations were delicate and quite wonderful. There was a small, low table between the Eames chairs. There were two electronic readers on the table.

I thought about the libraries I'd been in recently: Gilbert Ryden's. Alice Burns', and my own, of course. They were wonderful – at least, I thought so. But were they mausoleums for housing what some people now called dead tree editions? Did such libraries belong only to the past? Gretchen was a designer. She knew how to help people arrange their lives. This room reflected her life, her own needs and desires. And all she needed in her library of the future was a few cherished collections of dead tree books – and electronic readers for everything else.

I went back into the hall. There was piano music coming from the first floor. I walked down the stairs and found Gretchen sitting on the living room sofa. She was wearing a bathrobe similar to the one I had on. She was reading a newspaper. Her hair was slightly tousled. She looked much younger than she was, but not young enough, I thought regretfully.

I stopped before I entered the living room. I remembered those times years ago when I'd thought I'd seen Patricia somewhere – the back of that tall blonde teenager in Saks, for instance – but I'd been mistaken. I'd felt such a rush of joy until reality intervened. When I'd first laid eyes on Gretchen, I'd thought she could have been Patricia come back to life in an older version. Could I possibly believe that last night I had slept with Patricia come back to life and not the woman actually sitting ten feet from me? That isn't living in the present, is it? I needed to find a way to do better. Clearly.

Gretchen looked up and smiled at me. I smiled back at her.

There were peeled orange segments, mugs, and a carafe half-filled with dark coffee on the low table in front of the sofa. I sat down next to Gretchen and took a couple of orange segments off the plate. She leaned forward and poured coffee. Her robe fell open a little. I made no effort to avoid looking at what was revealed. Gretchen made no effort to prevent me from seeing what there was to see.

There was no cream or sugar in evidence. "I figured you for black," she said.

"Spot on."

The pianist on the CD had a nice touch. "I trust the Fauré is to your liking."

"Good choice."

"I washed your clothes. They're in the dryer."

"I thought you might have burned them, so you could keep me prisoner here."

"Don't you wish."

I had to admire Gretchen's technique. If her purpose in bantering with me and letting me have a peek at her breasts was to keep my focus on her, and not let my thoughts drift off, possibly to Patricia, the effort was enough of a success that I knew that I could convince myself that I was feeling better than I had for a very long time. I wondered if the feeling would last.

I stayed away from any complexities. "I feel great," I said.

"A little nookie goes a long way," Gretchen said.

We were dressed and out of the house around nine. We walked left, and then turned left again in a couple of blocks. A few minutes later, we entered a store called the Butcher Shop. There was a long display case on the left and an opening along the right-hand wall that led into a restaurant. A pretty redhead was behind a high counter.

"He needs a big breakfast," Gretchen said to the redhead. Gretchen turned and cupped a hand around my ear. "You earned it, big guy," she whispered.

I cupped a hand around *her* ear. "You're a right bitch." I whispered.
I blew gently into her ear.

Gretchen stifled a fit of laughter. I made the click-click sound with
my mouth that she'd made earlier. The redhead gave the two of us a
deadpan look.

We both had egg-white western omelets, home fries, and toasted
poppy seed bagels – "the works," Gretchen called the meal, as she pushed
my money away and paid herself.

We drank more black coffee. "The sort of breakfast Jack Reacher
would scarf down," I said. I wondered whether Gretchen would pick up
on the reference.

"Another three or four inches taller, plus fifty or sixty pounds
heavier, and I'm sure I wouldn't be able to tell the difference between you
and him," she said. "But then I'd have to see if you could take out half a
dozen mean guys in under a minute." She'd nailed it.

After breakfast, we walked through Wayland Square, where we'd
had dinner the previous night, and a few blocks later down a ramp to a
parking lot in front of a block of stores. Gretchen linked her arm in mine
and guided me into the Eastside Market. She pulled a loaf of bread from a
shelf. She handed the bread to me after she'd paid for it. It was in a Seven
Stars Bakery bag. The label said Durum Stick.

"It's good as is for today and for tomorrow, as well," Gretchen said.
"Then it's wonderful toasted. Or you can cut it up and freeze it sliced."

Something to remember you by, I thought. "Thanks for the
present," I said.

"My pleasure."

We walked to the beginning of Blackstone Boulevard. There were
several dogs on the path through the center of the median. Gretchen
stopped to pet all of them. She didn't seem to be in any kind of a hurry,
but when we turned onto her street, I had the sense that it was time for me
to go.

We stood in her driveway facing each other, less than two feet
apart. I put my arms around her and drew her into an embrace. Her cheek
pressed against mine. We didn't say anything. I didn't know what to say.
The sex had been terrific. I thought that Gretchen's friskiness indicated
that she agreed with my assessment. I felt grateful. I'd gone without sex
for too long. At the same time, I felt panicky. I felt as if I was losing
Patricia all over again – although I knew damn well that it was Gretchen,
the older version of Patricia only in my fevered imagination, who I was
leaving.

Gretchen and I leaned back and looked into each other's eyes.

"Don't lose your bread," she said.

"I'll be careful with it, not to worry."

We didn't say anything more. Maybe there was nothing more to say. I couldn't bring myself to talk about a future together. I thought my doing so might offend her, I feared that she might find me condescending. A million questions occurred to me. Should I ask her to meet me for dinner again? Should I talk about spending the night with her again? What would I say to her if she brought up the difference in our ages? How would I answer her if she asked whether I still believed that she was an older version of my dead wife? How would I react if Gretchen said that a relationship with me was impossible? I didn't ask her anything.

I had no way of knowing what she was thinking at that moment, and I didn't have the courage to ask. That pretty much defined me, I thought – a bloody coward. Then Gretchen took my hand and squeezed it. I didn't know how to interpret the look in her eyes. I squeezed back, and then I turned, unlocked the car, and tossed the bread gently onto the passenger seat. I turned back to Gretchen. The look in her eyes was still there. I still wasn't sure what it meant.

"A snack on the way home," I said. "Knowing me, I'll finish the whole loaf on the road."

She smiled at me and waved her hand across her face, just one time. She had turned and was walking across the small plot of grass toward the entrance to her home as I backed my car out of her driveway. I eased the car up the street, stopped behind a parked car, and looked in the rearview mirror. Gretchen had gone through the gate at the side of her house. She hadn't turned to watch me drive away. They only do that in the movies, I thought. I set up the navigation system for the long drive home and put the car in Drive.

The next morning, the phone in the upstate house rang before six, when the clock-radio was set to go on.

"I need to see you," a female voice said.

I looked at the caller ID. "Maggie? Do you know what time it is?"

"Meet me at noon." She named a restaurant not far from the Institute. Whenever I'd driven past the place, I'd wondered if anyone ever ate there.

"I'll be there," I said. Maggie hung up.

"I love conversations that sound like they come from third-rate detective novels," I said into the dead phone.

I got myself out for a brisk walk through town. My standard route takes me first through winding suburban residential streets. Except for the school busses, there isn't much morning traffic there. I can walk in the middle of the street much of the time. Many of the houses are modest and look like they date from the Twenties through the Sixties, although there are some sections where the houses are larger and grander. They're mostly fairly well kept on the outside. Inside, however, some of the more modest homes can be surprisingly shabby, especially those that have been occupied by older people who haven't spent any money on maintenance for some years. Patricia and I had learned this by attending estate sales.

The middle stretch of my route goes up the town's main commercial thoroughfare, which is lined with a mix of one- and two-story buildings. There are medical offices, a large chain drugstore and one small, locally owned pharmacy, where I have prescriptions filled, restaurants, including just one fast-food place, four gas stations, an auto repair shop, and other businesses. There's an astounding number of bank branches, all with tellers, in addition to ATMs. There is a bookstore. It has large greeting card and children's book and game sections. A couple of places sell the *Times*, and I stop briefly to buy it, before I go back into the residential streets for the last leg of the walk.

The streets are clean. Maybe once during my walk, I'll pass some fast-food trash that was ejected from a car during the night. That's the extent of debris, although I suspect that if the population density were markedly higher, there'd be a lot more of a mess.

There's hardly any crime, although there was a gruesome family homicide a few years ago that made the national news. Patricia was murdered miles from here.

She used to run with me in the early mornings. But now I walk alone, of course.

When I got back home, I made my standard breakfast, which was guaranteed to make me feel virtuous – a fresh orange with a banana, oatmeal with the big flame raisins, and black coffee – and read the *Times* while I ate it. After I put the dishes in the dishwasher, I poured another cup of coffee, cleared the newspaper away, and sat down at the kitchen table.

I thought again about how lonely my life was. I had hardly any friends, even counting Bob Steinberg, who was really a business colleague, and Rita and Brian Cassidy, who were in categories all to themselves, as far as I was concerned. Bill Kramer was a good friend. Did Maggie Hartnett count as a friend? Probably not. Had Sanford Glickauer? I hadn't known him long enough to find out, and, in the event, I'd begun to wonder about the true nature of our relationship. I had no family left, on either my side or on Patricia's. Finally, I doubted whether there was a future with Gretchen Carmichael.

It didn't matter where I lived. I could sell everything I owned and buy a new place just about anywhere – the States, Europe, Central America, it didn't matter. My kind of work lived in the ether. In fact, I thought, I could live a virtual life. Sort of like the fictional Jack Reacher – never putting down roots, just roaming from place to place, going wherever the action was.

I arrived at the place Maggie had designated a couple of minutes after noon. The restaurant was in the ground floor of a chain hotel that backed onto a street that climbed the hill half-a-dozen or so blocks from the north edge of the Institute. Parking was around back.

There wasn't much action in the place. There were a few people at the bar, and only two tables were occupied. I walked past a glossy easel on which a couple of specials had been written in green and red.

She was sitting in a booth about halfway back, not too close to the kitchen doors. There was a smart phone on the table in front of her. She tilted it up toward herself and pressed a finger against the lower part. "You're late," she said to me, as I slid into the booth opposite her. She turned the phone around so I could see the time before the screen went dark. 12:05 it said.

"What's up, Maggie? Anything I can do to brighten your day?"

She took a swig from a bottle of beer on the table. "You're always so smart, Mordecai. Do you know that?" Her blue eyes behind the oversized lenses bore into me. Nothing moved on her smooth, perfectly made-up face. I'd seen that expression before, trained on Bill, and sometimes on Sanford. "Don't fuck with me," it said.

"I really do try to not come across as a smart ass," I said. I tried a smile and got nothing in response. I wondered how a face could be made to look so perfect. Still, I liked Maggie. Maybe the hard time she gave everyone was part of the allure – the vital part. Although she also had a great body.

"You can't control yourself, is that it? The devil makes you do it? Or is it god?"

"Neither. I just try to get along with everyone. Always the diplomat, my father used to say about me, especially when he was irritated about my negotiating style."

"You tried to be so cool with Sanford, always trying to keep him from playing with you while he was playing with the rest of us during those games of his."

"You used to guide me in my responses, as I recall."

"I hated it when Sanford targeted another victim. And I knew that it didn't matter to him who the players in his games were."

"I thought you were an enthusiastic participant in Sanford's games."

"I could be, oh yes, I certainly could be. I'm a senior member of Sanford's firm, after all." There was sarcasm in her voice. She lifted the beer bottle to her lips and drank from it. Her pink tongue darted out like a cat's to wipe some foam off her upper lip.

"No, really. I thought you liked to play."

"Sometimes Sanford went too far. When he did, I didn't care for his behavior."

"I thought he tried not to embarrass the subjects of his public games, like the ones he had us play in the restaurant in our building."

"Not hard enough sometimes, I'm sad to point out."

"Why do you say that? Do you know anyone who got hurt in one of Sanford's games where you were a participant?"

"No, not really."

"Then what's the problem? I mean, the games I sat in on involved people who couldn't have know they were the butt of the joke. They were far enough away from where we were sitting, out of hearing."

A young woman dressed in a black waitress uniform appeared at tableside. I pointed to Maggie's bottle of beer, which was nearly empty. Then, with the fingers of my other hand, I made a sign indicating 'two more.' The waitress turned around and headed for the bar.

"I was never completely sure of that," Maggie said. "I was always warning Sanford to keep his voice down."

"He did used to whoop it up whenever he was victorious, which was pretty much all the time." I laughed at the memory.

"So you agree that it was possible that there were people who knew damn well when they were the subjects in one of Sanford's games."

The waitress had moved quickly, and she was back at our booth with two Amstel Lights that matched the beer that Maggie was just draining out of the bottle. It would have taken an awful lot of bottles of regular beer to do any harm to Maggie's perfect figure. I caught her looking up at the waitress. There was a tight smile on Maggie's mouth. The lips weren't parted. Then I looked up at the waitress. *Her* face lacked any expression – on purpose, I surmised. She looked exhausted, with dark smudges under her eyes. But she also looked like a tough Irish girl, hardened by a difficult life. She handed us menus.

"Give us a few minutes," I said.

"Just give a holler when you're ready to order," she said, and walked back towards the bar.

I took a swallow of the cold beer. I was playing for time, trying to decide whether to tell Maggie what I'd learned about Sanford and several of his more private games, during my visits to Kiawah Island and Rockville, Maryland. Maggie sat silently, looking at the menu, waiting me out apparently. Then I realized that I'd already told Bill Kramer about the Sanford's game involving Harlan and Alice Burns and Bethia Davenport, and it was entirely possible that he'd relayed the story to Maggie.

I took another swallow of beer and leaned forward, my hands on the table. "I've spoken with Bill about a game Sanford played back in the day involving Harlan and Alice Burns and Bethia Davenport. Has Bill spoken with you about this conversation?"

"No, he hasn't, Maggie said.

"Then I'll tell you all of what I told him." I started with Gilbert Ryden's account of the American Tractor meeting where Harlan Burns had embarrassed Sanford, went through the revenge game that Sanford played, and concluded with Alice Burns sending Sanford packing.

Maggie took a swallow of beer before she spoke. Then she looked at me with her unblinking blue eyes behind the oversized lenses. "Here's what I knew," she said. "Sanford started the firm when he got the opportunity to represent Alice Burns in her divorce action. But I didn't know how strong a role revenge might have played in the matter. And I didn't know about the relationship that Sanford and Alice had. It's not a pretty story, none of it."

"I've been trying to avoid passing judgment on it, at least for the time being."

"That's your prerogative."

"What's your take?"

"I need to hear more, if there is more."

"I talked to Phoebe Armstrong, Sanford's second wife. But before I tell you about my meeting with her, let's get our lunch orders in. I'm starving."

When we asked the waitress for a recommendation, she mentioned the chef's salad. Maggie and I both ordered it. She got her Russian dressing on the side; I asked for my salad to be tossed.

The salads appeared before I'd gotten very far into the story involving Phoebe Armstrong, and I really was hungry, so I ate while I talked, which dragged the story out somewhat. Maggie pecked at her salad and let me go through the whole story without stopping me. "You must know this story," I said, "or at least a lot of it. The first I heard about Phoebe was from Bill, your law partner, after all."

"But I didn't know all the details. I doubt that Bill does, either. Neither of us goes that far back in Sanford's life, for one thing. And for another thing, the Phoebe story never was a subject of discussion with Sanford. It was off-limits – it doesn't show Sanford in the best possible light, which wouldn't have pleased him and would have prevented him from discussing all aspects of it. He liked to play the hero, not the villain."

"That sounds like the Sanford I knew, however briefly."

"You're not judging Sanford, are you? You wouldn't want to be caught doing such a thing, would you?" There was a devilish, gotcha smile playing around Maggie's lips, maybe her first smile of the day, I reckoned. Would there be another one before bedtime? One could hope. The day wasn't half over, after all. I chewed a forkful of salad and a bite of a roll, and washed them down with a swallow of beer.

"And where did Gwennie fit into these stories?" Maggie said.

"She was always in the background, not forcing herself into the center of the action.   Gwennie had other interests that occupied her. What's more, she was secure in a belief that sooner or later a game would be brought to an end, and Sanford would be back in her arms – or in the same house with her, at least."

"That's the picture that was painted for you, I take it."

"I have no reason to dispute it."

"Not do I. Gwennie's a woman of many interests. That's for sure."

"And worrying about the whereabouts of Sanford's affections wasn't one of them. That's your point, isn't it?"

Maggie paid attention to her salad for what seemed like half a minute. Maybe she was waiting for me to say something more, and reckoned that the best method for getting it out of me was silence. But I could wait her out. Finally she looked up and met my gaze. "Word about a person gets around," she said evenly, as if she'd weighed each word carefully before it passed her lips.

"Why did she and Sanford leave the city and move upstate?"

"Sanford explained the move as a concession to Gwennie, who wanted to live close to nature, not to concrete."

"So the move was her idea? And it wasn't to tear him away from temptations of the flesh, because she didn't care whether he gave into them?"

"The answer to both of your questions is yes."

I busied myself with the rest of my salad. I hadn't mentioned Gretchen Carmichael, and I wasn't about to. Gretchen was my business –

unfinished or not, I didn't know, but mine nonetheless. In any case, Gretchen's involvement with Sanford was long past.

"Tell me Maggie," I said, "why did you set up this lunch?"

"OK, I'll cut to the chase. I believe that Sanford's death wasn't an accident. He was murdered."

"You can't be serious."

"Oh, but I am. The proper expression would be dead serious."

"Come on. It's my understanding that the police looked at the accident scene exhaustively. They found nothing that implicated anything or anyone in Sanford's car plunging off the road except the rain, which made the road treacherous suddenly, and Sanford himself, who must have misjudged the situation and the amount of danger he was in."

Maggie leaned forward and pointed her fork at me. "Let's look at another case, Mordecai, to get your opinion of how well the police are handling that one."

I knew what was coming, but I didn't protest. All that I said was, "I know where you're going."

"Of course, you do. But let's go there anyway. What have the police told you about your wife's murder? Oh, yes, this: they've found nothing to contradict their theory that your wife's murder was the result of a robbery gone bad. My husband's been pillow-talking, if you want to know." I stared at Maggie and tried to control my facial muscles. She stared back and went on: "And you subscribe to that theory without reservation, right?"

"Why in hell would you expect me to do so?" I spit the words out.

"I wouldn't. Of course not. So don't expect me to believe that Sanford's death was an accident, despite what my husband and his colleagues say. Besides, I think my husband's bored with his job. I keep telling him he would have been better off going into coaching after his football playing days were over."

"What does he say about that."

"He just grunts and stares at me." Maggie took a sip of beer. "Let's get back to the topic at hand," she said.

"OK, let's not get into the issue of how Sanford's supposed killer made murder look like an accident to trained investigators. Let's go right to the next question: Who do you believe the perpetrator was? Who did the dastardly deed?"

"Don't try to be funny Mordecai. You're not that good at it."

"I thought I was, but no matter. Let's get back to the question of who you think murdered Sanford. Alice Burns? Phoebe? Sanford was long in the past, as far as they're concerned. If they didn't kill him when he was an integral part of their lives, why would they years later? Or was it one of the subjects in a recent Sanford game who overheard Sanford and his tablemates discussing the game? That seems extraordinarily far-fetched."

"I don't know who killed him. But I now know more about Sanford's life than I did before we started this conversation."

"Why don't you search the firm's files – or your own memory, for that matter? You've been at the firm for a long time. The fact is, Phoebe split up with Sanford decades ago, and he handled a great many divorce cases between then and his death. A lot of divorcees - relieved as well as bitter – fell into his orbit. So there was plenty of opportunity for starting and playing private games – serious games, involving revenge and personal issues, not the trivial games he played in public." I was finished with my lunch. I lined up my knife and fork diagonally across my empty salad bowl.

"I believe that all the private game playing ended when Sanford left the city and moved upstate. That's my understanding, at any rate."

"So we're left with the theory that Sanford died in an accident. Unless you think Gwennie did him in. But I'm sure your bored hubby and his friends on the force have investigated that possibility. Or maybe Bill Kramer employed an undetectable method of dispatching the firm's founding partner. Or maybe you're Sanford's killer. Is that why you had me tell you what I know about Sanford's life – to see whether I might have a clue that you killed him?"

Maggie's eyes bore into me. I smiled at her, hoping she didn't see a smirk instead of a smile. "Just kidding," I said.

"I became a lawyer," Maggie said, "because I hate injustice. I want bad guys to be punished. That's why I take the battered wives cases that Gwennie's supposedly such an expert on. But I really do something about those cases. Anyway, that's why I'm not satisfied that an accident took Sanford's life. If someone killed him, I want that person brought to justice."

Maggie took a lipstick and compact out of her handbag and refreshed the bright red gloss on her lips. She patted her hair, put the cosmetics back in her bag, and slid quickly out of the booth. Standing at the side of the table, she looked as perfect as she usually did – hair in place, lipstick fresh, not a wrinkle or a crease in her clothing. "I'll have the waitress bring you another beer," she said. "You've earned it. I'll take care of the check on the way out."

Should I have been comforted that this was the second time in two days that a good-looking woman had told me that I'd earned my food and drink for services rendered? I didn't think so.

CHAPTER TWENTY

Maggie's idea, that Sanford hadn't died in accident but had been murdered somehow, struck me as preposterous. I was determined to put it out of my mind.

I drank the second Amstel Light, left the restaurant and got into the car, and drove down the hill to the entrance to the highway. Twenty minutes later, I pulled into the parking lot several blocks from my office. As usual, I didn't see anyone I knew as I walked through quiet streets to the building. I rode the elevator up to my floor. The key, which I hadn't used for some time, met no resistance in the lock of my office door. The air inside was warm and there were no unpleasant smells, which wasn't surprising. This was a smoke-free building, after all, and the basement restaurant was many floors away.

I couldn't remember when I'd been here last. I reckoned it must have been before Sanford's fatal accident. I would have liked to have checked postmarks on any mail that the letter carrier had pushed through the slot in the door, but I got all my mail at home, and when I picked up the pile of paper from the floor I found nothing but restaurant take-out menus.

I sat down in the large easy chair in the office's outer room and let the two lunchtime beers catch up to me. My head jerked when I dozed off, and I woke abruptly. I slid down in the chair so my head was supported and settled in for an afternoon catnap. I was escaping into sleep quite a lot these days, but I decided that I wouldn't let that bother me.

When I awoke, I looked at my watch. I figured I'd been asleep for fifteen minutes, which qualified as a catnap, I supposed. I got up, and felt a bit groggy. I needed some exercise so I could fully wake up. I took the three backrests off the sofa and piled them on the seat of the chair where

I'd been sleeping. Then I began to lift each of the sofa's three seat cushions so I could pound them back into shape. When I lifted the middle cushion, I found an iPhone that must have gotten wedged between the middle cushion and the one to the right. This must be Sanford's phone, I thought. No one else had sat on the sofa since the last time he'd been in my office.

I tried to turn the phone on, but the battery was dead. I thought about recharging the phone, but then I remembered that my charger was at home, and I didn't have another one in the office. So it would have to wait.

It seemed to me that there was no point in calling Hartnett about my having found the phone. After all, Sanford's death had been ruled an accident, no matter how Maggie felt about it. Besides, I wanted to hang onto the phone for awhile. Sanford might have stored some contacts or other information that would be of interest to me as I delved further into his life.

Was I doing something illegal? I decided not to let such niceties dissuade me.

I wasn't sleepy any longer. I fired up one of my computers and checked my email. Rachel Gormsby had sent a progress report with the status of the table of contents for the book she and I were working on. She hadn't been able to get several of the contributors I'd proposed to agree to participate in the project. I looked around on the Web for a couple of hours, wrote up suggestions for additional potential contributors, and sent them to her. By the time I'd finished it was late afternoon.

I locked up the office, took the elevator to the lower lobby, and walked back toward the car. The streets were more crowded than usual. People were leaving their offices and beginning to make their way out of the small downtown office district. As usual, I didn't speak to anyone, although I nodded to a few people whose faces I recognized, and who appeared to recognize me. We'd passed each other in the street on other occasions without stopping to chat. We didn't really know each other.

I picked up a take-out dinner box from the Asian place uptown that I liked. When I got home, I didn't bother with a plate. I ate the food out of the box in the dining room, and drank a glass of red wine with my dinner. While I ate, I read the latest *New Yorker*. After dinner, I plugged the charger into the iPhone that I strongly suspected was Sanford's.

Then I went into the living room and settled down on a comfortable wing chair with a second glass of wine and a Martin Beck mystery from the Seventies, *The Locked Room*. It may have been suffused with murder and mayhem, but it was high-quality escapist reading, perfect for a quiet evening at home, it seemed to me. I kept the house silent; no music, not even some mournful cello stuff, tonight.

After an hour, I went to check on the iPhone. It was charged. I unplugged the charger and took the phone into the living room. I sat down in the wing chair again, tapped the button that lit the screen and swiped it to unlock the phone.

I looked for any apps that had been downloaded. There was a Scrabble app. When I tapped the icon, I found a game with an opponent called MagHar1, most probably a handle that Maggie Hartnett used for Scrabble. She hadn't resigned after Sanford's fatal accident, so the game was still alive, and it was Sanford's move. I resisted making the move for him. It would have been a cruel joke to play on Maggie, and I wasn't up for having to explain such an attempt at humor to her, not with that "don't fuck with me" attitude of hers.

There was a TuneIn Radio app. When I tapped the icon, I got the local public radio station. The left arrow took me to a "Recents" list. WEEI, the first station on the list, was identified as "Boston Sports News." I saw this as further evidence that the phone had belonged to Sanford, who'd been passionate about the teams from his boyhood home town.

On the upper left hand corner of the screen, there was a Contacts icon. I tapped it. An "All Contacts" list appeared on the screen in alphabetical order, but arranged by first name, not last. I had such a list on my own iPhone, so I knew how you created one. Sanford had typed his contacts' first names into the "last name" box, and done the opposite with their last names.

I scrolled down to the B's and found Bill Kramer's phone number. I had no doubt now that I had found Sanford's phone. I found Gwennie's number in the G's, of course, but backed up, because another name close by had caught my eye as I'd scrolled past it. It was Gretchen's name. Surprise, surprise, I thought. I saw that the telephone number was up-to-date. I heard the words "what the fuck" come out of my mouth without my being conscious of speaking them. Then I moved on until I found Maggie's name. I continued to scroll slowly through the list, which must have contained dozens of names.

I froze when I got to the P's. There it was, and the cell phone number was correct. Patricia Bornstein. My dead wife's name and number were in Sanford's cell phone contacts list. Why? I asked myself. I'd been led to believe by Sanford and Gwennie at the Kramers' dinner party that Patricia and Sanford had never spoken. But there it was: Patricia's number. He'd used it to call her. Obviously.

I could delete Patricia's name and number now. But that wouldn't change what had happened in the past. Of course not.

I'd learned what Sanford had been like, how he had treated women. Is that why I hadn't called Hartnett and turned the phone over to him? Was it because I'd expected to find something awful in the phone? Had I kept the phone so I could look for Patricia's name and number – the very thing that would destroy me?

Before I realized it, I was crying uncontrollably. I couldn't stop myself, and I must have cried for several minutes. When I finally stopped, I realized that Sanford's phone was still in my hand. I unlocked it again and found the Camera icon. I tapped it. I tapped the tiny picture at the lower left-hand corner of the screen. I tapped it again, and a picture of Maggie appeared on the screen. She was sitting at a desk in what I surmised was her office. Sanford had caught her looking up in surprise at him. It looked as if he'd taken the picture when he'd walked into her office without warning.

At the top of the screen, it said, "65 of 65," which meant that there were that many photographs stored on Sanford's iPhone. I tapped a right-facing triangle at the bottom of the screen, and a slideshow started to play. There were pictures taken at a party somewhere, then motion pictures, with sound, taken of a waterfall, then pictures at another party, this one outdoors, then pictures of the Sam Hudson paintings that hung in the Glickauers' house in the hills, and then a picture that sent a chill through me. I tapped the screen, the slideshow stopped, and the picture remained.

When it comes to looking at pictures, an iPhone screen is hardly ideal. It's rather small, of course. And the picture that was frozen on the screen was of a woman taken from a distance. But I could tell, without any doubt, that the woman in the picture was Patricia. I knew her body's proportions so intimately, and the woman in the picture had those proportions. Wind had blown her jacket and skirt against her long, slender body, which made my identification even easier.

It seemed to me that the photograph had been taken without Patricia's knowledge – and probably without her permission, besides. What was it with these long distance photographs of her? I remembered the Stantons' album of pictures of a teenaged Patricia. Why had Sanford taken her picture surreptitiously, as they had?

"So why the long distance shot?" I realized that I had asked the question out loud. The answer's obvious, I thought. I wasn't speaking out loud. I had myself under control, I figured. And now I had the whole business worked out. Patricia hadn't wanted her picture to be on Sanford's phone. It might have led anyone seeing the picture to surmise that there was a relationship between the two of them. So she must have demanded that Sanford not take any pictures of her. But he'd taken one from a distance, without her knowledge. Just as he'd put her contact information in his phone without her knowing. He hadn't been able to resist, just as Joanna Stanton, enabled by her by her complicit husband, hadn't been able to.

Then, without warning, a wave of nausea struck me. I got up, dropped Sanford's phone onto the seat of the wing chair, and rushed to the first-floor bathroom. I knelt in front of the toilet bowl at the moment my insides lurched violently and I vomited the Japanese and the wine I'd consumed at dinner. I flushed the toilet and vomited a second time, probably the rest of dinner and some of lunch, as well – the beer and the ingredients of the chef's salad. I flushed the toilet again and stayed on the floor for awhile, slumped against a wall. I was covered with sweat, but I felt cold. My insides hurt. The vomiting had been violent.

The house was very quiet. I hadn't turned the bathroom light on, but there was a small nightlight plugged into a wall socket near the medicine cabinet, so the bathroom wasn't completely dark. After awhile, I staggered to my feet and washed my face with cold water. I put a little of the water in my mouth and spit it into the sink. I didn't turn the light on. I didn't want to look at my face in the mirror.

I went back into the living room, picked up Sanford's phone again, and sat back down in the wing chair. I sat silently, without moving. I didn't want to unlock the phone again to look at Patricia's picture and her contact information. Crazy thoughts were whirring around in my head. They made little sense to me. I'd known Patricia so well, hadn't I? The questions that kept assaulting me seemed absurd. Was the stuff on Sanford's phone evidence of Patricia's infidelity? Had she been his mistress?

I couldn't believe that she could have betrayed me. But that was where the evidence on the phone was pushing me. But why had she been unfaithful? Was her infidelity payback for my night at the Washington publishers' conference all those years ago? Had she waited until she found someone exciting and forceful enough? Had she been willing to go away with him, to leave me? I hadn't been worthy of her. I'd never been. Should an affair with another man have come as a shock? Live a life without illusions, I'd always told myself. My hoary dictum. Now I could put that cheap philosophy to the test. Isn't life grand, as someone said – said it more than once, no doubt.

I forced myself to unlock Sanford's phone again. I went through the pictures he'd taken until I came to the long-distance shot of Patricia. I stared at her. I couldn't believe it was her, captured in Sanford's phone, like she'd been captured in the Stantons' photograph album. But the small figure in the snapshot Sanford had taken was Patricia. I had no doubt.

I made myself continue through the pictures. More outdoor scenes followed Patricia's picture. Then I came to a picture of another woman. It had been taken indoors, in a room with a bed. Something about the bland décor indicated that the woman was in a hotel or motel room. I recognized her immediately. It was Gretchen. I knew immediately why her picture was in Sanford's phone. I had no doubt.

I let the phone fall out of my grasp. It landed on my lap. I picked the phone up again and put it down carefully on the end table next to me. I realized that I'd been gasping for breath. I sat without moving, until my breathing returned to normal.

I got up and turned off all the lights in the living room. The windows in the house are all uncovered. Patricia and I never had a problem with a passerby being able to look inside the house. The only exception was our second-floor bedroom, where we would shut the blinds at night. Despite leaving the windows uncovered, the house can be dark at night. There are no streetlights in our part of town and, with crime almost nonexistent, neighbors haven't bothered with installing their own outside lights and leaving them on all night. And there was no moonlight tonight, so the house was as dark as it ever gets.

I sat on the wing chair in my dark and silent living room. My head whirred with recriminations and the horror of Patricia's infidelity. As the night wore on, I became more and more certain that she'd been unfaithful, until finally there was light in the room and I had to face a new day. I might have slept for brief periods during the night, but by morning I wasn't sure whether or not I actually had.

I caught up to Bill Kramer at seven-fifteen in the morning, as he crossed the street from the parking garage he used to the double doors to the lower lobby of our office building. I came up behind him and put my hand on his shoulder. I didn't say anything. He stopped and turned around. There was a mixture of fear and annoyance in his eyes. Then he registered who I was, and the look in his eyes softened. "Mordecai," he said. There was warmth in his voice. Then he said, "My god, you look like shit." He said it in what came across as a kindly way.

I didn't argue with him. I'd taken a shower and changed my clothes, but I hadn't shaved. I still hadn't dared to look in a mirror. In any case, I was sure that he was right. "I haven't slept," I said by way of explanation.

"For how many nights?" Bill grinned at me. I looked at him blankly. "Just kidding," he said.

"I couldn't stop the whirring in my head."

"I don't know what that means."

"It's when I can't get something out of my mind and I can't keep myself from going over it, over and over again."

"I've never experienced that. It sounds like an awful affliction."

"You're very fortunate."

"Come on, you'll feel better when I buy you some breakfast and you tell me what it was that was whirring around in your head."

Bill guided me around the corner to a deli that served breakfast sandwiches and coffee. Most customers got their food to take out, so we had the place pretty much to ourselves. He got sandwiches and coffee for both of us and carried a tray with our meals up a ramp into the deli's windowless back room. Except for the two of us, the room was empty.

Bill pushed my sandwich toward me. "Sit down and take nourishment," he said.

I took a bite. It was good, but I knew I'd have to force the food down. I put the sandwich back on the paper plate, sipped my coffee, and told Bill about finding Sanford's cell phone in the sofa in my office. I didn't tell him immediately about what I'd found when I'd looked through the phone's contents.

Bill had devoured his sandwich before I'd finished telling him about the discovery. "It must have slid out of his pocket when you two were working on his profile," he said. "How's that project going, by the way?"

"I'm still talking to people who've been in Sanford's life. At this point, I'm not sure where the project's going." I took a small bite of the sandwich and washed it down with a few sips of coffee. I knew what the ingredients of the sandwich were, but I couldn't taste any of them. I felt queasy, and I didn't know whether to eat or not. "Aren't you going to ask me more about the cell phone?"

"You know me, Mordecai. I've learned to be patient. But, OK, let's cut to the chase here. I'm going to take a wild guess. You powered up Sanford's phone and found something on it that has unsettled you. In fact, it kept you up all night." Bill swallowed some of his coffee. "I'm right, aren't I?"

"You're right." Then I told Bill about finding Patricia's name and cell phone number among Sanford's contacts. I also went into detail about the pictures I'd found on the phone, and my reaction to discovering the long-distance shot of Patricia among them. I could hear the despair in my voice. I kept the phone in my pocket. I didn't want to have to look at Patricia's picture on Sanford's phone again.

"Oh, dear," Bill said simply. He didn't ask to see the phone. I knew why he was keeping his distance from it. "You should have turned it in without looking through it," he said. "But let's not get into that. I'm sure you'll do the right thing eventually."

I ignored the admonition. "From what I've been led to believe," I said, "the presence of Patricia's information and picture on Sanford's phone should make no sense. According to what Sanford and Gwennie said at the dinner party at your house – which was the first time I'd met them – Sanford and Patricia didn't know each other."

"That's been my understanding, as well. In fact, I don't believe they ever met."

"But when you really think about it, haven't you found their never having even met odd, considering how prominent both of them were in this town?"

"I suppose I never really thought about it. I had no reason to, when you come right down to it."

"And there's another thing that makes their never having even met, let alone become business associates or friends, odder still. I mean, they were both celebrities in the art world. She was a museum director and he was a big-deal art collector. I've been to his house. I've see those large Sam Hudson canvases."

"So have I, of course, on numerous occasions. Just the fact that Sanford owned those big paintings must have made him a player in the art world. I can make that judgment even though I don't know squat about that world. It's out of my league."

"If it hadn't been for Patricia, the art world would have been out of my league, as well. But because of Patricia, I've been conversant with artists, old and current, particularly painters. So I'm familiar with all of Hudson's work. And one thing I can say about it is, his style doesn't fit in with the current holdings in Patricia's museum. Plus I don't think she was planning to take the museum in a modernist direction. I mean, one of her big deals was finding those old paintings of Nineteenth Century industrial scenes somewhere in the museum basement. So their interest in art wasn't what could have caused Sanford to put Patricia's phone number in his contacts list and taken her picture. They both had interests in art, in other words, but those interests were divergent, and it's unlikely that they could have brought the two of them together as business associates or even acquaintances."

"It seems to me, Mordecai, that you're leaving out another possibility: that Patricia might have been in contact with Sanford because she was hitting him up to become a benefactor of her museum."

"I suppose it's possible. But think back to that dinner at your home – which was some time after Patricia was murdered and was when I met the Glickauers for the first time. Remember, they talked about where the Hudson paintings would end up after they died. They – well, Gwennie, especially – were adamant that the paintings would go to a museum in New York City, where they were created, after all. I got the distinct impression that they'd never been approached by Patricia to leave the paintings to the museum here in town. And, as I said a moment ago, they would have been out of place here, in more ways than one, what with the nudes."

"So what you're telling me is that there was no *business* reason for Sanford and Patricia to have been in contact. But what about the possibility that Sanford didn't want Gwennie to know that he was thinking of bequeathing the Hudson paintings he owned to Patricia's museum? Or maybe he didn't want his wife to know that he was contemplating a major cash donation to the museum.

"Sure, sure. But the Glickauers sounded pretty convincing to me when I met them at your home, at least with regard to the two possibilities you've just mentioned. Those possibilities were not the reason Patricia and Sanford had been in touch. And I'm certain the two of them had been. The evidence is all over his phone. So I'm sure that phone company records would show that they spoke numerous times before Patricia was murdered."

"You can't be sure of that."

"Why can't I? It's hardly much of a leap of logic."

"I know what you're thinking, Mordecai. I've been involved in enough divorce work to be able to come up with a reason Patricia and Sanford could have had for talking on the phone." There was great sadness in Bill's eyes when they met mine. "You and Patricia were together for a great many years. You knew her so well. You knew how much she loved you. You couldn't possibly believe that she'd ever been capable of such a thing." He paused and leaned forward across the table. "You and she weren't having any problems before she died, were you? I'm sorry that I even have to ask you such a terrible question."

"It's all right," I said. "You can ask me whatever you want." I looked down at the breakfast sandwich. I hadn't eaten much of it. I picked it up and put it back down on the paper plate without taking another bite. The sandwich had gone cold. That was just as well. I was in no mood for eating anything.

"So were there any problems? Not that such things would have driven Patricia toward Sanford necessarily."

"There weren't any problems that I knew about. But the husband's the last to know, isn't that what they always say?"

"I'm sad when I have to agree with any cliché, but this one's often true. But you and Patricia communicated with each other very well, didn't you?"

"I thought so. I'd always believed that we told each other everything."

"Wasn't that the case?"

"After Patricia was murdered, I learned some things about her high school years that she never told me about."

"At the risk of your thinking that I'm a nosy bastard, may I ask what they were?"

Had I been feeling better, I would have agreed that Bill was indeed a nosy bastard. But I passed on the opportunity. My mind went off in another direction. "I can't believe I'm talking like this about Patricia," I said. My voice was low and hoarse. "I loved her so much. I'll always love her, no matter what. I'm being so disloyal to her."

I banged both hands on the table. My coffee container, which was still half full, went over the side. "I feel so dirty," I said, my voice cracking.

One of the countermen bustled up the ramp into the back room. "Everything all right in here, Mr. Bill?" he said.

"Everything's fine," Bill said. "My friend here has been telling me an emotional story, that's all. We'll help you clean up the mess." Bill nodded toward the spilled coffee on the tile floor.

"That's all right, we'll get it later, before the lunch crowd," the counterman said. He was a large, balding man in his fifties, about my age, I guessed. "It doesn't look too bad," he went on. "Just be careful when you get up to leave."

After the counterman walked down the ramp into the main part of the deli, Bill looked at me and smiled. "Patricia wouldn't blame you for telling me all that you've been telling me," he said. "She'd say that you have to get it out, that's all."

"How do you know what she'd say?"

"You were with her a long time. Sometimes things happen. But they don't cancel out what went before and what came after."

"I have to believe that, don't I? In order to maintain my sanity."

I hit the table again. There was nothing left on it to spill. Bill sat silently, watching me warily.

After I'd gotten myself calmed down, I went into an account of my visits to the Stantons and Mary Howard, which was when I'd learned about Patricia's high school abortion and the little film she'd made with Mary's boyfriend Ted, who had gotten Patricia pregnant.

"Let's talk about all of this as dispassionately as we can, OK?" Bill said. "I know that's hard for you, but you have to at least give it a try."

"OK, I'll try," I said.

There was pause before Bill gathered himself to say, "I can understand how Patricia might have forgotten about the little film, but the abortion is another matter entirely, I'm afraid."

"I can't understand why she never told me."

"It must have been too humiliating. Or maybe she feared you'd castigate her if she told you."

"She had to have known me better than that. Besides, I didn't know her when she was in high school. I could hardly have condemned her for being unfaithful to me." An unbidden thought suddenly struck me that I had never told Patricia about that night at the Washington publishing conference when I'd been unfaithful to her. So how could I have expected her to have told me about getting pregnant and having an abortion when she was in high school?

"Whatever, those events were in the distant past."

"The trouble is, there were things that were much more recent." Bill frowned. He looked away from me, and then his gaze met mine. I told him about Patricia's solitary lunches in the out-of-the-way diner and about the mysterious slush fund she'd created at the museum. I told him about her clandestine (that was the word I used) visit to Sam Hudson's apartment/studio and Sanford's subsequent visit there when he'd discussed commissioning a painting with himself and an unnamed woman.

"Those things amount to circumstantial stuff. They don't prove anything. Her meals at the diner don't prove that she was meeting Sanford in the middle of the day or at any other time, for that matter. The potential commission could very well have been for a painting with Sanford and some woman other than Patricia. You said that she'd been in New York on another errand. When she realized that she'd have a few free hours before her train home, she'd seized an opportunity to visit an artist she'd heard about. Had Hudson's name been in the news?"

"I don't remember," I said. "But there's something else." And then I told Bill about my meeting Gretchen Carmichael. I didn't tell him about the sex or even about how well she and I had hit it off.

"So she looks like an older version of Patricia. What does that prove?"

"Not like an older version. Gretchen's a dead ringer for Patricia plus fifteen years or so."

"I still don't know what that proves."

"Gretchen lied to me. She told me that she hadn't seen Sanford for years, since before she'd gotten married, when she was in her twenties."

"Come on, Mordecai. You're going further and further off the deep end. How do you know that she lied?"

"I found her picture on Sanford's cell phone. He took it in a hotel or motel room some time after he took Patricia's picture."

"You certainly sprung that one on me. Good lord. So now I suppose you've woven all of what you've told me about Patricia and this Gretchen Carmichael look-alike into a theory."

"Of course. It should be as obvious to you as it is to me. Here's how it goes in the Cliff Notes version. Sanford never stopped seeing Gretchen after she got married and he married Gwennie. In fact, he kept seeing Gretchen during the five years he was married to Phoebe Armstrong."

"Wait a second. How do you know that last part?"

"Phoebe told me she suspected Sanford of seeing someone else during their marriage."

"And that woman was definitely Gretchen? How can you be sure?"

"It fits, that's all I can say. Just like the fact that Patricia and Gretchen look so much alike. Which Gretchen pooh-poohs, by the way – but for her own purposes, I'm sure." Bill started to say something, in rebuttal, no doubt, but I held my hand up in a stop sign. "The reason I'm sure," I went on, "is that Gretchen wants to distract me from realizing that Sanford replaced her with Patricia – until Patricia was murdered. Then he went back to Gretchen."

"Are you about to tell me that a jealous Gretchen murdered Patricia?"

"I don't think so, but I don't know. She didn't strike me as the jealous type, whatever that means. I mean, I just don't see her as a murderer."

"Or perhaps it was a jealous Gwennie."

"The problem with that theory is that Gwennie never showed any signs of caring one way or the other about Sanford's affairs with Bethia Davenport and Alice Burns, or even about his marrying Phoebe. That's according to Alice and Phoebe. I haven't questioned Gwennie about that subject."

"That would be a matter for Hartnett and his buddies on the police."

"Of course, but only if Hartnett ever can shake himself free of his theory that Patricia was murdered during a robbery, not for some other reason. Maybe he will, now that there's a motive for her murder."

"Possibly," Bill said, "but I'm not convinced. Although lawyers do like a good theory to explain events." He leaned back and folded his arms across his chest. "There's one other thing, Mordecai. Let's suppose you're right, and Sanford had an affair with Patricia. Let's even assume that it was a serious affair. Why, after she was dead, did he arrange with you to write a biographical profile of him?"

"Sanford loved to play games."

"Of course. I sometimes thought he lived for his game-playing."

"And think about all of them. Love games, hate games, revenge games, silly games not meant to hurt anyone, although they could be cruel games nevertheless."

"Sure, but we went along with them. Even Maggie did, although she balked at games after Sanford was killed. You were there, in fact, when she blew up over a game I wanted to start."

I didn't picture Maggie. Instead, I pictured Sanford's tender smile, the one he'd directed towards me on occasion. "Look, Bill, you were with Sanford for many years. But I don't think you fully understand Sanford's game-playing. In fact, I don't think you fully appreciate the rationale for the elaborate revenge game he played on Harlan Burns, with Bethia Davenport and Alice Burns as collateral damage. I thought you'd get it, but I guess you didn't."

"You don't mean to tell me that you believe that he was playing an elaborate game with you, do you? Are you asking me to believe that he talked you into writing his life story so you would eventually arrive at the conclusion that he and your wife had had an affair? That seems far-fetched to me."

"Well, not to me. I think he was entirely capable of such a thing. I didn't see that he had contempt for me, but maybe it was there, and I didn't allow myself to see it."

CHAPTER TWENTY-ONE

Bill left me alone for awhile. I sat at the table without moving, afraid that the whirring in my head would start again. When he returned, he was carrying a tray with two containers of coffee and a hard roll on a paper plate. He put the roll and one of the coffees on the table in front of me.

I took a bite of the roll. "Thanks for having this buttered, otherwise it would have been too dry for me," I said. Bill gave me an "it's nothing" smile. I tried to sip the coffee, but it was too hot for me to drink. I watched Bill gulp his coffee down. He seemed impervious to its temperature.

"So why have you been pouring out your heart to me?" he said.

"It's like you said, I have to get the story out. If I keep it in, I'll go insane."

"I can understand that. And it's not an easy story for you to tell, is it?"

"There is a part of the story that's easy tell, the part about the wonderful life I had with Patricia. Everything seemed perfect. She was a goddess – intelligent, beautiful, loving, warm – more than I deserved. The amazing thing is that I actually threw away the possibility of a wonderful life with her after a single date that went badly, as far as I was concerned. She moved far away - across the country, in fact. Miraculously, five years later, we found each other again, and I had a second chance at having a life with her."

I took another bite of the roll. The coffee had cooled enough so that I could take a couple of sips.

"You told me about your courtship and marriage one day on the golf course, before Patricia was murdered. You loved telling me, I could tell. You've never played better than you did that day."

"But then comes the part of the story that isn't easy for me to tell," I went on, "but I had to tell it to you. I had to get it out, like you said. It's the part that comes after Patricia was murdered, when I learned things about her past I hadn't known and discovered that she'd been doing things that she'd never told me about, including, I'm convinced – though with all my heart I don't want to be – her affair with Sanford."

"When I ask 'why me?' it's because of our relationship, Mordecai. We do play golf together, I did invite you to have lunch at Sanford's table, and you have had dinner at my home. But I can't be among your closest friends."

"The fact of the matter, Bill, is that I don't seem to have many friends. There's my main editor in New York, but I strongly suspect that if we didn't have a working relationship, we wouldn't be friendly at all. Then there's a couple in the New York area who were friends with Patricia and me. But that friendship's been blown up."

"That can happen, I'm sad to say, when half of a couple isn't around anymore. I've seen it happen with many of the couples whose divorces our firm has handled."

"They didn't just drop me. That would have been fine with me. No, what happened is that one afternoon the wife showed up unannounced for purposes of uninhibited sex."

Bill threw his head back. "Holy crap! Where was the husband?"

"She'd left him," she said.

"As in heading for divorce?"

"Precisely. Or so she said. But I haven't followed up to see whether she was telling me the truth or not."

"So what happened when she was in your apartment?"

"I didn't perform the act she had in mind." I didn't have the courage to tell Bill that I hadn't been *able* to perform.

"We could play WWSHD, I suppose."

"Which stands for?"

"What Would Sanford Have Done?"

I rolled my eyes. Then I laughed. I had to. After a moment, I said, "So that's it in the friends department. Not many, are there?"

"I'm sorry to hear it."

"Don't be. You see, except for my work, Patricia was pretty much my whole life. I didn't really need anyone else. I thought we'd go on forever together. I never imagined she'd be snatched away from me. And I certainly never imagined she'd have an affair and might consider separating herself from me."

"Mordecai, please. You don't have proof of an affair. You only have a theory."

"A theory is good enough for you lawyers, as you say. Besides, it's based on enough circumstantial evidence that adds up. I wanted to try the theory out on you, and it seems to me that you haven't really shot it down."

"You need to test the theory with someone besides me. You need to talk with Tim Hartnett. What's more important than anything, however, is that you can't deal with this by yourself. It's too important. And it's potentially too dangerous. It's a murder case, for god's sake. You don't have the right experience to handle it. You're a writer and an editor, not a private eye."

"I'll do what I have to do. If I get into trouble, so what? What happens to me from here on out doesn't concern me all that much." And when I came right down to it, I had no faith in Harnett. He lacked imagination, it seemed to me. He couldn't envision the passions, the jealousies, and the desire for revenge that had led to Patricia's murder. That was my theory, at any rate, and armed with it, it was up to me to find Patricia's killer.

"You have your whole life ahead of you," Bill was saying. I swam up out of my daydream into the air and heard him speaking, "That's what our parents always said when we were young. But it's still true, Mordecai. Believe me. So be careful. I don't want anything bad to happen to you."

"It already has, in Spades." I drained my coffee and got up from the table. Bill stood up with me. "Don't worry about me," I said, as we started out of the deli. "I'll be just fine."

The counterman must have heard me. I saw a doubtful look on his broad face.

Out on the street, I asked Bill to call a number on his cell phone that I remembered without any hesitation. "When a woman answers, just say 'sorry, wrong number,' and hang up," I said. He looked at me quizzically. "I just want to know if she's home," I said.

Bill made the call, listened for a moment, and then said, "Sorry to have bothered you. I dialed the wrong number." He ended the call and looked at me. "Anything else, Sam Spade?" he said.

"That's it for now," I said. "My people will be in touch with your people when there's something else." The "my people" stuff was a running joke with Bill and me.

"I await further instructions," he said. He smiled and held my shoulder for a moment. It was an expression of solidarity, I figured. I smiled back at him and then moved off down the street toward the parking lot where I'd left my car before the attendant had arrived for duty.

When I got behind the wheel, I turned Sanford's cell phone on, and made a call to a number on his Contacts list.

"Who is this?"

I thought I could detect a note of alarm in the voice. I said my name.

"What are you doing with my husband's phone, Mordecai?" At the beginning of the sentence, Gwennie's tone was harsh, but she must have realized it and softened it by the end.

"I found it in my office, when I was straightening out the sofa cushions. It must have fallen out of his pocket and gotten wedged down between the cushions the last time he was there."

"Didn't he call you to say that his phone was missing and ask if you'd look through your office for it?"

"Maybe he didn't miss it. There's no way of knowing whether he did or not, is there?"

"No, there isn't. But I missed his phone. I've been wondering what happened to it. When did you find it?"

"Just yesterday afternoon. I hadn't been back to the office since the last time I'd been there interviewing Sanford, which was right before the accident."

"And you just happened to find it."

"In just the way I've described to you, Gwennie."

"Have you told anyone about finding the phone?"

"Only you," I said. Everyone had been lying to me. Why should I care about me lying to anyone?

"Please don't tell anyone about finding my late husband's phone. Its existence isn't anyone else's business but mine. It belonged to my husband, and how it belongs to me. It's nothing more than one of his effects."

"I understand completely."

"I have to ask you this, Mordecai. Don't take it as criticism, implied or otherwise. Have you done anything with the phone besides turning it on and making this call to me?"

"No." This was another lie, of course, but the effect on me of lying didn't appear to be cumulative. The second lie bothered me even less that the first one had.

"Please don't use it anymore. Just turn it off and return it to me in person. Don't send it in the mail or by FedEx or anything. I don't want it to be lost again."

"You don't have to be concerned with that possibility. I'll bring the phone to you tonight. How late may I come to your house?"

"Don't worry about the time. I'll wait up for you."

"It will be sometime after dark, I'm afraid."

"That will be fine. By the way, I'll be the only one here, so you don't have to worry that there'll be another car on our narrow road. You'll be able to drive freely."

It was only ten to nine when I pulled out of the parking lot. I drove across the river and eventually entered the Mass. Turnpike. It was cloudy, so there wasn't sun in my eyes as I drove east. But I was exhausted, and several times I veered off the left lane onto the warning rumble strips. The tire noise brought me back into consciousness, and I steered the car back onto the road.

The navigation system indicated that the efficient way to get to Providence when you're heading from the west on the Turnpike is to get off at Exit 10A and take Route 146. It's an old-fashioned four-lane freeway that cuts through a portion of Massachusetts, starting at Worcester, and a stretch of Rhode Island, ending at Providence. I'd taken 146 only a couple of days earlier, on my way back home from Gretchen Carmichael's. Now I was reversing that process.

I made fairly good time, and I was in downtown Providence before eleven-thirty. The navigation system took me over the hill to Gretchen's neighborhood, and a few minutes later I pulled to the curb in front of her house.

I rapped on the glass of the side door and waited. When I didn't hear any sounds from inside the house, I rapped on the glass again, harder this time. The glass rattled a little, and I eased off, afraid I'd break it. When there were still no sounds inside the house, I walked around back to see if Gretchen's car was there. It was. The garage door was open, and I spotted her bicycle.

She might have gone for a walk, and I thought about driving around the neighborhood to look for her. Instead, I went back to side door and rapped on the glass again. Finally, I heard the sound of heels striking a hardwood floor, and then Gretchen was coming down the short flight of steps to the side door. She opened it halfway and stood facing me.

"You've been making an awful racket," she said. "You could have broken the glass."

"I'm sorry," I said. "I was just trying to make sure that you heard me."

"I was upstairs taking the rollers out of my hair. Robert's picking me up in fifteen minutes. We're going to lunch at my favorite Italian place on Atwells Avenue."

"Not that it's any of my business, but who's Robert?"

"Robert is Robert Silver. He's a banker. Well, not just any banker. He was an executive vice president for corporate and government relations at State Street Bank in Boston. He retired a few years before the financial crisis hit. He lives in a stately brick home on Commonwealth Avenue in Newton. He wants me to move in with him. I'll undoubtedly do so. You see, Robert is a very suave and persuasive man. That's why he's my fiancé. There, Mordecai, does that answer your question?" Gretchen smiled triumphantly.

"Your *what?*"

"Fiancé, Mordecai. It's not an unusual term, even in these free-floating days of hooking up, or whatever it is that young people do now."

"I don't pretend to understand you, Gretchen."

"I don't expect you to, and, frankly, I don't care whether you do or not. I've never much cared whether anyone's understood me and what I choose to do with my life." She laughed and put the palm of one hand against my jaw. "Don't tell me you're shocked at my behavior."

"Actually, I'm in awe of you."

"That's good. Now tell me what you're doing here, arriving without any warning, I might add." She arched an eyebrow. "Oh, wait. That wrong number this morning. You got someone to call to establish that I was at home."

"I need to talk to you."

"What's wrong with the telephone? You could have called me when your friend did. You didn't have to drive for three hours just to talk to me."

"I need to do this in person."

"Do what?" When I didn't answer, Gretchen said, "You'd better come in. But you can't stay long."

I followed her up the stairs. She was wearing a loosely fitting blue blouse and a full black skirt, with low-heeled black pumps. I couldn't keep my eyes off her. I was certain that she knew it.

We stood facing each other in the first-floor hallway. "Now what is it that made you drive all this way so you could talk to me in person?" Gretchen said. Her eyes, inches away from mine, were wide with amusement.

"You lied to me," I said, keeping my voice as calm and steady as I could.

The amusement in her eyes turned to confusion. "I didn't mislead you," Gretchen said with emphasis. "When you spent the night here with me, I never intimated that we had a future together. I like you, Mordecai, and I wanted to be intimate with you. And we did have fun. The companionship and the sex were both outstanding. I'm sure you felt the same way. You seemed reluctant to leave after we got back from breakfast. I had the sense that you were waiting for me to turn around and look at you when I was walking back to the house and you had pulled your car into the street."

"Don't try to distract me, Gretchen. Our time together is in the distant past, as far as I'm concerned." Did I believe what I'd just said? I had no idea.

"You're an attractive man, Mordecai. Don't try to act like you're not. It's not becoming." Gretchen folded her arms under her breasts. "God, I must sound like I'm your mother." Now her hands were on her hips. "Now tell me what it is that I'm supposedly distracting you from."

"I came here to talk to you about your relationship with Sanford Glickauer. You lied to me about it."

I saw her eyes flash with anger. "What business of yours is my relationship with Sanford? It's ancient history. After I married my husband, I never saw Sanford again."

"Stop lying to me, Gretchen. I know otherwise."

"You son of a bitch." Her right arm wind milled, and her hand smacked against the side of my face. Gretchen was a tall, fit-looking woman, and her arm had moved with some speed. But I outweighed her by sixty pounds or more, and I didn't move when she hit me.

She glared at me. I could see that she was making an effort to remain composed. She wind milled again, and her hand struck the side of my face again. The blow stung, but I held myself steady. Then I bent down, pushed my left shoulder into her waist, and lifted her off the floor. I heard of gasp of surprise.

I carried Gretchen on my left shoulder into the living room. She flailed at me with fists and feet. I flipped her over an arm of the sofa. She landed on her back, legs in the air. Her skirt fell, exposing white thighs and black underpants. She tried to rearrange herself. I pushed her against the back of the sofa, which made room for me to sit down next to her. I grabbed her wrists and held them down against her stomach. She tried to buck her way out of my grip, but she didn't have the strength. Finally, she lay quietly, her skirt bunched up around her upper thighs.

"This is a hell of way to treat me," Gretchen said. "Throwing me around like I was rag doll. I'm old enough to be your mother. Well, barely old enough."

"There'd never be a time when I'd mistake you for my mother," I said. "And it's not because you're a foot taller."

"I'm glad to hear it. I don't want you pretending that you slept with your own mother. Pretending that you slept with your dead wife – that I can handle."

I raised my right hand. I couldn't stop myself from doing so. Gretchen flinched, and I put my hand down. "There's a more important way you're different from my mother," I said. "My mother told the truth. You ought to try it sometime. It'll do you good, as Sanford used to say."

"Don't lecture me, you son of a bitch. Why don't you just hit me instead? You probably get off on hitting women." She glared at me.

"Hardly. As a matter of fact, I don't want to hurt you. I threw you on the sofa so you'd stop hitting me – and so you'd talk to me."

"All right, I'll talk. But let me sit up first. I can't talk with you looking at me like that."

I stood up. Gretchen got up from the sofa, pulled her skirt down, and straightened her clothes. She ran a hand through her hair. I didn't see hatred in her eyes when they met mine. Perhaps there was a sign of relief in her eyes, but I wasn't sure. She sat down again, with her back straight, and pulled her skirt over her knees.

"Give me a phone," she said.

I handed her a cell phone.

"Whose is this – yours?"

"It's Sanford's, I believe."

"Get me the house phone, please. It's on one of the kitchen counters."

When I returned with the phone, Gretchen made a call.

"Robert.

"Yes, it's me, darling.

"Yes, I know you're almost here, but something important has come up, and I can't have lunch and spend the afternoon with you today. Please pull over, if you can, so we can talk." Gretchen waited for about ten seconds, and then she said, "I'm sorry, too, darling.

"No, I can't tell you why, not now, anyway. I will tell you tomorrow. The situation here will get sorted out expeditiously, I promise you.

"No, it doesn't involve the two of us.

"Yes, I agree. Nothing can tear us apart. We won't let it.

"That's a dear. I can always count on you.

"Yes, I'll see you tomorrow.

"Love you, too."

Gretchen shut the phone off and put it down on the sofa.

"He's a nice man, your Robert, isn't he?" I said.

"Everything about him is impeccable." She looked up at me. "Please stop looming over me. I promise I'll tell you whatever it is that you want to know, providing I know it myself." I sat on a black Barcelona chair to Gretchen's right. "That's better," she said. "Thank you."

"Start from the beginning with Sanford," I said.

"Do you want me to go back to when Sanford and I first met?"

"Actually, no. I think I know that part of the story, if what Sanford told me was accurate – and I'm guessing that it was, because he had nothing to hide when he talked about the years before you went off to get married to your late husband. But you and Sanford both led me to believe that your marriage marked the end of your affair. Sanford's reliability ends at that point. So does yours."

"How do you know that?" Her voice was low, but firm. She looked at me impassively.

"Let me show you." I turned on Sanford's phone and found the pictures he'd taken. I moved over next to Gretchen and showed her Maggie's picture.

"Who's that?" Gretchen said.

"She's a lawyer in Sanford's firm. The picture was taken in her office."

"She's very attractive."

"Extremely." I started the slideshow. When I got to Patricia's picture, I paused. "That's my late wife, of course," I said.

"I can see now that there's some resemblance between her and me."

"More than you're ready to admit." Gretchen said nothing. I resumed the slideshow. When I got to Gretchen's picture, I paused again. "Where was this picture taken?" I said.

She turned to me. Her face was close to mine. The look in her eyes was impassive. I had a moment before she started to speak to examine her face again. It wasn't the face of a woman in her prime, but it was a face with unmistakable virtues. The brow was clear, the eyes were large, the cheekbones were prominent, and the jaw was still firm. It was a face you could look at across a table or beside you on a bed without regret that you'd married its owner. It wasn't a face that you would easily tire of and want to get rid of. I'd lived with the face for only a single afternoon, night, and a morning. I knew that had circumstances been different, I could have lived with the face for much longer than I had. Robert Silver was a lucky man, I thought.

Finally, Gretchen gathered herself and began to speak. "There's a Marriott Courtyard on Route 1, about forty-five minutes to an hour from here, if there's not much traffic. Sanford used to take a room there every few months. We'd meet in the afternoon, order room service, watch TV, and do other things. We had a taste for each other. Sometimes we spent the night together. Jack was easy to fool. I'm sure he let himself be fooled. We never discussed it. The bottom line for him was, he didn't like any trouble. Besides, I always came home to him, and he had no doubt that I always would."

"What about your boys?"

"We had a housekeeper, who lived with us. I think that the boys found her more motherly than me. She was white, but she was like the black maids in *The Help*, if you know what I mean. She was, in some sense, the boys' real mother. The fact that they hadn't sprung from her loins, to use an old expression, but from mine, was of no consequence. They didn't miss me when I was away for an afternoon or even for an entire night."

"So when you left Washington, did you and Sanford have a plan for continuing your relationship? According to him, your leaving to get married marked the end of it."

"There was no plan. But we'd both been bitten, and those bites turned into itches that we both had to scratch. It was only a matter of time, I guess, before we had a need to see each other."

"So Sanford called you."

"No, I called him."

"How did you know where he was? There was no Internet in those days."

"During dinner one evening, Jack mentioned that he'd heard from a classmate that Sanford was in law school. I've never been able to figure out whether Jack was innocent of anything between me and Sanford or he cunningly planned a reunion to keep me happy. I went to the school one morning and hunted Sanford down – the same way he'd hunted me down when I was at Wellesley, although when I walked up to him after one of his classes, I couldn't pretend that I'd run into him by accident. At the same time, I had the impression that he was expecting me, that he'd been waiting for me to make a move. We went to his room that afternoon. Two days later, I learned that I was pregnant, but given the timing, I knew that the baby was Jack's, not Sanford's."

I tried to compose my features so I would be looking at Gretchen impassively, the same way she'd looked at me a few minutes earlier. "You almost make it sound like you just couldn't live without seeing Sanford." I was blunt, but Gretchen didn't flinch.

"I couldn't stop myself from wanting to be with him, from looking for him, and then from being with him, from going to bed with him. I felt trapped. I couldn't get help, even if I asked for it. It felt like I was buried in a coffin under the earth, but I was still alive, and I was beating on the wood cover, even though I knew that no one would hear me and no one would come to dig me out."

"Did you think about going to a shrink?"

"I did go, once. It was a woman. She had her practice in Brookline, on Beacon Street near Coolidge Corner."

"How did you find her? You were living in Providence."

"I called one of the synagogues near Coolidge Corner and chatted with the rabbi. I figured that a rabbi would be sympathetic to the idea of my consulting a shrink. He provided the name of one that he knew who could help me with the problem I described, which wasn't the problem I actually had, but a less salacious one."

"And the reason you saw a shrink up in Brookline was so your husband wouldn't know about the visit."

"Yes, of course. Remember, I told you that I compartmentalize. Visits to a shrink weren't intended to fit into the Jack box."

"I remember. You're in the John F. Kennedy class of compartmentalists." I tried a small smile. "That's not a criticism, Gretchen. I actually admire your ability to put different aspects of your life in separate boxes, just as I admire Kennedy's, or Bill Clinton's, come to think of it."

"Thanks, but I'm not all sure that it's made my life easier. As I look over my life, I think that compartmentalizing everything might have made it harder."

"So did the shrink try to get at the root of why you were doing what you were doing, and let you come to your own conclusions, or did she give you advice?"

"She was a middle-aged Jewish woman, still attractive, although she'd put on a little weight. She was well-dressed, in a suit with the skirt above her knees and heels. She showed off a lot of leg when she sat down in front of me. I can still picture her, although it's been decades since I saw her. I expected her to want to delve into my relationship with my father, but I quickly realized that she was a no-nonsense kind of woman who fancied herself a problem solver. She was a forerunner of the type of shrinks who, as I understand it, predominate today. You know, the behavioral, or clinical, or whatever they call the type. They don't get you to talk about your past and the demons who may reside there. Instead, they recommend solutions to today's problem that you can put into practice. Or they prescribe medication."

"So she understood the problem and told you what solution to apply to it."

"Exactly. She listened to me for forty-five minutes, and in the last five minutes told me that I had to give Sanford up. I didn't argue with her. I told her that I would follow her advice. Then I walked out of her office and never went back."

"And you didn't follow her advice, did you?"

"Of course not. I was still in that dark coffin under the ground, with no way out. As I told you, that's how I saw myself. The shrink certainly didn't dig me out, didn't even come close." Gretchen rubbed her face. There was an exhausted look in her eyes. She slumped against the back of the sofa and crossed her legs. I watched her skirt ride up, exposing her knees. She closed her eyes then.

"You never got out of that coffin, did you?" I said. I leaned forward, my forearms on my thighs.

"I'm not sure I ever wanted to. Or maybe it was that Sanford recognized what my plight was and decided to take advantage of it. It was working out for him, when all was said and done. He had a piece on the side, no matter what." Gretchen laughed tiredly. "A pretty good piece, if I say so myself."

"Did you ever talk to Sanford about how you felt, ever tell him about the coffin image?"

"Whenever I would, he'd laugh and say that it was all nothing but a game, that life itself was nothing but a game."

"That sounds like Sanford, all right. Part of the game was keeping knowledge of the affair from spouses. You told me that your husband didn't let on as to whether or not he knew of the affair, or even suspected there was one. It must have been because he didn't want to lose you, is that right?"

"I've always believed that. Poor Jack. But otherwise, I was good wife to him. I always believed that, without any irony." Gretchen ran her fingers through her hair again. It seemed to fall back into place. She was still a very beautiful woman. Like Patricia would have been, if she'd lived to Gretchen's age.

"What about Gwennie?"

"I've never understood Gwennie. I've never met her, so how could I? What I mean is, I never detected behavior on Sanford's part that would have indicated that he was reacting to her being angry or even just upset with him. So, for instance, he never told me that he couldn't see me for awhile because Gwennie had confronted him about me. So what I mean about not understanding Gwennie is, how could she have remained so distant from whatever Sanford did?"

"Maybe she was behaving the way your husband did – not letting on that she knew about anything because she just wanted to keep Sanford no matter what it took to do so."

"Perhaps that's the explanation for what I imagined her behavior was. I was willfully blind to a lot of things, I'm afraid. In any case, whenever I asked Sanford about Gwennie, he said she had other interests and that some of what he did was of no consequence to her." Gretchen laughed, a little less tiredly now than she had before. "I should have realized that any explanation on his part for anything was only part of his game, as far as he was concerned."

"Phoebe Armstrong told me that she suspected that Sanford had carried on an affair while they were married, but she never found out about you."

"Poor little Phoebe. Did anyone actually believe Sanford's tale of leaving her because she didn't warm the dinner plates? Who could believe that was the reason he went back to Gwennie? It's laughable, isn't it?"

"I don't think that Phoebe can laugh about it."

"No, I suppose not, poor little thing. Sanford used her, and then he threw her away when he was tired of her. He was such a prick. But men do those kinds of things, don't they?"

I winced, and then hoped that Gretchen hadn't noticed. I'd been like Sanford. I'd thrown Patricia away when she'd disappointed me, instead brushing the disappointment off and finding my way forward with her. I'd lost five years with her because of my stupidity. I shook my head involuntarily.

"Mordecai, what's the matter?" Gretchen said. "You look like someone made you pay attention to something that you've wanted to forget about." I thought that I detected genuine concern in her voice.

I didn't want to talk about what I was feeling at that moment, but I also didn't want to say that I didn't want to talk about it. So instead I said, "When did Sanford finally tell you he wouldn't be seeing you anymore?"

Gretchen's head jerked toward me. She uncrossed her long legs and stared at me for awhile. I remained silent, waiting her out. Finally, she said, "about a year ago, I think it was – something like that. But how do you know?"

In as even a tone as I could muster, I told Gretchen my theory about the relationship between Sanford and Patricia – how she'd been a younger edition of Gretchen, how they must have gotten together whenever she'd had lunch at the out-of-the-way diner, and how Sanford had discussed commissioning Sam Hudson to paint himself with Patricia. It all sounded so convincing to me. I told the story without irony or any sarcasm, just straight, in a matter-of-fact tone.

"My theory makes more sense to me now, after hearing how powerful a hold Sanford had over you," I said to Gretchen.

"But I was different," she said. "I was damaged emotionally. Why I was isn't as important as the fact that Sanford recognized it and saw that he could take advantage of it."

"But I believe that Patricia was emotionally damaged, as well, because there's a crucial part of the story that I've left out. I can't bear to talk about, but I have to," I said, and for the first time I told someone about my one-night stand at the publishers' conference in Washington. When I came to the end of the sordid tale, I started to cry. I couldn't help myself. And I hated myself for being so weak. Gretchen hadn't cried when she'd told me about her affair with Sanford. What was wrong with me? She turned and held out her arms to me. I moved over to the sofa, beside her, and buried my face in the hollow between her neck and shoulder. She stroked my back slowly, tenderly.

"Poor Mordecai," she said softly, her voice soothing. "You loved her so very much, didn't you? Poor boy."

Poor Phoebe; poor Mordecai. Two losers. We were in the same category, in Gretchen's mind. This is what my life had come to. Mine was a poor contrast to another man's life, if that man was like Sanford – powerful, ruthless even. I felt grateful towards Gretchen, although at the same time I felt a tinge of resentment for her pity. But it didn't seem to matter. I felt myself relax, more and more, and let the warmth of Gretchen's body flow into mine. The last thought I had, absurdly, was of the sight of her landing helpless on the sofa, with her long legs in the air. Then I slept.

CHAPTER TWENTY-TWO

When I awoke, the afternoon light was fading. This was the second time in a matter of a couple days that I'd awoken next to Gretchen. But this time was very different than the last, which I knew would never be repeated. I wouldn't pursue Gretchen. She needed to be able to attempt to live her life in peace, not trapped in a coffin constructed of her self-destructive needs and desires, and buried deep underground. I hoped that Robert Silver was wise enough to help her achieve that peace.

I lifted my head and kissed Gretchen lightly on her cheek. She pulled back and smiled at me. I smiled back at her.

"It's been a hell of an afternoon," she said. "I'm starving. How about toast and an omelet? Ham or cheese, or both?"

"Both," I said. "Then I have to get on the road."

"Where to? Home?" She stood and smoothed out her clothing again.

"I need to see Gwennie. She's expecting me, in fact. I made the appointment before I drove over here."

"Gwennie? Why her? Why now?" There was concern in Gretchen's voice.

"She asked me to return Sanford's phone to her."

"How do you come to have it, anyway?"

"I found it buried between cushions in my office sofa. It must have fallen out of Sanford's pocket the last time he was there, during one of our interview sessions. On some level, I think he left it there on purpose."

"Why would he have done such a thing?"

"It was part of some game, involving my finding out that he had seduced my late wife.

"Mordecai, I'm worried about you." Gretchen was whisking eggs, ham, and cheese in a large bowl. Seven Star Bakery bread was in the four-slot toaster. We were sipping glasses of Fleurie.

"My editor said the same thing to me not so long ago, when he derided my last book as fucking turgid, as he so delicately put it. Don't be worried. I can take care of this."

"Why don't you just send the phone to Gwennie?"

"Because she asked me to bring it to her."

"So what? You don't take orders from her. What's the real reason you're going there?"

"OK, the truth is, I want to confront her."

"About what?"

"Don't you see, Gretchen? If my theory about Sanford and Patricia having a relationship is correct, there's a motive for her murder."

"I understand that, but haven't the police already figured that out, as well?"

"Well, no, they haven't. According to the detective in charge of the case, Tim Hartnett, Patricia was killed during a robbery gone too far. He's refused to consider any other possibility for her death. Oh, by the way, he's the husband of one of Sanford's partners, Maggie Hartnett."

Gretchen divided the omelet in halves and put them, together with the toast, on plates, which I carried over to the table. "Mordecai," she said, as we sat down to eat, "you're a writer and an editor, and you've done some great investigative work, but you're not a homicide detective. Leave this in the hands of the police."

"I can't do that. I've just told you why I have no faith in them. I have to go to Gwennie's myself tonight, so I can at least make an attempt to get to the bottom of things."

"Since you're so determined, I'm coming with you."

"You are not."

"Try and stop me. And don't even think about throwing me on the couch again." Gretchen pointed the sharp knife in her hand in my direction. "I'll cut your balls off if I have to."

"You not only look just like Patricia," I said, with a smile that Gretchen returned, "you even act just like her." I intended my words to sound carefree, but the truth was that I was apprehensive about Gretchen's accompanying me. I didn't know what I would find when I got to the Glickauers' house in the hills, and that troubled me.

As I drove the car up what Gretchen informed me was College Hill, she pointed out Thayer Street, Brown University's main commercial drag, and some of the school's landmarks. We made our way through a part of downtown Providence, then the navigation system took the car to Route 146, and the miles began to tick by.

I did all of the driving. Gretchen slept during the first part of the way, with her seat tilted back. I kept the volume down low on the Sirius Real Jazz channel and listened with half an ear. My mind was occupied with my theory of Patricia's relationship with Sanford. I was still convinced that they'd had one, and as each moment passed without her, the Patricia that I'd known seemed to recede further and further from my memory, and I kept finding it easier and easier to imagine that she'd deceived me.

Gretchen didn't sleep for more than ten or fifteen minutes, and she started to talk to me when we had to stop for a traffic light on 146.

"You like that music?" she said.

"That's why I have it on. Want me to turn the volume up?"

"It's fine where it is."

"I take it you don't like jazz."

"I like the crooners and especially the female singers from before rock took over, although some of them, like Tony Bennett, are still active today. I'm talking about the likes of Margaret Whiting, Jane Froman, Eydie Gorme, and Jo Stafford. I guess that's what I wished I could have been – one of them. I even like it when opera singers, like Eileen Farrell, do the American Song Book."

"That's funny. Patricia and I had a conversation like this when we first knew each other, except it was about female jazz vocalists."

"I have a problem with them. They change the songs. I like hearing them the way they were written."

We went back and forth on this tropic until we entered the Turnpike at Exit 10A, and then we started talking about our professional lives – her decorating business and my writing and editing. We didn't talk about the upcoming meeting with Gwennie, although I did tell Gretchen about the Glickauers' house and the Sam Hudson paintings that were in it.

"Did Sanford ever talk to you about being a patron of Hudson's?" I asked her.

"Once, when we met for a long afternoon in New York," she said. "He was very excited about having bought the large female nudes from that Baltimore dowager."

"I've heard Gwennie complain that Hudson and his dealer took advantage of Sanford."

"Do you really believe that Sanford would have let himself be taken by a painter and his dealer?"

"I doubt it. It's more likely that he was playing some sort of game with them and Gwennie."

"Maybe letting all three of them believe that he'd been taken, when he'd figured out that it was the reverse that was really the case."

"Something like that sounds like the Sanford we knew."

Once we'd cleared the Sturbridge exit, which takes you toward New York City, the traffic became lighter than it had been. It started to rain as we climbed through the Berkshires, and the rain got heavier as we approached the New York State line. Even with a stop for gas on the Turnpike, we crossed the river in well under three hours from the time we left Gretchen's house. I began to point out landmarks as we left the expressway and went up the hill to the long street that would take us to where the Glickauers' house was.

"My favorite old bookstore is a couple of blocks to the right," I said.

"The Kindle hasn't closed it down yet?"

"Not yet. In fact, the owner tells me that even if new books stopped being published in paper editions tomorrow, he'd still have a great business, what with all of the old physical books that exist."

We passed the multi-screen art house, crossed the bridge, shot past the shopping plaza and all the other businesses, banks, and restaurants on the long street, and then the high school was on the left. There weren't many cars on the road. It was close to midnight. Gretchen turned to me when the car started to climb into the hills.

"Have you thought about what you'll say to Gwennie?"

"I've tried, but I can't seem to come up with anything that sounds useful to me. We'll have play it by ear."

"We should have rehearsed something."

"OK. You play Gwennie."

"Mordecai, you have a wicked sense of humor. I guess it would be better if we shut up until we get there."

I'd turned off the navigation system when we stopped for gas on the Turnpike. I didn't need it. I remembered the turn onto the road into the Glickauers' house quite clearly.

It was still raining when I made turn. It was very dark. I had both the high beams and fog lights on, and I must have been going about twenty miles an hour. I didn't want to risk looking down at the speedometer. I wanted to keep my eyes on the road. I was focused on what had happened to Sanford, and he'd known the road far better than I did.

I could hear the tires crunching on gravel as we approached the elbow in the road. Then, as we made the turn, Gretchen cried out.

"Watch it!"

But it was too late. We were already on top of the large animal that was standing in the road. In the split second before we hit it, I realized what it was. So I didn't hit the brakes. I let the car slam into the animal and flip it over. We pushed it for maybe twenty or thirty yards, until it went over the side of the cliff on the left-hand side of the road.

"What the hell was that?" Gretchen shouted.

"That was the stuffed animal that Gwennie bought and put in front of the house to ward off unwanted varmints. She told me that she bought it after Sanford's accident." I eased the car to a stop and turned to Gretchen. "Which I now know has to have been bullshit," I went on.

"How do you know?"

"There was a cold rain the night of Sanford's supposed accident. Everyone thought he'd skidded on the wet road at the elbow and couldn't keep the car from going over the cliff. It was a logical assumption. There was no evidence that anyone had tampered with the road. So there was little investigation. Accidents happen, even to good drivers who are familiar with a road, especially a dangerous one like this.

"The thing is, Sanford had never seen the stuffed animal. So when he came around the elbow, all he saw was a large animal in the road, which looked real, and he did what most drivers would do: he hit the brakes. Hard. Which may have put him into a skid on a slick road – remember the cold rain – and he lost control of his big Lincoln."

"Was it a new car?"

"Yes, and it was loaded with everything you can possibly think of. He took me here in it once. He drove way too fast on this road, which he was probably also doing that night, despite the rain."

"Wouldn't a new Lincoln's braking system have prevented a skid?"

"Maybe it would have, had there been more room on the road, and had Sanford not probably been driving too fast. Maybe Sanford did something else that contributed to taking the car over the side of the road. It's a long, steep drop. Once you go over, it's impossible to survive."

"Why didn't you hit the brakes?"

"Because I instantly knew what it was in the road, and what must have kicked in was, there's no need to stop, just plow into the damn thing."

"Just because you'd seen the stuffed animal one time in front of the house here?"

"No, actually I've seen two of these big fake animals. The one here is the second. The first was at the golf course where I like to play. They installed it at the edge of the pond on the seventeenth fairway, to keep the geese away, I guess, although it doesn't seem to work now that it's been there for awhile. Familiarity breeds contempt, as they say. So I had no compunction not to ram into the damn thing. I'm sure the bumper's going to have to be replaced, at a minimum."

I put the car into drive and started to move forward.

"Mordecai, stop," Gretchen said emphatically. "We need to call the police. We're dealing with a woman who's dangerous."

"Not just yet. The police have been no help to me since Patricia's murder. I don't want to have to put up with them now."

She tried to reach the gear shift, but I held her hand down against the top of the padded compartment between the seats. "Let it go," I said.

When I braked to a stop in front of the house, I saw a figure going up the steps and into an open front door. I killed the engine, got out of the car, and ran up the steps. I sensed Gretchen's presence right behind me.

There was just enough light in the house so that I could make my way straight ahead, into the room with the two large Hudson nudes and *The Afternoon Party*. I felt a hand on my upper arm. I turned. It was Gretchen. Then the lights snapped on. It took a moment for my eyes to adjust to the sudden brightness. Then I saw that Gwennie was standing in front of one of the nudes, facing us. Her hair was in disarray. Her disheveled clothes had mud on them. There was a gun in her hand.

"I told you we should have stayed where we were and called the police," Gretchen said in a low but insistent voice.

"What are you, his mother?" Gwennie spat the words out with a heavy dose of sarcasm.

"I'm not his mother, I'm Gretchen Carmichael."

"I know who you are. One of Sanford's whores. That's all you've ever been."

I needed to change the subject. I stepped across and in front of Gretchen and pulled her behind me. "What were you going to tell Sanford if he'd managed to control his Lincoln and not go off into the ravine that night when you put the big stuffed animal in the road?" I said to Gwennie. I watched a smile slowly take over her stolid face.

"It's way past time you figured out how I got Stanford to kill himself, isn't it, Mister Walk Behind?" Gwennie leaned to her right, as if doing so would allow her to see Gretchen, who I'd tucked behind me. "That's what he was known as, when that fancy wife of his was strutting her stuff before the high and mighty. Mister Walk Behind. Walk. Behind." She measured the words out, and then she paused and laughed. "Behind. Ass. That's what you are: an ass."

"What were you going to tell Sanford?" I kept my voice steady.

"If he'd somehow managed to survive? Is that what you're asking?" Gwennie spat the words out, her voice louder than normal. Then she switched gears and affected a Southern drawl. She batted her eyes at me as she spoke. "I would have said, in my sweetest manner, that I was teaching him a lesson about driving too fast down this dangerous road that somehow reminded him of that hallway that he ridden his tricycle down when he was a little kid. The hallway was safe; this road isn't. That's what I would have said."

Gwennie dropped the Southern belle shtick and started talking loudly again. "He would have laughed at me and told me I was worrying too much. But he wasn't around to laugh. I had the last laugh – until now, that is. Besides, I didn't care whether he lived or died. He – his behavior, his endless fucking - was making me sick."

It was hard for me to believe that this woman - talking at me in a loud voice, then playing the Southern belle, then nearly shouting again, a woman with a goddamn gun in her hand - was the same woman I'd met on earlier occasions. She'd been cool, self-possessed. Her speech had been barbed, not off the wall, or affected. I'd thought she was a strong woman. Had she been so weak that Sanford had been able to drive her around the bend?

"I was like one of those battered women I worked with," Gwennie went on, her voice almost normal suddenly. "Except that I wasn't battered physically. My scars and bruises didn't cover my body. They were mental. Sanford abused my mind, my soul – which can be much more painful than taking a blow from a man's fist, although I could never say such a thing to a woman who'd been beaten up over and over again."

She looked intently at Gretchen. "Sanford battered you, just like he did me," Gwennie said. "I need to make you understand that."

"We've got to get out of here," Gretchen whispered in my ear. Her voice had no hysteria in it. She seemed calm, although I couldn't turn around and look at her. I wondered if she had a plan, and if so, what on earth could it be? I decided to ignore her, at least for the time being.

"Why didn't you just divorce Sanford?" I said to Gwennie.

"That's what he wanted. I knew he was baiting me, because he'd figured out how things would be different when we got divorced this time. He'd get his possessions this time. I wouldn't be able to keep everything. Which wasn't right. Oh no, it wasn't right. Everything Sanford got in his life was due to my father."

"He told me about your father," I broke in.

"Did he tell you how my father guided him, like Sanford was his own son, into a career in the law? Once Sanford submitted to my father, he was on Sanford's side. It was my father's tutelage which made Sanford wealthy. My father enabled him to be a patron of artists, like the wretch who paints the filth you see in this house. If these disgusting paintings weren't worth a ridiculous amount of money to some stupid Russian or Japanese, I'd burn the lot of them."

"I'm sure your father's old firm would have come to your assistance." I tried to keep my voice as soothing as I could, the way Gretchen's voice had comforted me earlier, when I'd broken down.

"I knew that. But there was something else. I didn't want Sanford to be able to go off with his whore."

"You mean me?" Gretchen said. Her voice was steady and loud enough to be heard. She was standing her ground. I had to hand it to her.

"Not you. You couldn't help being his whore. Even though Sanford abused you, he had pity for you. I could always tell."

"How?" Gretchen said. I could tell by her tone that she really wanted to know.

"It was because he didn't feel he had to hide his fucking you from me. That's why everyone thought I didn't care about it. But the real reason I didn't care about it was that you weren't a threat to me."

Everyone had been wrong about Gwennie, I now knew. It wasn't that she hadn't cared about what Sanford did with women. She was a battered woman, unable to help herself. Did that exonerate her from having murdered Sanford? Wiser people than I would have to judge her. Whatever that verdict, to my mind, her condition certainly didn't excuse any other murders.

I felt Gretchen slump against my back. Her arms were around my chest now. She wasn't in her coffin of sexual desire now. Now she was slipping underwater, she was drowning. I needed to help her, no matter what it cost me. I didn't care. So much of my life was lost to me now.

"Who was Sanford going off with?" I said to Gwennie. I knew what her answer would be, but I feared hearing it nonetheless. Yet when it came, I didn't flinch from it.

"Your wife, Mister Walk Behind. You must be an idiot not to have noticed anything, not to have suspected that your wife had become Sanford's new whore. A younger copy of this one." Gwennie waved the gun at me and Gretchen behind me. "And so much smarter.'

"How did you discover their relationship?" From the beginning, I'd been unable to say the word affair when I spoke about about Sanford and Patricia.

"Sanford developed diabetes," Gwennie said, and Gretchen and I murmured "I didn't know that" in unison. Gwennie ignored us. "His internist put him on a special, carb-restricted diet. The doctor employs dieticians, whose job it is to help patients avoid using insulin by providing them with low-carb menus. Sanford took the dieticians' advice to heart and started coming home for lunch a couple of days a week, so he could prepare the low-carb meals himself. He was eating a lot of canned salmon, certain veggies, and salads. No bread or crackers, of course, which had to be tough on Sanford, because he loved that stuff so much."

Gwennie smiled at the memory. She seemed calmer now, as if telling the story that she had to tell was lifting a burden off her. I watched her body relax. She was holding the gun at her side now, pointing it toward the floor. I could feel Gretchen, still behind me, relax, as well.

"I kept to myself," Gwennie went on, "when Sanford was home those lunchtimes. I usually skipped lunch, and besides, I had my volunteer work to do. It can be very time-consuming. Sanford didn't mind. He liked to read with meals, so eating alone was preferable for him. But I was aware of his presence, and I began to listen to his movements and follow them. I was quite sure that Sanford had no idea about any such interest on my part."

Gwennie paused and seemed to drift off. "Why would that have been?" I interjected. It seemed to snap her back to the present.

"I'd never been much interested in the minutia of Sanford's life before, according to him, so why should he have been alert to any change on my part?"

Gwennie seemed to drift off again. I began to wonder if her efforts tonight had left her exhausted. "Did you notice anything?" I said.

"I could hear him moving about, talking on his cell phone. I knew it was the cell, because when I picked up one of the regular phones to make a call, I noticed that the line was free. I thought Sanford's using his cell was a bit odd, because he preferred the regular phone in the house. He used the cell sporadically. He didn't seem to care much for it. In fact, he was somewhat absent-minded about it. Some mornings, after he left for the office, I would come across it on the breakfast table or on the bed. I'd put it on his desk. I never searched through it. I just wasn't interested.

"But, as I said, I could hear him talking on it. He was quite animated, and his voice had that low, sexy lilt that he sometimes used."

"I know that lilt," Gretchen whispered in my ear.

Gwennie paid no notice to Gretchen and me. "I heard part of several conversations. Sanford was laughing quite a lot. They all seemed to be with the same person, because he kept saying Patricia this and Patricia that. Always the same name.

"I thought it might be the name of a client. It was an easy thing to check. Sanford kept copies of his current and recently completed client contracts in a folder in one of his desk drawers. I went through the contracts. The only Patricia I found was a woman in her eighties who I knew was divorcing her elderly husband, who was suffering from dementia. So the Patricia who Sanford was happily talking with when he came home for lunch probably wasn't one of his clients

"The first chance I had, I went through the Contacts list on Sanford's phone. That was when I found Patricia Bornstein's name. It was easy, because Sanford arranged his contacts by first name, not last. I vaguely remembered who she was. I don't read the newspapers much or watch the local TV news, but I recalled that one of the women I volunteer with had mentioned that the museum downtown had hired a new director by that name, a beautiful, quite tall blonde.

"That same day, I took Sanford's cell and camped out in my car across the street from the museum's front door. I don't know why I expected the woman to come out the front door, rather than the back door into the museum parking lot, but I just did." Gwennie smiled. "And my expectations were rewarded. A quite tall blonde, who looked to be in her forties emerged from the museum's front door. It was a windy day – the evidence of that was in the photo I took. When I snapped the picture, the wind flattened the blonde's clothes against her tall, skinny body.

"I watched her walk into an underground garage in another building several doors down from the museum. I waited until I saw her drive out of the garage in a gray Honda – I think it was an Accord. I followed her out of town. There was plenty of traffic, and I was driving our third car, which is dark and non-descript – it's a dark Chevy– so I hoped she didn't notice that she was being followed. She drove over the river. I slowed down and pulled into a parking lot across the road when I saw her turn and head down a driveway into the opposite parking lot in front of a strip mall. I went in on foot and saw her eating in a diner. It was a non-descript place, and seemed to be a strange choice for a well-turned-out woman with a museum director position.

"I noticed where she'd parked her car. I went back, got my own car, and drove into the parking lot. It wasn't very full, so I could park in a space where I could see the driver's side of her car. She didn't linger in the diner. When she came out, she got in her car and sat reading for a few minutes. Then she put her cell phone to her ear and began to talk. I had no doubt about the identity of the person she was talking to. It had to be Sanford.

"I drove home. I found the picture of this Patricia Bornstein that I'd taken with Sanford's phone, and I downloaded into my computer, so I could really see it. I remember gasping in surprise. She was a dead ringer for Sanford's long-time whore, but a younger version. You, missy."

Gwennie pointed the gun at Gretchen and me, and then her arm fell, and the gun was pointing at the floor again. I hardly paid attention. My mind was occupied elsewhere. Was the relationship between Patricia and Sanford limited to lunchtime phone calls? How had my imagination conjured up an affair? But Gwennie's had.

"Another underfed blonde giraffe," Gwennie was saying, when I refocused on her. "But smarter than this whore. And much, much younger. The fucking was going to continue, and I could see no end to it. He didn't deserve to enjoy it. I needed to put a stop to it.

"I listened to Sanford's next lunchtime phone call very closely. I was glad that I had. He made a date to get together with the Bornstein woman. I heard him say, 'all right, in the parking lot where the diner is. Don't worry, I'll find it. I'll be there at nine, two nights from tonight.'

"I needed to get Sanford's cell away from him. I burst in on him immediately. He did what I hoped he'd do. He put his phone down on the dining table where he'd been eating lunch. He left it there when I asked him to join me at my computer and look at a garden furniture set I was thinking of buying. I found one on a web site I was familiar with. We discussed the set for some time. I managed to distract Sanford enough so that he forgot all about his cell phone, which he was prone to do anyway. It was still on the dining table when he left the house.

"I quickly sent a text message to the Bornstein woman. I told her to meet me on the next night – same hour, same spot – instead of two nights hence. She needed to reply only if she couldn't accommodate the change. Needless to say, she didn't reply, and I could act out my plan – which I did, as you well know, Mister Walk Behind. Too bad you weren't standing in attendance, as you usually did, I learned later, when my friends talked about how sad your wife's death was and how devastated you were. But then, you were never around when she and Sanford were together - unless you're one of those pitiful creatures who like to watch when your wife or your husband is fucking someone besides you yourself."

I felt Gretchen, who was leaning against my back, stiffen again, undoubtedly at the thought that while she and Sanford had been having sex, Gwennie might have been watching. Had she? If so, when? How many times? These were questions that I was sure that Gretchen would be very reluctant to ask. Nor would she want to know whether Sanford had made it possible for, or even encouraged, Gwennie to watch, as part of some filthy game he was playing.

"Would you like the graphic details of how I killed your wife when she uncoiled from her car seat?" Gwennie said. She was smiling. I took a step toward her. Gretchen hadn't expected me to move and she fell forward against me, her arms tightening around my chest. But that wasn't what froze me. What did it was the sound of a voice to my left, at the entrance to the large room we were in.

"Stupid. Fucking. Cow." I recognized the voice. It was Maggie's. I turned to look at her. She was standing at the entrance to the large room, at the edge of the brightness. I could see mud on her shoes and legs. The bottom part of her raincoat was wet, but her head and shoulders were fairly dry in comparison. She must have been carrying an umbrella when she was out in the rain. Then I finally noticed the gun in her hand. All these guns. Had the NRA hierarchy witnessed this scene, they would have been proud of it. I saw that Maggie's gun seemed to be pointed at Gwennie.

"Put the gun on the floor," Maggie said to Gwennie. Gwennie bent over and complied, and then straightened up. She looked exhausted.

"It's Maggie Hartnett," I said to Gretchen, under my breath. She's a partner in Sanford's law firm."

"I see," Gretchen murmured.

"What are you doing here, Maggie?" I said.

"Bill came to me this morning and told me about your conversation with him. He said he was worried about you."

"Why you and not the police?" I said.

"One, I'm his partner. We don't do secrets. Two, he said you asked him not to go to the police. I've been waiting all day for you. When you drove down the road, I walked in after you. And, by the way, who's this?" Maggie jerked her chin in Gretchen's direction. "She looks like she could be your late wife's mother."

"A friend," I said. "She's not Patricia's mother."

"I met Sanford when we were in college," Gretchen interjected.

"What are you doing here?" Maggie said.

"When Mordecai told me he was coming here, I insisted on going along."

"She was Sanford's whore," Gwennie said in a loud voice, "until Sanford took up with the younger model." I turned to her and saw that the crazed look was back in her eyes.

"This is so pathetic," Maggie said.

"I'm trying to be realistic," I said. Even as I did, I knew I was being ridiculous.

"Realistic?" Maggie snorted. "Paranoid is more like it. Topped off by delusional." She shook her head and laughed at me. "You have no faith, Mordecai, in that goody-two-shoes wife of yours. Why can't you let her rest in peace? Why do you have to invent things about her? What *is* the matter with you?"

"He's damaged goods, I'm afraid," Gretchen said. "We all are - you, too, unless I miss my guess."

"Collateral damage from Sanford's games – that's us, all right. Especially Gwennie – poor Gwennie, stupid and mad Gwennie." Maggie ground the name out between her teeth. "Such a stupid old cow. Didn't it mean anything to you that Sanford wasn't particularly broken up by Patricia's death?"

"What are you talking about?" Gwennie said. Her voice sounded dull, as if her mind was befogged by a realization she couldn't comprehend. "Sanford was going away with her. He was leaving me for good. I know it."

"No, he wasn't," Maggie snapped.

"How do you know?" Gwennie said, her voice sharper now.

"Let me tell you a little story," Maggie said. "Sanford went to that painter of his to commission a painting of a loving couple. Himself and who else, Gwennie? You think it was Patricia Bornstein? Have another think." Maggie paused for a beat. "Ready with your answer? No? Cat got your tongue? Let me help you out, then. The painting was going to serve as an announcement of the love that Sanford and I shared, that's what it was going to be."

"That's wrong!" Gwennie cried out. "It was the Bornstein woman he was fucking, not you!"

"Patricia? You're mad! All she wanted was the goddamn paintings Sanford owned for her museum's new wing," Maggie said.

"But the ones Sanford had bought weren't appropriate for Patricia's museum," I said, still half-believing my own theory.

"Mordecai, you know nothing. Let me enlighten you. Your wife convinced Sanford to swap the two nudies in this room for two other paintings by Sam Hudson – one of workmen installing a chandelier in his apartment, the second a view from the apartment of tugboats on the East River. She knew she'd never have been able to exhibit the nudies in a publicly owned museum in this town. It took her countless phone calls to get Sanford to go along with this plan. All during the negotiations, he made her keep everything secret. He even demanded that she call him on his cell phone in the middle of the day, when he was out of the office, from that godforsaken diner parking lot, where she was murdered eventually, so no one could overhear her. He also had her create a fund to compensate Hudson for agreeing to let Sanford and other patrons make the swap that Patricia desired. No one was to know the purpose of the fund, of course. No one was to know anything. Except for me. Sanford confided in me. He was happy to do so. He knew his secret was safe with me."

"Oh, Mordecai," Gretchen said. She put an arm around me. I stood still, mute and feeling profoundly stupid and guilty of disloyalty to the woman who had been my world.

Maggie wasn't finished. "What was that loud bang I heard when I walked in after you started driving down the road into this place? I thought you might have done a Sanford and gone off the road."

She was talking to me, I realized. "Give me the gun, Maggie, and I'll tell you," I said.

"You don't have to," she said. "It doesn't matter how the stupid cow took Sanford away from me. All that matters is that she succeeded. And now it's her turn to pay the piper. That's me. I'm the piper. Toot, toot."

"I'm not the one you should kill," Gwennie shouted. "He went back to her." She pointed at Gretchen. "Look on Sanford's phone cell phone. Her picture's there. See for yourself. It's the last one he took before he died."

Maggie grinned, and then her face suddenly scrunched up, as if she was going to cry. She recovered herself just as quickly and said, "Let me show you how well my husband Timmy schooled me."

Maggie fired just once, and once was all it took. The bullet went through Gwennie's right eye. Blood, bone, and gristle splattered on one of Sam Hudson's paintings. Gwennie fell over onto her back.

Maggie moved into the bright light. She looked at Gretchen. "Save me the trouble, you old bitch. Tell me Sanford didn't go back to you."

"We met at the Parker House. He took a room there. He wanted one last time with me, he said.   I told him I had a bladder infection and I didn't want to have sex. So we talked."

"Did he mention me?"

"No, Maggie. I'm sorry."

I pulled Gretchen behind me again.

"I've had enough," Maggie said. "Get out of the way, Mordecai."

I wasn't about to move or let go of Gretchen. I didn't care what happened to me – hadn't for a long time. Even though the truth was less painful now, Patricia was still lost to me forever. And what made her loss even worse was that Gwennie had made such a stupid mistake.

I didn't have to move. When the shot rang out, it was Maggie who fell to the floor, blood pumping out of her wounded chest, soiling her usually perfect clothes. "Oh, Timmy," she said, blood gurgling out of her mouth, "I'm so sorry I hurt you."

Hartnett moved in front of the undamaged nude. He looked through me, his eyes fixed on some distant place, maybe that better place where some people say we go when we die.

"I kept tabs on you from the get-go, Bornstein," he said, without any emotion in his voice. "With freelancers I had to hire, for Christ sakes. All that goddamn travel money. I had the idea you had a hand in doing your wife yourself, no matter how good your alibi was, though the I-just-knew-she-was-in-the-parking-lot crap didn't wash. And rejecting any eye-for-an-eye retribution didn't ring true for a Jewish guy, no matter how liberal you must be."

"It's what I believe. It has nothing to do with my politics." Or everything, but I didn't want to go any further.

In any case, Hartnett didn't seem to be paying any attention to what I had to say. "The robbery stuff I kept feeding you was bullshit," he went on. "It was meant to lull you into giving yourself away. You led us on a merry chase, to hell and gone." He laughed. "You never glommed on to all those people I had watching you. You'd make a lousy private eye, Bornstein. Stick to writing the books." Then he fell silent, the faraway look still in his eyes.

I remembered the man in street clothes on the beach on Kiawah, the woman on the empty block where the Hudsons' apartment was, and the car on Gretchen's otherwise empty street. I wondered how many other operatives I'd missed. It no longer mattered, of course. It no longer mattered that Hartnett had strung me along, believing that I might have murdered Patricia and would give myself away somehow. But I still resented it. Then I realized that I had to let it go.

"How do you happen to be here?" I said.

"A trooper I know prowls the back roads around here when he can't sleep or find anything else to do. His wife left him a long time ago, so he has plenty of empty hours to fill. He saw Maggie's car parked near here early this afternoon, and tonight, when he saw it hadn't moved, he gave me a call. He wasn't sure what to make of it. He'd seen the car heading this way a number of times, mostly late at night, and he thought he had to tell me about that, too. Like he was doing me a favor."

I remembered seeing a pair of taillights from the Town Car taking me home late on the night Sanford had shown me his Sam Hudsons. "How much did you hear just now?" I said to Hartnett.

"I didn't have to hear much of anything to finally figure this out, did I Maggie?" Hartnett looked over at his wife. She lay on the floor motionless. There was a puddle of blood on her. "Such a gorgeous woman," he went on. "It's a pity. She was more than I deserved. Like you, Bornstein, with your wife."

"I've always believed that," I said. I was telling the truth. "What are you going to do about all this?"

Hartnett's eyes finally focused on mine. "It's somebody else's problem now," he said. He seemed to be pushing the words out of his mouth with a grinding weariness. "Let them sort it out. I'm sick of everything – and everyone. I can't have what I thought I had. Once upon a time, as they say. Now it's time for my last party. It was going to be my retirement party next week, when the force and I are scheduled for a divorce. But why wait?"

He winked at me. Then he spat a toothpick out, put his gun in his mouth, pulled the trigger, and made a mess of the painting behind him.

EPILOGUE

The stench of blood and gunpowder was nearly overwhelming. The bright light spared Gretchen and me from none of the horror in the room. Human debris dripped down the two large paintings of Sam Hudson's nude models, as if a performance artist with a taste for self-mutilation had picked up where Hudson had left off.

I put my hand on the back of Gretchen's head and drew her into me. She put her arms around my neck, and then said softly, "I'll be all right." I tried not to look at the bloody bodies on the floor. *The Afternoon Party*, on the other side of the room, caught my eye. The people in the painting seemed to be passively in attendance to the carnage.

I slid my hand into my right front pants pocket and shut off the small tape recorder I'd put there earlier and switched on when Gretchen and I had followed Gwennie into the house. Then I took out my cell phone and punched in 911. Gretchen dropped to her knees beside Maggie, and then bent near her face. "She's still breathing," Gretchen said. "Tell them to hurry."

"I'll get some towels," I said. I talked into the phone while I headed for the bathroom. When I got back, Gretchen and I used the towels to staunch the bleeding as best we could. It appeared that Hartnett had shot Maggie on the right side of her chest, away from her heart, as if he'd wanted her to live. Why, I wasn't sure, unless it was that he wanted her to live to tell the story.

Police and three ambulances arrived nearly simultaneously, in about twenty minutes from the time I'd called. Two burly EMS guys moved Maggie out first, on the run. Other EMS personnel took their time with Gwennie and Hartnett. Everyone knew immediately that there was no point in hurrying.

The cops made sure that there were no firearms on Gretchen and me. Then they led us out toward waiting squad cars. As Gretchen and I left the abattoir, I noticed that her clothes were heavily bloodstained. It wasn't until then that I looked down at my own clothes and saw how much blood had gotten on me.

Bill was waiting at the station when the cops brought Gretchen and me in from the squad cars. They'd handcuffed both of us – just a routine precaution, they'd said – but they removed the cuffs once we were inside the interview rooms. I didn't know what the rules were, but I wasn't worried. Bill had drawn me aside to tell me that I didn't have to say anything, but I'd brushed him off, and in the interview room I handed over the small tape recorder and then calmly told what I'd witnessed at the Glickauer house. Gretchen must have told the same story, because after an hour or so, we were both brought to the station's front desk and were told that we were free to go home.

When I saw Iris Kramer, I asked her if Gretchen could go to their house. Iris rolled her eyes and said calmly, "What do you think I'm doing here?"

"I need some warm milk and a bed," Gretchen said. I patted her on the back.

"I'll take you to your house," Bill said to me. As he drove, I began to fill him in on the events of the night. I didn't finish until we'd been in the house for awhile and had drained three or four fingers of a bottle of Bourbon that had been sitting in a cabinet for several years without having been touched for all of that time, even after Patricia's murder.

"I can't tell you how rotten and guilty I feel," I said, when I walked Bill to the front door. "The way I talked about Patricia was vile."

"You haven't quite been yourself," Bill said. He yawned. "It will be great to have the old Mordecai back." He looked up at the sky. It had stopped raining, and the clouds had parted to reveal a half moon and a sky full of stars. Bill got in his car and drove down the street, very slowly.

Whether I was even beginning to get back to the old Mordecai or not, I had no idea. I did get back to work on my book projects. Rachel Gormsby was still her efficient self. She tiptoed around me, however, and didn't ask me anything about either my personal life or the horror I'd witnessed. Steinberg behaved as I expected. He tried every technique he knew to worm details of the carnage out of me, but I fended him off. I wasn't shy about being rude to Steinberg – I never had been, I realized – but that didn't bother him.

I began to feel uneasy about the profession I'd fallen into so seamlessly and had been reasonably successful at. I'd always known – at least, I thought I'd known – that a writing/editing career in most cases made you an observer of what others did. You were the chronicler, not the protagonist, much less the hero of the story, although the telling of it could bring you acclaim. There was no use kidding yourself that the financial rewards were totally satisfying. They weren't. But at this point in my life, there was nothing else I felt qualified, or even motivated, to do.

Robert Silver showed up on the afternoon following the night of slaughter. I found him pleasant and very well-mannered, and very much in control of any room he happened to be in, no matter who was in there with him. From the first moment I met him, I wondered whether his presence in the Glickauer house on that awful night would have made any difference. He was a trim man, elegantly dressed, with a full head of silvery hair, maybe an inch shorter than Gretchen, although when they stood together she seemed smaller than he did.

When I asked myself why she'd bothered to have sex with me, what with this strong man in her life, the only answer I could come up with involved some mumbo-jumbo about sex being her way of staying alive even while she felt trapped by her need for it. That coffin image was the key, I figured. I would have made a lousy shrink, I decided.

Gretchen and Silver stayed with the Kramers while the police sorted things out. It took them a week. Maggie had survived her gunshot wound, and she showed no hesitation, I was told, in corroborating the accounts that Gretchen and I had provided. Silver accompanied Gretchen to the police station when she and I were summoned to sign those accounts. I bid them goodbye then, and they headed back east in Silver's black Jaguar.

When it came to Maggie's acting as Gwennie's executioner, I was conflicted. As Hartnett had said, I wasn't an Old Testament eye-for-an-eye Jew, so Maggie's putting Gwennie to death for Sanford's murder – and for Patricia's murder, as well - didn't satisfy me. But the idea of sitting through Gwennie's trial would have been unappealing, to say the least. I wasn't at all sure that I could have endured it with any semblance of sanity intact. I was certain that I would have gotten zero hours of sleep. And if prosecutors would have determined that two trials were appropriate, I would have been more than doubly devastated.

As it was, however, Maggie would be going on trial for Gwennie's murder, and I would have to be present as a star witness, so I wouldn't be able to escape courtroom presentations of the events leading up to the night of carnage at the Glickauer house. There was no avoiding additional mental torment, I realized. Worse yet, Maggie's trial would be drawn out. Murder trials are not fast-moving affairs. Still, the trial was nine months to a year away, according to Bill Kramer, so there was time to let my psychic wounds begin to heal. Maybe getting through a trial would be a bit easier than I was imagining.

I wasn't sure what made me pick up the phone and get Bill on the line a day after Gretchen and Silver's departure. But when I heard Bill's voice, I said, without any thought, "You told Hartnett that I was going to Gwennie's that night, didn't you?" I tried not to sound like I was condemning him.

"I had to. The police wouldn't have been pleased with me if they'd found out what you'd told me and I hadn't reported it. I'm sorry, Mordecai."

"You have nothing to be sorry about. It was a good thing that Hartnett showed up when he did. If he hadn't intervened, Maggie might have killed Gretchen – and me, as well. But he gave another reason for showing up when he did: Maggie's empty car had been spotted in the vicinity of the Glickauer property. Not that it matters now, but I wonder why he did that. Maybe it was because he needed to highlight Maggie's betrayal, although that was hardly necessary."

"I just wish he hadn't felt so destroyed by Maggie's betrayal that he felt he had no choice but to kill himself after he shot her."

"Which brings me to another question. Before Hartnett pulled the trigger, he mentioned that he was retiring from the police force in a week. He didn't say why he was retiring, and I've gotten curious. Think you can find out the reason?"

"I have my contacts. I'll get back to you."

My question had its origins in articles I'd been reading in the *Times*. It's a treasure, but I have to wonder sometimes if it has much usefulness to me other than being a companion during my solitary meals. Now I had good reason to view the time I spent with the paper as worthwhile.

I'd read several articles about severe concussions and brain damage that football players had suffered. It had led to numerous cases of significant physical debilitation and instances of suicide. The problem was ongoing, undoubtedly. I'd learned from Maggie that Hartnett had been a running back who'd been noted for charging headfirst into bigger players he couldn't run around. I'd begun to wonder what his medical condition had been on the night of carnage at the Glickauer house.

Bill called back in a couple of days. "It was a medical condition that caused his early retirement. He was suffering from severe depression."

"I suspected that," I said. "Do you think Maggie knew?"

"Someone will undoubtedly ask her. I don't know what her answer will be. My informant tells me that Hartnett kept knowledge of his condition as hidden from everyone as he could. And Maggie was so involved with Sanford that she might very well not have noticed any changes in her husband's behavior."

"I guess that's a possibility."

"You know, I'd forgotten about his football playing. So you think it was the cause of his suicide?"

"That, and possibly his lousy shot at Maggie. We'll never know for sure."

I began to spend more time in my office downtown. I was there one afternoon, several weeks after the shootings, when Bill rushed in through the unlocked door, waving a piece of paper. He put it down in front me.

"I wanted you to be the first to read this!" he exclaimed.

It was a badly typed memorandum, which said, in somewhat stilted legal terms, that Sanford Glickauer, upon his death, and after the death of his wife, Gwennie, bequeathed his collection of Sam Hudson paintings to the Museum of Art and Industry, and that the museum was free to exchange any of said paintings for other works by the same artist.

"Sanford typed this memo on the old Smith-Corona portable that he kept in his office," Bill said. "I checked the typefaces, etc."

"So the memo's not in your firm's computer system," I said, in as bland a tone of voice as I could muster for this occasion. It meant, of course, that there was no date stamp on the memo.

"That's right."

"And where did you find it?"

"In the file drawer in Sanford's desk, slipped into his estimates for this year's taxes."

"And the signature at the bottom of the page is genuine," I said in the same bland tone of voice that I'd used a moment earlier.

"I have no doubt. I was with Sanford for a long time, and I handled a lot of his papers."

"Will anyone come out of the woodwork to contest this?"

"Sanford and Gwennie were the end of the Glickauer line. I don't recall mention of any relatives. Did he mention any to you during your interviews?"

"Nary a one," I said.

"Well, there you go," Bill said with a grin. "It looks like Sanford's collection will go where it really belongs and be part of Patricia's legacy."

The Hudson paintings that had sustained damage during the shootings were quickly restored. But were they originals or copies? If Sanford had actually hired some artists to execute copies of Hudson's paintings, where were the other versions? No record of his having hired any copyists could be found. Nor could another set of paintings be located. I suspected Bill's hand in all this, but I didn't ask him about any of it. There was no word from Sam Hudson, as far as I knew, about the matter.

There was something in the back of my mind about my visit to the Hudsons' apartment and studio. I couldn't bring the thought into the foreground, and that began to bother me. So a couple of days after Bill had burst into my office, I took the train down to New York and walked from Penn Station up to the Hudsons' building. This time their block was completely empty of strangers; the older woman in the broad-brimmed hat wasn't on the opposite sidewalk.

Deborah Hudson answered the door.

"Mr. Bornstein!" she exclaimed, a bit too excitedly, I thought. "What brings you here?"

"I wanted to speak with you and your husband."

"Well, you should have phoned first. Sam's in the studio just now, and no one's allowed to disturb him when he's working."

I reached for her left hand and brought it up near my face. "Let's go disturb him together," I said. Keeping the anger out of my voice took some effort. "I think he'll talk with us." I kept her hand in mine as I started to walk through the apartment.

"Please let go of me," she said. There was fear in her voice.

"When we get to the studio," I said. "Don't worry. I won't hurt you."

We went through the studio door without knocking. Hudson was sitting on a stool in front of a blank canvas that was mounted on an easel. Paints, brushes, jars, and cloths were arrayed on small low tables around him. The shades were drawn. The studio was filled with steady bright light from overhead. The skin of a naked blonde, who was sitting in a chair reading one of the tabloids, looked very white, as if she hadn't been out in the sun for a very long time.

I turned and saw the projector. It was turned off. Behind it, there was a carousel of slides on a table.

I pulled Deborah around her husband and held her left hand about six inches from his face. He looked at the hand, and then up at me. I'd expected fear, but what I saw in his eyes was sadness.

"I'm sorry," he said. That was usually my line, but I bit my tongue.

"What were you doing there?" I said. I was surprised by my level tone, although I shouldn't have been. Nothing could reverse the events of that night. Why get worked up over it? But I had to know what had actually happened.

"Jasmine, why don't you take a bathroom break? There's coffee in the kitchen. Deborah will let you know when we can resume."

The blonde picked up a bathrobe, put it on her shoulders and wrapped it around herself. She moved past me. My eyes returned to Hudson's face. There was no expression on it.

I hadn't let go of his wife's hand.

"What's this about, Sam?" she said, after the blonde had closed the studio door behind her.

"The ring," Hudson said.

"My ring? What about it? You gave it to me just a few months ago. It was in a Tiffany's box, like I'd always wanted. It was so sweet."

Hudson looked at his wife with an even more intense sadness than he'd directed at me.

When she started speaking again, she turned to me: "I've wanted a ring from Tiffany's from the first time Sam and I were together. But we didn't have the money when he was starting out. So I waited. I never brought it up. Then one night a few months ago, out of nowhere, it seemed, there was a blue Tiffany's box on the dining table with this exquisite engagement ring inside. It was polished, but I could tell that it was an estate piece that someone had cared for lovingly."

"Yes, she did," I said.

"I don't understand," Deborah said.

"I'm sorry," I said to her. "It's not your fault." I turned to Hudson. "Patricia's sudden visit must have rattled you a hell of a lot. Why?"

"She was the head of a museum in Sanford Glickauer's town. I thought he might have asked her to do some detective work."

"About your method?"

"Of course."

"Who the hell cares about your method? My guess is that that you project a photo onto the canvas so you can get the lines right, and then you use live models for color and context and depth, etc. It sounds like a perfectly respectable way to paint. There's no shame in what you do."

"Some of my art school teachers don't agree with you. They were always on me about the poor quality of my draftsmanship."

"And you thought that my wife was here to expose you."

"Until I heard about Sanford's bequest, I couldn't come up with any other reason for her sudden visit. I thought she'd come here to catch me out."

"So you went upstate to confront Patricia. What were you going to do? Kill her? But Gwennie beat you to it. Or did she?"

"I didn't know what I was going to do. I'd googled her, so I knew what she looked like, but until I saw her come out of the museum, I hadn't realized what a beautiful woman she was. I thought then that I could have painted her without having to take a photo first."

"But you never got the chance," I said. Deborah had removed Patricia's ring and put it in my hand. I looked at her. Her eyes were closed, as if she didn't want me to see inside her. "What happened after Patricia left the museum?" I said to Hudson. My eyes hadn't left Deborah's face.

"It was night," Hudson said. "I followed your wife out to a diner. I stashed my car far away and then went and hid in the woods across the parking lot and watched her eat her meal. When she came out finally, she walked over to her car and got in. She didn't start it up right away. It was as if she was waiting for someone. I'd come all that way, but when the time came to confront her, I froze. Then a figure in a coat and hat materialized from out of nowhere and rapped on the driver's side glass. I suppose the police figured out what happened next."

"How did you get the ring?" I put it carefully in my jacket pocket. I noticed that Deborah had gone over to the windows and raised the shades. I watched her turn out the studio lights, so daylight could take over. Then she sat down in the chair where the model had been reading the paper. Her eyes were open now, but I couldn't read the expression on her face or tell what might be going through her mind. I doubted that it was anything Hudson would want to know about.

I turned back to Hudson when he answered my question. I could tell by his thick voice that his mouth was dry. "The person who'd attacked your wife dropped it on the pavement," he said. "I picked it up."

"Did you check to see whether my wife was still alive?"

"There wasn't time. I had to leave. But from what I'd seen, I was pretty sure she was dead."

I heard Deborah retch, and then she vomited on the floor. She took off the cardigan she had on and threw it down on top of the mess. She looked whiter than the blonde model. I was sorry that I was putting her through this, but not sorry enough to ask her if I should stop.

"Did you recognize the murderer?" I said to Hudson. He looked composed, as if what he had done in a moment that had tested him could be comprehended.

"I thought it might be Gwennie Glickauer, but I wasn't totally sure."

"Why didn't you go to the police?"

"You don't understand, do you? How would I have explained what I was doing there? I didn't want to become a suspect. And I was certain that if I went to the police, discovery of my painting methods would be collateral damage. Only Deborah and my models know about them, and the models sign non-disclosure contracts."

"For Christ's sake," Deborah snarled. The color was back in her cheeks, and she was glaring at her husband. "Why didn't you just leave the ring on the pavement? Or once you'd taken it, why didn't you come to your senses and throw it away?"

"I wanted you to wear something a remarkable woman had worn," Hudson said. He put his face in his hands. Then he removed them and looked at his wife. Was he trying to make her understand a motivation only he had been able to understand? I couldn't tell.

"Weren't you afraid that someone might notice something unusual about the ring and wonder about it?" I said. "I had them use a band wider than normal for an engagement ring, so that it would look right on Patricia's very long fingers. It looked like it fit Deborah's hand, which is also long-fingered, although not as much as Patricia's."

"I thought I could brazen it out," Hudson said. "I didn't think you – a guy – would notice a ring."

"Besides," Deborah said, anger in her voice and on her face, "how could you have asked me to remove it? What reason could you have possibly given to me?"

I didn't let Hudson answer. "Of course, the ring is hardly the worst of it," I said.

"Yes, there's worse, isn't there," Deborah said. It wasn't a question. She was still looking at her husband.

I was looking at him, too. "If you'd gone to the police," I said to Hudson, "you might have prevented Sanford's murder. You realize that, don't you?"

"Of course, I realize that," Hudson said, anger in his voice. "I'm not stupid."

"And Gwennie came close to killing me and the woman who was riding with me. The same way she disposed of Sanford."

"I didn't know that," Hudson said, the anger gone, at least for the moment.

"And you could have prevented Gwennie's death and what happened to the Hartnetts."

"I don't know who the Hartnetts are," Hudson said. I noticed that Deborah was staring down at her hands. Only her wedding ring was left on her fingers now.

"Don't you read the papers or watch the news on TV?" I said. "The story's been everywhere."

"I haven't had time lately," Hudson said, looking at me directly. "My work is very demanding."

"You're much too busy to care about anyone but yourself," Deborah said. The anger at her husband was back on her cheeks. "None of what happened to those people means anything to you."

"I can't explain what I did," he said.

"Or what you didn't do, because you were too frightened for your precious reputation," Deborah said, her voice steady and hard.

"I can't explain any of it," Hudson said softly.

There was nothing left to talk about. I wasn't interested in Hudson's state of mind – either now or on the night of Patricia's murder. There was only despair to confront now.

Of all the terrible things I'd seen in the world since the last time I'd been with Patricia, only her death seemed to me more terrible that what Hudson had done – with her ring and, even more terribly, by not contacting the police about what he had witnessed. But it wasn't just those actions that twisted my heart. He was making it exceedingly difficult for me to separate the gifted artist from the flawed man. If Patricia's museum decided to accept the Glickauer bequest, I would have to disregard the man's character and behavior and join in the celebration. I would have to bury any objections to exhibiting his paintings for an admiring public that could not be told the truth about him. I had to guard Patricia's legacy from my own disparagements.

"What are you going to do?" Hudson asked. He'd turned to me. The smugness I'd sometimes seen in his face was absent, replaced by uncertainty.

"I think," I said, with a forced smile on my face, "that it would be an act of great generosity on your part if you were to donate a new painting to my wife's museum – maybe of Patricia herself. It's entirely up to you, of course. I wouldn't want go through the rest of my life thinking of myself as a blackmailer."

I'd answered, even though I knew that it was Deborah to whom Hudson should have directed the question. I also knew that one way or another, she would deal with him later, if only to make sure that painting he would donate would be one of his finest. There would be more reckoning after that, I was sure. Whatever it would be, it would be harsher than anything the courts or I could come up with, and it would last a lot longer.

A week after Bill showed me Sanford's memo, Helene Finckel called from the museum. "The trustees have voted unanimously to do two things," she said right after we'd said hello. For the first time I could remember, there was warmth in her voice. "The first thing is, the museum will accept the bequest by Sanford and Gwennie Glickauer of their collection of paintings by the New York artist, Sam Hudson, under the condition that two of the paintings – the nudes, which aren't appropriate for our attendees - be exchanged with two others by the same artist. There's some notoriety attached to the Glickauer name, as you know, of course, but the trustees have been able to keep their eyes on the prize, so to speak.

"The second thing that the trustees voted for unanimously calls for the museum's new wing to be named after your wife, which, as you no doubt remember, was the plan originally. I'm sure these actions will prove to extremely popular in the community. In fact, I'm happy to say that the local bloggers have weighed in positively already."

"I'm very appreciative," I said, "to you, Helene, to the trustees, and, of course, to the bloggers." Any of the misgivings about Hudson I harbored had to go unmentioned, I knew, and I kept them to myself. So I laughed appreciatively.

Helene laughed along with me. "I trust that you'll find time to be at the opening ceremony," she said.

"Even though there'll be no one for me to walk behind, I wouldn't miss it for the world."

Helene laughed again. "I have a husband. Even though he's very powerful, he sometimes has to walk behind me. So I know what you mean. We'll be honored by your presence."

I thought she was about to say goodbye and hang up. "Oh, I almost forgot, with all the other news," she said quickly. "Sam Hudson called me. He'd going to donate one of his new paintings –he hasn't done it yet - to the museum. We're all so very pleased."

"So am I. Does the painting have a title?"

"Not yet, as far as I can tell. But what a wonderful gesture."

"It is, indeed," I said. I was determined to say no more about Hudson.

I thought I wouldn't be talking with Helene for awhile, but two days later we were together in a studio with Martin Fantock, recording an hour of reminiscence about Patricia. I spoke about her life and Helene talked about how much Patricia had accomplished for the museum. Martin was planning to use the hour as part of an upcoming million-dollar fund drive. He put these drives on three times a year to raise money to keep the station, with its comprehensive local programming, on the air. The hour on Patricia would be played while listeners were asked to make pledges that would be matched by much larger pledges on the part of some of the wealthy people who served on the museum's board.

After forty minutes or so, I found my thoughts drifting off. For the first time since the bloody confrontation at the Glickauers' house, I came out of the shock of having learned that Patricia's murder had been caused by some combination of Sanford's need for secrecy about his intentions for his Hudsons, his affair with Maggie, a damaged Gwennie's misunderstanding of the whole business, and, so terribly sadly, Patricia's ambitions for her museum – perfectly reasonable, except not at that moment. I'd seen those ambitions on display during our first Frankfurt Book Fair trip. I never could have imagined that they could have done my dear wife any harm.

Sanford, Gwennie, Maggie, and Hartnett were like parts in one of those self-destructing machines that the Dada sculptor Jean Tinguely had designed and set off years ago. The four of them had destroyed each other and themselves, and Patricia had been killed by flying debris while an evil genius had been turning the crank in order to keep the machinery in motion.

The stage had been littered with bodies in the operatic last act. The svelte lady – they weren't fat anymore – had sung, and the curtain had come down. The audience had little to do but file silently out of the theater. The patrons were as mute as the figures in Sam Hudson's *The Afternoon Party*. No one, it seemed, had anything enlightening to tell me.

The harder I looked, the more senseless and heartbreaking it all was. I didn't bother to speculate as to why Sanford had never talked to me about what he'd been up to with his Hudsons and Patricia. Maybe even he couldn't have brought himself to speak candidly to me about it after her death. I refused to wonder whether he'd ever thought that his involvement with Patricia and her ambitions for her museum had led to her murder. And I didn't wonder how I would have reacted to any unburdening on his part. There didn't seem to be any point.

Then I noticed that Martin had picked up the faraway look that must have crept into my eyes and had skipped me for the moment and was asking Helene a question out of turn.

After I left the radio station, I got on the Internet and booked a one-way ticket to Paris. I had no idea when I'd be coming back. The price was exorbitant, but I didn't care. I threw a week's worth of clothes and a pair of running shoes in a suitcase. In a side pocket, I put the latest Lee Child novel, another readable, over-the-top Jack Reacher crime story. Despite what I'd been through, I hadn't lost my taste for that sort of stuff. The mind works in strange ways. My mind certainly does. At the last moment, I unlocked the window of the barrister's bookcase, so I could get at the shelf where Patricia had kept her journals, saw that one of them was jutting out a bit from the others, and pulled it out. Per our agreement, I was now allowed to read them. Maybe I'd finally make a start on the memoir I'd thought about writing.

At the airport, I used my iPhone to book a room at the hotel - in the Seventh, around the corner from Rue Cler - where Patricia and I had stayed on our first trip to Paris, following our first time in Frankfurt, when the blue-blazered smoothies had been all over my beautiful and brilliant wife.

I spent my days in Paris doing things that helped me feel Patricia's presence. I didn't expect to encounter her shade around some corner or to hear her voice. I don't believe in the supernatural. I just wanted her image to be in my mind. So in the early mornings, when I got back from long walks on familiar routes along the Seine and through districts on both sides of the river, I ate breakfast at the bar/restaurant on Rue Cler where she and I used to have our buttered half-baguettes and strong coffee. The schoolchildren at the tables outside the café might have been the children of the kids who'd been at the same tables when Patricia and I ate our first breakfast there.

I spent much of the days wandering through the city on streets that I remembered taking with Patricia. I bought books at the English language bookshop, on the Rue de Rivoli, where Patricia and had often gone to find something to read. I went to the restaurants we'd loved – Chez Andre, Boeuf sur la Toit, Brasserie Balthazar, Brasserie Flo, and all the others. I ordered the same things we always had.

I walked by myself. I ate alone. I spoke only to people who waited my table in restaurants or to the women who ran the hotel where I was staying. If you'd noticed me when food was first brought to my table, you would have seen me pause before picking up my utensils, and you might have thought that I was saying a blessing for what I was about to receive. But what I was doing was asking Patricia for forgiveness.

The obvious part, at least to me, was forgiveness for my dreaming up and broadcasting my fevered theory of her supposed, but not actual infidelity with Sanford - and forgiveness for my own, actual infidelity on that terrible night at the publishers' conference in Washington all those years ago, a profoundly stupid and potentially hurtful act, which I'd never had the courage to confess to Patricia.

But as I thought about forgiveness more and more during the days in Paris, I came to the realization that I needed it more and more for something else – which was for my ever thinking that Patricia was perfect. There were many, many wonderful things about her, and I would never tire of thinking about them. But to say that she was perfect would be to render her less than the terrific human being she actually was. Was she captive to her passions and her fears, like the rest of us have been throughout human history, almost without exception? Of course. To have expected her to have grappled with her passions and the things in her past in some perfect way was an insult to her as a real person. I realized that my own expectations, and not what Patricia had done, had led me to the bout of paranoia that I had suffered through. I worked hard to jettison such expectations and the harm they did to Patricia's memory. I owed that to her.

As the days went by, I gradually began to feel better, and my mood slowly brightened. This wasn't the false summit I'd reached with Gretchen. I began to feel I was finally about to reach the mountaintop. I began to enjoy the food more and more. It began to taste the way it had when I'd the same meals with Patricia. I remembered more and more details of those wonderful meals. At Brasserie Flo, I thought of dropping some chocolate sauce on my shirt front, the way Patricia had when she'd attacked a full portion of profiteroles with wild abandon.

Late one evening, I stopped at a table outside a small brasserie in the Seventh and ordered a beer. When I looked across the street, I realized that I was looking at the same curtains behind the same second-story windows that I'd put in the poem I'd written for Patricia on our first Paris trip. I watched figures moving behind the curtains, just as I had that other time, when I'd sat here with her. I thought I might have to hide some tears, but I found that I was smiling.

Then, just as suddenly as the smile had appeared, it faded. And I began to wonder if I could trust the good feelings of the past several days. My emotions were on a rollercoaster, I decided, and I hoped I could slow it down when I had to.

Late one afternoon, I walked out of the hotel and headed for the bridge that Patricia and I had crossed together at the same time of day on that first Paris trip. The misty atmosphere was the same as I remembered. I remembered, too, her saying, when we stopped on the bridge, with no one else around, "We're the only people in the world." I'd put those words into the poem I'd written soon after. I could still recite it, and I would have if she'd been there with me.

Instead of proceeding across the bridge, to look at the statues of the black horses rearing up with flaring nostrils, which I'd also put into the poem, I wandered off the bridge and onto the grassy river embankment. The third bench I came to was unoccupied, and I sat down. I pulled from my jacket pocket the volume of Patricia's journal that I'd packed in my suitcase. I hadn't looked in any of the volumes, except the last one, since her death. I hadn't had the heart.

But now I found myself idly riffling through the pages. I stopped where two photographs had been inserted. One showed Patricia and me dressed up for a party. I remembered that party. We were about thirty. We were standing side by side, me in a dark suit and tie, Patricia in a very short black dress with thin straps and on very high heels. Her long legs looked slender but strong. We were wearing black eye masks on our smiling faces. We looked so comfortable with ourselves, like we belonged together and hadn't a care in the world.

When I looked at the second picture, I instantly remembered the wedding where it had been taken. We were in the middle of the dance floor, standing together. I had on a double-breasted, chalked stripe gray suit and a bold red tie Patricia that had bought for me at Charvet in Paris. Her dress was also red, but a couple of shades lighter than my tie. It was cut in a deep V, and it was hemmed higher in the middle, between her long legs. A saucy number, I'd called it. Her hair was swept up from her forehead. We were in our early forties, and we were smiling. Patricia had on beige high heels – I loved those shoes – and when the picture was taken, she'd tilted her head toward mine, so that our eyes were on the same level.

And then I remembered how relaxed, how at ease with myself, I'd always felt standing beside my willowy wife, taller on her high heels than me, just the two of us, alone together in the whole wide world, if even just for a moment.

She'd left the shoes under the table when we'd gone onto the floor to dance to a slow tune the DJ was spinning. When the crooner got to the line, By the time I get to Phoenix/You'll be waking, I asked Patricia to retrieve her shoes. I told her it felt more natural if she was wearing them when we danced. She melded into me, her arms encircling my neck, her body so warm, so tall and so slender, like she had been on that night long ago at the Inn on the Lake.

My mind wandered to another time with those beige shoes. Patricia had taken them along to a house on the Maine coast that we'd rented sight-unseen. "Tobacco Road," I'd said, as the car bounced into the yard. The mattresses were made of rubber, there was only a wood stove in the kitchen for heat, and the bathroom was unspeakable. But there was a hibachi for cooking fresh swordfish, and we could walk to a store that improbably carried fresh crusty bread and the *Times*.

Nevertheless, or possibly because the place was such a dump, we had a wonderful week there. I wrote a poem about it – Beige Shoe Nights – that celebrated grilling on the hibachi, finding the bread and the newspaper just down the road, and Patricia's marvelous tallness in the shoes and the touch of her cool dry skin as I embraced her nakedness.

I would place her against a pillar in the living room and stretch her up in those beige shoes. I'd move my hands up her arms to her wrists, and hold her arms over her head. It was easy then to caress her with my mouth in the hollow between her neck and her shoulder. I would bend my knees so I could take her nipples between my lips, and then I would lower myself down onto my knees so I could move my tongue around her mound and between her thighs, Then I would carry her up to the bedroom.

One night we were lying on a sheet that we'd spread over the thick shag rug in the living room. Our clothes were in a pile. Patricia wrapped her long slim legs around my midsection and squeezed. I was startled by her strength. I gasped. I saw her large gray eyes widen, perhaps in appreciation of a taste of physical power over the man who was always lifting and carrying her. My expression of appreciation was an enormous erection.

I'd watched her take notice of it. She released me and stretched languidly on her back. I thought I heard a purr, and it wasn't from a cat who'd wandered in. I crawled over Patricia. She put me inside her.

"I love you so much," she'd said.

"I love you, too, more than you could ever imagine."

I felt a stirring of my flesh under the journal, which was resting on my lap. Then I lifted the volume and began to read:

Friday – February 5

Mordecai returned home from the Washington publishers' conference tonight with a distressed look on his handsome face – the face I love. He's miserable, I know that, and I believe I know why. In fact, I know him well enough that I have no doubt. He did something in Washington that he feels horribly guilty about, and I'm pretty sure I know what that something could be — he gave in to temptation, to a moment's madness. If only I could have attended the conference, to see him collect his award; what is bothering him so terribly would have been avoided. But I can't redo the history of the last two days. Should I confront him, and ask him what's making him so miserable? I think not. I'll have to bring him out of his misery without letting on that I can surmise what happened in D.C. I don't think he can take making a confession — and I don't want him to. I can tell from how miserable he is that he'll never fall again. So I have to be strong — for both of us. Like I've been strong all the years of our marriage, and always will be, like whenever those blue-blazered smoothies — as my Mordecai loves to call them — come on to me. Goody Two Shoes, that's me. But it's worked for us, and always will.

When I finished reading the page, I put the photographs back where I'd found them, closed the journal, and put it back in my pocket. I realized that I was breathing heavily through my nose. I closed my eyes and tried to get my breathing under control. I needed to calm myself.

And then I thought that I could feel long cool fingers caressing my face and cupping my chin, the way Patricia had so many times, when she sensed it was what I needed. My breathing became regular. Patricia wasn't there with me physically. I knew that. But I felt at peace, for the first time in a very long while - since her death, it seemed. And then I thought I could feel Patricia's fingers slide away, and I knew she was releasing me, not physically, but from the stupid, thoughtless act that had been tormenting me. And that, I knew, was the most wonderful gift she could have given me.

I sat quietly on the bench, not moving, while the natural light around me died and the yellow haze across the river resolved itself into individual points of light.

At that moment, just as clearly as I saw the lights across the river, I could see that my life was preordained, as if there really was a god with a plan that I could not escape from. A god with a malicious sense of humor, who had sent Patricia to that better place I thought Hartnett had been looking toward before he'd shot himself. But first she'd had to die. That god.

I could see my fate. I could see that even as Patricia had released me from one torment, other torments would, in an instant and without any warning, wrap themselves around me. You must live a life without illusions, I'd always told myself, and now I knew that I had to face the knowledge of how I would be summoned by a force I could not hope to understand to live my life.

I had worshipped Patricia. When I'd told her, many, many times, that I loved her more than she could ever imagine, it was the truth, even though I had sinned against her. And I had no doubt that she had loved me – unconditionally, I now knew. But her love for me wasn't the sum total of her existence. She also had her career and her ambition, which I'd welcomed with all my heart. And she had something else - the secrets I'd learned about after her death.

Patricia had guided me to the page in her journals that she knew would sooth my troubled heart. But what else had she written over the years in those books that were to remain unopened until her death and I would never have read had I died before her? Did I have the courage to look through them? Or was I too afraid of what I might find – a hint or an allusion, an uncharacteristically careless word here, or a phrase there, something that I would feel compelled to investigate?

And what might arrive in the mail someday that would lead, as Joanna Stanton's sympathy card had led, to the discovery of more secrets? Would a phone call – from California, say, where Patricia had spent five years and had an affair with an older man – prompt me to another fateful journey? Would a stranger accost me in some lonely street and thrust a photograph in my hand that would shatter me?

I could feel, again, that I wasn't alone on that Paris bench by the river. I realized that while Patricia wasn't with me physically, she was with me again in some other, non-corporeal form. Somehow, it would still be the two us, once more, alone together, like our bodies were in the photographs I'd been looking at earlier – so long ago it had been, when our lives had been full of such passion and promise.

Yes, I could see my fate.

I would be going to the same places I'd gone to with Patricia, staying in the same hotels we'd stayed in together, walking the same streets we'd walked together, frequenting the same restaurants, and ordering the same dishes, as we had done together, so joyfully, so many times.

Patricia would always be with me. I would see her in the eyes of any woman who would beckon to me, who would hold out her arms to me, who would offer her lips to me, who would make love to me, even. It had already happened with Gretchen, if I was willing to face the truth.

I didn't believe that I was going mad. I had no doubt that I would still be able to function. And I was under no delusions. I wasn't about to imagine that Patricia's arms could still encircle my neck. Her thighs could no longer lock themselves around my waist. I knew that - rationally. I knew that her long, slender body, which I'd adored, was gone.

But I also knew, in the deepest part of me, that there would be no tearing myself away from Patricia's embrace. Even should I want to. Which I knew I never would.

Made in the USA
Lexington, KY
21 September 2012